Third Time is a Charm

The Richard Jackson Saga, Volume 7

Ed Nelson

Published by Ed Nelson, 2024.

Table of Contents

Other books by Ed Nelson

The Richard Jackson Saga
Book 1: The Beginning
Book 2: Schooldays
Book 3: Hollywood
Book 4: In the Movies
Book 5: Star to Deckhand
Book 6: Surfing Dude
Book 7: Third Time is a Charm
Book 8: Oxford University
Book 9: Cold War
Book 10: Taking Care of Business
Book 11: Interesting Times
Book 12: Escape from Siberia
Book 13: Regicide
Book 14: What's Under, Down Under?
Book 15: The Lunar Kingdom
Book 16: First Steps

In the Richard Jackson World
Mary, Mary
Stand Alone Story
Ever and Always
The Cast in Time series
Book 1: Baron
Book 2: Baron of the Middle Counties
Book 3: Count
Book 4: Earl
Book 5: Earl of the Marches

1

Dedication

This is dedicated to my wife Carol for her support and help as my first reader and editor.

Also, the BHS class of 1962 just because.

Professionally edited by Janet E. Rupert

Quotation

That is exactly how it happened, give or take a lie or two.

James Garner as Wyatt Earp, describing the gunfight at the OK Corral in the movie *Sunset*

Copyright © 2021

ISBN: 979-8-89434-012-8
Library of Congress Control Number: 2022911369

Chapter 1

I had to hit the ground running Monday, well, not hit the ground, but I had a busy day ahead and had to get moving. Up at five, I still did not beat Ben Carpenter to the stables. Bob had been told of Ben's coming on board, so there was no surprise.

Bob acted relieved to be going back to the ranch. I think all the socializing he had to do was getting to him. Though I must say, his nods were more at ease than they had been. I don't think he was quite the introvert he thought he was. Why, he had a three-second nod last night, and it had a little side-ways bob to it. Neat, Bob was bobbing his head.

I hate Mondays!

Anyway, before I started my run, I oversaw the handover from Bob to Ben. Bob explained the daily routine to Ben. I found out Bob had been holding out. He could speak in complete sentences. Last night Dad had tipped Bob one hundred dollars for his efforts, which might have helped his mood.

Ben and Bob had a good conversation about each of the horses. I understood about half of that and learned a few things along the way. The horses had been vaccinated for strangles last month, so they should be good for a year with the usual precautions. They had been dewormed before leaving the ranch so that they would be due next month, and none of them had the laminitis stance.

I pretended to know what they were talking about, but I don't think I fooled anyone. I finally broke down and asked questions. Turned out strangles is distemper. All horses need deworming regularly, depending on the climate. There was laminitis, which results in sore feet, and hunching of the back from too much grain. Good to know.

The last instruction was to watch out that Mary didn't overfeed Misty. Misty would let Mary get her so fat her belly would drag on the ground.

After that short education, Bob and I helped Ben move his things into the apartment above the stable. Bob had his truck all packed and ready to go, and with a sharp nod, he headed out. It was a nice nod, saying, "Hey, I enjoyed this. You aren't too bad for a bunch of city slickers. Let's do this again, and if you're out my way, look me up." Well, at least that is what I thought it meant. At long last, I was able to go on my morning run. I saw the couple who helped with the girl with the sprained ankle and waved. I couldn't remember their names.

Breakfast was busy. First, Dad reminded me we had a full business review at the office on Thursday. Then Mum informed us that Sybil and Popeye would arrive tomorrow and stay through Saturday. They will be going to Boeing with them on Wednesday.

Next was Susan Wallace, who had joined us in response to the beach party news, but I had to talk to her about Dennis anyway.

Our first discussion was about the tabloids and Alice. Pictures were everywhere. I loved the one that identified her as an incognito Hungarian princess. I wondered if Hungary had princesses anymore.

Susan told me that I would pay for that. The tabloids were a vengeful bunch. I wasn't too worried. It wasn't as though I were courting public opinion like I was running for office.

Sometimes things work out. The phone rang, and Mrs. Hernandez answered it with her usual, "Jackson House." It was for me, one of the tabloid's competitors was on the line. They were one of the few that had not run the story. They wanted to know about the Hungarian princess.

I explained that the other tabloid had made a terrible error; she was not a Hungarian princess but rather a Bulgarian princess.

They were excited by the chance to point out their competitor's poor investigative reporting.

Susan was shaking her head the whole time.

"You will have an alien love child by the time it is over."

"What's an alien love child?" asked Mary.

I urgently needed to use the bathroom, so I quickly left the table. I don't know what was said while I was gone, but Mary told me I was bad when I got back.

The truth about Alice: she is a sixteen-year-old sophomore at Hollywood High; her last name is Liddell, and her dad is a key grip at MGM. I wouldn't mind getting to know her but thought I would let things settle down before I tried to contact her.

Next, I told Susan about how I had hired Dennis Lawson as a Jackson Enterprises publicist. I could see she looked uncomfortable when I started explaining things. It dawned on me that she was in charge of my acting publicity, which came under Jackson Enterprises.

"Susan, it has just occurred to me that I haven't thought this through very well. I do need someone to publicize the manufacturing side of Jackson Enterprises. While Dennis has a general business background, he doesn't know the publicity side of things. I should be offering you the vice president of publicity position for all of Jackson Enterprises, with Dennis reporting to you."

"Rick, you have started a mess. Think about what I do; it is a very specialized form of marketing. I'm marketing Richard Jackson, the performing artist. Dennis will be bringing higher visibility to the Jackson Enterprises brand. Do not confuse visibility with selling the product.

"Think about it: companies publicly traded need visibility so people will know about their products and services so that they will invest in the company. In your case, you don't need that. What you need is marketing.

"Since you have licensed out most of your inventions, the licensees perform the marketing. The only place you don't have marketing is the containerized shipping business. There you are the only game in town, so you don't have to market."

"Cripes, I see what you are saying. I have screwed up. I shouldn't have hired Dennis, but I refuse to let him go. That would mess up his life for my mistake."

"Not my point at all. Yes, you have charged into this without thinking. So now figure out how to use Dennis's talents in your business to achieve a win for everyone."

The whole family sat at the table listening to my latest faux pas. Mrs. Hernandez spoke up in Spanish, "What about your dad's newspapers?"

Talk about a lifeline. None of the adults sitting at the table spoke Spanish, but of course, my brothers and sisters did. They all made positive sounds.

I asked Dad if he needed a business editor for his papers. He thought for a moment.

"Rick, my papers are local, same for the TV and radio stations. The only business news they carry is local. Anything other than that comes off the wire."

"Could you use someone to expand coverage?"

"That was not in the business plan. I'm not opposed to it, but I'm unsure if we can recover the cost."

"It's my error. What if I cover the cost of starting a business news department that provides stories for all your outlets?"

Susan said, "Rick, your creative mind is getting ahead of itself again. First, Dennis could provide print stories for the papers with no problems. That is his background. I'm not aware of anyone providing the same services on-air other than snippets when a major company has a breakthrough or a problem."

"So, we could set Dennis up as business editor for stories in the paper, then record radio programs with those stories and some discussion about them. Do you think we could sell the programs to other stations?"

"I don't know, Rick; you must have a sales and marketing group to handle that."

I groaned and said, "Okay, Dad, if I funded it, would you let Dennis start running business stories in the paper?"

"I will, Rick, but realize the cost is more than Dennis's salary. It takes time to set type while the price of paper and ink in that quantity is not cheap."

"This is my error, and I will pay for it. But I'm going to try to make lemonade out of this mess."

Susan asked, "What money have you offered Dennis?"

When I told her there were groans around the table. Well, Mary didn't groan. She just got a calculating look. I think Mum and Susan would be facing some negotiating of their own with their miniature reporter.

"Rick, what do you know about newspaper pay scales?" asked Susan.

"Nothing."

"I don't either, but you may have another problem."

Dad spoke up, "I know he has. I've just been through the budgets for all these operations. That is as much as or more than the top person on each paper. Then there is another issue. I've no doubt Dennis is a good reporter, based on the one big story he has gotten into print. That doesn't mean he will be a good editor. An editor of a newspaper not only makes certain a story is written but that the story should be printed in the first place."

I hate Mondays.

Mum threw in her thoughts. "Why don't you tell everyone that you want to create a new business unit? Assign a senior editor to review Dennis's stories and let the editor pick the stories to print. Send those stories out on AP or UP and see which ones are picked up. Those picked up but don't have a critical time factor can be used to create a package for radio stations. Since it is a special project paid for by Rick, it shouldn't cause pay problems. Just be certain that Dennis knows not to discuss his salary."

Dad then built on it. "We can easily track the audience on radio programming. The Nielsen rating service does that. If the ratings are good, the stations do have advertising salespeople in place. We will pick one of the better ones to pitch the program to other stations outside our broadcast area. If we get lucky, maybe one of the networks will pick up the program."

Even Denny got into the act. "Once that is going, you can see if a show on nothing but business will work on TV. Maybe you could have a group of businessmen talk about one of Dennis's articles."

I love my family.

"Okay, Dad, what would you have to do to start Dennis up at the papers?"

"Since I'm the owner, I could force it down their throats, but I don't like to work that way. Why don't you come up with a presentation on how you would like to use a column on business to expand into the broadcast world?"

"That sounds doable. Susan, would you work with Dennis and me to develop a presentation?"

"Rick, I would love to. Do you realize that your error may result in an entirely new business? I wouldn't miss this for the world."

"Now I have to break the news to Dennis. Susan, I told him that you and I would meet him at my office this morning."

"Okay, we will go directly there when we are finished eating."

"Mum, change of subject. I need your help in finding a beach house in Huntington Beach. Nancy Katin helped me realize that I don't know the first thing about selecting a house."

"It seems to be your day for education, Rick."

"Schoolwork is so much easier than this life stuff."

"Bingo! Anyway, what are your concerns?"

"Well, Nancy put the question to me: was it a place to change clothes or a place to live?"

"What was your answer?"

"I would get back to her after talking to you."

"Good answer. I suggest you think of it in the long term. Do you want a shack to change clothes in that inevitability you will treat as a shack or a place to live which you will take care of, and that will have future value?"

"Uh, that answers the question, doesn't it?"

"If money was the concern, no, but since it isn't, yes."

"Would you help me find a place?"

"Rick, how could you!"

Oh, oh, what have I done now?

"I'm sorry, Mum. Shouldn't I have asked?"

She was laughing her head off. Well, it didn't fall off her shoulders or anything.

"Ask a woman if she wants to go house hunting? You do have a lot to learn. Susan, would you like to go with me?"

"I would love to, Peg."

Mary piped up, "Can I go too?"

"Certainly, dear."

I think I hate my family.

"After we speak to Dennis this morning, I have to pick up my dry cleaning, and then I want to stop by the studio and talk to them about that fiasco sock hop."

When I mentioned the dry cleaner, there was no reaction from my parents. Their tradecraft was excellent. I would have to strive for that level.

At last, the breakfast from hell was over. Well, to me, it was hell.

Chapter 2

As we were leaving, Dad touched my arm and directed me into the library.

"Rick, you did well. There was a problem you created, and then it was brought to your attention. You didn't get defensive. Instead, you faced it directly, recognized a solution, and accepted other help. Most importantly, you were concerned about the people involved, not the cost."

I love my family. What a great day!

Susan and I arrived at the same time as Dennis. He wore a suit and tie for his first day at his new job. We settled into the conference room with coffee and a closed door. I introduced him to Susan, and they made the obligatory noises. I then started to explain my problem to him.

From the look on his face, I jumped ahead.

"Oh, you have a job, just not the job I first had in mind."

You could see the relief wash across him.

I then started over and explained what we had in mind.

"Rick, this is great. I was worried about the publicity end. I know nothing about it. The reporting is different. I think any reporter would give his eyeteeth for this opportunity."

"The pay stands as is. I would like you to consider Susan as a mentor. Even though she doesn't know the reporting business, she certainly knows which buttons to push to get a story out there. I think you would be a formidable team."

Susan and I had discussed this and other possibilities in the car on the way down to the office, so I hadn't stepped into it again.

I then had the embarrassing task of informing Jim Williamson of my error. However, I try to learn from my mistakes, so I led off by telling him there would be no changes in our planned raises but that we were taking a different direction with Dennis.

He told me he wondered but didn't know if it was his place to question my decisions. I informed him it was very much his place. I also made a mental note that Jim was more of a yes-man than a no-man and that I should keep that in mind when I had my brainstorms.

Susan rode with me on to Chinatown. I asked her not to mention to my parents about the pay raises I had given. She grinned and asked me what it was worth to me. As I gaped at her, she giggled.

"Gotcha! Of course, I won't. It sounded like it was time for a series of increases anyway. I'm surprised the compensation committee on your board of directors didn't address the issue."

I changed the subject.

The stop at the dry cleaners was short. I had remembered my "tickee," so I was prepared to hand it to the grandmotherly type at the counter. The beautiful Chinese girl at the counter may have been her granddaughter.

She told me, "Bring some more clothes in for cleaning next Monday; there will be an envelope to pick up."

She smiled, winked at me, and added, "Besides, we need the business."

I was all flushed when I returned to the car. We were parked directly in front of the cleaners, so Susan saw the transaction. She also saw how I looked.

"Cute, huh?"

"Very."

We went back to Jackson House. I turned on the radio. We heard songs about "Louie Miller," "Mm dooby do, dahm dahm, dahm do dahm by do," "got stuck on a subway train," and "powdered an alligator's behind." I think we had the best music ever.

Susan was going to get in her car and leave, but Mum waylaid us first.

"How was your trip to the office?"

"It went fine. Dennis is very much on board with the news program. Susan has graciously agreed to help mentor Dennis."

"Good. Did you remember to go to the dry cleaner?"

I knew this was the real question, and she didn't have to ask as I had my suit in hand.

"Oh, he remembers and will be glad to go again," replied Susan.

"Why is that?"

"I think Rick is in love with the girl behind the counter."

Mum raised an eyebrow at that; she had that one eyebrow trick down.

I ignored her.

As Susan left, she told me we had to talk.

"Rick, this could be a honeypot."

"Besides the obvious, what is a honeypot?"

"In our world, it is common to place someone attractive in front of you. The ideal outcome for them is to have some film of you in compromising positions for blackmail."

"I don't think I like our world."

"It is what it is."

"So, if she acts friendly, just ignore it?"

"Yes, there is nothing to gain by leading her on and possibly a lot to lose."

"With my luck and girls, maybe I should find a Hungarian princess."

"Don't give up, Rick; you are still young."

"I know, but it is so discouraging. Every time I think I have a girlfriend, it goes bad."

"As I said, don't give up."

It had been a busy Monday so far, and it was only lunchtime. I decided to head for the studio. I could eat there.

When I got there, I was told Mr. Monroe wouldn't be available for at least an hour, so I went over to the commissary. Mr. Monroe wasn't around, but Mr. Wayne was there.

When he caught sight of me, he yelled, "Hey, Pilgrim, come on over."

I joined him and Katherine Hepburn. They were working together on a film and had come to the commissary rather than eating with the crew on set. From the way they were passing a flask back and forth, I think I knew why.

It didn't take long to figure out that they were more interested in drinking than eating or acting. I made an excuse and wandered off.

Over at the stunt yard, I worked on my archery as it was my hardest skill to keep up. The sword fighting seemed ingrained in my muscle memory to the point that I just needed to refresh it occasionally. Of course, I could always learn new thrusts and parries.

After an hour, I went back to the main office. I was told I had just missed Mr. Monroe as he went from one meeting to another. It would be another hour.

I went back and taped my hands, then worked on the heavy, reflex, and speed bags for an hour.

Again, I had missed him between meetings. His secretary assured me he had been informed. I asked which meeting room he was in. She pointed at one door across the hall, so I sat in a chair and waited. I was beginning to get suspicious. After half an hour, Mr. Monroe came out.

Chapter 3

He didn't seem surprised that I was there. That may have something to do with the receptionist making a call, and my hearing the phone ring in the conference room. It was also strange that he was the only one in that room. He didn't seem thrilled to see me.

"Hey, Rick, I hear you have been trying to catch up with me all afternoon."

"I have. Do you have a minute to talk about the sock hop?"

"Not really, let's do it next week."

"Okay, I will wing it in the press conference."

"What press conference?"

"One of the papers got wind that the sock hop was not as presented and wanted to get my side of it."

Of course, there was no interview; well, maybe Dennis could interview me. Suddenly, having our media outlets made a lot of sense.

"Rick, don't do anything hasty. Let's go to my office. We are trying to straighten this mess out."

We moved into his office, and he closed the door.

"What happened anyway?" I asked.

"A case of too many Indians, not enough chiefs. Do you realize that all the studios, eight different consulate schools, and three networks were involved with this dance? Each of us was assigned one low-level person to represent us. Remember, it was just a school dance in the gym.

"Things went awry when one of the low-level people at a network decided it would be a good TV special. They then set it up for one of their mobile TV crews to be there. Then someone else decided if it were going to be a TV special, then they just couldn't let the riffraff be on screen. They would hire professional dancers. Next thing you know, Dick Clark is hired; the red carpet is rolled out.

"The result: I have over twenty calls from irate agents. You are the only person who has come in to face me themselves."

"What is going to happen?"

"I'm the leader of a group of executives deciding how to handle this. At this point, we are inclined to embargo all the tape and declare it a non-event."

"Why would you do that?"

"Because there is no way we could get the releases signed now for a reasonable rate. Some of the agents think they have us over a barrel."

Sometimes, inspiration hits at the right time. For me, it is normally when the time has passed. You know the perfect comeback when you are on your way home.

"Don't pay anyone. Make it a charity event."

"That won't work; we still have to pay to scale. Some will refuse that."

"You can pay them much more than scale."

"How?"

"Pay them in kind?"

"What do you mean?"

"Have them list their time as a charitable donation. You issue them a letter stating their time as a charitable donation is tax-deductible. I mean, do the charity for real like the March of Dimes telethon."

"Do not put an amount in the letter; let each person decide their worth. Their agent will get ten percent of that deduction."

"What if they decide they are worth some ridiculous amount?"

"That's between them and the IRS; it's just like when you donate to the Salvation Army, they have you do the valuation. That way, they are not in the middle. As they say, pigs get fat, hogs get slaughtered."

"We would have to get everyone together again for the show."

"Use the footage you have, then have volunteers who were present like me make the on-air pleas."

"Would you do that?"

"For the right charity, I would."

"Rick, once again, I owe you big time. Now to decide which network will carry it."

"That's easy, the one that created this mess. They can carry the cost, that or be sued by everyone else."

"I love it."

I told him I had to go, but he stopped me.

"Rick, what did you think of the class ring designed by committee?"

I didn't know how to answer that. Mr. Monroe laughed at me.

"Horrid, gaudy things, aren't they?"

"Uh, yeah."

He went to his desk and picked up a small jeweler's box.

"You told me why you wanted a class ring. When I saw those monsters, I knew it would not work. So here."

He handed me a box, and when I opened it, I saw a normal-looking and correct-size class ring with WBHS on the sides. It was perfect. It was what a real high school student would give his girlfriend.

"Mr. Monroe, I don't know how to thank you."

"You have more than thanked me today, Rick. I mean it. If you ever have problems, the studio will do everything in its power to help you out."

Knowing what I did about Hollywood's past, that was an enormous promise.

"Thank you, sir."

His phone rang at that time. After answering it, he told me he had to get moving. Hepburn and Wayne were raising hell on the backlot.

I had spent the whole afternoon at the studio, so I headed home for dinner. We talked about the day. I related my ideas about the sock hop fiasco. Everyone thought it was a good plan. Denny and Eddie didn't pay much attention as they were in a big argument about who would win a fight between Batman and Superman.

I was learning to keep an eye on Mary. She was listening to the TV plans avidly. I wondered what was going through her devious little mind.

After the heady adventures of the day, reality crept in as I headed to the library to do schoolwork. After several hours, the day caught up with me, and I went to my room and crashed.

As I ran Tuesday morning, I tried to sort out yesterday in my head. I had wins and losses. The biggest win was the charity telethon idea. The loss was my impulsive decision to hire Dennis.

My family had come together to develop a plan to straighten out the situation. The question was, how did I get there in the first place? After some thought, I realized I had decided when I didn't have to.

As I thought more, I decided my order of decision-making should be people, then cost. The first question on any decision is, do I have to make that decision right now? If not, put it off until I consult with those whose opinions I respect. If I can't put it off, make sure everyone involved knows why I'm making the decision and what may cause me to change my mind later.

If I have to decide immediately and there is no way to reverse it later, learn to live with the consequences. The important thing is to put off decisions until they are thought through if at all possible.

I resolved to stop whenever I was thinking about an action that would affect other's lives.

I was thinking so hard about these issues that I completed my run with absolutely no idea of what course I had taken. When I got back, Ben was out in the yard working with the horses. I asked him how it was going. He told me that the position was so far beyond his dreams he didn't know what to say.

I asked him how his grandmother was doing.

"Not so well. She didn't recognize me the last time I went in. She kept calling me Jason."

"I'm sorry to hear that."

"Thank you. It is hard. She raised me after my parents were killed in a car crash in 1952."

"It has not been easy, has it?"

"It was a wonderful life until recently. Now, the nursing home costs are eating up the last of her money. I don't know what we will do when it runs out."

I was ready to open my mouth but shut it as I realized no decision had to be made right now. Instead, I changed the subject and asked how the horses looked to him.

"They are in great condition. I checked all of their shoes this morning. None of them need new ones yet. That reminds me, what farrier do you use?"

"As far as I know, none has been set up."

"I can recommend one that will come here if you need her."

"Her? I didn't realize there were female farriers."

"Jane is one of the few and probably the only cute one in the country."

I could see which way that wind was blowing.

"I will check with my parents. If we don't have anyone set up, there is no reason she couldn't do the work."

"Thanks, Rick. I appreciate it."

"Okay, see you later."

"It will be much later. I have some things to do after this."

"Okay."

Uncle Popeye, as he now was to be called, and Aunt Sybil were at breakfast. I hugged my aunt and shook Popeye's hand. We exchanged a few inanities as none of us had had coffee yet.

I brought up the farrier issue. We didn't have one, so Dad was going to tell Ben to go ahead and have her stop by when needed.

I asked him for a private moment after breakfast. In his office, I explained about Ben's grandmother. He told me he would take care of it. The family would pay for her care. To be blunt, it was not entirely out of the goodness of his heart, but a desire to bind Ben closer to the family so he wouldn't spill our secret hideaway.

As I left the room, I realized this delaying bit had something going for it. In the end, Dad decided, not me, and he was paying for it!

I went into the library and sat down for a thinking session. There was a problem that I had been putting off. Namely, I'm sixteen years old and have soloed. What's next?

I can try to become a private pilot with instrument ratings. Then, I can get instructions on flying a multi-engine aircraft. I can't get a commercial license yet, but that wasn't in the plan.

My new Cessna 310 will be delivered in early March. They had moved the date up; the demand was so great another production line had been added. There was no reason I couldn't start my multi-engine training before that as soon as I had my private certificate in hand. My parents weren't aware of any of this. They left all the details to me.

My question now was where to go and who to see to start my instruction. Ideally, I would be ready to go when my plane was delivered. I needed to ask Mr. McGarry for advice.

As arranged, I spent the rest of the morning with Mr. McGarry, working on my instrument rating. In a way, it was like flying a 707. You had to have faith in your instruments. Maintenance and flight checks make one heck of a lot of sense.

For the fun of it, we buzzed Mr. Tunstall's ranch. At least, that's what Mr. McGarry told me I did. He had a hood up, and I couldn't see anything out of the canopy.

I did ask him about multi-engine training, and he recommended a school at LAX. I would have to check into that. Hmm, maybe I would get a beach house sooner so I wouldn't have so far to drive for lessons.

Chapter 4

When I arrived home for lunch, Popeye and Aunt Sybil were there. Anna Romanov joined us at lunch. After lunch, the men were informed that the ladies were going shopping. We could entertain ourselves.

Our entertainment consisted of going to the library where Dad and Popeye had a whiskey while I had my Coke.

Popeye described what he had seen in the various ports he and Sybil had visited. He had changed his opinion on several ports since our last meeting.

He thought that Singapore would hold promise if it could get out from under British rule and get its corruption under control. He and Dad agreed it wasn't likely to happen.

Haiphong wasn't in the running because of the past problems between the French and Vietnamese. The country still hadn't stabilized.

Sydney, Manila, Tokyo, and Hong Kong in the Pacific; London, Liverpool, Rotterdam, Antwerp, Marseille, Hamburg, and Valencia in Europe; Colon, Buenos Aries, and Santos in South America; Savannah, Charleston, Houston, New York or more likely New Jersey, Long Beach, and Seattle/Tacoma in the United States. Others were interested, but these were the ones he thought would come through the quickest.

If China ever opened up, it would be Shanghai, hands down, but don't hold your breath.

Dinner was very pleasant with Popeye and Sybil. I just couldn't bring myself to call him Uncle Popeye like the other kids. He didn't seem to mind, so the other adults let it go.

We all related all our recent adventures. Aunt Sybil turned out to be the storyteller in the family. While Popeye would relate facts, she provided color and interest. After dessert, we adjourned to watch

TV, but the set never got turned on as Sybil told us about the various cities and countries they had visited.

I realized that while I had been to a few places, it was nothing compared to them. I vowed to change that in the future.

My morning run gave me time to think through my day. Mum and Dad were heading to Boeing. The boys were going to a homeschool outing with some friends and their parents. Mary would be taken care of by Mrs. Hernandez. I needed to check on the commercial pilot's school at LAX about multi-engine training.

Part of my new morning ritual was checking up on Ben and the horses. Everything was fine. Ben, as he put it, was in pig heaven. The horses were looking comfortable in their new settings. How does one tell a horse seems comfortable? They just did.

Popeye and Sybil had gone with Mum and Dad, so it was just us kids at breakfast. The boys were chattering on and on about the tar pits. They hoped a dinosaur would float to the top while they were there. I didn't think it worked that way, but it would be cool if it did.

The phone rang, and Mrs. Hernandez summoned me.

"Hello, Rick Jackson speaking."

"Rick, this is your favorite redhead from Katin's."

"Hi, Nancy, what's up?"

"I just had the most disturbing phone call from the accountant on your movie. They are refusing to pay for your charges from the other day."

"That doesn't surprise me. I figured I would owe for it. How much?"

"The total is two hundred twenty-seven dollars and fifty-six cents."

"Wow, that was a lot of swimsuits. Were the fifty-six cents for a bikini?"

"Very funny, Rick. That's not the worst part. They are withdrawing support from Corky Carrol and the world surfing competition."

I got a cold feeling.

"Let me check into it. Don't worry about Corky. I'm good for all of it."

"Rick, that's a lot of money."

"I have a lot of money, and I take care of my friends when needed. I will be down this morning. I need to go down to LAX anyway. I'll be there before lunch."

"Okay, see you then."

I immediately redialed the studio and asked for Mr. Monroe. He took my call right then.

"Rick, I guess you heard you were next on my list to call."

"I've heard that the surf movie has refused to pay some bills at Katin's and has withdrawn support for Corky Carrol's world tour."

"It's much worse than that; the production company has gone broke."

"How did that happen? I thought money was in escrow?"

"A lot is, but it covers future expenses like your salary for the movie. Carrol's tour would come under advertising, which is not included."

"So, what happens now?

"The movie has been canceled. It will go into bankruptcy; the judge will order escrowed commitments paid. Everyone else will have to haggle for anything they can get."

"So, I make money for doing nothing?"

"Consider it lost opportunity money. You could have been making another movie. Remember, you had points in this. They are worth nothing now. Luckily, your points were in lieu of salary, so they are a debt to you and not considered part ownership, or the debtors would be coming after you."

"Well, this is a kick in the head."

"Rick, don't whine. Think of all the production crew who thought they had a job. They aren't under a contract, so they are out."

"Sorry if I sounded like that. This has taken me by surprise."

"Me too. I think the accountants are going to uncover some fraud. This happened too quickly, as though the money disappeared overnight."

'Okay, please keep me posted on what I should know."

"You should talk to your lawyers. You may want to sue some people just to protect yourself."

Now that was plain crazy, but I made a mental note to talk to the company lawyers about that. Then I had a thought.

"Should I turn this over to Mr. Baxter as my agent to be my front man?

"Good idea, Rick. John will be like a pit bull. It's also his livelihood."

I already had a lawsuit against me for flying an airplane to save us all and now faced another to protect myself from other people's bad decisions and possible theft. What is the world coming to?

After our goodbyes and hanging up, I headed down to LAX. I had to be quick about this as I had a full day ahead.

Of course, I had time to stop and talk to the nice police officer who let me off with a warning about going too fast. I even took the time to sign an autograph to "Ponch from Sir Richard."

After that interruption to my day, I slowed down a bit and went to the commercial pilot's school at the LAX airport. I noticed some work had been started by McKee Construction in the center of the terminals. I wondered what it was.

After I drove around the terminal twice, I figured out I was in the wrong part of the airport. Another nice police officer gave me directions to the civilian side of the airport.

There I found the school I was looking for. I had to ask at an information desk about who I needed to see for lessons. They seemed reluctant to give me the time of day.

Finally, a pale-looking young man came out of an office and talked to me in the lobby. When I explained what I was looking for, he made a face and informed me that it would be expensive, in the hundreds of dollars, and unless my parents were paying, I should wait until I grew up.

Maybe if my day had been going better, I would have been more of an adult about it. However, the day hadn't been going well. I pulled out my money clip and counted out five one-hundred-dollar bills.

"Will this cover it?"

He blushed clear from his throat to his hairline.

"Yes, I am sorry, Mr. —?"

"Jackson, Sir Richard Jackson." The day hadn't been going well.

"Come this way, Sir Richard."

We went into his office, the smallest in a short row of offices. He rummaged in a mess on his desk and pulled out some forms.

"You want multi-engine training. Is there a specific purpose in mind?"

"Yes, I am taking delivery of a new Cessna 310c early next year, and I want to be able to fly it. Oh, by the way, I paid cash for it."

Maybe later, I would feel like an ass, but not now.

"Okay, these are the forms you must complete and return. You will need a copy of your current physical, logbook, and pilot's certificate. We require two hundred dollars down. The rest will depend on how many hours you need to qualify."

I was starting to feel embarrassed about how nasty I had been, so I thanked him profusely and got out of there.

I had mellowed a bit by the time I got to Katin's. I had my checkbook, so I wrote a check for the swimwear and Corky's sponsorship money.

I explained that I was on a tight schedule and moved along.

I went as quickly as possible, keeping an eye out for motorcycle cops up to Hollywood and Mr. Baxter's office. I was taking a chance on his being in. I got lucky.

The receptionist directed me to his office immediately. From the look on his face, I knew he had heard about the movie's cancellation.

We exchanged a few pleasantries and got down to business.

"Rick, how do you feel about this?"

"I think I'm upset, but I'm not emotionally involved. I think other people have more problems with this than I do."

"I know, but you have points in this movie, so someone might try to say you own part of the movie and should share in the losses."

"What does my contract say?"

"From that point of view, you are in the clear, but some idiot will sue over anything."

"I know that well. Did you know I am being sued for landing that 707 without the proper training?"

He looked at me as if I were crazy, or at least what he heard was crazy.

"You're kidding. Is it a passenger or a concerned citizen?"

"A passenger."

"You save his life, and this is how he pays you back?"

"Yep."

"Mr. Baxter, I have a question. This is on the spur of the moment, and I haven't thought it through, but I would like to ask anyway."

"Go ahead. I'm always intrigued about how you see things."

"After your percentage, how much money is in escrow?"

"It should be a little over twenty-thousand dollars."

"The way I see it, it is found money for me. Besides getting a good tan, the only thing I have done so far is learn to surf."

"That's one way to look at it. So what do you have in mind?"

"A lot of people depending on that movie for next year's living will be in trouble. I want to help them in some way."

"There are about fifty people involved, some who can afford the setback, and others who will be devastated."

"I wouldn't want to give money where it's not needed, and I don't want to do just charity."

"So, how will you get the money to those who need it?"

"I could hire those who need a job, giving first preference to those out of work because of the movie's failure."

"What would you have them do?"

"That's the hang-up, I don't know."

"Well, if there is anything I can do to help, let me know."

"I will, and thanks for listening to my thoughts."

"Rick, it will be interesting to see where your thoughts take you."

Chapter 5

Returning home, I found out that I had missed the lunch layout. The cook was helpful in the kitchen as I made a small sandwich. Well, she kept laying out items, and I kept piling them on. Before it was over, I had a real Dagwood. That and a Coke would tide me over until dinner.

Wondering what to do with my new leisure, I took the elevator to the tower. No sign indicated ladies were sunbathing, but I was cautious as usual, having learned my lesson well.

Sitting there, I realized that my life was out of control right now; things had changed, and maybe I wanted to re-evaluate where I was headed and how I would get there.

Not having a movie to do gave me a lot more time on my hands than I had planned. Hmm, I wonder if that meant I was unemployed. Could I draw unemployment? I knew some actors that did. Nah, I didn't need it, and I would be so embarrassed. I could just hear Mum and Dad now. And lord knows what Mary would write.

Did I want to find another movie? Not sure about that.

What about school? Eleventh grade would have been tough as I would have been in Hawaii then. It would be a real snooze if I didn't get involved with another movie. I wonder how my credits stand? Could I maybe do twelfth grade before next summer?

The family wanted me to keep to a grade level close to my age so that I would socialize with people my age. That ship had sailed.

No movie, and I would be able to bang out my multi-engine training.

So, after high school, what? I knew I would be going to school, and it would be as a major in engineering. Mechanical or electrical was the decision, or maybe a double major?

Then, a Master's in business. I don't know what good a Ph.D. might do me, but I didn't need to decide on that for a long time.

I would also have time to finish my unarmed combat training, Marine Corps style. I'm not sure I needed the black belt level, but it sounded cool.

The more I thought about it, the more I liked the idea of finishing high school instead of working in a movie.

After all that deep thinking, it was still the middle of the afternoon, so I drove over to the studio, looking out for motorcycle cops all the way.

When I got there, neither Mr. Danson nor Miss Sperry was at the schoolhouse. I returned to the front desk and asked when they would be in. I was informed they were working in offices down the hall to the right, second door on the left. I found the green door, and now know what's behind it. Two teachers, not what I had pictured.

They were performing a teacher's favorite pastime, grading papers. They welcomed my interruption.

"Rick, long time no see; what's up?" inquired Mr. Danson.

"I would like to know if it is possible that if I doubled up and took some extra courses, I could graduate by next summer."

'Hmm, let me look at your record."

He extracted a folder from a stout wooden file, which I assumed was mine.

Leafing through it, nodding as he went, he smiled, frowned, and grimaced. Trying to read something into that was impossible.

He then silently handed the file over to Miss Sperry, who went through the same process, including the facial gestures. They were driving me nuts!

"It's doable, Rick. It's not the total credits that are an issue; it's the extra courses. You would need to add a semester of Solid Geometry, another of Trigonometry, a year of Physics, English, and American Civics. This is the required curriculum by the State of California. All this is on top of Chemistry, English, American

History, and Plane Geometry, which you would have to take starting in January."

"One thing going for you: you don't have to worry about electives such as music, art, typing, driver's education, or even study halls."

"I can do all those; remember, no movie. I will have the time to be a full-time student if need be."

"What do your parents have to say about that?"

"Before talking to them, I wanted to know if it was even possible."

"With most students, I would say no, but you have shown the required self-discipline, so if asked, I will support you."

Miss Sperry added, "I will also, Rick. Will the studio let you continue here if you aren't making a movie? The State School Board normally only lets child actors attend the studio schools if they are working on a movie."

"Ouch, I hadn't even thought of those hurdles. I'm still going to try for it. I am still an employee of the studio, so that might help."

"I'm not sure about that. All the regular employee's children attend local schools."

"Oh, I may have more of a problem than I thought. Thanks for your help."

Closing the misleading green door behind me, I headed towards Mr. Monroe's office. He was in a meeting, but it would only be another hour. As I headed to the archery range, I arranged for a runner to be sent for me.

"Hi, Rick. Time for some practice."

"Mr. Bell, I was hoping you would be here. I have an hour to kill and wondered if you would help me with my long-range bow work."

"Your lucky day. I have an hour."

My gear was in a locker in the workshop, so it took only a few minutes to be ready. Mr. Bell had me shoot several arrows at a target one hundred yards out to warm up. After that, I worked with butts at two hundred yards. There was something cool about the swishing sound of an arrow as it flew to the target.

"Rick, your form is good; the only way you can get significantly better is to be out here several hours a day. You could perform some exercises so you don't get carpal tunnel syndrome, but then again, you don't use the bow that often. The archers in the Middle Ages were prone to it. Many of them took up juggling to use a different hand motion to ease or prevent it."

"Juggling would be cool."

The next thing you knew, I had several leather bean bags in hand, learning to juggle. I could keep three of them moving for several minutes but would lose my concentration, and they would go flying. I had seen guys on Ed Sullivan make bowling balls and ten pins look easy. It gave me a new appreciation of what they were doing.

If nothing else, it made the time fly. The runner showed up in what seemed a few minutes but was an hour and a half. Mr. Bell gave me the leather bean bags to take with me.

I found out that Mr. Monroe's meeting was going to run awfully long, and he wouldn't be available until Friday. I made an appointment for Friday morning and returned home.

My parents weren't back from Boeing yet, so it was just us kids. Without saying anything, I started juggling. Fortunately, I didn't drop the balls immediately, so it looked like I knew what I was doing.

Mary was the first to notice. Her eyes got as big as saucers.

"Rick, teach me how to do that. Oh, please teach me."

This got Denny and Eddie's attention. The next thing I knew, they were taking turns. Like me, the first few attempts had leather balls everywhere.

Impatient Denny found three baseballs to practice with. He was handling them pretty well.

Eddie went on a search mission because Mary wouldn't share. He returned from the basement with three pool balls. Now, what could go wrong? I barely opened my mouth to stop him when there was a crash.

We were in the small dining room, and a pool ball had just taken out a glass window in a China cabinet. Everyone froze.

Denny had the presence of mind to yell, "No chips on windows."

Mary said, "Rick, you're in trouble."

She was right. I had been left in charge of the kids.

The sound of glass breaking brought several people to the room, Mrs. Hernandez leading the pack. She quickly took charge of the cleanup, banishing the children outside so they wouldn't get cut.

"Mrs. Hernandez, do you know how I can get this glass replaced?"

"There will be a glass replacement business in the Yellow Pages. Look it up."

I found one and called them. I was told to bring the door in, and they would look at it. Luckily, the door came off easily with the removal of a few screws. I took it along with a large glass sliver to them.

A mere fifty dollars later, I had returned home and reinstalled the door. I hoped that would mitigate the chewing out I was certain to get.

Mum, Dad, Popeye, and Sybil arrived home. There was a great hubbub as everyone tried to talk at once while Denny and Mary demonstrated their newfound juggling skills. Eddie was wisely refraining from joining in with his pool balls. In fairness, practicing outside, he was getting the hang of it.

I was hoping to skate through the broken glass incident, but of course, Mary spilled the beans. She told Mum how she had a new Rick story. I got the evil eye from Mum with a promise to talk later.

Dad and Popeye thought it was great about the juggling and immediately had to give it a try. It probably would have gone better if they hadn't started drinking Mexicali Delight at the same time.

It seems Dad already knew how to juggle. He quickly graduated from leather balls to full beer bottles, handing his second half-empty bottle to Popeye.

"Hold my beer and watch this."

I must say Dad did very well for the first several rounds. Then he lost concentration, and beer bottles went flying. In trying to catch the one that got loose, all three ended up smashing on the kitchen floor.

Mum and Sybil looked at each other, grabbed a beer, and left the room. Maybe my talking to about being responsible would be put off.

I also decided I wouldn't bring up my school situation tonight.

It was a quiet evening at Jackson House. Well, almost quiet. The adults were playing Canasta. The threats and groans were loud and often.

In my room, I thought about tomorrow's business meeting. Did I have a vision for my businesses, or would I be an absentee landlord, letting others manage for me?

That didn't mean that I would possibly try to run the operations. I didn't have the skill sets or, frankly, the desire. It was the higher-level directions that were my concerns. The movie falling through reminded me of how fickle life can be.

Just because a company was big didn't mean a thing. Look at Ford's Edsel. What a fiasco.

Besides my business direction, I thought about how I could help the other people who were losing out on the surfing movie not being made.

A few things became clearer, others less so. I gave up and went to bed.

Chapter 6

I woke up Thursday with no sudden revelations. The same mice were running around the same racetracks in my head. They even continued with me on my morning run. It was nice to have company. The trip went faster that way.

At breakfast, Dad had some cheerful news. The lawsuit brought against me had been thrown out of court figuratively and literally. The judge summarily dismissed the case as being beyond stupid; his words, not mine, and then had the bailiff remove the plaintiff from the courtroom.

Looking professional in good suits and ties, Dad and I were driven to the office in a limo. I had seen the vehicle around so much I wondered if we now had a car and driver. Before I could ask, Dad brought up a subject.

"Rick, now that your movie has fallen through, what are your intentions?"

That was a good start. It appeared as if my choices might count.

"I've considered doubling up studies the first half of next year and trying to complete the eleventh and twelfth grades."

"Mum and I wondered about that, and after that?"

"That's where I'm lost. My finances are such that I don't need to do anything. Now, I have to figure out what I want to do. "

"It's amazing, Rick. So many people go through life being pushed by events, never having to make real decisions. They dream about your situation, not realizing it has its own problems."

"I know that I want a useful life, not be like Tommy Manville."

"I don't think you have to worry about that, Rick. Now, what about college? Have you given any thought as to your major?"

"I haven't given any real thought about going to college. Most people get a degree so they can get a job."

"You will need the knowledge, not the degree."

'I've read that college teaches you how to learn. I think I already know that."

"Yes, you do, but depending on what direction you want to go, the information gained lets you head in the right direction. I'm talking about a degree in the sciences, not a general liberal arts degree."

"It would be a science degree, preferably engineering of some sort."

"What sort?"

"Electrical or mechanical,"

"Why not both?"

"Uh."

Changing tactics, Dad asked, "Where would you go for a double engineering degree?"

"I don't know, I know the names of MIT, Stanford, Georgia Tech, Princeton, and Purdue. Which is the best for me? I have no idea. There might be others that I don't know about."

"There is the Imperial College of London. It has a good engineering reputation. Studying in England would please your Mum, and maybe even your godmother."

"That's food for thought."

We arrived at the office about that time, so that conversation ended. Of course, the mice got busier than ever.

The first meeting we had was attended by Roberta Grimes, Sam Wingate, Dad, and me. We were the newly created compensation committee. Frankly, I had dodged several bullets recently with jobs and increases given on the spur of the moment.

A newly created committee was an understatement. After talking with Dad last night, I had to make several calls to form the group. I hoped he would call for me, but I knew it was part of my learning experience.

Mr. Wingate, our corporate council, had done the needed investigation as to where we should be. He had a presentation on a flip chart that looked at the organization from the top down and the bottom up. He also had comparisons for similar jobs in other companies and industries.

It quickly became apparent that the entertainment industry pay scales were toxic to the rest of the organization. They were different worlds. We could have very few if any employees working in both. Paying prevailing entertainment rates would destroy the other operations' profit margins.

Once that point was driven home, it was easy to come up with proper pay in each business segment. I had no problems with any of it until they started talking about what my pay should be.

I like my toys and work hard, but no sixteen-year-old is worth one and a half million dollars a year!

Pay rates from public companies with similar positions were presented until I finally yielded. My arguments against paying me so much took us an hour over the schedule. It was lunchtime.

Lunch was brought in to save time. While we ate, I brought up my concern about the movie workers who depended on the surfing movie and now would have to scramble for a job.

Dad asked, "Do you have a plan?"

"I would like to make a movie/television production on what is happening to make the containerized shipping business a reality. That includes container manufacturing, shipbuilding, port conversions, railroad and truck line interfaces, and setting up a network of brokers to use it.

"The way I see it, several things will be accomplished: a chance to make money off the film, employ the surfing movie crew, give Jackson Enterprises good publicity, and most important of all, make the world aware of containerized shipping and its possibilities."

Of all the responses to my statement, Mr. Wingate surprised me the most.

"Rick, that is one of the most well-thought-out and succinctly put plans I have heard in a long time."

"Thank you."

The plan is what I had been thinking about last night.

"Bring it up as new business when we have the official board meeting, and we will approve," said Dad.

After lunch, the first group we met with was Jackson Personal Products, about the hairdryer and the new curling iron patent we had purchased. Don Pearson presented his charts, graphs, and spreadsheets with projections for the next five years. He showed us his plans to arrive at sales agreements with companies in South America, South Africa, Australia, New Zealand, and most of Europe.

Altogether, he was projecting ten million dollars a year in profit; based on that, we agreed to his request to invest a million dollars in an R&D group for Personal Products.

I asked him to let me know when R&D was up and running so I could visit them.

Next was Jackson Home Products, which included the showerheads and flexible shower hose.

Mark Downing was there to present, but to my surprise, Sharon Bronson accompanied him. They were still together. I saw how together they were when I noticed the diamond ring she was wearing on her ring finger. I had to play a little.

"I see you are engaged, Sharon. Anyone I know?"

She opened and closed her mouth before responding.

"I'm going to get you for that, Rick."

I quickly stood and shook Mark's hand while congratulating him and Sharon. At least she didn't hit me when I hugged her. After all the handshaking and hugging settled down, we got down to business.

Things were going great, to put it mildly. Profits were way up. Mark was ready to either expand the plant or buy another company for the equipment and infrastructure. This was a recent conclusion, so he was just starting to price out expansion and look at what was on the market.

Sharon brought us up to date on her venture with Anna Romanov. Things were going so well with them. They were talking to some other named stars to represent them at specific home designs and the resulting parties. They were calling them "reveals". That was a new way to use the word, at least to me.

When all was said and done, this Division was adding three million dollars a year to the bottom line.

Susan Wallace presented the Entertainment Division along with Mr. Baxter. There were still residuals from *Bandits of Sherwood* and *Sir Nickalous*. For some reason, they loved *Sir Nickalous* in India. Go figure.

The failed surfing movie had little discussion other than a close eye would be kept on legal actions. It would be some time before my money would be released from escrow by the judge assigned to the bankruptcy.

I brought up my thoughts on producing a show about the building of the container business. I made a point that everyone who thought they had a job in the surfing movie was to be given the first right of refusal on a job with us on this project.

Susan was excited about the new production and the fact that I would be ensuring employment for those who lost out.

Mr. Baxter, while smiling about taking care of my fellow workers, didn't show the same degree of excitement as Susan. I uncharitably thought it was that he would not be getting a percentage off me. Instead, he asked me.

"Rick, should I be soliciting scripts now?"

"I don't think so. I'm going to spend until next summer completing high school."

That statement sort of brought things to a halt. Here we were discussing a multi-million-dollar business, and I was talking about completing high school!

"This timing makes it easier for me," Mr. Baxter responded. "I've been ready to retire for some time. I think the time is right."

We all made supportive noises. I mean, what do you say to that? I made a mental note to come up with a retirement gift. I think he deserved more than a gold watch from me. It also made me feel bad about my earlier thoughts.

No sooner had I thought that than Mr. Baxter brought up, "Of course, if Rick does any narration, I will expect my commission on his salary."

I hadn't thought about narration, but Susan said it was a given. I would also be appearing with various heads of state where port expansions would occur talking about the opportunities for their countries.

Mr. Baxter then asked who he should talk to about my remuneration and his commission in accounting. Roberta told him she would be his contact.

Hurray for human nature, so much for my uncharitable thoughts.

The most surprising item to me was that money was still coming in from my song with the Beach Boys and "Brothers".

Chapter 7

The last and longest was the session on Jackson Transportation. Present for that were Todd Goodson and Popeye. Mr. John Churchill (distant relation) from the Scottish Lines and Mr. Robert Wilson (Bob) from Narrow Freight were new to the group. We had just bought both of those operations.

Each group gave a presentation in which they all requested expansion funds.

In my thinking during my daily runs and session last night, I had considered one thought about this division.

"Before we address specific funding requests, I have one question for this group. Where are we going to be making money in the long term? I don't mean maintaining constant income in a mature market. I mean long-term continuing growth?"

I wish I could claim credit for that question. It was in one of the economic books I had read. It said all businesses had to face that question.

Each person made a pitch that there would be a continuing need for more ships, trucks, and containers. Roberta pointed out that while the economy would continue to grow, there would be times when it would be flat and growth income would slow down.

I sat there and listened while the group discussed how the growth or at least income could continue if we weren't building more trucks, ships, or containers.

The shipping and trucking lines were continuing income. So were replacement containers. But overall, a stagnant economy would cause a significant loss of income. We would have an idle shipyard, and I shuddered to think of layoffs in Pittsburg.

Of all people, Dad's secretary Helen brought up the fact that the people who arranged transportation would continue to have income while their costs wouldn't go up.

Popeye expanded on that with the fact he didn't know of a worldwide brokerage firm. At most, there were national companies. Some were in several countries, but nothing truly worldwide.

That broke the conversation wide open. Should we start a new brokerage or buy existing ones to set up a new network?

Again, those books I had been reading came in handy.

"Why don't we buy an existing high-end brokerage and then set up correspondence with brokerages in each country we have or will have an interest in? As we see how each country progresses, we can then buy out the brokerages where we can. That will get us in the market without a huge initial outlay and position us for the future.

"It's sort of like we are building razors, but the real money is in the razor blades."

After that statement, the room became quiet. The silence continued until Dad broke it.

"Rick, you just reminded us of whose ideas got this business going. We had fallen back into thinking of you as a teenager at the table. Well, you are a teenager, but you also own this table."

There were some head nods but no further conversation on the subject. It took a few minutes, but it was decided that Dad would detail a person to get up to speed on the brokerage business. Their job would be to find someone who knew the business internationally. We could go from there.

The last discussion was about money. There was a ton coming in and a ton going out. All that would be left this year was a mere ninety-three million dollars. Maybe a million and a half dollars for me wasn't out of line.

The very last item on the agenda was an official board meeting. Mum joined us, and we voted on making the decisions of the day official. We would start a production unit to make a movie about the container business. Mark would be supported in growing his division. The money would be invested in expanding production in Jackson Transportation, but not unlimited.

We would open an international brokerage firm.

Also, I wouldn't let Eddie juggle pool balls in the house. That was from Mum. Helen started to write it in the minutes until she heard the laughter.

Afterward, we went out as a group for dinner. It was fun getting to know the people who were running my business. Mr. Wingate turned out to be a really funny guy, not the dry-stuffed shirt I thought he was.

He and I also had a pleasant conversation about "idea people vs. doers." It was a variation of what I had learned in my economics books. Those who had the original ideas could only take them so far.

The successful ones knew when to turn over the leadership to those with the skill set of running a larger business. Even then, some could run a business at a certain level, like under ten million a year, ten to fifty million a year, and then actual big business.

At each step, the organization had a different level of engagement. Many a good idea had failed the first time through because the idea man didn't have the business acumen required for that level. If it were truly a good idea, some other person or group would pick it up.

Then there were the ideas whose time had come and gone. How would you like to invent the perfect buggy whip the day the first Model T came off the line?

That was the only serious discussion of the evening. I heard Dad and Popeye talking about the Order of the Purple Porpoise, both putting it on their bucket list. I was glad to see that Dad wasn't drinking tonight. The alcoholism in our family was a genuine concern.

After my morning workout and breakfast, I got ready to accompany Mary for her show and tell. At the table, she drilled into me how I was to relate Misty's heroism in rescuing her from those thugs—her words, not mine.

We were driven to the school in Mary's limo. Well, not her limo, just the one she usually rode in. I knew it was the one she usually rode in because she had drawings pinned to the back of the seats in front of her.

I was flattered by a small movie poster from *Bandits*. Well, it was one from one scene in which Mary appeared, so maybe it wasn't about me.

I didn't know we had two limos at the house and others on call as needed. The security firm provided the drivers.

As we rode over, Mary continued prepping me for the event. Her teacher, Mrs. Boynton, couldn't be called by her first name Connie. She was new at the school, having just come from Miss Nestor's. Her husband Philip was a dreamboat.

I was to remember that Patty's grandfather owned a newspaper chain larger than ours, and their house was bigger. She didn't have a pony, so she had no right to be nasty.

Female logic is beyond me. Five-year-old female logic is beyond Einstein.

Mrs. Boynton was nice, but I wouldn't want to be on the receiving end of her sharp tongue. The kids took my relating Misty's heroics as hoped for by Mary.

Mary had told the class a few things about me because the boys all pretended to be gunfighters or swordsmen. The girls just sat there with big eyes.

I never even figured out who the dreaded Patty was, so it was a nonissue.

Rather than have the limo driver make an extra trip, I waited in the car until class was over, and then we went home. Planning, I had my English literature book along.

I was rereading the story about the Puritan lady who had to wear a badge of shame on her dress. I liked the fact she embraced it rather than let it shame her. I had first read it several years previously but was not taking chances with my upcoming exams.

Chapter 8

Saturday and Sunday were golf days at Calabasas. I called ahead for tee times and arranged for John Jacobs to be my caddy. We were comfortable together, and he knew the course.

I was allowed to play alone, so I had time to work on shots out of the rough and sand traps. I normally avoided trouble, but it wouldn't hurt to know how to make a long shot when a tree branch impeded your club.

All in all, I had a good two days. It even helped my tan for the movie I wouldn't be in.

My morning routine was getting more complex all the time. I was doing pushups, chin-ups, sit-ups, running, and now riding. I limited it all to two and a half hours, finishing by eight every morning. That still had me up at five thirty, which had me in bed by ten or eleven every night.

A quick shower and shave had me down to breakfast with the rest of the family. Popeye and Aunt Sybil left for London early this morning. Mum told me she had several houses at the beach to look at. We could also stop at the dry cleaners on the way there.

She also reminded me about Friday's fundraiser for Deputy Burrill's sheriff's campaign. Then I got a new assignment. Saturday, there was to be a charity fundraiser at the house. The whole family was expected to be there in costume.

"Mum, I'm too old to wear one of those cheesy Halloween costumes from Murphy's Five & Dime."

"I agree, dear. I'm certain you can arrange something from the studio wardrobe department."

"Oh, I will just wear my cowboy gear."

"I knew you would think of something."

Why did that come across as sarcastic?

"Mary, will you be a princess or a fairy?"

47

"Stupid boy, I'm going to be a newspaper reporter with my camera. That way, I can get pictures for my article."

What's with this stupid boy thing? It sounds like a story of some sort.

"Good thinking. You can be a miniature Walter Winchell.

"Richard Edward Jackson, apologize to your sister right now!"

Oops, I had stepped into it. I knew Mum and Dad hated Walter Winchell and Drew Pearson. I just named the first gossip person I could think of. They both thought Winchell was a bucket of slime and Pearson a Communist.

"Mary, I am sorry; I didn't mean that."

"That's okay, Ricky."

Ouch, Mary knew how I hated the use of Ricky when I was a kid. It was okay, but now I am more dignified. Now was not the time to correct her. I knew enough when I was in a hole to stop digging.

Mrs. Hernandez just looked at me and mouthed *niño estúpido*. Some days, you can't win.

Dad saved me by changing the subject. He wanted to meet with me and an architect he had found for the garage workshop expansion. This caught Mum's interest, so she invited herself to that meeting on Wednesday. She was concerned about the men messing up the Jackson House image; her words, not mine.

To keep the subject changed, I mentioned that I would be stopping by the flight school later today to get registered to start. Also, I would go by the studio tomorrow to find out the latest on the failed movie and try to sort out my schooling. Plus, I was trying to get more golf in as I would like to qualify for the US Open next year.

I had been playing around with the golf idea for a while. I needed a physical challenge.

Mum and I headed down to the Huntington Beach area. Our first stop was at the dry cleaner. I dropped off a pair of slacks. In exchange, I was given a large, sealed envelope to deliver to Mum.

That was the easiest handover yet. She slid it into her large open-top purse.

We enjoyed the drive with the top down on the T-Bird. On the radio, we listened to the "terror of Highway 101," the man who lived at the Carlton Hotel and played chess, and an absolute favorite of mine, "lift six-foot, seven-foot, eight-foot, bunch."

A little Nash Rambler pulled up to us at one intersection with a ramp onto 101. The driver asked Mum if she knew how to shift gears on the Nash. She told him no. He couldn't get it out of second gear. She told him to ask the driver of the caddy in the next lane over.

About that time, the light changed, and the caddy took off. The Nash followed him onto the 101, but I doubted he would ever catch him.

At the beach, we were met by a realtor. I didn't catch her name. Mum introduced me as my son Rick. She had two properties to show us. One was nice. It came across as a home. The other looked like a bunch of college boys camped there.

Mum asked, "What do you think, Rick?"

"The first one looked in a lot better condition. I would go with that one."

"It's closer to the water; the other is next to the highway."

"Being right on the water is what I had in mind."

The agent said, "How about the price range? Would you pay more to be on the water?"

"Sure, when I was thinking of a beach house, I was thinking of being able to go right out and surf, swim, and spend time on the beach."

The agent looked nervous as she told Mum, "The nearer to the water is a lot more expensive. It could run up to five hundred thousand dollars."

"Don't look at me; Rick will be the one paying."

I thought the poor woman would cry as she saw any sale going out the window.

"Half a mill for the right place works for me."

Heck, that was only a third of a year's income for me. I liked this being rich.

Eyes darting back and forth, you could tell the poor realtor didn't know if this was a bad joke or what. I took pity on her.

"My full name is Richard Jackson, and I'm an actor. I really can afford this."

We went back to the one on the water and went through it closely. My time spent in Bellefontaine working on rentals with Dad came in handy.

"You can see where they added on this section. Since an electrical plate is missing, I can see it is not to code. We will want a home inspection with a licensed engineer. This will affect my offer."

"I can arrange that if you want."

"Mum. Do you think we could get the same firm that inspected Jackson House?"

"I'm certain we can. Do you want me to call them for you?"

"If you would be so kind, I would appreciate it."

Wow, we sounded like someone was writing a script for us!

"Coastal Engineering will be contacting you to arrange a time for an inspection."

"So, you are interested in this property?"

"Yes, I am; however, while we are waiting, there are several others I'm interested in further south on the beach."

There were no such units, but we did buy and sell in Bellefontaine. I didn't want her to get too comfortable with a sale. Let her work for it.

The drive home had us on a two-lane highway with some blind curves. They weren't terrible, but the yellow lines meant something.

There was a guy on a motorcycle in front of us. It was a heavy old bike, like a Harley or Indian.

An idiot came up behind us, speeding way over the limit. He attempted to pass us on the yellow in front of one of those curves. A moving van was coming towards us. As soon as he cleared my car, which I started to brake heavily, he pulled over in front of me.

I don't know if he saw the cycle, but the result was it pulled over into the side of the motorcycle, driving it off the road. The cycle hit a pole, and the rider went flying.

I was torn for a moment between chasing the car or stopping and helping the rider. Mum made the decision.

"Pull over, Rick."

It was in a voice I didn't hear very often. Dad called it her command voice. I pulled over.

She was out of the car in a flash. Running over to the rider, who was unconscious, she checked him out quickly. A part of an old fence post had gone deep into his leg.

Mum rolled him over and, using her scarf, put pressure on his leg. She was pushing all of her weight on it.

"Rick, his femoral artery has been punctured. I can reduce the bleeding, but we need to get him to the hospital right now, or he will bleed out."

I had read about this; Mum had lived it during the war.

The moving van driver and his helper had joined us by this time. The driver had brought a moving pad with him, so we were able to place the injured man on that and move him to my T-Bird. Thank goodness the top was down.

All this time, Mum kept the pressure on his leg. The rider was starting to regain consciousness while we moved him, but he didn't fight us.

As we were putting him into my car, a motorcycle cop pulled up. A quick conversation and I was to follow him. It wasn't my buddy Ponch. His name tag said Jon.

We hit ninety on the way. Within five minutes, we were pulling up to the emergency room. It would have taken fifteen or more minutes for an ambulance to arrive after we found a phone, so this guy was lucky.

After we knocked on the door, the place went into full take-over mode. Someone, I think an intern, took over for Mum. Others wheeled him off to surgery.

The policeman, Jon Baker, took our statement.

When this was done, an administrative person from the hospital approached us.

"The gentleman has no ID on him. Do you know him?"

We explained our position in the events.

"Oh, we have to provide him the immediate treatment, but I don't know about afterward."

Mum spoke up, still in command voice, "I will sign and guarantee payment."

"You realize he is a Hells Angel?"

"No matter, he is a person in trouble, and I can help."

That explained the death's head patch on his jacket.

Mum signed a bunch of papers, and we headed out. The T-Bird was a mess with blood everywhere. The state patrolman was still there, and he gave us a note including his station phone number. People got suspicious if you brought in a blood-covered car to be cleaned!

We sat on some old beach blankets from the trunk and went home. We were done for the day. I called the flight school right away and let them know I would be in tomorrow afternoon.

Once home, after changing clothes, Mum and I got buckets of cold water and started cleaning. I would have used warm water, but

Mum explained that would cause blood stains to set in. My, what an interesting life she has led.

After that, I went riding on George. I then sat down for some of the seemingly eternal homework.

At dinner, Mum and I regaled everyone with our day's adventure. The boys thought blood everywhere was neat. Mary wished she were there with a camera. Dad just shook his head and hoped a motorcycle gang wouldn't show up on our doorstep.

I wasn't up late; I don't know why, but the day had tired me out.

Chapter 9

Tuesday started normally. That lasted until we were having breakfast. The front gate guards called. There were two Los Angeles plainclothes detectives asking for Mum and me.

Dad took over immediately. He instructed the guards at the front gate and, after a ten-minute wait, had the police escorted to the reception.

One of the guards nodded at Dad, and they left.

The cops identified themselves by flourishing their leather badge wallets. They went by so fast they could have been the school safety patrol for all I knew.

My parents must have felt the same way because they requested politely to see them again.

The smaller of the two not-large detectives asked in a snarky manner.

"Are you Rick and Olive Jackson?"

Mum nodded at me and replied, "Yes, we are."

"You need to come downtown with us."

"You need to provide proper identification and explain why you are here."

They turned to face Dad; from his tone of voice, this would not end well for someone.

The little one turned to his partner and told him, "Cuff them."

His partner just stood there with wide eyes. The little one turned to see what had disturbed his partner.

At that point, we all heard a distinct metallic sound—a pump shotgun being racked.

Mum held it, pointing at the floor, but she could move it before they could react. You could tell she knew what she was doing from the way she held it.

"Now, once more, may I please see your identification?" Dad said quietly.

This time, they carefully pulled out their wallets for Dad. He noted their badge numbers and names.

"Now, gentlemen, what's this all about?"

"We have been ordered to bring Olive and Rick downtown for questioning."

Patiently, Dad asked, "Questioning about what?"

"I don't know. We were just ordered to bring them in."

"May I see your warrant?"

"There isn't one. The captain just told us to bring them in."

"Well, gentlemen, we are at an impasse. You have no legal authority in the county, you do not have a warrant, and you don't know why you are here. Now, why would my wife and son go with you?"

The two cops weren't stupid. They knew they were in over their heads.

"Can I call my office to see what is going on? We were expecting to pick up two motorcycle gang members for questioning."

I couldn't keep my mouth shut, "Yeah, this is our gang's clubhouse."

The larger of the two cops winced, "We started to wonder when we pulled up."

"But you still proceeded stupidly. Yes, you can make a call. But before that, please set your weapons on the side table."

Mum still had the shotgun out, so looking at each other, they gingerly set their pistols down.

Since I didn't remember their names, I began to think of them as Mutt and Jeff.

Jeff dialed the phone and asked for some captain. We heard his end of the conversation. He described their entrance to a swanky castle high in the hills, and no way was it a motorcycle gang hangout.

It had a professional guard service at the entrance, and we seemed like posh people.

There was no mention of shotguns in his conversation, just that we were reluctant to come downtown without a warrant. Lastly, he asked what they should do since it was out of their jurisdiction.

He ended up with, "Sir, that isn't going to happen. That is an illegal order. You will have to send someone else."

He was hung up on.

"Well, there is my career down the drain."

"Maybe not," came from a new voice.

Our favorite sheriff's deputy, George Burrill, had just walked in. Now I knew what Dad had arranged before he let the cops in.

"Now, what's going on here?"

Mum, whose shotgun had disappeared, smiled at George.

"Let's all have a seat, and may I offer anyone coffee or tea?"

The detectives retrieved their weapons.

Deputy Burrill noticed this and reprimanded them with, "Not a good idea parting with your weapons, boys."

Mutt replied, "You had to have been here," while he glared at Mum.

Mrs. Hernandez had been listening in on all this. She wheeled in a trolley with coffee, tea, sugar, cream, and some pastries. She approached each of us and fulfilled the requested refreshments.

She didn't ask me; she just poured black coffee and handed me a plate with four pastries. She must think I'm a pig. They were good.

As Mutt and Jeff explained their side of the story, Mum and I gave ours. It became clear what was going on.

A known motorcycle gangster was injured. We had picked him up and seen to his treatment. The Los Angeles organized crime unit wanted to know if we were connected.

Looking around, the two cops had concluded that we weren't. However, their captain wasn't convinced and had us ordered in no matter what the law said.

Once he understood this, Deputy Burrill borrowed our phone. Looking up a number in his little black phone book, he made a call.

He knew the captain in question.

"Hey, David, I have two of your detectives here operating out of their jurisdiction without a warrant. Were you planning on calling me?"

He listened for a while.

"Do you realize you ordered your men to arrest Lady and Sir Richard Jackson illegally? May I mention that Lady Jackson's husband is a personal friend of the mayor?"

"Yeah, you have stepped in it. Here, you can tell the Jacksons how sorry you are."

Dad took the phone from the deputy and listened to a long-winded, what I guessed was an apology. After a few minutes, I ducked out to my room and grabbed my honorary LA police badge.

On returning, I handed it to Mutt, who I since learned was John. After looking at it, he handed it to Jeff, AKA Peter.

Dad had just hung up, so I was asked how I got this. I related the story of the bank robbers and my bow.

They both got excited as they remembered the incident.

"Wait, you are also an actor, aren't you? And you saved the Queen of England and landed that jet plane."

I nodded my head modestly, well, as modestly as one could after that mouthful.

The two detectives looked like they would pee their pants. They were laughing so hard.

"This story will become a legend at the station!"

Peter added, "I don't think we need to remember the shotgun."

Deputy Burrill had a puzzled look but kept his mouth shut. I think he now understood why the detectives had parted with their weapons.

Both detectives apologized for their rough behavior, but Mum and Dad shrugged it off. Then a serious conversation proceeded where Mum and I explained our involvement, to the point of showing them Jon Baker's note.

Chapter 10

By the time all this drama was done, the morning was shot, so I studied for a while. Well, I typed up a paper that interested me. It would have been extra credit at Bellefontaine High; here it was for my pleasure. When you are essentially a class of one, you are the valedictorian, also last in your class. Hmm, I wonder, class valedictorian, salutatorian, and president would be neat on a college application.

I could be captain of the Archery and Golf Teams and the Fencing Club. Or I could just not get myself in trouble by needless bragging. Fun thought, though.

After lunch, I finally made it to flight school. It was a different experience than learning from Mr. McGarry. He taught by doing. They wanted me to do the bookwork first, followed by simulators, and finally, flying time.

They were working with multiple students simultaneously, so I understood why they did it that way. His way was more fun.

There were eight of us who wanted to be multi-engine pilots. The instructor went over our paperwork while we were doing our reading assignment.

At one point, the instructor asked, "Jackson, McGarry of the Flying Tigers was your first instructor?"

"Yes, sir."

"Well, don't strafe the flight line."

I guess they all knew Bill. He had given me approach pointers for that very same operation. I thought it was all in fun. Now I wonder.

We were asked if we had any questions at the end of our time. A couple of eager beaver types kept us there for another fifteen minutes.

The instructor caught me as I was leaving.

"Got a minute?"

"Certainly."

"Bill McGarry is one of if not the best pilot in the world and an excellent instructor. I assume you had one on one with him."

I nodded yes.

"You will find most of this boring then, but stick with it. You will get what you need out of this course."

"I do have one question."

"Shoot."

"Why are we reading in class? Shouldn't you be teaching, with us doing our reading outside?"

"You are correct, but unfortunately, most of those in class wouldn't do their homework and would waste our time catching up, so I let everyone read in the first class. On Friday, we will quickly review this material once more. You will be surprised at the questions. Then I will have everyone read the next chapter.

"That way, I get everyone through the ground portion of the class at the same time. If you were alone and did your reading outside the classroom, it would only take one-third of the time."

He chuckled, "And we could only charge one-third as much."

I gave a dutiful laugh, assuring him I would stick with it. It reconfirmed my thoughts about all schooling. The courses were all set for the slowest and consequently held the rest back.

That thought stopped me. I turned around and caught the instructor.

"For a price, can I get individual instruction?"

"For a price, you can get almost anything. If you're serious, let's go to the front office."

We did exactly that. It turned out there was a twenty-five percent surcharge for a private course. That made sense. The school could have had multiple students with the same instructor and a better profit margin. The only catch was it was to be on a time available with my current instructor, Hank Smith. The single-student course was a private deal between him and me.

I think they did it based on Mr. McGarry being my flight instructor more than anything else. He had one heck of a good reputation locally.

After that was arranged, Mr. Smith gave me my next assignment. I was to read and be prepared for an examination covering the contents of the next two chapters. The exam was to be given immediately after the scheduled course on Friday.

Holy cow, what had I done?

Later, at dinner, we discussed the day. There were no further developments about the motorcycle gang. Well, Mary wanted a picture of me and Mum on motorcycles, but that wouldn't happen. Denny and Eddie thought motorcycle jackets would be neat. That wasn't going to happen either.

We did talk about the garage expansion. We have a meeting scheduled with an architect tomorrow afternoon. Mum also reminded us about the Friday fundraiser for George Burrill and then the Saturday charity event. Costumes were discussed; threats made; pouty faces formed (Dad), Mary waffled on the reporter idea vs. princess vs. fairy, all the usual as the Jackson family got ready for an event.

I spent the evening reading my assigned multi-engine chapters.

Before going to sleep, I read for pleasure about little Nat and sailing by log, lead, and lookout. His *American Practical Navigator* was a must-read for even today's sailors.

After my morning workout, I hung out at the stable briefly. I wasn't being nosey. Okay, I was. Everything was fine. The place was clean and well-kept. As far as I could see, the horses were all in good condition.

At breakfast, I read several letters that I had received yesterday. One was a puzzler. It was from the Valley Forge Military Academy.

A Cadet there, Cadet Rylski #6883, asked me to stop making fun of his beloved Bulgaria. I had trouble remembering when I had made fun of Bulgaria. Dad reminded me of my Hungarian and Bulgarian princess remarks to the tabloids. I shrugged as it was a dead issue I wouldn't bring up again.

The other letter was from Judy King. I hadn't heard from her for a long time. Her opening paragraph reminded me that I had owed her a letter for months. Maybe that is why I had not heard from her.

She forgave me anyway and then caught me up on her life. She had been dating but nothing serious. She hoped I was fine and kept up with me in the fan magazines. She had read I was dating a Bulgarian princess. Ouch. Other than that, it was a friend's letter reaching out to maintain contact. As time passed, we seemed to have less and less in common.

I reflected on that thought. She was the only constant girl in my life since, well, ever! I wonder what that meant. I did make a mental note to write her a reply immediately. I went directly to the library after breakfast and started a letter. I cleared up the Bulgarian princess comment I had made. I even shared Cadet Rylski's request.

Before lunch, we met with the architect on the garage extension. He had drawings that fit all our criteria. Mum's were all about maintaining an integrated look on the outside of the structure. It was to be as though it was part of the original building and not added on.

Mine and Dad's were all about the interior functionality. Dad had included a lift to work on cars. Since it was additional space, it took nothing away from what I wanted.

I desired a lot of workbench space and electrical outlets, up to 220 AC. Compressed air would be available, and all the space would be well-lit, plus plenty of storage. The storage was to be a series of cabinets, open shelving, and tool chests under the workbenches.

There would be a mezzanine for additional storage. Altogether, it would be almost two thousand square feet.

The architect asked me what I intended to build. I shrugged and replied, "I will think of something."

Dad proudly told him about how I was the inventor of the first genuinely usable hand-held hairdryer and about the cargo container business. The way the architect's attitude towards me changed was noticeable.

We were to expect drawings within two weeks, but it would be four or more months before construction was completed after the go-ahead had been given. That included putting the construction job out for bids. All in all, that sounded reasonable to us.

Lunch was a laid-back affair with a spread of deli cuts. I noticed Dad pull a Mexicali Delight beer out of the refrigerator as we headed into the small dining room, but Mum gave a headshake before he opened it. He put it back.

Chapter 11

After lunch, I called the studio to see if Mr. Monroe was available. He could work me in, so I headed over. I drove the non-bloodied T-Bird. The other was clean, but something about it gave me the heebie-jeebies.

The guard on duty was new, so I had to show my ID. How soon they forget in this business.

I only had to wait a few minutes for Mr. Monroe. He welcomed me.

"Rick, I'm so glad you stopped by. I was going to call you about the telethon. It is on for the last week in January. Not much is happening at that time of year, so we thought it would do well. Please keep that date open.

"Speaking of keeping that date open, how are you doing on a new movie project?"

"I'm not. I will spend the rest of this year and the first half of the next completing the eleventh and twelfth grades. That, of course, depends on me being able to stay with the studio school."

"Is John Baxter aware of all this?"

"Yes, sir, he is taking this as an opportunity to retire."

"Good for him. He has earned it."

"Now I'm disappointed about no movie, as we always need projects, but the school is no problem. Remember, we carry you as a permanent employee doing bit parts in movies."

"I forgot about that; I haven't been called for any."

"And you probably haven't noticed the money being deposited into your checking account every week."

I was embarrassed that I hadn't, but it always had at least one hundred thousand dollars in it. I had given up paying attention. That blew my mind. I had to change my ways. I could remember when a two-dollar allowance was big money!

"Mike Todd has a project underway. You might be called on for a cameo for that. There will be a lot of big names in it from all over the world."

"Okay, sounds good."

"I will let the school know nothing is holding things back."

"I appreciate it."

"If I may ask, what are your plans after you graduate?"

"I'm thinking of a good technical school like MIT or Stanford."

"So, your movie career will be on hold?"

"I'm afraid so. It is only fair to tell you with my other ventures, I may never make another one other than the one we are doing for Jackson Enterprises. Even then, I don't have that much to do with it.'

"That movie or information commercial you are doing is good for all involved. You have always had a good reputation, but this has put it over the top. People want to be involved with a Jackson project."

"Why is that?"

"Rick, I had my people following this debacle about the bankrupt movie. Do you realize everyone involved who needs or wants a job already has one? That is unheard of in this industry."

"There can't be that many projects go bad."

"You would be surprised by the bankruptcies or, like a few years ago, the McCarthy blacklists. Think about those. Yes, some stars were fired, but if they were in the middle of a project, then everyone lost their job. I take no sides on the political issues, but it wasn't right that everyone paid for it, especially when some of the charges were false."

"One thing for certain about the bankruptcy—there was fraud involved. It looks like the money man had gambling problems, and the mob wanted their money one way or the other. He chose the other."

We finished, and I went to the schoolhouse, but no one was around.

From there, I headed over to Calabasas Country Club and played eighteen holes.

After dinner, it was more time in the schoolbooks. This session was spent on scholastic matters.

At breakfast, I brought up the subject of the bloody T-Bird. It turned out that Mum shared my feelings about the car. It had cleaned up well, but there just was something about it now.

A thought had occurred to me last night.

"It makes no sense to own two identical cars. Do you have any objections to me trading in the bloody bird?"

It was neat to call it the "bloody bird." When I was younger, Mum would have considered that swearing, but she had to accept that it wasn't swearing in America. I felt that I was getting away with something.

Anyway, she and Dad had no problem other than asking the basic question of why I should replace it. Why not just sell it outright and forget it?

I stammered a bit as I tried to come up with a rational defense for my other thoughts last night.

"Give it up, Rick. What do you want to buy?"

"Well, the Chevy Corvette looks like a nice car."

"Just what a teenage boy needs—an over-powered sports car."

This was from Mum.

Dad commented, "I read they now have a small block fuel-injected V-8 with 290 HP."

This earned him a glare from Mum.

"Jack!"

"Well, it is a good-looking car. The kid here hasn't gotten into trouble recently, so why not?"

"And I don't want him to get into any trouble."

I just had to say, "Well, maybe I could get a motorcycle instead."

"You most certainly will not, young man. A sports car is one thing. A motorcycle is another."

"Okay, I will stick with the sports car."

"Good!"

After she said that, Mum got a stricken look on her face.

"Oh, very well, buy your new toy."

It's not very often I get one past Mum. I have learned that when you do, you shut up immediately. The next is to go do what you just got away with. Don't give her time to change her mind.

I left the breakfast table quickly. I was almost to the bloody bird. Dad came with me.

"Is the title in the glove box?"

A quick check found it there.

"Let's go before she catches up with us."

We headed off to a local Chevy dealer who Dad knew.

As we parked, the first lot lizard approached us. Dad told him we were here to see the owner, so we broke free of him. The next one was at the door. Picking up the pace, Dad skirted around him and headed to the receptionist.

The owner was in and glad-handed Dad. You could see his eyes light up when our mission was explained. He introduced us to his sales manager, who in turn gave us to a salesman. He wasn't either of the two we had first seen.

He had the same last name as the owner, so I think I knew how that worked. The sour look of the guy at the door confirmed my thoughts. The guy outside would be chewing nails when he heard as it was his up.

I could not do anything about it, so I explained what I was interested in.

They had three Corvettes on the lot, two red and white, one black and silver. I gravitated to the black and silver convertible with the power top.

The salesman pointed out the 8000-rpm tachometer in the center in front of the driver. He confirmed it was a small block V8 with fuel injection, which gave 290 HP. He explained because of all this speed, there was a new safety feature: seat belts.

The seat belts looked flimsy to me after the five-point belts on the 707, but I let it go. I did like the shifter with the T handle.

I was ready to take a test drive, but the salesman continued his pitch.

The salesman demonstrated the power windows, a new feature to me. He also spoke about the RPO 684 heavy-duty brakes and suspension system. This thing could take a corner.

The 276 15" x 5.5" wheels looked good. I knew the size because he told me.

Now, I was getting impatient to drive the car.

Instead, he went on about the black interior and the fact the louvers and chrome strips from 1958 had been removed.

I want to drive the car!

When he started to point out the four headlamps and chrome grill, I had enough.

"May I please take a test drive?"

"Why certainly; I wasn't sure if you were interested."

"I'm interested now. Can we go?"

As I was getting behind the wheel, I saw Dad's smirk. That was when I realized that the salesman had dragged his feet deliberately. I had just lost some negotiating power by my eagerness.

I didn't care right then as I fired up the machine.

I loved the rumble of the exhaust.

It drove like a dream. Several cute girls waved at me as we pulled out of the lot. Were they part of the sales effort?

After driving the car for several miles, I was ready to sign on the dotted line. Well, at least ready to write a check.

While I had been taking my test drive, they had been checking the bloody bird out. We had cleaned it well, so they didn't know its recent history.

Chapter 12

When we sat down to talk about the price, they got cute with showing what they would give on my trade-in. The number was written down on a strip of paper. It was four digits. The salesman had them covered with his fingers.

The first finger he removed covered the last number. It was zero. He kept patter up, trying to build some suspense, but I ruined his game by pulling the paper out from under his hand. The actual number seemed fair, so I didn't understand what he was trying to accomplish.

He was not a happy camper, but I was the customer, so he continued.

"What sort of payment can you handle?"

I understood this part: he wanted to know if I was a price or payment buyer. He would prefer a payment buyer as he would have more freedom to make money on financing and any other terms they could dream up.

I was about to say I would pay cash when Dad interrupted.

"That would depend on what you offer. What is the price of the Vette, less the trade-in?"

This put the ball in the salesman's court. Good job, Dad!

He wrote down a price. Why don't they say these things?

Dad continued, "What would be the payment if Rick put ten percent down or twenty percent?"

Numbers were calculated, his machine clacking away. He gave the two numbers, the twenty percent down resulting in a lower number.

"Okay, now refigure after the dealer's discount. Also, I saw in the paper that Chevy was making an allowance, so include that in."

With a frown, the salesman entered the numbers and spoke directly to Dad.

"So, here's the payment for twenty percent down."

The guy had finally figured out who was running this show.

"If there was a larger down payment, could you come down a little more in the price?"

"I could only reduce the amount of the payment."

"Well, then, we need to be going. There is a dealer out in the Valley that can do better."

We stood up to leave. The salesman had the T-Bird keys in hand. I reached for them, but he pulled back.

"We need to talk about this some more."

I just kept my hand out for the keys. He showed no sign of giving them back.

Dad asked, "So what else can you offer?"

The salesman sat back down with a small smile. He figured he had Dad and me trapped as long as he had our keys. I changed that game by grabbing his wrist with my left hand and twisting the keys out of his hand with my right.

"I could have you arrested for assault."

"And you for attempted car theft."

Dad said, "Now, boys, settle down, and what do you have to counteroffer with?"

I found that a little funny as we, well, Dad, had offered nothing yet.

"I will have to get this approved by my sales manager, but this is what I think we can do."

He left the room, and I was about to open my mouth when Dad held his finger vertically over his lips. Was this office wiretapped? After five minutes of letting us stew, the salesman and his manager returned.

"Well, this will take us to the bone, but we can do it."

I took a chance, "Another one percent, and I will sign the deal here and now."

As I said this, I laid out the T-Bird title and set my checkbook beside it. The sales manager hemmed and hawed but came around to my price.

The number I was interested in was the cost of the car, less the trade-in, but apparently, they thought I was going to put twenty percent down.

"Before I finalize this, Rick, we also sell car insurance on the vehicle and insurance to cover the loan if you have to default. Also, there is undercoating for rust."

"We have an insurance agent we use; I don't need insurance on a loan, and I haven't seen much salt on the road here in California to need a rust inhibitor."

"Except being next to the ocean will cause rust."

"We live inland, so I'm not worried. What is the price of the car?"

Finally, I had a price.

"I will set you up for financing with our local bank."

"Not needed."

"Oh, are you going to use your bank?"

"No, I am writing a check."

"We can't do that; the price was contingent on you financing the car."

"That has not been said. You have written down what you will sell the car for."

The sales manager got red in the face and was about to throw a fit when the owner stepped in.

"What's the problem, Jack?"

"We were quoted a price, and now he is trying to welsh on it."

It took a while, but it straightened out. When I wrote a check, the sales manager tried to get us to sign loan papers, "Just until the check clears."

The owner told him that it wasn't necessary.

We then had to wait for the Corvette to be prepped. While they did that, I double-checked the T-Bird for anything left. Other than a dried-out sock left from some surfing outing, it was empty. Now that the car was going, it didn't bother me at all.

It took another hour, but finally, the paper temporary tag was in place, and I drove away. They took the fun out of buying a car with their games. What a turn-off.

On the way home with the top-down, Dad and I listened to classics about "bearcat stew" and "he's a clown, why's everybody always pickin' on me?" Also, I never did figure out if it was purple or its food purple.

We got home for a late lunch. Mum took one look at the car, held out her hands for the keys, and took it for a spin. It is a good thing security had the gate open for her when she returned as she blew through the entrance and brought the car in sideways.

"Nice car, Rick. I would like to take it out occasionally."

"Sure thing, Mum."

Not what I was expecting. From someone who didn't drive in Ohio who became this maniac was impressive. I later learned she and Anna Romanov had taken driving lessons together to learn to avoid pursuit.

Anyway, Mum seems to have accepted my new car. Hope I get to drive it.

While we ate lunch, Dad read the reviews of Dennis Lawson's first business article in the paper. They appeared yesterday and were well received by the paper's readers. The most common comment was the hope that it would be a regular feature.

It wasn't too late, so I went to Calabasas and practiced golf. I worked on getting out of the rough and from under tree limbs. I wasn't in trouble on the course that often, so I needed to work on these areas.

I knew today would be busy, so I called my office early and let them know I wouldn't be in today.

After breakfast, I called the studio schoolhouse. They were in, so I decided to stop by. Both Miss Sperry and Mr. Danson were waiting for me, plus a person from the State of California.

Surprisingly, they were all supportive of my plan. The lady from the state expressed her office's feelings, "You are so far out of the norm we just want to get it over with. There is no sense in trying to fit you into the school system. It would be too disruptive."

I was asked if I had any plans for the rest of the day. I had my flying class. They asked if I could skip it. I called the school, and I explained I couldn't make it. They told me to stop by tomorrow morning to speak to my instructor.

The next thing you know, I was taking the end-of-the-year tests in all my subjects. My studies had covered all the material for an entire year, so it wasn't a wipeout, but it was a stretch.

As I completed a test, it was scored by the lady from the state. I never did learn her name. My lunch was ordered from the commissary. I was given half an hour for it and a bathroom break.

By three in the afternoon, I felt like a dishrag. While I grabbed a snack, they graded my last test.

"Congratulations, Rick, you now have passed the tenth grade."

"Thanks, how did I do?"

"You passed the tenth grade, not with your usual straight A's, but you passed."

"Won't that hurt me later?"

"Think about it, Rick, what university in the world wouldn't want you as a student and, more importantly, as an alumnus? As long as your scores aren't embarrassingly low, you are in. Even if they are at the bottom, you could buy them a building or two and get in."

"I hadn't thought of that. I guess follow the money is a truism."

We agreed to meet next Monday to develop my schedule for the eleventh and twelfth grades.

Chapter 13

I still had some time before I had to be home to get ready for the fundraiser for George Burrill for sheriff, so I headed over to the archery area.

Mr. Bell welcomed me; my gear was still there in storage, so I spent an hour and a half keeping my skills current. I was a little rusty, but not that bad. It came back quickly. I doubt I was good enough for Agincourt, but I could hit the target at a distance.

Our house was, as expected, a bit of a madhouse. The valet parking and catering people were setting up. Mum was on Mary about leaving some of those little wax Coke bottles with sugar water in them on the reception couch. Seems they melted in the sunlight. I snuck by the two of them to my room.

I showered, dressed, and spent my time with my flying manuals until it was time for the cocktail party and dinner for sponsors. By donating a larger sum as a sponsor of the event, people were invited to the pre-event. They got to hobnob for a fee.

The Burrill fundraiser started with a one-hundred-dollar semi-formal dinner for the sponsors. Of course, George made a few remarks. They centered on the local hot-button issue of the homeless moving into the area. I had heard this small variation on his law-and-order stump speech several times, so it wasn't too exciting.

Watching the people in the room as they had cocktails before dinner was interesting. Everyone was on their best behavior. People who had lunch together today acted like they were newly met after a long separation. There were more air kisses and handshakes than in a European court. Well, maybe not more. It was hard to beat the Europeans in fake greetings.

Mum had hired a catering service for the evening, so there were canapes on top of canapes. I had several coconut shrimp, well, maybe a half dozen. Later, I denied I ate a dozen angels on horseback. Since

I didn't keep track, there was no way to challenge my story, and I'm sticking to it.

There was an open bar. Luckily, they had plenty of Coke.

It was fun watching people circulate and contact each other. They had all been registered at the door. Invitations had been sent out to the A-list of the Republican powerbrokers. Anna Romanov and Sharon Bronson were there to give the party a bit of Hollywood glamor. They posed for a lot of pictures with people.

People had also brought their cameras. I would have dots in front of my eyes from the blue flashbulbs going off all night.

I was even asked to pose with some people. I had a special place to stand. It was in front of the tiger skin, which had been mounted on the wall for the evening.

Dad would take a small group of men at a time into his study, where he had his Holland and Holland rifle out to show. Pictures were also taken there, with the attendees holding the triple-checked unloaded rifle.

You could see business contacts being made left and right.

I saw an unusual sight as I circled the room doing my glad-handing. There was a very frustrated-looking young man standing there. He looked to be nine or ten years old.

He was dressed almost identically to me: Brooks Brother's dark blue sport coat, white shirt with a button-down collar, regimental striped tie (I think Coldstream guards), black shoes, socks, and belt.

He was the only one his age in the room; my brothers and sister were lucky and didn't have to attend. Some people couldn't get sitters, so their kids were in the basement.

I went over and introduced myself to him. We shook hands, and he extended a business card. It read (David "Davy" Dawson) and gave an address and phone number. On the back was a brief sentence, "Interested in Politics."

"Davy, you don't look very happy. Can I help?"

"Sir Richard, I am trying to make contacts in the political world. If I start now, by the time I have finished college, I will know all the movers and shakers. The problem is when I try to introduce myself, I get blown off immediately. I don't know how to handle this."

Several things came to mind. I had introduced myself as Rick, but he had been paying attention to the world. Next, this kid is planning years out. I'm proud to sort out the next six months.

"Are you here with anyone?"

He blushed from the top of his head to as far down as you could see.

"Not exactly."

"Not exactly how?"

"My parents received an invitation but were not coming. They left it on the kitchen table. I bought a certified check with my newspaper route money and sent it in. I received my ticket in the mail at my girlfriend's house.

"I told my parents I was going to stay with a friend. I had my clothes stored at her house, so I changed there and took a cab."

"She must be a close friend."

If humanly possible, he blushed even more.

"Yes, she is."

"Well, let's see if I can get you started."

"That would be great!"

There's no reason not to start at the top.

"Mr. Burrill, I want to introduce a young fan and contributor. He has a project where he has to contact people in the political arena by exchanging business cards."

Mr. Burrill graciously exchanged cards, asked a few questions, and moved on. Those around us were not surprised when they were approached and willingly did the card exchange.

I made certain he had a picture with me in front of the tiger skin and holding the rifle.

Then, after nine or ten people, I told Davy he was on his own. Again, he thanked me profusely and went back to work. The way I had presented it implied that it was a school project, and Davy continued that misleading line of thought.

Off to a good start for a budding politician. I will probably go to hell for this.

I watched him for a while and saw he was doing fine. We will hear more of Davy Dawson in the future; he certainly isn't a stupid boy.

I also pointed him out to one of our security people and asked them to make certain he didn't have any problems getting a cab ride home.

After the cocktail party, the doors were opened for all the donors. There must have been over a hundred people sitting down for dinner. Side tables had been set to accommodate the crowd. I had an assigned table where I had to entertain and be certain that everyone had a chance to donate again.

After dinner, it was more posing with the tiger skin. I was thankful for all my practice in acting. I said the same words with conviction over and over again. I wondered why we hadn't seen any big-name actors in the political arena. They would be naturals at the campaigning part.

As all events do, it came to an end. George's campaign accountant reported that the fundraiser brought in over twenty thousand dollars. We were told that was an enormous amount of money for a local campaign. This would all be reported in Dad's papers. Of course, they had a reporter and photographer there all evening.

After checking with security about Davy getting a cab ride, I excused myself and went to bed.

I was at the flight school as soon as it was open. Hank Smith was okay with me missing the class. He gave me the exams on the three chapters, which I aced. He told me that was what he expected, so he wasn't upset, but please try not to miss others. I promised not to. My next assignment was due Wednesday of next week. It covered another three chapters. I would have done six chapters to the class's two.

I spent the rest of Saturday morning playing golf. John Jacobs was my caddy, as usual. I wasn't trying to set any course records, just enjoying the day. During the extended walk, I told John I would like to qualify for the US Open. My first step would be to win the local qualifying round at Riviera Country Club in Santa Monica Canyon on May 15 next year, then the sectional the following week.

John had been my caddy enough times to know that this was a real possibility.

"Rick, have you ever played that course?"

"No, but I suspect it can be tough."

"You are right about that. It is a private club. How will you get permission to practice."

"I think as a member of Warner Brothers, I have guest privileges."

"That sounds like it would be fun. Wish I could go with you."

"You can. I will hire you as my caddy for the event."

"I would like that, but I don't know that course."

I had some thoughts on that, and so negotiations began. The upshot was that John would get a strong recommendation from our local pro. He would start caddying as soon as possible at Riviera.

He would be on my payroll. Since I had no plans on becoming a professional, his salary would be respectable. He would keep all money earned as a caddy plus tips. This was all to be written up in a personal services contract. John had just tripled his income.

After the round, we talked to the pro. He made a phone call then and there. Speaking with the Riviera Country Club pro, the pro told the whole story of why John needed a job as a caddy.

I guess my local golf reputation was in good standing as it was approved immediately. There was also the fact that professional caddies were always in demand.

It was confirmed that I had guest privileges.

I called my offices and explained to counsel what was needed in a contract. John was to stop at our offices next Monday for the signing.

I ate lunch at the club.

It was so neat driving the Corvette home. I know every girl turned to look at me. Well, I think they did.

When I got home, there was a little excitement. A package had arrived in the mail addressed to me and Mum. She opened it, and it contained two motorcycle vests. They had the distinctive Hells Angels' Death's Head on the back. There were a half dozen other patches on it. If we interpreted them correctly, Mum and I were now full-fledged Hells Angels members.

It was a shame they got here just before the costume party. It was too late to gather any accessories. We did have a good laugh about where we could wear them.

Mum thought hers would go well at the White House. I was going to the investiture at Buckingham Palace in the spring. It would be just the thing. Well, maybe not.

Chapter 14

I then spent an easy afternoon studying my flight manuals.

At dinner, I shared my plans to qualify for the US Open as an amateur. No one at the table doubted that I could do it. Dad thought my plan for John to learn the course was sound.

After dinner, it was time to get dressed for Mum's Halloween charity party. I was taking the easy way out as I dressed in jeans, cowboy boots, belt, and hat. I had a Western shirt under my vest. Pinned to the vest was my honorary Texas Ranger Badge. I thought long and hard about it but finally buckled on my gun belt with my real 45 Colt revolver. It was a present from John Wayne from our first movie. I made certain it was unloaded but did keep live shells in the loops at the back of the belt.

I ambled into the reception (cowboys always amble) as Dad and the head of the security shift talked.

"It's the same valet and catering crews as last night, so no changes. They have all been vetted. We will not let anyone in without an invitation."

"Well, let's use a little common sense; if someone shows up with an infant with them having only an adult invitation, let them in. Any kid who looks more than ten, ask me or Peg."

"Okay. Many of these ladies will be wearing a fortune in jewelry."

I had thought about that. Last night they hadn't, but this was a different crowd. This was the high society of Hollywood.

I got to see Mary practicing her stunt. Yes, her stunt. Her costume was a fairy princess. She had changed her mind about being a reporter. Not being able to choose between a fairy and a princess, she chose both. Well, it seems fairy princesses could fly and wave a magic wand that gave off sparkles.

The little monster had talked Mum and Dad into hiring Dick Wyman to set up a wire and harness for her so she could swoop off the second-floor stairs at the entrance hall and soar over the crowd while she waved her wand and threw sparkles over the gathered group as they arrived.

It looked cool.

Denny was a pirate helping to welcome guests. He had a hat decorated with a skull and crossbones, an eyepatch, and a stuffed parrot on his shoulder. I thought it was stuffed until it said, "Ahoy." Of course, Denny used "arrr" a lot.

Eddie was a hobo and seemed mundane after the other two, but he looked happy as he begged from the guests with his tin cup. I later learned he made thirty-two dollars, so he should have been happy.

There was a table set up where people dropped off late donations. Most had sent them in with their checks.

I watched the guests as they arrived to see what the costumes would be. There were several Cleopatras and Mark Anthonys. Many of the characters were from *The Wizard of Oz*. Several others were cowboys. Maybe we could have a shoot-out later. I was glad to see Superman and Batman there. Fred Flintstone and Wilma looked good. Some I had no idea what they were.

A gangster and his moll looked dangerous. He had a violin case, which I suppose held his Tommy gun. His moll was ugly for a woman. I think it was a guy in disguise. The third person in their party was dressed as an FBI agent. I know that was what he was supposed to be, as he had a big badge with "FBI" handwritten on it pinned to his coat.

Guests gathered in the entranceway and reception until the appointed hour. At that time, the ballroom doors were opened, and everyone poured in for the dance.

Once all were in, the doors were closed, and people started to sit at their assigned tables. These were assigned by number in advance.

Except then, all hell broke loose. Hell in the form of a real Tommy gun being fired into the ceiling.

"This is a robbery. Everyone stay right where you are. My two helpers will collect your wallets, purses, and jewelry."

The guy with the machine gun pointed at his two cohorts, who now had what looked like pillow covers.

I worked my way deeper into the crowd while I pulled bullets out of my gun belt. Carefully loading the six-shot revolver, I thought furiously. Opening fire in this crowd would be too dangerous, but I would watch events unfold.

The collectors, the gangster moll, really a guy, and the fake FBI guy were working their way through the crowd. This didn't look too smart to me. The only thing they had going for them was the guy with the Tommy gun.

The guy with the gun spoke.

"You must be wondering how we will get out; I will take a hostage or two, starting with that little fairy princess right there."

That was a mistake as I worked my way to the center of the room. Mary had started forward, but Mum grabbed her. This led to the gunman looking at Mum.

That gave me an opportunity as I stepped forward and, using a two-handed grip, shot the gunman in the chest. It must have been his lucky day because he was holding the machine gun in a loose form of port arms. I shot the machine gun right in the trigger.

This had the effect of blowing off his finger and knocking him down. The bullet ended up in his lower stomach, but I was told later it didn't bounce around and tear him up.

That was all it took for the rest of the crowd to beat the others into submission.

From start to finish, the whole event took about two minutes if that. Unlike that bank in Colorado, there was time to think, not much, but some. I would have let them rob us but not put Mary in danger.

Deputy Sheriff Burrill was in attendance, along with several other law officers. They took control immediately. The bandits were searched and cuffed. The one I shot had lost a finger but was lucky to be alive.

Everyone was asked to take their seats. Some wanted to leave but weren't allowed as statements were to be taken. Mum and Dad were having a hurried conversation with the deputy. One of our security people came in with a stack of invitations.

Deputy Burrill announced to the crowd.

"Okay, folks, only people with invitations were let in. Now the questions are whose they did use, and are those people okay? So, we are going to call out the names we have. When your name is called, stand up. Anyone who recognizes them, please hold up your hand, so we know they are that person."

Other police started arriving.

They got halfway through the invitations when three names were called. No one stood up. They quickly checked the names versus a list Mum had retrieved, and four deputies headed out.

One of the first things that occurred after the bad guys were down was that my pistol was confiscated. Luckily, people had seen me loading it, so I didn't look like a nitwit.

Since it was a charity event, several society reporters and photographers were there. They were interviewing like crazy. The police kept me separate from them. There were plenty of pictures taken at a distance.

I had to sit at a table hastily moved to the front of the room as an ad hoc command center and write my statement. It was pretty simple, "They announced a robbery. I was okay with that until they threatened Mary. I shot the guy."

Mr. Burrill chuckled at my honorary Texas Ranger badge.

"We will have to get you a deputy sheriff's badge."

After the robbers were hauled away, Mum had the band start playing, and the dance was on. I did give interviews on the side but kept them as simple as my police statement.

Would you believe I won the prize for the best costume?

After all that happened on Saturday, we did nothing on Sunday. I rode George around the park. Mum had a thousand or so phone calls. I also had a bunch but wasn't talking to anyone.

At lunch, it was reported the three invitations were to a couple and their adult son. They weren't coming, so they told a maid to pitch them. Instead, she gave them to her boyfriend; the rest is history.

I went out to Ontario, rented a plane for the afternoon, and just flew around the area. Dinner was a quiet affair. Mary kissed me on the cheek for saving her from the bad guys. Not a bad reward.

Chapter 15

Monday morning, the phone started ringing. The Halloween Nightmare Party, as the press had christened it, was national news. The stories were all over the place. A big deal was made of me shooting the bad guy; that was to be expected. What surprised me was all the criticism of continuing the event.

From some of the tabloids, it appeared that we danced and laughed on blood-soaked floors. We knew what the tabloids said because Mum had gotten a copy of every one she could find.

I found out that my date, the Bulgarian princess, was either mad at me, in love with me, carrying my child, or dropping me for another guy. I wondered if I should write Cadet Rylski #6883 and tell him she wasn't there. Heck, I don't even know if she exists.

Mary was pleased with the photograph of her flying through the air. The question in the paper that asked, "How many will die for her?" left us uneasy. Mary had never been told the details of the Russians who kidnapped her.

The NRA called me a hero for defending our home. Others called me a lunatic for carrying a weapon and shooting in a crowded house. I agreed with both of them. It could have gone very badly. But don't try to harm Mary!

We talked it over at the breakfast table. In the end, we all decided that I had to give some interviews. Dad's papers, of course, then the *LA Times*. I had several calls to go to Washington for the Sunday morning shows but didn't want to spend the time traveling. It was the same with the New York talk shows.

The Beach House home inspection was scheduled for this afternoon. Dad and I both wanted to be there for that.

I had a busy day. There was a business update; I had missed going to the office last Friday. Also, there was the John Jacobs contract to get signed and, finally, to pick up my books for the eleventh and twelfth grades.

My first stop was my office. There wasn't that much new business to review. Most of it centered on the information commercial. That was a mouthful to say all the time, so I kept calling it the infomercial. It worked as our in-house slang. No one else would probably ever use it.

This was not a time-critical project, but we did want to wrap it up. My role would be all voice-overs on pictures of the various ports, ships, and factories. It would start with me being interviewed on how I got this idea. There would be shots of crews loading ships and trucks the old way, then shots of containers being loaded.

It was a blatant advertisement. We were trying to have President Eisenhower say a few words on how this would help America trade worldwide. World War II had destroyed the manufacturing capability of most of the world. They needed our products while they rebuilt. How this would work out in fifty years, I had no idea.

Hairdryer sales were continuing upwards. Being able to dry your hair at home and style it appeared to cross all age and economic groups of women. Now, if long hair came into fashion for men, that would be something. Not that it is going to happen.

Jim Williamson went over the financials with us. I was beginning to believe that I could end up as the richest person in the world. That was cause for concern. Would I live my life as I wanted or as the money dictated? I didn't want to become a recluse scared to go out. Being able to do what I wanted was nice, but at some point, security would become an issue.

Would the world put expectations on me that I couldn't live up to? A loud exhaust pipe going down the road saved me from these morbid thoughts. I wondered if I could take it with my new Corvette.

There was a formal request from the Prime Minister of Australia to be present at the opening of the new facilities in Sydney. This wouldn't be until the fall of next year, so I asked for a draft letter for my signature as I gave a tentative yes. Who knows where I will be in a year?

John Jacobs was waiting in the outer office to sign his contract. He looked uncomfortable in a suit and tie. I think the suit was from the 1940s, as it looked like a zoot suit. At least he didn't have one of those silly hats. The one sitting in his lap was a modern fedora.

I welcomed him and did my best to make him comfortable. The contract was here, ready to be signed. I asked if he wanted to take it with him for his lawyer to review. He informed me that if he didn't bring home a copy of a signed contract, his wife would probably shoot him. This was the best thing that ever happened to them.

I inquired about his family, as I didn't even know he was married. It turned out they were newlyweds and wanted to start a family. This job would allow them to do so. I still had our lawyer review each paragraph with him in plain English. It was not a complex contract. If he didn't commit any criminal acts, his income was secure for the next two years with a continuing option on both sides.

There was also no penalty for John if he walked away. My lawyer wasn't wild about this, but my argument was that it was such a good deal it would take something serious to make him leave.

At last, John was able to leave without being shot at home. I saw him out the front door. He had an enormous smile as he was taking that tie off.

It had taken all morning. Dad had things to do at his office, so I headed towards the studio.

When I exited the office door, I smiled as I lost my tie.

Tooling down Rodeo Drive in a Corvette with the top down is good for the ego. Women would turn and stare at me. Men would look at the car. At least, I hoped it was in that order.

At the studio school, they had a stack of books for me. It filled the boot of the Vette. I was also scheduled to attend Chemistry at Hollywood High. A syllabus had been printed out with a timeline of work due and several exams. The exams would have been like the six-week tests if I had regular classes. There was no mid-term, just a final.

While a lot of work, it seemed doable.

I dropped the books off at home and scarfed some lunch to the annoyance of Mrs. Hernandez, who thought lunch should be a leisurely affair. Mum agreed with her, but fortunately, she was not there. I asked where she was; apparently, she had a luncheon date at the British Consulate in Central City. I wondered what that was about.

I met Dad at the Beach House. The real estate agent and the home inspector were already there and started. The inspector had some concerns. The wiring was not to code. Every electrical plate in the house would have to be removed and checked. He recommended an electrician be hired. Some receptacles had to be replaced.

The main electrical panel looked good, and he didn't think any new wires would have to be pulled, so it was not a deal killer.

His primary concern was the addition I had noted. He had to check to see if permits had been pulled. The house did not have a smooth, professional look where the added room joined. That is why I had noticed it. If there were no permits for the job, the room would have to be torn out and either replaced or the house made smaller.

That would be a deal killer unless the price were reduced dramatically. The inspector told us he would go downtown and check on the situation as his next stop. Needless to say, the real estate agent was not happy.

Dad and I went our separate ways, his back to work and mine returning to the house to study. I had a ton of schoolbooks to get set up in the library. That project only took half an hour, so I took my new World History text to the top of the tower.

There were no signs out that sunbathing was going on. I had it to myself. Mrs. Hernandez had seen me go up as she showed up with a pitcher of lemonade and a cheese and cracker plate. This was to make up for my lunch, which I ate too fast. She was certain none would have stayed in my stomach, so I must be hungry.

Well, I'm a teenage boy, so I'm always hungry.

With a full tummy sitting in the sun, I dozed off. I would tell Mrs. Hernandez about my siesta. It would gain back some of the brownie points lost at lunch.

My history text was interesting. I relearned that the Holy Roman Empire was not Holy, not Roman, and not an Empire. Talk about false advertising!

Dinner was a quiet affair. At least the phone had stopped ringing about the Halloween Party. Dad had heard the guy I shot was going to be fine. He would get more jail time for his fully automatic machine gun than the attempted robbery. Of course, besides the robbery, there would be charges involved with the threatened hostage-taking, which is a form of kidnapping.

We wouldn't see those guys for a long time. The only good to come out of it was the money raised. They had collected a record thirty-five thousand dollars for the women's shelter they were sponsoring. That made their entire annual budget.

Denny wanted to know if they could arrange a robbery every year. I think he was kidding.

After dinner, I went back to my history text and looked at the suggested readings at the end of the chapter. I would have to obtain a copy of every book in the bibliography to maintain my current standard of learning. There was no reason to back off just because I wanted to finish high school.

When you started looking at sources other than the official school textbook, the different viewpoints found were amazing. It was like someone, somewhere, had decided what their take on history was, and they were making it the official version.

Then, to cover themselves, they added in the bibliography with other texts, knowing full well that few, if any, would read them. Yet they could claim all facts were presented.

I had been skeptical about textbooks since the fifth grade. I will never forget reading in my social studies textbook that southern children walked barefoot. This led to hookworms, which caused Southerners to talk slowly. My neighbor Eugene Wilson was from South Carolina and talked as slow as all get out, but he wore shoes.

Anyway, I talked to Mum, and she would have someone order all the books listed in my text. We had so many books that our library shelves should be checked to see if we already had a copy before ordering. After thinking about it, she decided we needed a card catalog for our books. I wasn't the only book collector in the family. She and Dad had bought a lot in the last year.

I studied until bedtime and called it a night.

Chapter 16

I hadn't ridden George for a while, so I took him out on the trails in the park behind our house. It was a pleasant outing. By the time I had finished my exercises, riding, and rubbing George down, I couldn't stand myself. The shower was exceptionally refreshing. I was going to have a good day.

At breakfast, everyone was cheerful. We were past Saturday night, and only one tabloid was wondering if my Bulgarian Princess was going to have a boy or girl. What was going on with that? I wasn't even sure if Bulgaria had a king, much less a princess.

It had me curious enough earlier that I checked in the Encyclopedia Americana and found there was a king in exile. Still, it gave no information about any brothers or sisters of the current monarch in exile. Wow, it must be a mouthful to say that all the time.

Dad changed the subject.

"Rick, I had a phone call yesterday from the membership chair at the Riviera Country Club. He told me that it would be viewed favorably if we applied for a family membership."

"I thought there was a long waiting list for places like that."

"There is no waiting list for Dame Jackson or her son Sir Richard."

"They are making an exception because of me and Mum?"

"Yes, because I asked about having a single membership, and I got the runaround. They want your titles."

"Have you decided?"

"We are joining. It's good business and tax-deductible."

Mum said, "The women there must be something else. They better keep their hands off my men."

"Oh, I doubt any of them would be interested in me."

"Christina would hang out at a place like this."

I shuddered. That was one English blonde I would never forget.

"I will be on my guard."

As we were leaving the breakfast table, an envelope was delivered. It contained the home inspection report. The house had some significant issues. It would need to be completely rewired, and no permits had been pulled for the addition. According to the city, it had to come down.

I figured that would kill the deal, which was a shame because I loved its location right on the beach waterside.

Dad had a different take.

"Rick, now these items have been found in the inspection, they have to be provided to all prospective buyers. Instead of a five hundred-thousand-dollar property, this is, at the most, a three hundred-thousand-dollar house. If they sell for that, you can add another one hundred and fifty thousand or so and have some major work done."

"The wiring will have to all be replaced, but instead of getting permits and replacing the one room, you could add two bedrooms and a full bath. There is enough room. The property is not wide, but it is long. It could be done."

"For another fifty thousand, you could add an enormous deck. So, you would have a considerably better house for the same five hundred thousand dollars."

"I wondered what the valuation would be after the rework."

"Let's pass it by one of our in-house people."

"Dad, it sounds like a good deal no matter what, so I would like to make an offer of three hundred and twenty-five thousand."

"Why so much?"

"I have learned it's best not to carve a deal to the bone."

"Whoever taught you that was a wise person."

"You did, Dad."

"Then they were super smart."

"Well..."

"Aren't you playing golf today at Riviera? You don't want to miss your tee time."

"Yeah, I had better get a move on."

John Jacobs had moved my golf clubs and gear over to Riviera, so I didn't have to worry about that.

They have valet parking at the front of the Spanish-style clubhouse. There is a really neat fountain in the front. All in all, a classy-looking place.

I managed to arrive with enough time to check in at the pro shop, put my shoes on, and gather my gear. I walked up to the tee box with two minutes to spare.

There is nothing like having time to warm up.

I was going out in a twosome. The other golfer was Steve Whitney, the assistant golf pro. He had been assigned to introduce me to the course. I guess they were serious about wanting our family's presence in their club.

Steve was a nice guy, and I felt at ease immediately. That was the last time I felt at ease until the round was complete. That course was tough!

We teed up on the black tees. The first hole was a par five 503-yard hole. It was a straight away fairway. Two enormous bunkers were guarding the green. The tee was elevated and the fairway narrow. The green was M-shaped.

Today, the pin was close to the furthest bunker, so while I had a nice drive that left me in what appeared to be a good position, it set me up for failure. My second shot needed a precision iron to clear the bunker, then immediately stopped to be near the pin. It cleared the bunker okay and then rolled past the hole by thirty feet. I felt lucky to three-putt it.

That was the story of the day.

We rounded the clubhouse turn and passed a couple of tennis courts. There were two lovely-looking young ladies, maybe in their mid-twenties, playing.

"Not very nice, are they," asked Steve.

"They look very nice to me."

He did a doubletake.

"Oh, the young women, yes, very nice, but I was talking about the tennis courts."

I felt like a fool, a one-track mind teenage fool.

"The club board of directors has been considering doing away with the polo grounds and putting in large tennis facilities. They are talking about world-class instruction. There aren't as many polo players as there used to be, and tennis is picking up."

"Nice to know, but I don't play either sport. Well, I do own a horse, but I don't think George would care for polo."

He laughed at that. "The guys who play will bring a string of seven polo ponies."

I can see why that is losing its popularity. It would cost a fortune to maintain that. Besides the seven, there would be backups at the stables and young horses being trained.

We started the back nine. I had managed to maintain par so far, but was a long way from setting any records.

The back nine threaten to kick my butt. It started with the tenth.

It was a par four 315 yards from the back tees. It looked very straightforward to me. My drive was to the green but hung to the right. It rolled off the green down a slope. I ended up with a double bogey.

I managed to finish the back nine one over, so I had a one-over-par seventy-two for the round. Not what it would take to win the qualifying rounds.

I must have looked very down when we finished because Steve asked me what my problem was. When I told him how disappointed I was with my score, he looked astonished.

"You walked onto a tournament-level course for the first time and scored a one-over? Talk about expectations!"

That did bring me back down to earth a little.

"That is egotistical of me, isn't it?"

"Well, I don't know about egotistical, but I would love to see you play to your expectations."

I gave a wry grin. "I'll have to work on that, won't I?"

It was a little late for lunch, but we hadn't eaten anything at the turn, so we went into the casual restaurant. This is opposed to the formal dining area where a suit and tie were de rigueur.

We were even allowed to wear our spike shoes here.

We were seated near a front window. As I studied the menu, which seemed to encourage a cheeseburger and fries, I noticed the two young ladies from tennis earlier.

Steve noticed them also.

"I should warn you about them. They are around thirty years old. Both married to physicians, both surgeons. They have a reputation around here."

"From my acting career and other events, I have learned to be careful about women. They may look inviting, but so does a coral snake."

"Oh, you have been burned."

As we finished up, Steve said, "Let's see if I can rescue you in advance."

He took me over to the ladies and introduced me as Sir Richard Jackson, the teenage movie star playing golf here to qualify for the US Open.

I think he thought them knowing I was a teenager would turn them off from the jailbait. If anything, it turned them on. They both preened and hand-combed their hair as they let me know in no uncertain terms they would like to get to know me.

It was like looking at two starving piranhas. I mumbled a "Nice to meet you" and moved on as fast as possible.

As we walked away, Steve shook his head. That did not go well at all. I think you are lost."

"Wait until they meet Mum and Mary. They will find out then who is lost."

This statement caused Steve to ask what I meant. I just told him it appeared my family would be joining the country club and that my Mum and my sister took a very dim view of certain types of women.

John Jacobs had been with us the entire day. He was learning the course as much as I was. He commented that he was impressed with my first outing.

"Rick, you had a bogey on ten, which you can avoid easily. You have it in you to drive to the left side of the green. It holds better there and, depending on the lie, a two-putt at worse."

"I will spend much of my time caddying here, learning to read the greens. While the fairways can be tricky, mastering the greens here is the answer."

"I suspect you are right, and of course, that is the weakest part of my game."

John snorted, then said, "Yeah, your weak spot is stronger than most people's strong spot."

"I hope you are right. At least we have time to work on this."

John took my clubs for cleaning while I changed into the shirt and slacks in the gym bag I had brought. As soon as possible, I had to arrange for a locker.

With that in mind, I stopped at the pro shop and asked about that. My question resulted in my being handed a locker key. The pro told me that since I had guest privileges, I had the right to use a locker. He was well aware my family was paying for a membership and that we would have full privileges as soon as the board voted.

Because of that, he assigned me to a full member's locker. These weren't your high school gym metal lockers. These were wooden full-length lockers with adjacent closet racks. There was a padded bench in front of each locker arrangement.

It was the poshest setup I had ever seen.

I retrieved the Vette from the valet and headed home.

At dinner, I told everyone about the country club. The building is what was called Spanish Revival. It was enormous and could hold events even larger than Jackson House. That got a few laughs.

I told them how hard the course was, and John Jacobs comments about it being a putting course, though the fairways could kill you. I went on to describe the tennis courts and plans for them.

I neglected to mention the two ladies at the club. That would take care of itself one way or the other. Why open a can of worms if you don't have to?

I spent the evening with my multi-engine textbooks. I wanted to do well on those quizzes tomorrow.

Chapter 17

The morning was a little brisk for California. It was down to forty-eight degrees last night. That was about five degrees colder than usual. It was just breaking daylight when I started running, so the temperature hadn't warmed up yet. It was a perfect day for a run.

I stayed out longer than usual, keeping a sharp eye out for tigers. I didn't see any. When I was going back to the house, I ran into Ben Carpenter. He looked upset.

"Ben, what's wrong?"

"My grandma Eunice died last night."

"I'm so sorry to hear that."

"We knew it was coming. She hasn't recognized me for days."

I did feel bad for Ben. His grandma was his only family left.

"Have arrangements been made?"

"The rest home is helping. There is no sense in holding a service, as no one is left of her friends or family. Having a chapel open with me the only one there would be silly."

"If there is anything we can do, let us know."

I had the horrible thought on the way into the house that now only Ben, the Wymans, and our family knew about the sub-basement. Shame on me. His only family had just passed.

I told the family at breakfast about Mrs. Carpenter's passing. We all thought it was sad that Ben wouldn't have a service because there would be no one to come. Mum got a determined look and said she would make some phone calls.

Dad also called his newspaper editor and had them get started on an obituary.

While this happened, I got ready to drive to the flight center at LAX. I had exams to take.

The exams were anticlimactic. I'm not that smart, really, but my study habits were standing me in good stead. I aced all three quizzes. Hank Smith was impressed that I aced them.

It was no big deal to me. The questions were well-written and multiple-choice in the standard format. That meant two of the answers were wrong if you knew anything about the subject. A third was the "distractor," which could be misconstrued as correct if you didn't know the subject, and finally, the right answer.

That meant if you had read the chapter, you had a fifty percent chance of guessing the correct answer. I had not only read the chapters several times, I had answered the trial questions after the chapter. They were the same questions worded a little differently. So, in effect, I had practiced on the actual exam.

I told Mr. Smith I didn't think it was that hard of a test.

"If you know the answers, it isn't. History says that half of the current class will fail these, and no one will have a one hundred percent on all three exams."

"Wow, I had no idea."

"Unfortunately, that is the way it is. People don't like to do schoolwork, or they have no aptitude for it. Anyway, I have you scheduled time in a simulator."

"That sounds like fun."

Well, it did sound like fun until I faced reality. I had read about what must be done to take off, fly, and land with two engines. Now, I was being thrown to the wolves. I thought I would go on some actual flights as an observer first.

There was a checklist for a Cessna 310b. The controls were set up in that mode. There was no interior as such, so the simulator could be modified to be one of several aircraft. Since they knew I had a 310 on order, that is what was set up for me.

I even had to mock the walk-around using the checklist. When I got to the flaps on a hunch, I wiggled them as I would on a real walk-around. The ones on the right wing fell off. I passed that test.

Learning from that, I checked the fuel and oil. The oil was low. Again, it was a setup.

The flap was latched back on, and I was assured that oil was not an issue since the engines didn't work.

Inside the structure, I firmly put it into my mind that I was in a real aircraft. If I acted like it wasn't real, there would be problems.

I was surprised when I fired up those motors, which didn't work. My gages said they did as oil pressure and heat indicators rose. The real kicker was the noise and vibration. It didn't take much to imagine I was in the real thing. Well, unless you tried to look out the cockpit window. There wasn't one. It would be all instruments this trip.

I had been informed this flight was considered local operations, so I didn't have to file a flight plan. Hank Smith was acting as the control tower. I said all the right words, filling in the blanks on the checklist, tail number, etc.

I received permission to take off. That was weird. No taxiing to the apron; just take off from where I was at. I suppose they can only simulate so much. It would be great if they had a moving picture screen with the actual airport, and I could move and see everything as though it was real. I couldn't imagine that would ever happen.

I successfully flew the aircraft up to fifteen thousand feet when a light on the panel showed the engine on the right wing was on fire, that and the sounds being made. I quickly grabbed the emergency checklist. I knew I would have to shut the engine down and activate the built-in fire extinguisher.

While doing that, I reported to the FAA flight tower that I had an emergency on board. I was asked if I thought I could safely land on one engine. I responded positively.

It seemed familiar when I had to fly low and slow while dumping fuel. From there, it seemed routine as I brought the aircraft into the flight pattern as directed by the tower. My instruments reflected the speed and altitude as though I was flying the aircraft as instructed.

Other than the plane wanting to crab, because of all the power being on the left-wing, it seemed like a normal landing.

I brought the plane down and signed off. Some joker had rigged up a fire siren and set it off as I reported being on the ground.

When I opened the hood, a smiling Hank Smith was waiting for me.

"Well, Rick, we have to get in your hours, in the air, but I think you can fly one of these."

"Thanks, Hank. That was so real working through the fire bit that I had no time to think. I had to follow through on the checklist to make it come out okay. I didn't have time to worry."

"I know, as you were reporting your action, you sounded almost bored."

"Then why is my shirt wringing wet?"

He laughed at that, and we started to leave the area. All of a sudden, there was applause. I looked around and realized that there was an audience of about twenty people. Most from the class I should have been in.

People seemed pleased that I had performed so well. One guy wasn't, as we walked towards him, I heard him say.

"Sure, the guy performed well in the simulator. Put him a real emergency in the air, and he would fall apart."

The guy who he was talking to whispered something in his ear. Whatever it was, it shut him up.

I couldn't help it. As I walked past, I winked at him. I know it was a cheap shot, but I felt so good about things I thought a little fun was in order.

The guy flushed red and muttered, "Sorry."

I heard him say to his buddy, "That's the kid who landed a 707?"

Mr. Smith brought me back into the real world as he assigned me more reading on instrument flying with dual engines. It was due next Wednesday.

It had taken all morning, so I headed home for lunch.

After lunch, I drove to the studio to see if anyone was in the stunt area. There was, but I got dragooned into being an extra in some movie. When I say dragooned, I mean dragooned. I was sent to makeup, where I had to don a British heavy cavalry uniform.

I tried to argue that dragoons weren't heavy cavalry. But the wardrobe department didn't care. That was what was ordered, so that is what I would wear if I were going to be in the scene. I realized it was only a movie and had seen grosser historical errors.

I'm not even sure what movie it was. My job was to wave a large sword around and die gloriously. No spoken words, just wave the sword, get stabbed, and fall. It's not what you could call a hard day's work, other than they shot the scene seven times.

I ran into Mr. Monroe on my way to turn my costume back in. He almost didn't recognize me when I said, "Hi."

"Hello, Rick. I'm glad to see you are earning your living."

"Yep, thinking of being a Viking next so I can go burning and pillaging."

"Oh, that is bad."

"I'm glad to be doing something to earn the money you pay me."

He got a serious look.

"Rick, you have more than earned the money we pay you. Your 'extra board' idea you guided my people into raised our profits by twenty-five percent last quarter. My bonus this year will be the highest ever given in the industry. If you never did anything else, you have earned your money several times over. That said, do you want to take a pay cut?"

"Uh, I think I am happy with things as they are.

"I thought so. See you later."

I was almost late for dinner by the time I got home. After the quick trip to the studio turned into a day's work, I was tired.

Taking my turn, I related my day at flight school and then the trip to the studio. The boys were still homeschooling, so they didn't have much news. Mary was on the outs with Patti again. Must be a little girl thing.

Mum told us there would be a memorial service for Mrs. Carpenter in the funeral home chapel on Saturday and that we would be attending as a family.

After dinner, I sat in front of the TV for several shows. When I realized I had no idea what I had been watching, I went to bed.

Chapter 18

It is another wonderful cool morning for running. Every step had a little more snap to it. Do steps snap? My other exercises flowed. It was a good day.

At breakfast, we talked about our plans for the day. Nobody had anything urgent. I had made a tee time at Riviera, so I had to leave in a while. Both Denny and Eddie had a lot of questions about the club, so I asked them if they would like to go out to their driving range with me on Sunday morning.

They were both enthusiastic about it. Denny was tall enough for a regular adult set. Eddie would need something shorter. I even asked Mary if she wanted to go, but she had plans with her friend Patti. At that moment, I realized I would never understand women.

I packed a bag with a change of clothes plus personal items like my favorite deodorant, toothbrush, toothpaste, shaving cream, and razor. I would leave these in my locker at the club. On occasion, golf can get messy. Try hitting a ball out of an inch of water or buried in a muddy lie.

It was a nice drive over to the country club. Today, I wasn't running late. I had the top down. It was such a perfect California day.

The way the valet eyed my car, I hoped he didn't take off in it. I realized I had a high opinion of my Vette when a Ferrari pulled up behind me. Oh well, if the valet were going to joyride, that would be a better choice. I wonder what one of those would cost.

At the Pro shop, I explained I was bringing my two younger brothers out to the driving range on Sunday. I needed a regular set of clubs for Denny and a junior set for Eddie. The Pro showed me what he thought would be good starter sets in their respective sizes. I paid for them and asked for them to be stored in my locker. We would pick up shoes, gloves, tees, etc., on Sunday.

While we were finishing up, a nicely dressed gentleman approached us. The Pro introduced him as Mr. Johnathon Whitestone the Third. Mr. Whitestone was on the Board of Directors of the Riviera Country Club. I took that formal introduction as a warning to play it very straight and be on my best behavior.

"May I call you Rick?" He asked.

"Certainly, you may, Sir."

Hey, I ran around with the Buckingham Palace crowd.

"May we have a word in private?"

I thought that meant that we would move elsewhere. No, it meant the club pro would leave us.

"I am so pleased that your parents have applied for a family membership in the club. I'm certain they will be voted in."

"That's nice to hear."

"Since you are going to be a member of our family, I invite you to join in one of our activities."

"I would love to. What is it?"

I can tell genteel blackmail when I hear it.

"We are having a charity auction two weeks from Saturday. We would like you to participate."

"That sounds like fun. What is being auctioned?"

"We are auctioning the young eligible bachelor members of the club for a dinner date."

"You realize I'm only sixteen, so can't be considered an eligible bachelor?"

Thank goodness. A nightmare avoided.

"We had a brief conversation about that. There will be a special category for future eligible bachelors. Bids can only be made on behalf of young ladies who are eighteen or under."

Cripes.

"Then I will be glad to participate. Count me in. The night of the auction, should I wear a tuxedo?"

"That would be very appropriate. We will mail the complete details to your parents."

"It was so nice to meet you, Sir, and I am going to enjoy being a member of the Riviera Country Club."

"We are glad to have you, Sir Richard."

I did wonder where else I could qualify for the open. Too late, I guess. My parents have applied for membership already. It would cause too much embarrassment all around. Who knows, it may not be too bad since the girls must be eighteen or younger.

After that, playing golf was a relief. Again, Steve Whitney and his caddy joined John Jacobs and me to play the round. I did a little better, coming in two under par for the day. Not good enough to guarantee qualifying for the sectional, but getting closer.

Driving home, I enjoyed the day with the top down. It was so neat driving the Corvette.

As I drove onto an overpass, the car's front end started shaking like I had a flat. I slowed down by taking my foot off the gas but not pushing the brake as I had been taught. The shaking got worse.

A bus coming towards me started to veer, so I had no choice but to turn to the curb and jam on the brakes to avoid it. The Vette came to a stop, but the shaking continued. That is when I realized I was in my first large California earthquake.

When the car stopped, I saw ripples going through the bridge's concrete. The blacktopped cement was flowing like water. Then there was a tearing, ripping sound. A crack opened in the bridge. It ran under the bus. If it opened anymore, the bus would fall through.

I climbed out of the Vette without opening the door and ran to the bus to see if I could help. People were trying to get out the door but were so slow! From the passengers' looks, it was a senior's tour of really old people who could hardly navigate the bus steps.

The first person coming down was a lady who had to hold onto the rail as she tottered down. I picked her up by her waist and set her on the ground. The next in line, a man, received the same treatment this time.

As I set the man down, another driver joined us and moved the elderly lady out of the way. Other motorists were coming to help. I didn't spend much time looking but instead helped people move out of the bus.

There must have been almost fifty people on that bus. What I thought was the last person off was the driver. He stopped in the doorway and told me two people in the back couldn't walk. They came with wheelchairs.

I could only head to the back of the bus and pick up the first person I came to. I got halfway back to the front and handed her off to the driver who had followed me.

I turned for the last man. He was rather large, and I had to put him in a fireman's carry. Halfway to the door, there was further grinding and groaning from the pavement. At that moment, an aftershock hit. I bounced my head off the bus ceiling.

It momentarily stunned me, but I recovered and kept going. Expecting people to be at the door, I was surprised to find no one there. They were far back, waving and yelling for me to move.

I took the hint and moved as fast as I could towards them. I was most of the way there when I heard a tremendous crash. Arriving at the apparent safe line, people were sitting or lying down everywhere. Several men helped me lower the man from my back.

I turned to find that the crack in the overpass had widened, and the bus had fallen through. The middle of the bridge was missing. Something was wrong with what I was seeing. No, it was what I wasn't seeing. My Corvette had gone with the bridge. Walking to the edge, I saw its mangled remains down below.

The perfect California day was not so perfect anymore. Everything seemed to be under control. People were being taken off the bridge. No one seemed to be hurt, which was a miracle. If nothing else, how I had been hauling people off the bus could have hurt someone.

I asked a policeman who had taken over the supervision of operations if there was anything else for me to do. He told me to help those on the bridge to be entirely off it in case it collapsed. It didn't take long. A convenience store was on the corner at the bottom of the bridge.

Two other guys and I went to it and bought several cases of one-gallon jugs of distilled water used for ironing and several packages of paper cups.

That done, I asked the store manager if I could use his phone but found out there must have been lines down as there was no service.

I did the only thing left for me. I turned around and walked home. It was about five miles. Add to that walking the golf course for eighteen holes and my run in the morning, and I was plain tired when I got home.

As I walked, I fretted about what used to be my shiny new Corvette. It was a total loss to an Act of God. I'm not a religious person by nature, but I had a few words for God on that walk. I would probably pay for them later.

I was the last one in, so Mum made a little fuss. When she realized I was fine, she was happy. I told her and Dad about the Corvette and the busload of people. I could have saved the Vette if I hadn't helped all those people. Even as I thought that, I knew the loss of the car was nothing compared to the lives of all those people.

When I expressed concern about losing the car to an Act of God, I was told not to worry. First, that amount of money was nothing to us, and secondly, we had comprehensive coverage with a rider for earthquakes on our personal property.

That is when I learned the difference between collision and comprehensive coverage and what a rider was. Good to know. Since it was my car, I had to call the insurance company, part of my learning experience, according to Dad.

Chapter 19

At dinner, we talked about replacing the Corvette. Dad was all for it. He hadn't had a chance to drive it. Mum didn't care. I had one car already. I was the ambivalent one. I knew I didn't need two cars, and I already had the Corvette experience. While it was nice, it wasn't going to become a religion with me like it had with some people. Now, that Ferrari I saw at the country club was worth a prayer or two.

Not that I was dumb enough to say I wanted one of those right now. Even though I am rich, there are limits to what my parents will let me get away with. There was no danger of me being a spoiled rich kid.

The subject of the bus rescue came up again. Denny wanted to know if I would get another Boy Scout award for it. I told him I doubted it because I wasn't going to come forward and take any credit. I had only helped a few people off a bus, big deal. I didn't even realize I was in any danger until the event was over. Nothing heroic there.

The subject changed to the retrieval of the corpse of the Corvette. The coin dropped first for Dad.

"Rick, you don't have to worry about taking credit. The reporters will be here in the morning."

"How will they know I was involved?"

"They can track you from the license plate on the Corvette."

"Rats!"

"That's the way it is, Rick,"

"Well, I don't want to go through all that again. I refuse to do any interviews."

"You have to give them something."

"Can it be in writing?"

"I don't see why not."

So, we, as a family, talked about what would be in my written statement to the press. I liked what Eddie said the best. He wanted to tell them I was a Boy Scout doing my good deed for the day by helping an old lady off a bus. I had to do so many because I was over a month behind on good deeds.

We all agreed that was a winner but wouldn't fly. It finally boiled down to a statement that I could see the people on the bus couldn't get off the bus as quickly as needed, so I was expediting matters but never felt myself to be in danger, so there was no hero to see here.

That wouldn't make them happy, but that was what they would get.

Dad would get a copy of my statement to his paper first thing in the morning. Power and telephones were out everywhere. Jackson House was running on its generators. The Wymans down the hill were also included in our little power grid, and Mum had checked on them.

The last conversation I had for the day was telling Mum and Dad about volunteering for the country club's charity auction. They agreed it was tantamount to blackmail.

Mum expressed her concerns once more about the sort of people that could be involved. While ninety percent or more of the club members were fine people, there would be some bad apples. She told me she would think of something.

I had been scheduled on the simulator at the flight center today, but that was out. I spent the morning riding George. We checked the area all around our house and found no damage. I thought I would go look at the Corvette, but Mum and Dad discouraged that.

I let, well didn't let, Denny, trounce me at eight-ball.

All our help had made it in to work, so we had a nice leisurely lunch. The only news we could get was on the radio, as the television stations were still out. The quake was 7.6 on the Richter scale, bad but not bad. It had done a lot of property damage, but there were no reported deaths.

The outages were all due to lines being down. It was hoped that service would start returning to Los Angeles County early this evening. The police were encouraging everyone who could to stay home.

Dad's old golf clubs were in the first basement, so we got those out. I spent most of the afternoon working with the boys on how to swing. They both had the natural tendency to try to pick the ball up with the club rather than let the angle of the clubface do the work. They started to get it and were hitting them pretty darn good. We had to quit when we had lost all the golf balls over the wall into the adjacent park.

Power was restored by Saturday morning in our area. There were not many areas left with outages. The phone lines were working everywhere. After my morning routine and breakfast, the rest of the family and I got ready to go to Mrs. Carpenter's funeral service.

Ben rode with us. He was quiet, and you could tell he was upset. We were escorted to a small chapel when we arrived at the funeral home. There was no casket, as she had requested to be cremated. There was the urn with her ashes and several pictures of her at various ages.

To Ben's surprise, there were about ten people there. He knew them all. Even though all of Mrs. Carpenter's age group and children were gone, Ben had friends. Even Jane, the blacksmith/farrier, was there. You could tell very quickly they were an item.

It appears Mum had Jane's phone number, so she contacted her and, from Jane, got a list of Ben's friends and called them. The service was really for Ben. That brought it home to me how much family and friends meant when you needed them.

There was a prayer reading, and then Ben gave a small talk with some of the highlights of his grandma's life. He did not refer to her wild youth, only the loving care she gave to an orphaned child.

Our small entourage followed the hearse to the cemetery where Mrs. Carpenter's ashes were interred in the mausoleum next to her late husband.

As a group, we all returned to Jackson House, where refreshments were served. Ben gave his friends a tour of his living arrangements and the stable for which he was responsible. You could see him become animated as he talked to his friends. You could also see the pain on Dad's face as they drank all his Mexicali Delight.

I spent the rest of the day studying both high school and flight school. After dinner, the family took a walk together. All in all, it was a nice day.

The phone started ringing early Sunday morning. The reporters had found the owner of the smashed-up Corvette. After the first three, Mary took over phone duty and read my statement. When pressed further, she told them she had an exclusive on the rest of the story, and they could read her column. Brat.

Denny, Eddie, and I headed to the Riviera Country Club. Waiting at the pro shop were their new clubs. They tried on new shoes, which were added to my account. When did I get an account?

Eddie's hardest decision was picking headcovers for his driver and three wood. He finally settled on Bullwinkle and Rocky.

The driving range was fun. We spent several hours there. We saw Dean Martin. Frank Sinatra came over and talked for a while. He was still interested in another song, but I had my doubts.

The boys were both learning fast enough that if they kept it up, they would be good golfers. Unlike playing pool, I did not intend to let Denny get the better of me.

The rest of the day was a lazy Sunday. On the way home, we drove down to the beach and admired the young ladies in their swimsuits. Eddie thought that was a bit of a waste.

I was very satisfied with my T-Bird and don't think I will defect to the Chevy ranks again.

Chapter 20

I went out for an early ride on George. It wasn't long, but he got pretty rambunctious if he didn't get out. Later, as I wiped him down, Ben came out to talk. I asked him how he was doing since his grandmother had passed.

"I'm okay, Rick. It was a long time coming. That wonderful woman who loved life hadn't been there for ages. There was nothing left but a shell. It is easy to say she had a good life, and it was her time, but I still miss her. I didn't visit her every day at the rest home, but I knew she was there. When I woke up this morning, my first thought was that I should go see Grandma today."

"That has to be hard."

"It is, and it isn't. I miss her, but she wanted to move on. Anything was better than lying in that bed, wasting away and slowly losing her mind.

"At least she went out like she wanted to. She didn't want to die in a sickbed. The home had called me and told me her time was near. I spent the afternoon with her, but she didn't know me. Later, I went out for dinner.

"When I was out, she asked for 'Help.' The nurse asked what sort of help. 'Up' is what she said. So, they lifted her into her wheelchair. She died sitting up about ten minutes later."

That left a tight feeling in my throat. After that, I went for my morning run and then lifted weights.

After that, I cleaned up and went to breakfast. Today was my British accent day. The kids and I would only use that. Tomorrow was Spanish day. We had been doing this for what seemed like forever but only since we had moved here.

Mum and Dad were debating whether we should learn French or German next. I was lobbying for Russian. Denny thought speaking Japanese would be cool.

Whatever was chosen would require adding someone fluent in the best accent of that language. I would hate to learn Russian with our equivalent of a hillbilly accent. This debate had been ongoing. I think the truth is that none of us kids were anxious to pick up more studies.

Dad, the fink, was getting by without learning any languages.

He claimed that as he was born in America, he didn't need to learn any other language. At the same time, it wouldn't hurt Eddie and Mary, who were born here, to learn other languages. As I said, he's a fink.

I was informed at breakfast that the insurance on the Corvette would pay out. However, my rates would be going up. Stopping to assist people in trouble was not a good reason to park over a crack that might open up and lose the car.

Dad didn't think it was going up enough to justify changing insurance companies. Mum begged to differ. It was a matter of principle. I stayed out of it.

Before the discussion could get heated, Mum had a long-distance phone call. The caller asked for Olive Jackson. This caused some confusion for Mrs. Hernandez, who answered the phone. She told them Peg Jackson lived here, but she didn't know of an Olive Jackson. I heard her ask who was calling. I don't know what was said, but she exclaimed, "The Queen of England?"

Mum stood up and held out her hand for the telephone. Mrs. Hernandez handed it off like she was getting rid of a rattlesnake very quickly.

"This is Olive Jackson."

Few outside the family knew that Mum's real name was Olive. Peg or Peggy, or even the more formal Margaret, was a nickname her father gave her, and that is what the world knew her as. She had no middle name, which was weird, especially when you knew that the people in her father's family all had four names.

"This is Olive," Mum repeated into the phone.

"Yes, I will hold."

"Your Majesty, it is nice to hear from you.

"We are alright. There was no earthquake damage at Jackson House. Rick had a little excitement, but that ended well, other than his car falling through a road crack.

"No, Liz, he wasn't in it. He was helping people out of a bus at the time. It also fell through after all were off."

"I know he is a regular hero. We keep a good supply of pins in to puncture his head if it gets too big.

"No, she has decided that being a real princess is too much work, though she liked the idea of being queen. All we heard for a week after we got home from our visit was, 'Off with their heads.'

"I know it's a shame the Crown had to give that up.

"Is there anything in particular that you called for?

"I will pass that on to him, and we thank you for the call, TTFN."

Mum hung up and asked Dad and me to accompany her to the library.

She relayed the gist of the queen's call. "Rick, the queen wants me to tell you two things. One, be careful. She would hate to see her knight in shining armor hurt; two, the messages you have been passing back and forth have been very promising."

"She didn't say what they were about or who they are really for?"

"No, not a word. Welcome to the world of intrigue. Most of the time, you will do things and never know what they were about or learn any outcome."

We returned to breakfast. We had no sooner sat down, and the phone rang once more. Mrs. Hernandez answered it, "Jackson House."

This time, she didn't miss a beat.

"It is the White House calling for Mr. Jackson."

Dad took the phone.

"Yes, I will hold for the president.

"Mr. President, how may I help you on this fine, smoggy California day?

"No, we had no damage. Yes, it was Rick that helped the people off the bus. I will tell him that."

Dad listened for a while without saying anything.

"Oh, I will certainly relay that information. Thank you for your call, Ike."

I think Dad was finally forgiving Ike.

"Peg, will you and Rick come to the library with me?"

Once more, we paraded out of the room. Everyone remaining behind must wonder what was going on.

Dad opened with, "That, of course, was President Eisenhower. He wanted to make certain we were alright. But he also wanted us to know that the CIA has a certain Chinese dry cleaner under surveillance, and they are curious about Rick's visits. There are many dry cleaners closer to home."

Uh oh, I didn't need problems with the CIA.

"Maybe I could talk the pretty young lady in there into having coffee with me? That way, they will think I'm chasing her."

"I don't think so, Rick. They will conclude that you are falling into a honeypot trap and take action."

"I hadn't thought of that, Mum. I guess doing nothing is best."

"It will drive them crazy when nothing changes about your visits. I am sure the president was asked to call to try to flush something out."

"It is interesting that we get calls from the Queen of England and the president of the United States within a few minutes of each other, and they both refer to a Chinese laundry."

"Rick, that is more than interesting. China has been effectively closed to the West since the Communists took over. I wonder what is going on."

"Dad, it looks like the British are having back-channel talks with the Chinese, and the CIA knows something is going on but not the details."

"Be careful, Rick, these guys play hardball."

"I wonder if the CIA knows I'm a Queen's Messenger?"

"One would think so, but it was never publicized to my knowledge."

"Would it hurt if they knew?"

"Not unless they wanted to try to intercept a message delivery. I don't think the higher-ups would let that happen. It would play hell with US-British relations."

"Mum, from what I saw of those clowns in the CIA that were here, I wouldn't trust them not to try something stupid."

"You're right, Rick. I will check back through my channels and see if they have any suggestions."

While these events and conversations were going on, those who remained at the table speculated on what was going on. When we returned, a wide-eyed group consisting of Mrs. Hernandez, Denny, Eddie, and Mary waited to hear what was happening.

Denny asked the question that they all had to be thinking.

"Rick, are you some sort of spy like James Bond?"

"Denny, you have been reading too much Ian Fleming. I'm sorry I loaned you my collection."

Mum broke in.

"Everyone, listen up. Rick has been acting as a Queen's Messenger. You all know he is one. He has been delivering some sensitive messages for Her Majesty's government. He is nothing more than a delivery boy."

"And I don't even get a tip," I joked.

Dad completely changed the subject.

"Rick, the property evaluation came in with the proposed changes. If the people are reasonable in their pricing, you should do okay in the short term and very well in the long run."

"Then you think it is a good idea?"

"Most definitely."

"Then would you please make an offer on my behalf?"

This being underage was a bother.

In the meantime, Denny, Eddie, and Mary had started a dialog.

"What's your name?"

"John Brown, ask me again, and I will knock you down."

"What's your name?"

"President Monroe, ask me again, and you still won't know."

"What's your name?"

"Puddin Tane, ask me again, and I will tell you the same.

"Where do you live?"

"Down the lane."

"What's your number?"

"Cucumber"

"What do you eat?"

"Bread and meat."

That's when Mum threw us out of the room to start our day.

Since I had no plans for the day, I hit the books. I was working on the first read-through of all my high school textbooks. Next, when they arrived, I would go through all the additional texts listed in the schoolbook's bibliography to see which ones were worth reading in-depth.

I discovered while all books were valuable, some were more useful than others. I think some of them were written by some professor who needed to be published, so he regurgitated common knowledge or theories and then forced the use of his book in his classes.

These had become easily recognizable to me as they were almost always published by the university's publishing house, and the prose was so stilted as to be almost indecipherable.

While browsing my bookshelves, I found an old favorite. It was about the French and Indian wars in Ohio. That was a brutal time.

Chapter 21

I broke for lunch and went right back to it. Around three o'clock, I went out and talked to Ben for a while and then took a ride on George. After that, it was time to get cleaned up and dressed for dinner.

Since Monday was British accent day, it was also British dinner day. We had a Yorkshire pudding. While Mum always threatened us with Tam Tattlers Tarts for dessert, there was a Strawberry Trifle. There wasn't enough for seconds. From the looks Mum and Mrs. Hernandez exchanged, I think I know where it went.

I returned to the books but was stuck with airplane stuff until bedtime. It was a quiet day at the Jackson House. Well, other than some interesting phone calls.

There was a call at breakfast. This one was from BSA headquarters. They wanted me to know they had reviewed the events during the earthquake and that while I demonstrated bravery, there weren't any special skills used that were learned in Scouting. There would be no award this time.

They almost seemed embarrassed by that, but I was more than okay with it. Enough of this hero stuff. How embarrassed do they think I got every time I received an award for what anyone would have done in my place?

I had just finished breakfast, and there was another call for me. This was from Mr. Monroe at Warner Brothers. I didn't think about it as I said, "Hola."

He answered with, "No hablo español."

"Oh, sorry, I forgot, it's Spanish day here."

"That's interesting, Rick. Are you busy this morning?"

"Not really. I have no real plans for the day except for some studying."

"Would you please stop by my office? I have a project that you might be able to help with."

"Certainly, Sir, I can be there in about forty-five minutes."

"That would be great. I will see you then."

Driving my only T-Bird with the top down was nice. It was a shame you couldn't even see the mountains because of the smog. Something had to be done. I know there was talk about changing the fuel in cars and how cars were made. As long as they could still go fast, I didn't care. Not that I was going fast. I had seen CHIPS too often recently.

Before the song played on the radio, I always thought of organs as solemn, boring things. Baby sure changed my mind.

Mr. Monroe had me admitted immediately. He got right to the point.

"Rick, you seem able to think out of the box. Your extra board idea has saved the studio a lot of money and made us more responsive. It is being adopted throughout the industry."

"What I need your help on is with a specific movie. Most of the movies made here are from producers who rent out facilities and services. We do produce movies of our own. These are both big-budget and small-budget movies. It is a small-budget movie I would like your thoughts on."

"We schedule each year movies of different types: dramas, comedies, and romance with varieties such as westerns, historical, modern kids, etc."

"There is a western getting ready to start. As you know, everything on TV these days is a Western show. The last thing we want is to produce a low-budget ho-hum. We want a low budget, gotta see."

"Gee, you don't want much."

Mr. Monroe had the grace to laugh, "Yeah, I know you get what you pay for, but I still want it all."

"That might be possible if we don't use many big names or have complicated sets."

"The only thing I would require is a more serious theme to attract adults, and the lead needs to be a handsome male to attract the ladies. I suppose a good-looking female lead would help also."

"Other than that, I am free to think outside the normal scenarios?"

"All yours or I think we will waste our budget this year."

We then got into the details of who I had to see. I would start with the in-house producer. His office was just down the hall, so Mr. Monroe escorted me to him and introduced us.

"Rick, this is Mr. Thomas James."

"Tom, this is Rick Jackson."

Standing and walking around his desk, he shook my hand. He was almost as tall as I and had a chiseled look. I wondered why he wasn't a leading man. That was answered when he opened his mouth, and his voice proved to be what I would call high-pitched. Not a leading man's voice.

His handshake was firm and gave an excellent first impression. However, with that voice, he would never make it in the movies.

"Rick, of course, I have heard a lot about you and watched your movies. More importantly, Mr. Monroe and I discussed getting your thoughts on this year's B western."

At least the way had been cleared.

"I will leave you two to get acquainted and briefly examine the plot synopsis."

At that, Mr. Monroe left. Tom, as I was asked to call him, to my Rick, suggested that we have a cup of coffee at the commissary and talk there. That sounded attractive to me, so we headed out.

As we crossed the lot, we saw the normal mélange of characters. President Roosevelt was being pushed to a set from makeup in a wheelchair.

I saw Robert Mitchum and Peter Ustinov walking across the way. They were dressed like a couple of hicks.

There must have been one of the many Homer hero movies being made, as there were a whole host of extras in costume.

I was tempted to stop and ask Peter Lawford, Sammy Davis Jr., and Joey Bishop for their autographs but decided that wouldn't be classy at work.

So, of course, Joey Bishop walked up to me and asked for my autograph. Fortunately, I wore a sports coat with some publicity pictures in the inside pocket. It was a habit Susan Wallace had encouraged. Tom had to loan us a pen.

It was almost funny as I was the only one with anything to sign. I am the proud owner of my picture, autographed by all three. I would like to see that explained one day.

After he bought our coffee, Tom explained that the movie they had scheduled was about some fur trappers who discover gold. They are chased by bad guys who try to get it from them. The story comes across as unreal and contrived. The Indians in it are a pathetic caricature of the real people. The ending has them losing a huge amount of gold in a river and laughing about it, then going back to fur trapping.

If there is ever a loser at the box office as he described, this was it.

"Rick, does anything immediately jump to mind?"

Chapter 22

"Something does. This morning, I saw my old Ohio History textbook on the shelf. It reminds me of people and events that would make a strong adult movie. Since it has Indians, it would be viewed as a Western, but it is set before and during the Revolutionary War."

"I don't know much about that period in our country's history."

"It is the story of opening up what is now Ohio, Indiana, and Michigan and adjoining areas known then as the Northwest Territory. It was a struggle that started with the Indians against the British, Indians against the French, French and the Indians against the British, the British and Indians against the French, the new Americans against the British and Indians, and the Americans against the Indians."

"Wow, is there a scorecard for that?"

"It's even worse than that. I have used Indians as though they were a single group. Each tribe is a separate nation, the same as France, England, and Spain."

"That is one reason there never was a workable peace treaty. The European and then the American governments treated the Indians as a single group. Even though they knew each tribe was separate, they never could understand it."

"When a treaty was signed, it was frequently like Spain ceding part of France. It didn't go over too well. Add that to the fact that the Indians didn't understand the concept of land ownership. To them, the land was there for all to use. They were hunters, not farmers."

"So, this is when traders sold the Indians infected blankets?"

"Some of that probably still happened, but for the most part, the tribes were already done for in the sixteen hundreds by smallpox. The majority had died from the white man's diseases. The population was so low they turned to kidnapping to grow their tribes. Historians reviewing newspaper accounts of the day say there were over ten thousand white captives during this period.

"This was now a time of hatred and feuds. There was no going back. The attitude of the day for the white settlers was shown in militia call-up notices during the Revolutionary War. They would simply read, 'Indian infestation.'

"Some complex characters result from these actions. One of the most famous was Simon Girty, of Irish descent. Indians captured him and his siblings. Previously, he learned to hate the British when they arrested his family for settling in an area that wasn't declared open. The British fined the family heavily and burnt their home and farm to the ground. His father was killed in a duel reportedly encouraged by the British.

"His mother remarried only to have the whole family captured by Indians. His stepfather was tortured in front of the family and then scalped. The children were split up among different tribes.

"Girty went to the Mingos; he was tested by sending him through a gauntlet. He survived that, so they pulled his hair out by the roots, leaving him only with a scalp lock to signify he was a warrior. What we consider torture, they thought of as signs of bravery.

"He lived with them for seven years, adopting their ways. At one point, he was traded back to the British as part of a peace treaty. Girty was brilliant. He spoke eleven languages. He worked as an interpreter between the British and the Iroquois for a peace treaty.

"At the start of the American Revolution, he was on the American side. He was so well thought of what Fort St. Mary's is now was originally called Girty Town.

"After he saw American atrocities against peaceful Indians he knew, he switched sides and fought with the Loyalists after discussing it with the officers in his group. While with the

Americans, he served alongside George Rogers Clark, Simon Kenton, and Daniel Boone. They all admired him.

"When he changed sides, he was called a renegade and has been known as that ever since.

"So, he will be the villain," said Tom.

"Actually, no, he is more of a symbol of the complexity of the time. He is a sample of the pioneers fighting themselves. The villain of the story was considered a hero at the time but now is looked at as a psychopathic serial killer."

"Who was that?"

"Lewis Wetzel, the Indian fighter. He was called Death Wind by the Shawnee. Again, he was captured as a young man but managed to escape. This marked him for life. He never did anything but hunt Indians after that. He would murder them all: men, women, and children.

"Even the Federal government had enough of him when he killed Indian Chief Tegunten, who was on his way to sign a peace accord. This set back the government's expansion plans. They charged him with murder, but he was set free by the settlers. Among those was Simon Kenton. They called him a hero.

"Without a doubt, he was one heck of a fighter. He could reload a muzzleloader while sprinting. His favorite method, though, was the ambush, thus Death Wind. He killed so many Indians that, to this day, the Shawnee leave charms on his grave to keep him in it.

"He was hired to guard a party for John Monroe, brother of the future president. He paid more attention to killing Indians rather than protecting his party, leading to Monroe's death.

"Then there is Simon Kenton, who led settlers and soldiers. He also was captured and forced to run a gauntlet. In movies, the gauntlets have ten or so people on each side, and the person would have to run fifty feet. Kenton had to run a gauntlet of half a mile.

"He was then sentenced to be burned at the stake but was saved by Simon Girty. Girty was credited with saving many captives, buying their freedom with money out of his pocket.

"Before you think too kindly of him, he also participated in the torture and burning at the stake of Colonel William Crawford at Zanesfield, Ohio. Crawford was a land speculator and personal friend of George Washington."

"So, who would your hero be?"

"It would be Oliver Spencer's father. In real life, he wasn't, but after Indians kidnapped Oliver, we can have him hunt for Oliver. He found Oliver, who was adopted and treated well. I don't know the real story, but for our movie, he was adopted by a young, beautiful Indian widow, thus our love interest. The icing on our cake is that in real life, Oliver was one of those that Simon Girty helped to be freed from the Indians.

"Of course, in the usual Girty style, he wanted to split Spencer's ears at the lobe so they would hang down as a souvenir of his captivity. Fortunately, Oliver was able to hide long enough to avoid that fate."

"I never heard of splitting the ear lobes."

"It was a bit of a fashion statement. One Indian Chief, during peace talks, would chew on his lobes as they hung so low. What an unnerving sight that must have been."

"Wow, Rick, that could be the basis of a powerful story. It's a shame we don't know much about how they dressed during that period. I suspect our Plains Indian costumes won't work."

"I know a man that might be able to help. He is Doctor Chief Alex Redfoot of the Shawnee Tribe. He is the Head Curator at the Shawnee Tribe Heritage and Cultural Center. Or maybe it is Chief Doctor? Anyway, if anyone knows, he will."

"We've never had much luck getting the real Indians to help us in the movies. They feel we always portray them poorly."

"Don't we?"

"Well, yeah, but that is what the public expects."

"It's time we woke them up a little."

"How will you get Chief Redfoot to help us?"

"Oh, I think I may have an in. I'm sure he will help out a declared friend of the Shawnee."

Tom started to open his mouth to ask a question, then shook his head.

"I'm not sure I want to know. If you had to scalp someone, I don't want to know about a crime."

"I swear I have never had anything to do with scalping people."

I hoped he didn't ask about carrying around severed heads in a bowling ball bag.

I changed the subject back to the movie. It is a story based on distant governments with agendas and not knowing or caring about the people. It was about two groups of people who could not communicate on basic lifestyles.

"I have another thought. I hate to sit through all those boring openings. Why don't we start the movie with a five to ten-minute action scene? That scene will only be an expectation setter, not part of the main story. It will introduce the main character as a strong frontiersman."

"It will draw people into the movie before they realize it, a real adventure."

"I don't know, Rick; that is not how we do things. People expect it that way. The opening credits give them time to settle in."

"Please give it some thought."

"By the way, if you and your writers think my storyline has merit, I can loan you my Ohio History books and some other references to give a better idea of what it was like."

"Plan on it. Mr. Monroe was the one who suggested it, and he signs my paycheck. Also, please call your Chief Redfoot for me to see if he is available.

"I will try this evening, but it might take several days. I will get back to you."

"Thank you. See you later."

I stopped by Mr. Monroe's office on the way out. He waved me in.

"How did it go?"

"Fine, I think. I suggested an early Indian story set in Ohio around 1770-1780."

"Tell me about it."

I gave him the short version. Since I had given it once, I think it flowed better when retold.

"I like it, Rick, a little bold for a low budget, but I don't see a problem."

"Just keep the mountains and cactus out of the shot, and we'll be okay."

"You mean Malibu is out?"

It took me a second to realize he was pulling my leg.

"Well, it would take some fancy camera work. Though it would be interesting to see if people notice the Pacific moved to Ohio."

"We've done dumber things. Anyway, I will follow up and see what they think. Our public opinion people tell us the country is looking for changes. This might be the vanguard for movies, more serious, and addressing social issues."

"Sir, remember we have to make money while doing it."

"Now you are stealing my line. Get out of here."

I laughed and headed home. I was at loose ends for the day, so as planned, I took the opportunity to plunge into my schoolbooks. They weren't going to do it themselves.

While going through my physics textbook, I saw a reference to Schrodinger's cat. I don't know why it hit me; it may have been something from a conversation on a movie set about acting. They were talking about the fourth wall and that it must never be broken. That is where the actor is aware of the audience and talks to them.

If Schrodinger's cat could break the fourth wall, what would it say?

"Meow."

I know I am weird. That was the high point of the session. It was also to absorb new information and take notes to help ingrain it.

Dinner was just us kids as Mum and Dad went to a charity event. It was pizza night, so we were happy to stay at home. Let me see, jeans and pizza or a suit and rubber chicken.

I'll suffer and stay home.

After dinner, I called the number I had for Chief Redfoot. He was not at home, but his wife took a message for him to call me when he could.

We had a rousing game of Monopoly after dinner. Mrs. Hernandez and Mary teamed up and beat up us boys.

Chief Redfoot called just as we finished the game. Why couldn't he have called before Mrs. Hernandez gave Mary Park Place?

I explained that I needed his help as a technical advisor on a movie with the Shawnee in it. At first, he was lukewarm. He got interested when I explained how I wanted to show the good and bad on both sides.

He finally agreed to come to Hollywood at our expense if the studio chose to follow up on my suggestions.

As he put it, "They always show the bad side of the Shawnee. It will be a victory for us if they show both our good and bad, plus the white man's good and bad. Telling the truth about that psychopathic Wetzel makes it worthwhile by itself."

I went to my room and read about a detective's first trip to Hollywood and the starlet with the gangster boyfriend. I guessed the sibs secret early on. I think the people in the book were modeled on some people I had met out here.

Chapter 23

I played golf early in the morning, going directly from breakfast to the course. When I signed in at the pro shop, they told me that there was a roped-off area on the edge of the fairway on the sixteenth hole.

A gopher was tearing the course up. They had tried trapping it, poisoning it to no avail. They were talking about dynamite.

I think they were joking.

Steve Whitney was with me as was becoming the norm. My caddie was with someone else today. I hadn't gotten the word to him on time. I was getting spoiled. Steve and I had two of the regular caddies, and they were good, just not my John Jacobs.

I was learning the course. It was straightforward in its presentation. It was just the execution that was difficult. Today's challenge was figuring out how to play the course to my strengths such as hitting a long ball, which would set me up nicely, but most players couldn't reach out that distance.

This, of course, led to some shots not doing what I hoped for. A missed shot at Riviera came at a cost. I had plenty of practice with nasty lies in the rough and fried eggs in the traps.

I learned a lot about what I could and could not do on the course, so it was a well-spent morning.

I was able to get home for a late lunch. A set of drawings for the garage expansion had been delivered; they were laid out on a large table in the library. Mum left a note that she liked the exterior shown. I liked the fact that there was plenty of workspace, enough power provided, and storage. Dad's note approved the oil changing area.

I initialed the drawing the same way Mum and Dad had to show that we wanted them to let it out for bids.

After that, I drove down to LAX for my multi-engine class. First, there was my quiz on the last chapters of the book. Again, I had no problem with any of the questions. I almost felt they were too easy.

When I shared that thought, I was told that the quizzes on these last chapters had an average score of seventy-eight percent. I guess hard work pays off. Well, not even hard work. It is more like my persistence of effort. Yeah, I like that thought.

Instead of the simulator, we went out to a real aircraft. I did the walk around very carefully, but apparently, there were no tricks since all was as it should be. I don't think Mr. Smith would let me take off if I missed a trick.

I used the checklist every step of the way. I was allowed to take off after taxiing and talking to the tower.

In the air, I continued being cautious, sticking with the checklist all the way.

Mr. Smith told me to turn off the starboard engine and restart it. I did, then repeated with the port. He had me change fuel tanks. The last thing he had me do was land with one engine down.

"Rick, we have to get the hours in your logbook, but I think you can safely fly this aircraft."

"Thank you."

"You are not what they call a natural pilot; you have to work at it. The point is you do work at it. With your attitude, I predict many successes in life. That is easy for me to predict when you have had so many already. That said, well done."

When I got home, I remembered to call the studio and let Mr. James know that if the studio chose to proceed, Chief Redfoot would participate if we paid his way.

He took Chief Redfoot's number as Mr. Monroe had instructed him to investigate this thoroughly. Travel expenses and a consulting fee for this and any other work he performed would be paid. He asked me to drop off the Ohio History textbooks I had told him about.

While I was on the phone with Mr. James, a delivery truck dropped off the books I had ordered from the bibliography of my textbooks. Of course, I had to unpack and place them in order on the shelves. This also included making up a card for them and a label with the Dewey decimal system number on the spine of each book.

I wonder when we will have enough books to justify a librarian on staff. I was not too fond of this job but would hear from Mum if it wasn't done promptly and correctly.

Life is unfair; the other kids would probably need these books later, and all this work would be done. Then I thought of Mary and the Dewey decimal system and had the grace to laugh at myself. She would probably color-code the books with crayons and glued-on sparkles.

No, this was a job that needed to be done and done now by me. I need to stop whining about things I can't control. Needless to say, I only got about halfway through the task as I kept stopping to glance through many of the books. Some of them caught my attention for many pages at a time. I broke for dinner and gave my report for the day.

"Fine."

I think that is the legally required teenage response to parent's questions. Then I went back to the books.

I was so engrossed that Mum told me it was eleven o'clock and bedtime. Since I had been getting up at 5 a.m. to work out every morning, this was late for me. I went to bed and looked forward to finishing my job with the books.

I gave riding George a pass in the morning. Instead, I ran an extra-long course, at least longer than I normally run. It had me deeper into the park than I had ever been. Ever alert for tigers, I explored new territory.

It is funny how being attacked by one tiger can change your outlook. I knew intellectually that my chances of ever seeing a tiger in the wild without going to Asia were nil. The reptilian part of my brain thought otherwise.

I didn't run into a big cat. It was a small cat, as a matter of fact, a kitten. It was sitting in the middle of the path as I came around a corner. It just sat there as I approached it. I slowed down so as not to frighten it, but the way it stood its ground, I don't think it scared easily.

Stopping short of it, I crouched down. It was a cute little black cat with two white front feet.

"Hey, little guy, what are you doing out here by yourself?"

I don't care what its tough-guy attitude thought. It wouldn't last the night with the coyotes out here. Of course, the kitten didn't answer me. It didn't run either.

I held out a hand. It sniffed and then moved a little closer to me. I patiently waited for it to come to me, which probably took five minutes for the whole process.

It finally was close enough to sniff my fingers. While it did, I ran one finger over its head. It backed up from me. Again, I patiently waited for it. We played like this back and forth until it let me scratch its ears. This, it liked.

I looked around, expecting to see a mother cat glaring at me. Mothers do that, you know. There was no sign of one. How did this kitten get here? She, I looked, wasn't more than two months old, barely weaned.

When I picked her up, she didn't fight me. I jogged back to the house, holding the kitten carefully. She watched the path as though she was a princess touring her kingdom.

Arriving back at the house, I sought out Ben, who was doing his morning chores.

"Ho, what do we have here?"

"It's called a cat, dummy."

The veterinary student gave me a look that resembled the glare I was expecting from the mother cat.

"I meant, where was the cat when you found it?"

"I found her way back on the trails. I have no idea how she got there. I couldn't leave her as coyote bait."

"Are you going to keep her in the house or the barn?"

"I hadn't thought of that. I suspect she will be more welcome as a barn cat."

"What's her name?"

Now, I hadn't given that any thought, so I was as surprised as Ben when it came out. "Schrodinger."

I then had to explain what the Schrodinger's cat would say when it broke the fourth wall. By the time I explained Schrodinger's box and what the fourth wall was, there wasn't a laugh to be found.

Ben volunteered to get her shots and spayed since she was to be a barn cat, but no declawing.

At breakfast, I told the family about our new member. That may have been a mistake, as Mary disappeared as soon as breakfast was finished.

I headed over to the studio. I needed to brush up on what I thought were my acting skills. I spent the morning with swords, fencing foils, sabers, broad and bastard, then daggers. I took on anyone who would pick up a bladed weapon.

It was fun.

A small crowd gathered, and before it was over, money was changing hands. I wasn't as rusty as I thought, and anyone who bet against me lost their money.

From sword fighting, I went to boxing. I was glad I wore a head protector and a mouthpiece because otherwise I would have been knocked silly. My coach must have been frustrated about something as he worked me over. My sword fighting may have been great, but while I knew the moves and could do a movie scene, a boxer, I wasn't.

Unarmed combat was fun. By this time, I was as loose and limber as I would get. The important thing was that I practiced this for real life, not movie scenes. My muscle memory was still there as I fought to a draw.

The crowd from the sword fight had followed me to each session, and money continued to change hands. I should demand a cut or arrange to throw the bout.

Nah.

My last session was with the bow. Here, I excelled once more. The next time I was in England, I might have a chance of doing well in a tournament.

I had worked through lunch at the studio and would have missed it at home, so I stopped at an In and Out on the way home. Two cheeseburgers and fries with a vanilla shake would last me until dinner.

When I got home, the guard at the gate had a message for me.

"Your mum needs to see you as soon as possible."

"Thanks, I will look her up immediately."

He must have called her because she was waiting for me at the garage's side door.

Chapter 24

"Rick, the Chinese laundry called. Your suit is ready and needs to be picked up this afternoon."

"They said it wouldn't be until next Monday."

"I know, but they stressed it needed to be picked up today."

"Okay, I will leave now."

"Remember, the place is being watched."

"No problem."

Yeah, no problem. You ever drive up to a place and strive to look nonchalant when you know the CIA has the place under surveillance? Well, it was probably the FBI doing it for them if the CIA was following the law. I am sure it would never occur to them to break the law.

Silly me.

Inside, I was given my suit and handed an envelope. The envelope was to be given to Lady Jackson at once. I transferred the envelope to an inside pocket of my sports coat to which I had affixed my greyhound pin.

As I exited the store, I looked around carefully but didn't see anyone paying attention to me. I relaxed once I was back in the T-Bird and was driving away. Several blocks down, as I was turning to join the freeway, a set of red lights came on behind me.

Wondering what I had done, I pulled over. I watched in my rearview mirror as a Los Angeles policeman got out of his cruiser to approach me. What made me wonder was a plainclothes man getting out of the other side of the cruiser. All of a sudden, this didn't seem like a traffic stop.

In a few seconds, as the cop walked up to the car, I withdrew the envelope from my coat pocket and placed it under the floor mat.

Holding his hand out, the cop said, "Driver's License and Vehicle Registration, please."

While I dug out my wallet and license, the plainclothes person picked up the suit from the backseat where I had placed it. He ripped off the paper wrapper and went through the pockets of the suit and pants. When he found nothing, he dropped them in a bundle in the car's back seat.

"It must be on him."

From saying please, it now was, "Out of the car."

Not knowing what else to do, I got out. I was taken back to the cruiser, where I had to assume the position seen on police shows. A quick search showed that I had nothing on me.

While the "policeman" was searching me, the plainclothes guy had looked through my car. It didn't take him long to find the envelope under the mat.

All of a sudden, cars pulled up all around us. Some were black unmarked, but most were Los Angeles police with lights flashing.

Men in suits came running up.

"FBI, hands in the air!" they yelled. That was a little weird as I already had my hands up. The men in suits grabbed the plainclothes guy and the cop who stopped me. They were taken to the ground and handcuffed before I could comprehend what was happening.

"You okay, Mr. Jackson?"

'Uh, yeah, what's going on?"

"This is confidential government business, and you don't have the clearance to be told."

"They took an envelope from my car that belongs to me."

"A US citizen could be in a lot of trouble if they had a communication from the Chinese government. I think it's best if we keep that letter."

I looked down in thought and saw that little greyhound pin on my lapel.

"What about a messenger for the Queen of England? Would they have diplomatic immunity?"

"I would think very carefully before going that route. If you claim diplomatic immunity, then you're declaring yourself a British citizen. You would keep the letter but lose your US citizenship."

He no sooner said that, and he clenched his jaw and started to grind his teeth. Something was upsetting him.

I didn't say anything; I just held out my hand. The man stared me in the eye for what seemed like forever. He changed from looking like he was grinding his teeth to having swallowed a lemon. He handed me the envelope.

I got into the T-Bird and drove away.

What have I done?

I drove onto the freeway and went several miles, checking to see if anyone was following. Of course, they weren't. They knew where I lived. I pulled off at a ramp and stopped on the shoulder. I broke out into a sweat and started shaking.

After a while, I settled down enough to drive home.

Mum and Dad were waiting for me. Someone had called them.

"Are you okay, Rick?"

"I just lost my US citizenship."

"No, you haven't."

I went on to explain what had happened.

"Here is what happened. The FBI called and explained what was going on. You have caused a real can of worms to be opened.

"The Russians were trying to intercept that letter. The FBI was watching both them and the Chinese. When the Russians stopped you, the FBI elected to arrest them rather than take a chance on that letter getting away.

"The US government wanted that letter to get to the British without being responsible. The agent who gave you the letter got himself into a pickle. He had the letter and no way to give it back to you legally until you declared yourself a Queen's Messenger. Unfortunately, his orders were not to touch any messages, to let them move on. He had the letter. His natural inclination was to keep it, but he would have ruined his career.

"He was obligated to give it to you by his orders. From a legal standpoint, possession would have been in his favor as he had taken custody of a Russian spy. Anyway, he spoke without thinking when he told you that you would lose your citizenship.

"He was correct in his statement, but he also realized that it would go to court, and that was the last thing the government wanted. It would deepen the rupture between the Chinese and Americans. He just got caught up in the moment."

"Oh."

What else could I say? Now I know why he looked so frustrated. I handed the envelope to Mum.

Unlike other envelopes I had delivered, this one was addressed on the outside to Mum. She opened it immediately. She read it and stated.

"The Chinese are bloody bastards."

Mum seldom swears, but when she does, she goes all out. She handed me the letter. It was an apology to me from the Chinese. The whole thing was a setup by them to get the Russians off their backs.

Suddenly, the Jackson, Richard Jackson image I had seemed naive.

Dinner was quiet. The kids knew something had happened, but no one was discussing it. I was still shaken up. I had not realized how serious things could get. I didn't want to lose my citizenship. It also brought home that this was the big league, and people could die. I didn't want it to be me.

After dinner, Mum made a long-distance call. She was on the telephone for a long time. She asked Dad and me to come to the library when she was done.

"Rick, you are done with the Chinese laundry."

I was scared for my life earlier, but this hit my pride.

"What do you mean? I'm not too scared to do it."

"Rick, in our world, you have been burned. You have been exposed as a messenger in this mess, so everyone will now follow you. New channels of communication will be opened up."

"Oh, just as long as everyone knows I'm not too scared to do it."

"What you are is sixteen. You should feel lucky you got out this easily."

Stupid, stupid, stupid!

"You're right. I am lucky to get out of this. Frankly, I'm very scared but would carry on."

"Anyone in their right mind would be scared of being caught between the American, British, Chinese, and the Russians."

Said that way, I didn't feel too bad. All of a sudden, I was exhausted. I went to my room and read. I went to sleep early. To this day, I can't tell you what I read.

Chapter 25

As I woke up on Friday, I reflected on what had happened yesterday. I had carried out my duty as a Queen's Messenger. I had been exposed as a messenger, so I could no longer be used on secret deliveries. I also realized that I had lived in a fantasy world all along, thinking I was James Bond.

I was no spy; I was a kid who could travel unnoticed until I was noticed. Then it was game over. Mum was right; getting caught up in those events could lead to a short life. It might explain why she always seemed to have a weapon at hand.

Knowing I wouldn't be asked to do anything like that again, I cheerfully got up, performed a full workout, and even rode George around the park; no tigers or kittens.

I wondered what Schrodinger was doing. Ben stopped by as I was wiping George down, so I asked him.

"Oh, I haven't seen her since Mary took her into the house."

Uh oh, sounds like trouble in the making. After cleaning up, I went down to breakfast. There was Mary with a kitten on her lap, with Mum and Dad's apparent approval.

"I see you have adopted Schrodinger."

"Her name is not Schrodinger, silly. No cat wants to be called that. Her name is Mittens for her two white feet."

"It's okay with me. She is now your cat. You should have Ben get her shots and stuff."

I'm not going to explain spaying to my baby sister.

Mary beamed at me.

"Thank you, Rick. You are the best big brother."

She told me this as she glared at her other two brothers at the table. I didn't ask.

"What are your plans for the day, Rick?"

"I thought I would call Hank Smith and see if I could get some flying time in. Then spend some time reading my new textbooks."

The first reading of new books was fun. The outlining, taking notes, and memorizing got to be a pain. It was fun again after reading the books in the bibliography and comparing what they said to the textbooks. There were so many different ways to interpret and report events.

I now see why they say the winner writes the history. It also explained why being the secretary of a committee was a powerful position.

When I called Hank, he told me he would have four hours open this afternoon, so I booked them. I read and studied until lunch. After lunch, I drove down to LAX and spent the rest of the afternoon flying.

As we fueled the aircraft, which I had to pay for, I realized why it took so long for many to get their licenses.

Flying was expensive.

It was a lovely day to be in the air. The only thing that marred it was this instructor who thought it his duty to make my life miserable by shutting off the engines, forcing stalls, and even into a spin. It was good to get the practice in. I was just feeling let down after yesterday.

After a few touch-downs and takes-offs at small airfields around the area, we called it a day. He countersigned my logbook, and we declared it a winner.

Returning home, it was back to the books. Well, after stopping for a milkshake on the way. As I rode home, I thought about next week's bachelor auction at the country club. I was dreading it, but there was nothing I could do. I hoped it was a nice young lady instead of a gold digger. Cute would be good, nice would be better. Cute and nice was almost too much to hope for.

At breakfast, I shared my concerns about the auction. Mum ignored me and changed the subject.

"Rick, there has been some interesting feedback on your little adventure at the laundry. The American CIA isn't happy with you, but that is nothing new. MI6 thinks you are wonderful."

"Now, what have I done?"

"The Americans have been considering the Chinese and Russians as joined at the hip. The fact that the Russians were trying to intercept a message in such a blatant manner says otherwise. This is counter to what the CIA has been telling the president."

"The Brits are happy because it adds to their theory that all is not well in Redland. The FBI is happy that the CIA has been shown up. The Chinese are probably happy because it gets the Russians out of the picture for a while, but with the Chinese, there is no way of knowing. The Russians are unhappy because this is going to cost them."

"In what way will it cost the Russians?"

"Several, it deepens any divide with China. The biggest immediate cost is the replacement of almost all their LA Consulate staff."

"Why do they have to replace them?"

"Because they lost their best people to you boys when you caught them spying on the CIA. Now, they have lost their second string. They need to bring in new people. They would be easy to spot if they only brought in a few new spies. So, they will replace the entire staff to keep us guessing."

"So, I have the Russian KGB and American CIA upset with me. How could that go wrong?"

"The Russians are now a concern. Before, you were only considered family and left alone. They learned that lesson the hard way. Now, you will be considered a player. I don't think they will come after you, but they will pay attention to you. MI6 will not use you anymore as they know you will be followed. The Russians have to follow you in case you are still active."

"Am I in danger?"

"Not unless you get involved with an active operation, which I will not allow. I talked to Elizabeth early today, and she told me she would handle it. As the boys said, heads will roll."

"What about the CIA?"

"Oh, they will follow you for certain. That makes them your insurance policy with the Russians."

"Should I do anything differently?"

"No, they will do it for a while. Then both groups will get bored and need the resources elsewhere."

"Okay, I'm going to play golf today."

"Good idea. All those spies need some exercise."

Now that was a thought, a parade of spies following me on the golf course. I would have my gallery.

At the pro shop, they told me the gopher was destroying the course. There was talk of getting a flame thrower.

Steve Whitney was off today, so I was put in with a threesome. They were a couple of doctors and a dentist. They talked shop most of the round and ignored me, which was fine with me.

At the half, they compared scores, which were all around ten over par. I was asked, and just said I was doing okay. The dentist started paying attention to me. After the eighteenth hole, he approached me apart from the others.

"If you played the entire round like you did the back nine, you are under par for the day."

I wasn't about to lie, but I wouldn't brag. When asked directly, I told him I was four-under for the day. He gave a low whistle.

"Now I know who you are. Could I have your autograph for my daughter? She won't believe me otherwise."

I had some publicity pictures in my golf bag, so I signed one made out to his daughter Alice. I wrote that her dad was a great golfer, and I enjoyed the day.

"This will get me lots of credit at home. Eleven-year-old girls are hard to impress. Not like when they were six."

We parted company, the dentist talking rapidly to the two doctors.

I headed home and hit the books.

Chapter 26

Sunday morning, after breakfast, I took the kids down to the beach. We drove by the house I was buying, but we couldn't go in. They all loved the idea of having a house on the water.

As Mary put it, "It will be nice to have a real potty at the beach."

That started the boys off about peeing in the ocean. I threatened to turn around if they didn't straighten up.

When did I start sounding like Dad?

We had a good swim, ate lunch at a hot dog stand, and then stopped for ice cream on the way home. I went back to the books. After dinner, we played Clue as a family. Colonel Mustard did it in the library with the candlestick.

All in all, it was a nice day.

I hope all the spies enjoyed the outing.

After last week, I knew this week had to be a whole lot calmer. At breakfast, we decided if the phone rang this morning, we would ignore it. Well, of course, the phone rang. After five rings, Dad couldn't stand it and grabbed the phone.

After answering, he held it out to me.

"There is a Tom James from Warner Brothers for you, Rick."

You could feel the tension leave the room.

"This is Rick."

He asked if I were available to talk about the movie this morning and reminded me to bring those books.

I thought of something that might get my books returned later and typed out a loan agreement. I then gathered them up and headed out to the studio. I got caught at a long light across from a middle school.

The young crossing guards wearing badges and waving flags came out to control the flow of kids streaming across the road.

There was a horde of children on the playground before classes started.

A group of boys was pushing the merry-go-round at a tremendous rate. They all tried to jump on at the same time. They all made it, except one kid lost his grip, and the centrifugal force sent him flying.

I bet he got skinned up on the gravel. That happened to me a couple of times.

One boy was showing off by walking on top of the monkey bars. If he slipped and straddled the bar, it would hurt!

They were having a good time on the swings. They were swinging them as high as they could go and jumping off. One boy went so high you could see the chain jerk.

That always scared me. I thought I was about to swing around the top bar.

The girls were a lot more sensible. They played hopscotch on a chalked grid on the sidewalk, other girls were double-dutching it with two long jump ropes.

A gang of boys was running around, making shooting motions with their hands. Others were using hand bows and arrows. Cowboys and Indians, I guess. None were good shots, as no one fell.

Two teachers idly watching while enjoying a cigarette kept the mayhem down to a dull roar.

I got too engrossed in the activities and missed the light change. Several helpful drivers honked their horns to remind me.

All that activity at school was mind-blowing when viewed all at once. Imagine those kids in the classroom if they couldn't work off all that energy.

They would have to put them on drugs.

At the studio, Mr. James and two other writers were waiting for me. Tom got right down to business.

"Marty, tell Rick about what you guys have pulled together as a first cut."

"From the notes taken the other day, we have a rough outline of what we want to do.

"The story will be about rescuing a young boy, Oliver Spencer, kidnapped by Indians. It will center on his father's efforts to find and bring him back. The Shawnee will have kidnapped Oliver.

"His father reaches out to Simon Kenton for help. In turn, Kenton approaches Simon Girty.

"The story will be set immediately before the American Revolution to avoid that complex mess between Indians, British, and Americans.

"In the opening scene, Oliver will be snatched. It will be part of a montage of violence by the Indians and settlers. It will be a mixture not favoring one side or the other. Whatever started it is long forgotten. We want to set a tone of hatred with no chance of reconciliation.

"There will be scenes set in England and France where decisions are made by their governments with no consideration of the realities of living there. It will show their elites acting to enrich themselves with no thought for the cost in lives.

"At the same time, we will work in that the Indian tribes treat each other the same way.

"On the local level, we will bring out the Indians and settler's completely different understanding of land ownership."

"Simon Kenton will be a very good guy who helps Spencer's dad using his contact with Simon Girty to find the boy.

"Once found, Oliver's dad, who has been a widower for several years, meets the Indian widow who adopted Oliver. It turns out she is a white woman who was kidnapped at a young age but not before she received a basic education. This is our romantic interest.

"Throughout the film, we will have instances where progress seems to be being made for peace between the Indians and the local settlers, but it keeps getting disrupted by the man the Indians call Death Wind.

"Death Wind will be a murderous psychopath, but at the same time, one heck of a fighter. We will show him loading a muzzleloader at a sprint, among other things.

"There will also be a very personable young man named Lew who will be shown playing the fiddle at gatherings. He will be very popular. At the movie's end we show Death Wind being chased and escaping, and not until then do we learn Lew Wetzel is the fiddle player.

"The movie will end with Oliver, his Indian mother, and his real father going back East to live. At the same time, we will show the killings and burnings continuing on both sides. This will include Simon Kenton running the half-mile gauntlet and being saved from burning at the stake by Simon Girty.

"In the after-credits, we will give a two-sentence crawl about the major characters. For example, Girty changed sides and became known as a renegade and died in bed of old age.

Or Wetzel ended up in New Orleans as a counterfeiter, died in bed, and the Shawnee put charms on his grave to keep him there."

"Oliver Spencer settled in Ohio as an adult and was a friend and supporter of the Shawnee around Wapakoneta, Ohio."

"Last we say a few sentences about Simon Kenton, who saved Daniel Boone, scouted for George Rogers Clark, and fought at Fallen Timbers with Mad Anthony Wayne, where Tecumseh was defeated, ending the warfare and opening up the Northwest Territory for the new United States of America."

"Wow, that sounds ambitious."

"There will be a lot of scenes without dialogue and scenes with dialogue set in the forest so that the set costs will be low."

"Have you given any thought to the actors?" I asked.

"Only two so far have jumped out at us. We think Sharon Bronson as the Shawnee widow, and the actor who will play Death Wind."

"Who is that?"

"Why, you, of course."

"First, why me, and second, I don't have time to do a movie next year."

"You are the perfect person for this role. You have such a clean-cut image that no one would suspect you until the big reveal.

"Second, it would only take a few days in front of the camera. We would use stunt people for the Death Wind scenes except when we see your face at the end. The shots of you playing the fiddle and being social could be done in several days. You will have no dialog."

"We talked to Mr. Monroe, and he is very enthusiastic about it."

I'm learning that there are some battles that you cannot win. You are better off not even fighting. Or take the fight to another front.

This was one of them.

"Okay, I will consider it. Please call my agent, Mr. Baxter, who thinks he's retired, and make him aware you are railroading me into a movie and forcing him to work."

I was putting the needle in since Mr. Baxter was winding his business down, intending to call it quits at the end of the year. I would call him today and tell him to play hardball with these guys. This battle would be on another front.

Mr. James held out his hand.

"I see you brought those books you promised. May I see them?"

"Yes, sign for them here."

I don't know why I thought of it this morning, but I typed a letter with a brief loan agreement. No charge, but the books must be returned when the movie is released or the project dropped.

There would be one hundred dollars per book if not returned. I figured they could be replaced for a lot less. Mr. James would be personally responsible. He frowned as he read it but had no excuse not to sign.

"Thanks. I need to get going if you don't have anything else."

"Not at this time. We are flying Chief Redfoot out next week, and you may want to sit in on that."

"I would like that very much. Let me know when."

"We will give you a call, and thanks for giving in so easily on the movie. Mr. Monroe told us it would be a hard sell."

They ain't seen nothing yet, as the saying goes.

I called Mr. Baxter as soon as I got home. I explained what was going on.

"What do you want out of this, Rick?"

"I want to own the movie. They used Mr. Monroe's name to put me in a corner. I want to repay the favor. They asked for me, they will get me. The cost will be the major profits from the movie.

"Let them explain it to Mr. Monroe. I bet they have sold this so hard to Mr. Monroe that they will not want to back down.

"At the same time, he knows he was used, so he will not feel kindly to them while feeling obligated to keep his end of the deal. I have learned that people will try to use me. It is not going to happen as easily as they think.

"So, how much should we ask for?"

"Scale for the part."

"That's all?"

"And thirty points for the movie idea and consulting."

"As your mother would say, you are becoming a right bastard."

"Mum doesn't talk like that."

I was conveniently forgetting her comments about the Chinese.

"Maybe not around you kids."

Things we don't know about our parents.

"Anyway, that is what I want."

"This will be fun and a good way to go out."

Since it was almost lunchtime, I ate at home. After that, I went to LAX and teamed up with another instructor since Hank Smith wasn't available and spent four hours touring the air and doing touch-and-goes.

The instructor was as bad as Mr. Smith, as he kept throwing emergencies at me. Somehow, I kept my cool and didn't crash. Unlike the simulator, this would be a bad thing.

After dinner, I took another shower, put on some comfy clothes, and hit the textbooks. I don't know if I would remember anything I read as my morning with the movie people kept going around in my head.

Try to help someone for free, and they want more.

Chapter 27

I had a good run to start the day. My weightlifting was now in maintenance mode. I wasn't looking to be Charles Atlas or Johnny Weissmuller.

At breakfast, Mary had a pathetic-looking kitten in her lap. Mittens now had mittens or rather bandages as she had been declawed. I guess she was the official Jackson Housecat. That gave me a thought for later.

I washed and waxed the T-Bird as it had been a while and looked a little worse for the wear. That didn't take long, and I easily made my 10 a.m. tee time.

John Jacobs was my caddie today, and we had a nice casual round with just the two of us. Today, I concentrated on layups at different points from each green. If there was a wind or other interference with my preferred landing spot for my drive, I wanted to be prepared for it.

I also realized this was much more preparation than I would have for the actual open when I qualified. There was no doubt in my mind I would win the local and regional rounds here at Riviera.

We had lunch at the club's outdoor restaurant. While eating, several girls close to my age came up to me and just gave me a good look over. When I asked what they were doing, they told me they wanted to check out the merchandise before bidding on it.

So many smart comments went through my mind, along with the humiliation of being thought merchandise, but I realized my acting career made me exactly that. Instead, I kept my mouth shut in line with Ben Franklin's motto of saying nothing and thought a fool.

Besides, I was taught you never used foul language with ladies.

Of course, I would have to look to find some ladies around here.

I'm more sensitive to these things than I thought, as it showed up in my golf shots later. John started talking to me in an obvious attempt to settle me down.

He knew nothing about the auction and thought it was funny as all get out when I explained it and my fear. Of course, he wouldn't be the one that no one would bid on.

I finally admitted it. My only concern for the auction was no bids.

Once I realized that was my problem, I decided to ask Mum and Dad to see if they would arrange for someone to bid on me, maybe Sharon Bronson, but then she was too old to win.

When I got home, there was a message to call Mr. Monroe. This was going to be good.

"Mr. Monroe, this is Rick Jackson returning your call."

"Oh, is this the snake in the grass who wants to steal the bread off my table?"

"Yes, that's me."

Hey, in for a penny in for a pound.

"Rick, I asked for help, and now you're trying to rob me."

"You asked for my help and then pushed me to appear in a movie when you knew I didn't want to."

"It would have been a perfect part for you. Now, since we can't afford you, I will have to cancel the project."

"Okay, I was only trying to help. You guys decided to up the ante, and I have called you on it."

"We can make the movie with someone else as Lew Wetzel."

"No, you can't. I talked to Mr. Baxter about it. We have a verbal agreement that I come up with a movie plot, which I did, and it was all discussed in front of witnesses. Even if you have someone else in it, I am owed for my work."

"Rick, this isn't like you."

"It isn't like you to help box me in against my will."

"Rick, this project is too good to pass up!"

"Mr. Monroe, you are teaching me some valuable lessons here. I helped for free with no expectations on the extra board concept. No worries, we won't be going to court over that. Just don't try to steal my movie idea."

There was a long silence on the other end.

"Rick, I had no idea it would come out like this. I just saw an opportunity to turn out a good movie, and your role would have put it over the top."

"You knew how I felt about taking the first half of next year off and maybe even ending my movie career. That carries a price. If you want to make the movie, please let Mr. Baxter know."

At that, I told him I had to go and hung up. Dad, who had heard the whole thing, was dumbfounded.

"Rick, I have never seen you stand up to anyone like that before."

"I think it is about time I start doing that, or the world will run over me. I know Mr. Monroe meant nothing wrong, but at the same time, he ignored what he knew I wanted. Now he is clear on the issue."

I went to study until dinner, but that conversation kept running through my mind. I finally concluded that there was no other way for me to handle it.

Once I arrived at that point, I was able to study.

During dinner, I raised my concern about no one bidding on me at the auction. They downplayed the idea and wouldn't discuss it any further. Mary had a funny look, so I knew something was up, so let it go.

After dinner, Mr. Baxter called.

"Rick, you have got Monroe's drawers in a knot. He is afraid he has lost your respect and friendship. You may not realize what you have done for the studio and him personally. He doesn't want it to end badly. In short, they are going ahead with the movie. You get thirty points. He is convinced they will lose money, but he doesn't care."

"I have mixed feelings about this. I don't want them to lose money, but I don't want to play silly games, either. "

"Well, I want you to take the deal. My percentage could make me a fortune. I want this last picture to be a huge moneymaker for me."

"Oh, we are taking the deal. If I let them off lightly, they will try the same thing in the future."

"What should I tell Monroe?"

"The deal is on, and I hold no grudge. Let's work together to make this a box office hit."

"That sounds good to me. Good night."

"Later."

I filled Mum and Dad in on the call. They agreed that it would send the wrong sign if I relented now. They also urged me to think that Mr. Monroe hadn't been playing a game with me. He saw a good business opportunity and, in the heat of the moment, didn't think it through.

I agreed that was most likely the cause.

Funny, a movie I hadn't heard or thought of until last week becomes such a contentious center of my life. I now wanted it to succeed beyond our wildest expectations.

At that, I called it a night and went to bed early.

Chapter 28

My only plan for today was further multi-engine instruction. It was coming together, and I thought I would be ready when my plane was delivered early next year.

Cessna marketing had sent me a welcoming kit that had me drooling and wishing time would fly. Somehow, that thought came out like a bad pun, but I was looking forward to it.

As the best of plans get mislaid, this one did, too. As we were leaving the breakfast table, Dad got a phone call. He talked for a few minutes. He wrote a name down and hung up.

"That was a John Forester from the FBI. He wants me to call the main switchboard of the LA FBI building and ask for him. Also, I am to get a description of him from the switchboard operator."

Mum had a puzzled look, "What's it about?"

"He wouldn't say other than I had to be certain I was talking to a real FBI agent before he would go into it."

Dad looked up the number in the blue section of the white pages and called. He explained who he was calling for and needed a description of the man. The switchboard people had been forewarned that it happened all the time.

Dad was connected and had a conversation. Mum and I heard only one side, but it was enough to keep our attention riveted. After Dad hung up, he explained what was going on.

"The CIA has questions about the park bench dead drop and how that happened. Since they cannot work on US soil, they asked the FBI to contact us and set up a meeting. "

"They want to keep it low profile, so we are to meet Forester at this address. It looks like it is out by the City of Industry in the warehouse area. CIA wants to question Rick but thinks it best if both parents were present. I agree. We have an hour to get there, which will be pushing it."

We piled into one of Dad's cars. He has several now. This one is a nondescript blue and white Ford Fairlane with a white interior. There must be thousands of them on the road.

We talked on the way down, but there wasn't much to say. Most of our conversation was about the Beach House and garage expansion. Something was niggling at the back of my mind the whole trip.

The address was a three-story building that looked like it had been empty for years. Just what the CIA would select for a secret rendezvous.

As we went up the short steps to the front entrance, the door opened. A man who fit the description Dad had shared stood there with a wallet and a badge extended. Dad looked at it and told us the name and badge number were correct.

Agent Forester started to edge past us, "I'm not part of this. My job was to get you here. They are in the last office on the right on the second floor. I will be going now."

All of a sudden, what had been niggling at the back of my mind came bursting out. As he walked by, I took him by the arm, twisted it into a half-Nelson, and took him to his knees.

"What are you doing, Rick?"

"Mum and Dad, to my knowledge, we never told the CIA or anyone else that the dead drop was a park bench. We just used the term dead drop. The only other people who would know would be the Russians."

Forester was struggling, but I held him in place. Mum and Dad both agreed they had never said anything.

Dad searched Forester, finding and removing his credentials, his weapon, and a set of handcuffs.

Dad expertly cuffed the guy and walked him into the building. A quick look around found no telephones. Mum tied Forester to a water fountain pipe using his necktie. The way she tied it, he could not get at the knots. She pulled out his handkerchief and stuffed it in his mouth.

"Mr. Forester, we may have to come down and give you our sincerest apologies in a few minutes. However, better safe than sorry, as they say."

Dad checked Forester's .38 revolver. Mum pulled out a .357 Magnum, which we both stared at.

She shrugged, "I like big guns."

I felt left out.

We went up the stairs as quietly as we could. They were expecting us so there would not be much of a surprise. The last door was closed, which was good.

Dad, holding his weapon in front of him, approached and checked each office. There was a restroom across the hall, which he ignored. When we reached the last door, he was on the doorknob side and Mum on the hinge. I was behind Dad.

He started to knock on the door when there was a sound behind me. A guy came out of the restroom. I didn't give him a chance, taking him down with a hold the US Marines would have been proud of.

I hope these were really bad guys, or I was in big trouble.

As my man hit the floor, Dad opened the door and charged into the room. Four or five quick gunshots followed. My first thought was, my parents!

Dad stepped out of the room to help me. Mum stood in the doorway with her back to us. She was keeping an eye on someone or something in the room.

Using the man's belt and tie, we got him under control. That is when I was able to look in the room. There were two bodies on the floor and a third person tied up in the corner.

Mum, keeping her gun out, stood guard while Dad kicked the guns on the floor aside and untied the third man. I recognized him as one of the CIA trainees from the tailing exercises. He was one of those whose cover was blown so that he couldn't do fieldwork.

As he was loosened, he told us what he knew from listening to them. They had kidnapped him outside of the local CIA field office. They intended to kill us and him and make it look like a CIA operation gone wrong. This would create a division between MI6 and the CIA.

He only knew this because he spoke Russian. They didn't realize he understood them.

Dad went downstairs to bring Forester up with us. After that, he was going for help. He brought Forester back, but there was blood all over him. Forester had spit out the handkerchief and tried to commit suicide by biting his tongue off. It was a mess, but he failed.

The CIA man expressed the thought that now he knew for certain that he didn't want to do fieldwork. I tend to agree with him.

Dad returned in half an hour, and the police and FBI arrived fifteen minutes later. I thought the FBI would have a hard time being convinced that Forester was a traitor, but it turned out he was suspected as a mole for the Russians.

While we waited for Dad, I asked Mum what we would do to the Russians.

"Nothing, Rick; this is in the hands of the FBI, CIA, and MI6. Even if we thought of something, too many people will be watching."

That made sense, but having a target on my back wasn't a nice feeling.

"I thought you said the Russians had lost most of their people, and we would be safe for a while."

"I was wrong."

We had to go down to LA police headquarters and to be interviewed, separately, of course. I didn't feel I was being accused of anything, but it was still an uncomfortable experience. After two hours, I thought we were done.

We were then taken to FBI headquarters for another round of questioning. These were more direct than the police. They were most interested in what tipped me off in the first place.

The lead agent asking questions expressed disbelief that a kid would pick up on such a small clue. The other agent was filling out form 302. Watching the agent fill out the form made me realize that the only record of this interview was what he was writing down.

"I think I need my parents in here as witnesses. You do remember I'm a minor?"

"What are you trying to hide?"

"I'm done here."

"You're done when I say you are done."

"Am I under arrest?"

"Not yet."

"Then I'm here as a voluntary citizen, and I'm now done."

About that time, the door opened, and Mum and Dad walked in with his lawyer. Sam Wingate may be a corporate attorney, but he knew his way around criminal law.

"Tear up that 302 or face felony charges for holding a minor against his parent's will."

The recording agent never hesitated as he tore it. "I knew this was a bad idea."

"Forester is one of ours!"

"He looks like he was on the Russian's team or whoever could afford him."

We didn't hang around for the rest of the conversation but got out.

It was a late, quiet dinner that night, and I turned in early with a million thoughts going through my mind.

The number one thought was *a target is on my back.*

Chapter 29

The next morning after a good night's sleep, the sun was out, and the world looked better. My morning physical exercise helped clear my mind. I may have set a pull-up record, but I lost count.

I ended up spending more time than usual and almost missed breakfast. Even then, I had to show up before showering. I think Mary spoke for the family when she said, "Pee Eww!"

I was allowed to eat but promised to shower immediately after eating.

It was a relief to get some normal grief rather than someone trying to kill me.

Mum, Dad, and I met in the library after I cleaned up.

"Have you learned anything about yesterday?"

"No, Rick. It is yet early days in the investigation. It will take a while. There will be an interrogation of the prisoners. The guy you knocked out is a low-level KGB agent, so he won't be able to tell us much.

"The FBI agent was real and a turncoat for money. He will know more about his control. We don't know which department his control is working for that wanted this hit or if it was some other group within the KGB. It could even be the GRU trying to cause trouble for the KGB."

"I have read about the Russian Military Intelligence group but didn't know they would try to sabotage the KGB."

"There is no love lost between the two groups; they are like the FBI and CIA, but unlike ours, they will try to harm each other physically. Thankfully, the American groups haven't descended to that level.

"At least MI5 and MI6 aren't like either of them."

She managed to say that with a straight face.

"Well, until then, I will try to keep myself out of trouble."

"Just be careful of your surroundings and any new contacts."

"I will. In the meantime, I think I will play some golf today. All those spies who are following me need a day of relaxation."

"That's the spirit, Rick. Watch out for your fellow man."

"Yeah, right. Anyway, I will be home in time for dinner."

Leaving the house, I made certain the gate guards knew where I was heading. They told me they heard we had some excitement yesterday. I confirmed it without going into the details.

I noticed the gun racks on the wall behind the front desk, which were usually empty, now had shotguns and rifles in them.

I felt safer at the country club than in most places. I had kidded about spies following me around. Any strangers on the course would stick out like a sore thumb.

John Jacobs was my caddy for today. I had not called ahead, but he was available. I agreed with him that if I called one day ahead, he would be my caddy. If I didn't call, he could get in the queue for the day. He would keep any tips made that way. It was accounted for in the deal. He was making out rather well the last two weeks.

Today, he was mine. We agreed that I would play the course for score today to see how much the practice and scoping out the course helped.

It helped a lot. I came in three under par. Not a course record, but it would have me in solid contention. Shaving two more strokes would give me an almost certain lock on being in the US Open.

When we made the turn at the ninth, we grabbed a bite to eat. Three women told me their daughters would bid on me Friday night. If they looked like their mothers, I couldn't lose.

More importantly, I now didn't have to worry about my nightmare. No bids.

I saw Mr. Johnathon Whitestone III after the eighteenth, but I made a point of ducking out of his line of sight. I wanted nothing to do with that man.

On the way home, I happened to look over at an automobile dealership and saw the perfect car. Not for me, for Mum. Dad had told me he was trying to find her a surprise present.

The small dealership had in its display window a sports car that looked perfect. It looked so good I pulled into their parking lot and went inside. Of course, a salesman was with me immediately.

He was polite in his approach, so I wasn't put off. I asked about the car. He proceeded to wax eloquent on the 1959 Morgan Plus4. It was a two-door Roadster with a four-cylinder 1991 cc/90 hp 2x1 bbl SU. This one was painted British racing green.

Mum would love it. It would remind her of the little sports cars she loved in the 30s and 40s. Yet it would have a more modern power train.

I thought it was neat that the body was framed in ash wood. There wasn't much weather protection, but that wasn't a concern here in California.

I called Dad from the dealership. His reaction was, "Yes!"

He told me to wait right there; he was on his way. When Dad burst through the door with a smile on his face, I knew the salesman's day was made. He had Dad over a barrel and would get the full asking price.

The car was factory new, so after a test drive, Dad told the salesman to write the deal up. Dad hadn't even asked the price. I watched carefully as the details were taken from the window sticker. The guy could have added ten thousand dollars, and Dad wouldn't have noticed. He was buying his girl a car.

He arranged for the car to be delivered to the house tomorrow morning. They showed us something I had never seen or heard of before. They had a giant ribbon that would be put on top of the car.

The car would be trucked to Jackson House, and the bow would be placed on top. They tried to haul it once with the bow already on and had to chase it down the freeway. That must have been a sight.

I asked, but we didn't get to keep the ribbon. We were only renting it. That was a shame; I had already thought of several uses.

Dad had a large grin at dinner but kept his mouth shut.

Denny was the one with news today. He had entered several of his pictures in a photo contest held at a local gallery. Mum worked with the gallery on charity events, so she knew about it and encouraged him to submit his work. It was accepted.

Denny's pictures were considered good, and he won the grand prize blue ribbon.

Besides the ribbon, he was to do a small photo shoot on the beach tomorrow morning for some group. I figured it was some team outing. We were all excited for him and wished him well on his shoot.

After dinner, Mum asked Dad and me to join her in the library. She updated us on the incident from the other day.

"The American government, namely the State Department, does not want to make an issue of this, so they have already exchanged the live Russian and returned the bodies. The FBI guy is going to secret court and will probably never see the light of day again. So, this is all over as far as they are concerned."

"The Russians are going to get away with this?"

"The Americans feel that the British, Chinese, and the Russians are playing games on their turf and don't feel any responsibility for what any of them do."

"So again, the Russians will get away with this?"

"Yes, with the Americans."

"Does that mean they aren't going to get away with it with the British?"

"Her Majesty's government would never try to undertake an operation of that serious a magnitude on American soil."

"I don't get it."

"You don't have to; you will have no involvement."

"Then who will?"

"Rick, you don't need to know, but you need to listen better. I said Her Majesty's government would take no action on American soil. I didn't say no action."

"Oh, I will watch the papers."

I should mention that I never saw anything in the papers, but several weeks later, Mum said a message had been sent.

Denny was all hyped up at breakfast. His photo shoot on the beach was to start at 9 a.m., so he and Mum had to take off. He had already loaded his equipment in our surfing Woodie. It wouldn't fit in any of the other cars. I hadn't realized that he owned so much stuff.

When Mum went out to drive the Woodie, there was the brand-new Morgan with a bow on top waiting for her. She jumped around like a little kid, hugging and kissing Dad. Way to go, Dad.

One of the security people was recruited to drive the Woodie while Mum followed in her new car. I bet it wouldn't take her long to pass them and fly down the road. Hope she doesn't meet my friends in CHIPs.

I had nothing to do for the day except stop by my office for a business review. I asked if it would be okay to stop by later to see how the shoot was going. Mum said I could, but I had to hang back out of the way. I was a well enough known actor who could disrupt Denny's big day.

Dad asked to speak to me before I left for the office.

Chapter 30

"Rick, your business is yours and seems to be under control. Mine is getting more demanding, so I can't afford to take the time out to attend these meetings. Mum and I have discussed it, and we think it is time for you to become emancipated. "

"What does that entail?"

"You legally become an adult. You have to abide by the age-related laws like drinking and driving, but you will be able to sign legal documents."

"Do you think I'm ready?"

"We wouldn't be suggesting it if we didn't."

"Okay, what do we have to do?"

At that, Dad brought out a stack of papers for me to sign. He asked Mrs. Hernandez to notarize my signature. It was really handy to have an in-house Public Notary.

"A judge must approve these after he interviews you. The interview is to ensure there is no coercion and that you appear to be mentally sound."

"Ouch, appear to be mentally sound?"

"You know what I mean."

"Now that I have signed these, when will I see this judge?"

"I will submit them to the judge's office, and his clerk will schedule an appointment. Ike tells me it will be expedited, so probably sometime next week."

"Why is the president involved?"

"Ike is the one who started this. He called concerned about the Russians being after you. He wants you to be armed and able to carry legally."

"Even if I am legally an adult, how can I do that in California?"

"US Marshals can carry anywhere."

"What!"

"Ike is using an old regulation in the Marshal's office. It goes back to the Old West. A marshal could deputize any adult to form a posse. It didn't stipulate an age."

"He, as president, is appointing you as a full US marshal as a one-man posse."

"Who am I supposed to be tracking down?"

"Judge Crater."

"He's been missing since before I was born!"

"Around 1930, if I remember right."

"What am I supposed to do about it?"

"Submit an updated report if you come across any new evidence."

"That's not likely."

"We know. It is just an excuse for the legal record. Ike's people came up with it as it can be a continuing appointment after he leaves office next year. It's set up in a way that most future administrations will never notice it, and then it would take an executive order of the president to cancel it.

"Those things get such scrutiny that it causes more trouble than its worth. As soon as you're twenty-one, it is all moot and by the system. By the way, you will not be paid. Your salary will go to the US Marshals Orphans and Widows Fund."

"That seems fair, but Dad, I don't know much about firearms. Only a little hunting with shotguns we did in Ohio and shooting I did with Elvis and John Wayne."

"You will be learning starting next week.

"Now, you'd better get to your office."

I left the house, my mind reeling from all the new information. Now I was to be an adult and a US marshal; talk about changes."

I arrived at my office and couldn't remember driving there.

Jim Williamson was ready and waiting. I told him that Dad wouldn't be attending in the future and about my pending emancipation. I didn't mention about becoming a US marshal. That seemed so unreal.

The business was doing fine. The company was growing faster than expected, and earnings were far beyond expectations. It only took fifteen minutes to go over everything, and there were no major corporate decisions to be made.

I thought I got off easy until Jim led me from his office to the conference room. There was a massive stack of cards for me to sign. They were for birthdays, anniversaries, birth announcements, weddings, condolences, and graduations, to name most of the events. One was congratulations on adopting a child by a worker in Pittsburg.

I signed until my fingers were cramping. I took a break and talked to the ladies in the office. Emily's aunt was there, and I spoke nicely to her but didn't inquire about Emily. Her aunt didn't bring her up either.

I finished signing and headed to the beach, hoping Denny's photo shoot was still happening.

The trip to the beach wasn't too bad as the morning rush hour was over. The beach was in Santa Monica. They wanted the Ferris wheel in the background on some of the shots.

I hadn't thought about who the subject of the shoot would be. Some local team or social group, probably. You could have knocked me over with a feather when I pulled up and saw several semi-trucks that had brought set equipment—photography sets.

A sign on the side of the semi-trucks said Miss California Teen Pageant.

My little brother had scored a beauty pageant!

I did as Mum requested and hung way back. Plenty of spectators stood behind the roped-off area, so I blended in with the crowd.

I was proud of Denny as he worked. He was a natural at putting the girls in poses that showed their best attributes, and man, there were some attributes! He also joked and laughed with them, keeping them at ease.

I watched it until their lunch break. The roped-off area contained portable picnic tables, and various people were cooking on grills. I took a chance and moved to the entrance to the site. Denny saw me and waved me over.

The guys keeping people out didn't give me any trouble. It was a low-key, enjoyable event. The people-watching would come and go without trying to join the proceedings.

Denny hustled over to me. You could tell he was bursting with excitement.

"Rick, have you seen all these girls? They are gorgeous."

"Yeah, they are kind of hard to miss, Denny."

"They are thirteen to eighteen years old!"

"Sounds like you have fallen into it."

"You bet I have. Some have been asking me if I would do sittings for their portfolios. Several even inquired about vanity pictures for their boyfriends."

Maybe I should take up photography.

"I can see it now. I will have a studio in the darkest corner of the basement and all these babes visiting me."

Somehow, I doubted it as Mum was standing right behind him. She held her finger to her lips and left.

Now that I thought about it, I didn't care that much about taking pictures.

I ate lunch with Denny while he continued to rattle on. As we ate, contestants would come up to our table. I didn't know if I should feel insulted or not. They wanted to talk to Denny and mostly ignored me.

Several of the older girls eyed me but didn't say anything. I kept my word to Mum and didn't try to butt into the events of the day.

As we finished eating, Mum returned with Sam Nielsen in tow. Sam was the professional photographer who had been dating Roberta Grimes. I heard that they were now engaged. He had his studio in our building.

"Denny, I brought Sam over as he would like to talk to you about your photographs."

Sam smiled as he spoke, "Denny, you have impressed me with your work today. You handle your subjects with ease and get the best out of them. I would like you to join my studio."

"It would be on Saturdays only, and you would handle all the young ladies who need portfolios and some vanity shots. By using the studio, there would always be the proper chaperonage. It would also provide you with the accounting structure for taxes."

Since Mum was standing right there, Denny couldn't object, but you could see a lot of dreams going down the drain. I should feel sorry for the poor kid. However, the poor kid would make money while meeting many pretty young ladies. Suffer, suffer.

I left Denny to his suffering and went home to study. I had been lax this week with the various excitements and didn't want to fall behind.

Chapter 31

I was starting to notice something in my work. It seemed like I already knew a lot of what was being covered in the textbooks. The extra reading and studies I did in the previous courses covered much of the "new" information.

The books in the bibliography did not limit themselves to the structure of the course work but to the writer's thoughts on what information needed to be conveyed.

This was even true in a limited sense in the math books. While not covering everything, it would make each chapter easier for me to assimilate.

Dinner was fun, with us teasing Denny about his newfound vocation. He enthusiastically described the studio arrangement with Sam Nielsen.

Mum winked across the table.

I had to wonder how much similar guidance I had been given in the last few years.

After dinner, we had a family game of Clue. This time, it was Miss Scarlet in the kitchen with a dagger.

Dad was the winner. Of course, we told him the winner had to put the game away.

While we were playing, Mary asked Denny about a folio. She had heard it being discussed and thought she should have one. What was it? After Denny explained it, she thought it would be a good thing for her acting career. We were surprised as this was the first we had heard of it.

"I'm going to be appearing in TV advertisements."

Mum looked surprised. Further questioning found that she had been talking to her classmates. Several of them were attending casting calls.

Mum and Dad told her they would have to talk about it. I don't think Mum was up to being a stage mother. I know Dad wanted no part of it, just from the panicked look on his face.

Mary also told us she had better have some vanity pictures taken while she was at it. That had Dad in a sweat.

Mum said, "Mary, vanity pictures are usually given to boyfriends or husbands."

"Oh, it might be a little soon then. Davey in our class doesn't like girls yet."

Poor Davey. He will never know what hit him.

I brought up the auction tomorrow night, but no one wanted to discuss it. Mary let out a little giggle, so I knew something was up.

I had an extra-long workout on Saturday. I cleaned up before breakfast but then rode George for an hour. After cleaning up again, I put it together that I was nervous about that dang charity auction tonight.

I called the country club and asked if it was possible to work me in. I was told to show up, and they would fit me in with a two or threesome.

John Jacobs had already gone out for the morning, so I had a different caddy. He was new to the course and wouldn't be much help. That was okay. I just had to keep busy today.

I was put in with a twosome. I walked up just as they were getting ready to tee off. We spent little time on introductions. I was Rick to their Jim and Troy.

As we teed off, it became apparent they were equally bad with each other. Well, not horrid bad but not the caliber I was used to playing with. They were having a good time talking trash to each other.

They paid little attention to me while they spent half their time looking for their golf balls in the rough or swearing when they went in the water. I just patiently hit the ball and then waited my turn.

I ignored my score, but my caddy didn't. At the turn after nine, he asked me if I knew where I stood. I told him I was just keeping myself busy, not shooting for score. He gave me a funny look.

We stopped for a quick bite at the clubhouse outdoor grill. I had two hotdogs and a Coke. The other two were now talking about a business deal of some sort.

My ears perked up when I heard Jackson Enterprises. I paid attention while not looking like I was paying attention. I think that was called eavesdropping. I preferred to think of it as industrial espionage.

They were thinking of putting together a proposal to clean the new cargo containers when they were in the Port of Long Beach.

This got my attention as we had not even considered this. The plan they fleshed out was a good one. They were concerned about doing the job correctly so they could expand to other ports. They cautioned each other to not get greedy as they talked about finances.

It sounded like they had enough backing to have a solid start. What impressed me was they both had experience working with truck lines and railroads in cleaning trailers and boxcars.

The only part they hadn't figured out was how to get to see Mr. Jackson. I think they meant my dad. I decided to keep my mouth shut until after the round was completed, as they would pester me to death if I introduced myself now.

Several young ladies approached me as we walked over to the tenth tee. They didn't say anything; they just looked at me. Then one told the other, "He's okay."

Thanks a lot!

My golfing buddies didn't see this, thank goodness. How humiliating.

Our caddies were waiting at the tee box. We hit off and continued around the back nine. After coming off eighteen, I offered a tip to my caddy.

He stared at me like I was crazy.

"Man, you just broke the course record and don't even know it!"

Unfortunately, my partners heard it. They insisted on signing my scorecard even though they had no idea if it was accurate. Heck, I had no idea if it was accurate.

I replayed the course in my head and realized I had set a new record.

They started yelling and cheering. Of course, this got attention in this staid country club. This brought the pro out of his shop. He congratulated me and asked if they could have the card for their records.

I couldn't see the big deal. It was just a relaxing round of golf, which had helped me get through some nervous hours.

During the commotion, my golf companions figured out who I was. They were torn between congratulating me and trying to get an appointment.

I solved that problem by giving them one of my cards and telling them to call Jim Williamson to set a meeting. I liked what I had heard. They fell over themselves, trying to assure me it was not planned.

I knew that as I had joined them randomly.

Troy, I think it was, joked that at least they wouldn't have to pretend that I was better at golf than they were. That got a laugh.

After things settled down, I went home. It would give me time to have a meal and get cleaned up. I knew they would serve dinner there, but I hated the food served at these events. This way, I could pick at the good stuff and ignore the rubber chicken. I would sweet-talk the cook at home into a cheeseburger and fries.

I wore a tux to the event. Since it was winter it had a black coat with a white cummerbund and tie. For the fun of it, for the first time, I wore the top hat the British tailor provided. I drew the line at the white spats and gloves. They stayed in the box.

When I went to reception at home where the family was gathering to leave for my ritual sacrifice, I received a mixed reception about the hat. The ladies liked it, and the men hated it. Denny and Mary both had cameras ready and took pictures. They probably had different goals in mind.

Eddie told me I looked like a Melvin. I conveniently left the hat on an end table as we walked out to the limo. There was no further to do about it, so I figured I might wear it at a wedding someday, but that's it for fashion statements.

Chapter 32

When we arrived at the Club, it was like walking on the red carpet. Pictures were taken, and interviews were given. I was asked how much I thought I would bring to the auction.

"I hope a lot, as I intend to match it."

"Rick, are you trying to drive your price up?"

"Yes, I hope it sets a record."

As I had picked up from Mum, in for a penny in for a pound.

"The record for this event is five thousand dollars, so good luck."

What was I thinking? I should be happy if someone wanted to pay one hundred dollars for a date with me. Heck, the guy typically has to pay for the date.

Our family's table was at the absolute back of the room. We didn't fill it up as there were empty chairs. Meals were served; speeches were given, and then it was time for the main event. All eleven of us eligible bachelors were invited up front.

They sat us in a line on the stage in front of the audience. There must have been five hundred people in the room. With that many people present, the room was getting quite warm.

Our table was so far back that I couldn't make out faces. All the chairs were now filled, but I couldn't tell with whom. It appeared to be a guy and two women.

The bidding started. The event was run in good fun, and no one was insulted. The average price was two thousand dollars, and one actor who just went through a messy divorce set an auction record of fifty-five hundred dollars.

Color me cynical, but I think his agent set up the bidding to reestablish his desirability. The audience was pretty quiet during this round of bidding. Only two women were involved, and they kept glancing at the well-known agent before raising their hands.

Once the record was set, he quickly drew his finger over his throat, and it was over, a little obvious.

As each auction was concluded, the auctioned-off guy would join the winner at their table. Waiters would bring a chair for them.

Finally, it was me alone on the stage. Of course, the MC and auctioneer had to give another speech extolling the virtues of Sir Richard Jackson, actor, golfer, business tycoon, hero, and all-around good guy. I wanted to throw up.

My acting stood me in good stead as I plastered a smile on my face and waited. I suspect I looked like I was waiting for a firing squad.

My fears of no bids quickly proved to be unfounded. A dozen different young ladies were raising their hands. It quickly went to one thousand, then two and three.

They began dropping out at four thousand. It came down to two young ladies at the front of the room. They edged it up towards five thousand. I glanced at the agent who had run up the record, who had a sour look.

When it got to fifty-four hundred dollars, the room got silent. That agent was sweating bullets. He kept wiping his face with a handkerchief. The room was now downright hot. The MC was playing up the bidding and drawing it out for all it was worth.

The silence drew out as the MC said, "Going once."

At that, a new voice came strongly from the back of the room.

"I bid ten thousand dollars!"

Well, there goes my allowance.

All pandemonium broke out.

The actor with the previous record was all over his agent as their plan fell apart.

All that was interesting, but my question was, who had won the bid?

A waiter led me back to the winning table, the Jackson family table.

There waiting was the winner, Judy King, and her parents. Judy jumped up and met me with a complete body-frontal hug. This somehow turned into a kiss. It must have gone on too long as we received parental clearing of throats.

As we separated, I started to ask how, but a look at Mum answered everything. By then, reporters had caught up with us and were at Judy with the questions. She gave short, complete answers.

She heard about the auction and, as a long-time friend, knew someone had to take care of me. So, her parents came out with her from Columbus, Ohio to see that I didn't get in trouble.

What a liar!

I lost it when Mary winked at me. I wondered how long this had been in the works. When I got a chance, I whispered to my parents.

"Thanks."

Dad whispered back, "This was the women's doing. Bob and I are innocent bystanders. Your Mum and Sandra arranged it all. Mary has had her story ready to go for a week. Judy was the surprise. We thought she would do it as a favor. I think there is more to it than that."

Mum just smirked. She had me fill out my matching check and the auction amount, twenty thousand dollars from my account. I later found out I was also paying for the King's expenses, including first-class airfare.

After more pictures of Judy and me, we managed to break away. Two limos were waiting, one a stretch and the other a town car. I don't know how it worked out, but Judy and I were alone in the town car.

When we got in the back, she scooted over next to me, and putting an arm around her was natural.

"This is such a pleasant surprise. It never occurred to me that you might be here."

"We flew in this afternoon, and they smuggled us into Jackson House where we hid in a guest suite. I can't wait to get a whole house tour."

"How long can you stay?"

"We have to leave early tomorrow; I have school on Monday."

"When can we have dinner?"

"I would love for you to fly to Columbus and escort me to our Winter Ball. It's on Friday, December 11th."

"I don't see any reason that I can't. I will check with my parents."

"Oh, they have already approved."

As Dad said, we men were innocent bystanders.

"Then it's a date. We should plan on dinner before the dance."

"I would like to go to The Top for a steak."

"Then that is where we will go."

"Did you notice the partition between us, and the driver is closed off from us?"

"Uh."

"We won't have any alone time once we get to your house."

I never realized girls were so soft.

We rearranged our slightly disarrayed clothes before we entered the house.

It is a party atmosphere inside. The Kings coming out here was arranged almost the day after I told Mum about the auction. She had seen the gold diggers at the country club and didn't want them near me. That was fine with me.

Judy was the one girl still around who knew me before fame and fortune. Wow, fame and fortune. Hard to think about, but it is real.

Mum and Dad took the Kings on a house tour, so I accompanied Judy. It was natural to hold her hand as we showed the house off.

The tower always impressed people the most. Judy wanted to know about the sign sitting near the entrance. I explained how I walked in on Mary and her girlfriends. She thought that was a hoot. She also agreed with Mum that it would be a wonderful place to sunbathe. That gave me thoughts about all those soft places. I started doing multiplication tables in my head. They saved the day.

After the tour, Judy and I settled in reception to talk as everyone else had gravitated to the kitchen. She told me about her school and how the tenth grade was going.

I shared what was going on in my world. I tried not to make a big deal about it but try to tell someone you are a multi-millionaire and not sound like you are bragging. One of the stuntmen told me if you can do it, it isn't bragging. I tried to keep it factual.

Judy was more interested in my plans beyond high school. Where was I considering going to college? I explained my choices. She looked slightly frustrated for a minute.

"Rick, I like you; I like you a lot. I would want to date you if we were in the same school. As it is, I don't see us ever getting together."

"Why not?"

"Stupid boy, you are here in LA, and I'm in Columbus."

"There is a new invention called the airplane."

That stopped her for a moment. Her eyes got big.

"You would fly to Columbus to see me? How could you afford that?"

"Hey, you're forgetting; rich boy here. If needed, I could buy a 707 to come to see you. Mum and Dad would have a cow, but I could do it."

She giggled at that.

"Well, I would love to see more of you."

"What about a date once a month and special occasions?"

You would think I had proposed. Maybe I had. She squealed a yes. It was loud enough to attract a mother and a mum.

Judy didn't hesitate to tell them I wanted to fly to Columbus every month for dates. I figured I was about to get an earful.

Instead, there were two smiling mothers. I raised an eyebrow at Mum.

"Rick, it is a win for both Sandra and me. You will be dating, and Judy won't be going out on many dates. You have had no social life, and Sandra has told me that Judy's has been a little too much."

Judy and I both blushed for different reasons. I suspect I now knew why Judy knew her way around the backseat of a car better than me. Not that I cared.

After that, we talked for hours, and every time we were about to run down, we started up again. Everyone else had gone to bed. Judy and I watched the sun come up on top of the tower. It was pleasant having coffee and croissants at daybreak.

Chapter 33

Too soon, we got in the limo to take her and her parents to the airport. I was the only one from the family to go. We had a pleasant conversation on the way to the airport. I saw Judy off at the gate.

The ticket agent standing there said I looked like I had it bad. I asked how she knew.

"Well, I don't think you put that tux on this morning."

"Busted."

"Oh, to be young again."

I went home and took a nap. Then I caught up on the exercises I hadn't done yet today. After a ride on George, the day was almost over.

There was one last item to cover. It was Sunday night, and *Maverick* was on. I had a call from Jim Garner earlier this week to tell me it was the episode I was in.

Watching it with the family, I about died. They played me as a naïve young kid. While not the blatant butt of jokes, I was the center of the humor of the show. It is incredible how they can take a series of scenes and string them together to tell the story they want. Thank heavens the news people don't do that.

My week started fine. Good weather, well, except for the eternal smog over the Los Angeles basin. We were up high enough it didn't affect us. It was like looking down on a sick miasma from the top of the tower. The city looked diseased. I hoped they could do something about it someday.

After my normal morning routine, I cleaned up and went for breakfast. The whole family was there. Mary was excited because Mum had agreed to take her to a casting call for a cereal advertisement. So, their day was planned. Dad was doing his usual work. I'm not even sure what all he is involved in these days.

Denny was still working on the photographs he had taken at the beauty contest. Eddie sort of looked lost. He was the only one of us that didn't have real plans for the day. Well, except for me.

Even that changed. There was a phone call for me. Chief Redstone was in Hollywood and would like to get together. After some discussion, I agreed to pick him up from the Beverly Hills Hotel and bring him out to Jackson House for dinner.

He wasn't due at the studio until tomorrow, so that would work out fine.

I hit the books for the rest of the morning and most of the afternoon. Around three o'clock, I was getting ready to leave to pick up the chief when I noticed Eddie sitting at the kitchen table looking bored. I invited him along. He was up like a shot.

I guess homeschooling has its drawbacks. We talked about that during our drive. He told me he made more progress at his own pace, but he missed his friends. He thought it would be forever until he got to go back to school after the first of the year.

Our taking over of the school was now complete. The name hadn't been changed, but Mum and Dad had put a new board of directors and superintendent in place. Each existing teacher was being interviewed for their job. A few who had known about the bullying environment and favoritism and had done nothing had been let go.

I asked Eddie if he had any money-making ideas, and he expressed frustration. Everyone in the family but Eddie had extra income. He felt like a failure.

I tried to tell him he wasn't, but you could tell he wasn't buying it. I wondered if Mum and Dad realized how he felt about things. When asked what he would like to do, he shrugged. I don't think most twelve-year-olds do.

I had a newspaper route when I was his age. It was different in California. Delivering papers on a bicycle in our area would be too dangerous. Lawn mowing, another mainstay of Bellefontaine youth, was carried out by landscaping companies.

He wasn't old enough to be a lifeguard. Caddying wasn't a kid's job, at least at the courses I played.

"Is it making money you want or something interesting to do?"

"Something to do, I guess."

"I have enjoyed the Boy Scouts. I know Denny had little interest in Ohio and didn't rejoin out here, but have you thought about it?"

"Not really. No one would have the time to take me."

"I do."

"You do?"

"Certainly. I am still a Boy Scout. I should join a troop out here. Would you like to go with me?"

"Wow, yes, I would. When can we go?"

"Well, let's find a troop first."

By the time we got to the hotel, Eddie was fighting bears and forest fires on our camping trips.

Chief Redstone was waiting in the lobby, so he joined us immediately when I pulled up to the entrance. He had two long hard cases with him. They barely fit in the trunk. The Corvette would have never held them.

We shook hands and proceeded to Jackson House.

He updated me on the Shawnee Museum and how the medals I had donated had put them on the map as a serious Indian museum. No one had caught on how they "discovered" them in the museum storage area, so there were no counterclaims for custody.

Eddie asked him if he was a real Indian chief. Doctor Redstone assured him he was. Eddie spent the rest of the trip in awe.

My parents were waiting for us at home, so we spent some time catching up with how everyone was doing. Dad and I took the chief on a tour of the house. He chuckled at how our circumstances had changed since he met us in Bellefontaine.

He brought in the two hard cases he had with him.

The first one contained a flintlock rifle. It wasn't in the best of condition. I examined it carefully as the chief explained it was a Northwest gun. The smoothbore full-stock musket had a brass sea serpent side plate.

Chief Redstone explained the 60-caliber weapon had what was called the tombstone fox. That is an outline of a tombstone with a sitting fox inside. This indicated it was probably made by Barnett.

He had brought it to present to the studio as a reward for trying to make the picture fair to both sides.

I asked if it was worth much.

The chief started laughing.

"Yes, it probably is, Rick. You don't see many of these about. They were used in the woods by Indians and used hard. That makes them rare."

"Why are you laughing about it?"

"Their value is in their rarity; at the time, they were pieces of junk the white man pawned off on the Indians. This is a trade rifle."

"I thought it justice that I return the white man's junk to him."

"That's harsh."

"Yeah, but it's funny."

I wasn't sure about that, but since Dad was laughing, I didn't continue questioning. I'm glad I didn't.

Chief Redstone then opened the other case.

"Now, Rick, the tribe has decided this is the rifle you should use in the movie. Even though you play the bad guy, you are our friend."

The flintlock rifle was beautiful. It had fancy brass fittings. The wood was curly maple. On the top of the octagon barrel, written in script, was the maker's name, J. Dickert. The mark on it was a tomahawk crossed with a bow contained within an oval.

"Dickert was an early Pennsylvania gunsmith who made rifles for Washington's army. These were used by the Rangers and credited with winning major battles. They were accurate out to 250 yards, while the British Brown Bess only did 100 or so.

"These later became known as the Kentucky long rifle. They were used in battles from the French and Indian Wars until the Civil War. One of these is the only known surviving rifle from the Battle of the Alamo. It is what Davy Crockett and the other frontiersmen used.

"This rifle is rare, top quality, and in fantastic condition. It is worth a lot of money."

"I will take care of it and return it in the same condition."

"Oh, you don't understand. It is a gift to you from the Shawnee. You are our friend."

That started to choke me up.

Chief Redstone then got a pensive look.

"You may not thank me later."

"Why not?"

"You're going to have to learn how to load and fire it."

"That doesn't sound hard."

"While running."

"Oh.

"Oh, how do you do that? It takes force to push the bullet down the barrel."

We waited until after dinner and adjourned outside at his suggestion. Dad and the kids joined us.

"Now, to answer your question about the force needed to push the bullet down the barrel. Usually, you have a wad of cloth wrapped around the bullet to keep it from rolling out and to contain the force of the explosion. It also keeps the ball turning against the grooves. The tightness of the wadding makes it hard to ram it home.

"For this, you don't use wadding. Since the ball will be pretty free in the barrel you will have to be careful not to tip it downward. Also, you will lose accuracy and force, but it won't matter at a close distance."

"What about spitting the ball down the barrel?"

"I don't recommend it. A good way to get a fat lip or lose a tooth."

He then walked me through the actions: first, the ramrod down the barrel to clear any embers from the last shot; a best guess at pouring the powder; the ball dropped manually into place; then the ramrod again to tamp the powder down. Lastly, I put fine priming powder into the pan.

It seemed easy standing there. Trying it at a jog was a different story. I commented that I don't think I could ever do it at a dead run. He agreed, but that was where the magic of Hollywood would come into play. The camera would make it seem I was running faster than I was.

After I showed him how fast I could run, he told me the cameras were needed. In the real world, I would be run down and scalped before I could load my weapon. Now, that was just mean.

I performed several run-throughs under his tutelage. I would need to do it several hundred more times to get it down pat, but I could see it was doable.

Dad and the boys had to try it. At least I wasn't the only one looking like a doofus. Mary watched for a while then told us she would hire soldiers to shoot for her—wise beyond her age.

I asked the chief about doing this at a dead run, not that my dead run was anything to brag about.

"You will be chased through the woods; you will have to keep your eye on your surroundings so you don't trip and fall. You will work on your loading only when on a comparative clear straightaway. This means the loading will be performed in stages rather than all at once. Your chasers will have the same problem."

So, with the help of cameras, I could appear to do this. Thinking about doing it in the real world, like Kenton and Wetzel, was mind-boggling. Though I suppose being chased by people intent on scalping you would be an incentive for speed.

After the guys all had a go at it and failed miserably, we called it a night. I returned the chief to his hotel. I agreed to return at nine in the morning to escort him to the studio.

Back at home, I spent several hours on my schoolwork. I wanted to be done with high school.

Chapter 34

I had a good start to my day: a little horseback riding, my exercise routine, and a large breakfast. What more could a boy ask for?

I picked up Chief Redstone as agreed. I took him to the studio offices, saving him a lot of nonsense at the gate. Mr. Monroe came out and greeted the chief. I received a curt "Sir Richard" as he led the chief away. He turned and told me they would take care of the chief's travel home.

Boy, I guess I had made him angry. Tough, he started it.

I spent the rest of the day flying. It was in two sessions, as the instructors didn't have more than four hours open at a time. I did eat lunch as they refueled the plane between instructors. I wanted to get this out of the way.

At dinner, I shared how I was in the doghouse at the studio. Dad thought it was funny, and Mum got that look on her face. I hastened to tell her that it wasn't that big of a deal with me, as I wasn't certain I even wanted to continue acting until I had completed all my schooling.

That opened up the discussion of where I would go to school. As usual, that went in circles. To break the circle, I brought up Eddie and me looking for a scout troop. Mum and Dad were supportive. Well, supportive to the point that I was tasked with calling the scout council to find troops in our area.

After dinner, I hit the schoolbooks but got sidelined in reading one of the referenced books in European history. It was about the kings of England. What a bloody bunch! Murder and treason were the names of the day. Talk about survival of the fittest.

Today's royal family had been out of true power long enough they shouldn't be included. Well, maybe they had gone from the sword to the stiletto, something to keep in mind.

That brought up the picture of Queen Elizabeth in crown and robes stalking the palace halls. It was good that I was in my room with the door closed as I laughed like a loon.

When I calmed down, I called it a night with the schoolbooks and read about the adventures of NYPD Detective Baley and his partner Olivaw.

The next morning, I had a typical start to the day. After breakfast, I call the BSA office listed on the white pages. They described several troops in the Beverly Hills area. The most likely was Troop 33, who met in a "scout house" behind El Rodeo School. Their meetings were on Wednesday at 6:30, so I planned to be there with Eddie tomorrow night.

I no sooner hung up, and the phone rang. I answered, "Jackson House."

It was for me. The studio wanted me to come in for some costume fittings. I told them I was available this morning and was told to come on over.

I noticed the T-Bird was low on gas. Mum was walking out at the same time, so I asked if I could take her Morgan instead. She just held her head high as she brushed by me.

I detoured on the way to the studio and filled the tank. Getting back to the route to the studio brought me to the school with the large playground. The light had just changed to yellow, so the three cars in front of me stopped. I hated this long light. It had been set so kids crossing the street to walk to school had it in their favor.

As I waited, I noticed something a little strange. There was a man holding something out to a little girl. She was coming through an opening in the fence for kids coming onto the grounds. As she neared him, he stepped forward and grabbed her, which brought out a scream from the girl.

This looked so wrong. I was out of my car and halfway to him before I wondered if I had put the car into parking gear. Later, I found out I had.

The girl's cries also attracted a teacher's attention, but she was too far away to stop the man before he could get to his car. I wasn't.

He had just turned the girl in his arms when I arrived. On seeing me, he dropped her. He just had time to pull out a revolver before I hit him. A moving six foot five two-hundred-and-ten-pound object hitting a five foot ten one-hundred and maybe fifty-pound object carries a lot of force.

Wrapping my arms around him, he went down hard. Too hard, as I heard his head hit the pavement. It was the most sickening sound I have ever heard. I was slightly stunned by the impact. By the time I shook it off, the teacher had arrived and had the little girl in her arms.

Whistles were blowing, and all the other kids were pouring into the school. This must have been a preplanned drill as two other teachers joined us while the rest herded students inside.

The little girl, who looked like a first grader, was asked if she knew the man.

"No, but he said my mother told him it was okay if I shared his candy."

I took a good look at the man. From his eyes and stuff seeping out of the back of his head, I knew he wouldn't be offering candy to little girls again. I told one of the teachers.

"Don't let her see him."

The startled teacher let out a gasp as she looked. As I went to my car, which was blocking traffic, she got between the girl and the body. I got a beach blanket out of the trunk and covered the guy.

It was about that time it came to me that I had just killed a man. I had to sit down on the curb.

Since my car was blocking traffic, it didn't take long for a police vehicle to show up. I got lucky as it was a sheriff's car. Since George Burrill had won his election, they might not shoot me on the spot.

The deputy didn't recognize me. He was calm and cool in taking my statement. He didn't imply by his questions that I did anything wrong. He was just trying to establish what had happened. I was feeling better as he finished. Then he made a statement that scared the heck out of me.

"At most, it is involuntary manslaughter."

I thought I was going to be sick. I had just killed what may be an innocent man. In the long run, it didn't matter as two teachers told him they had seen the guy trying to lure the girl to his car but couldn't get there in time. I was a hero.

That was a relief. Not the hero part, the witnesses.

An older gentleman showed up. He must have been the school principal. He sent most of the teachers back to their classrooms. I heard him ask the deputy an interesting question.

"Do you think it is the predator we have been looking for?"

"I hope so," was the reply.

It took several hours before I was allowed to leave. Of course, reporters and even one radio station had shown up during that period. Shame it wasn't Dad's.

When allowed, I drove back home. The entire time, I kept hearing the thump of his head like a pumpkin hitting the sidewalk. At home, I showered, remembered to call the studio, and told them I had been detained and would try to make it tomorrow. From there, I went to the tower top and sat looking at the world below.

I had been there for about an hour when Mum and Dad showed up. Dad had heard about it on the radio and called Mum, and they returned home hoping I would be there.

They sat down with me.

Dad softly asked, "You okay, Rick?"

"I think so. It seems so weird. One minute, I'm stopping at a traffic light, and next, I'm killing a guy. How should I feel?"

"Like you saved a little girl. They went to his house. He lived alone. When the police went in, they found the bodies of three other children in his basement."

"Oh."

"There are reporters at the front gate. Do you want to talk to them?"

"No."

"Rick, do you feel guilty that you killed him?"

"No, first of all, it was an accident, and second, he needed to be stopped. He was dead the moment I saw him try to kidnap the little girl, if not at that moment, then later in jail. From what I read, people like him don't last in prison."

"Then what is bothering you?"

"Mum, it is the sound of his head hitting the sidewalk. It keeps playing over and over in my mind."

Dad spoke up, "I still feel the ax biting into those Russian's heads. It does get better with time. Instead of the actual feeling, it becomes a memory that isn't as vivid, but it never seems to go away."

Mum added, "For me, it's a knife slicing into a neck."

I looked at her incredulously.

"It's memories from the resistance in France."

"Oh." I seemed to be saying that a lot recently.

"Rick, the guy also had a gun, so taking him down quickly was the only solution."

"Oh."

Dad snorted, "I thought he knew more words than that."

That broke me up a little. I gave a weak laugh.

"I thought I did. I think I will study for a while to take my mind off things."

"Sounds like a plan."

Dad said, "Rick, time helps. The feeling will always be there, but it will get duller until it becomes a faint echo. The frequency of remembering will drop off, just like other significant events in your life. You will remember, but there will be a distance, and the details will fade.

"Thanks, Dad. It can't come too soon for me."

I typed papers on my good old IBM until lunch. By then, I was able to keep a train of thought going without going back to the guy hitting his head on the sidewalk.

At lunch, I was reminded that I had an appointment at the LA Federal Office building. I was to appear before a judge, take an oath as a US marshal, and sign my emancipation papers.

Dad drove me there. The traffic was horrible. It took almost an hour to get from home to downtown LA. They said it was going to be worse in the future. I think I will have to move if it gets that bad.

Chapter 35

It took us a few minutes to find the right office at the courthouse. Once there, we were almost immediately escorted into the office of the Honorable Thurman Clarke.

After introductions, the judge informed me he had heard about the attempted kidnapping I had thwarted, and that was good quick thinking.

We chatted for a few minutes, and then Chief Deputy US Marshal Bill Tilghman arrived. Obviously, he and Dad were well acquainted as they served together during the war. They hadn't seen each other since and decided to meet later and catch up.

After a "Harrumph," the judge returned to the business at hand. First, he had Dad and me sign my emancipation papers, which he countersigned.

Then he read aloud a letter written by an assistant US attorney general directing him to swear me in as a Special Deputy US Marshal as per 28 CFR 0.19a (3) of the US Code.

After I was sworn in, Marshal Tilghman handed me the traditional five-star marshal's badge and a .38 special revolver. The badge was in a leather folder with my identification card. The revolver was in a shoulder holster rig.

Marshall Tilghman thought I was starting right by taking out a bad guy on my first day on the job. He was one person who didn't appear squeamish about killing homicidal criminals. His off-hand comment made me feel a little better about the event. I did what I was supposed to do.

He also added, "I understand you will be taking shooting lessons. If you pull that gun before you are qualified, I'm going to kick your ass seven ways till Sunday."

Well, that was pretty clear.

"Rick, I hope to never hear of you again other than in your singing and acting. You have been made a marshal to protect yourself, not to arrest bad guys. I haven't been given the details, but I understand some foreign government has been after you for unknown reasons."

"Never fear, my singing days are over, and maybe my acting. I'm concentrating on school right now. I have one movie project, and that is it. As to the rest, I'm not trained as a police officer, so I won't attempt to be one. Regarding foreign governments, I guess I upset one of them."

The judge was interested in the movie project, so I briefly described my appearance in the movie I had written. Well, at least I came up with the scenario.

The judge gave me a copy of the letter from the AG's office. From there, Dad and I headed home. It took even longer as we got into the "Rush Hour".

At dinner, I discovered I wasn't the only one with an exciting day. Mary had tried out for a cereal advertisement. They had her do several pose shots and read some lines. She did well enough that they had her do a practice ad.

"How did that go, Mary?"

"The cereal tasted awful! I spit it out."

"Well, that ended your career, I bet."

"No, I begged for another chance. I did very well in faking as though I loved it."

I looked at Mum.

"She did, Rick."

So, did you get the job?

Mary shook her head sadly. "No, they decided since I didn't like the cereal, it wouldn't be right for me to represent them. The ad agency did say they would call me for other projects."

"Well, there is hope then."

"It wasn't as much fun as I thought it would be. It was real work."

"I know."

"I think I will stick with my newspaper column for now."

"So, you are giving up before you have even really started?"

Eyes flashed at me, both Mary's and Mum's, I suspect for different reasons. Mary's for calling her a quitter; Mum's, because she wasn't wild about Mary doing this.

"I'm not quitting. I will keep at it, just not with this advertising agency!"

"Rick, I'm certain you have homework to do."

Not completely clueless, I escaped to the library and grabbed a flight manual.

After half an hour of figuring out how airplanes stayed in the air, I gave up.

I understood the Bernoulli principle of airflow and lift. It was that pesky Newton that was giving me fits.

There is air pushing down on the wing. Lots of it clear out to the edge of space. But there was an equal and opposite reaction for every action, so the air below the wing was pushing back. But there was less below the wing than above. Of course, it was compressed by all the weight above it.

So, it was equalized and should not have an effect. However, the curved shape of the wing left fewer square inches below than above, so there would be more pounds per square inch pushing up than down. But then the top of the wing would have more area.

The air below was denser, so would gravity affect it more? Maybe I could drop different-sized cannonballs on Newton to prove the point? Nah. That experiment has been done, and our tower doesn't lean. At least I hope that apple hurt when it hit him.

The more I tried to sort it out, the worse it got, so I gave up and read fiction for the rest of the evening. I read about the adventures of

Matt, Tex, Oscar, and Pierre aboard the *PRS James Randolph*. They
didn't have to worry about how their craft stayed up in the air.

I called the studio right after breakfast to reschedule my costume
fitting. I was told they could take care of it this morning if I were
available. So, I headed over.

Passing the intersection at school was strange. It was like nothing
ever happened. The playground was empty, as it wasn't recess time. I
don't know what I thought would be different, but nothing was.

At the studio, they had two costumes ready for me. They had me
sized pretty well, so it didn't take long. There was an outfit for the
woods and another for in town. One left me dark and foreboding,
the other cheerful and outgoing. This was to contrast even sharper at
the end when it was shown that I was the psychopathic Lew Wetzel.

When in town, I was to be seen playing a fiddle and singing at
several barn dances. This would be a neat trick, as I could do neither.
Well, I could sing, but it sounded horrible to me. But I had never
touched a fiddle or other stringed instrument in my life. I got a drum
for Christmas when I was three, but I don't think that counts. I could
beat on it, but not in time.

I asked about that and was told the director would like to discuss
that with me, but he wasn't available today. Could I call and make an
appointment with him? Since Thanksgiving was coming up, I told
them I would call on Monday.

After getting back home, I returned a call from Susan Wallace.
She guessed how I would feel about publicity on the kidnapper, but
she had called me anyway. It seems the talk shows wanted me to
make the rounds again.

I told her she was correct in my not wanting to go on the shows
about this. I didn't currently have any movies to publicize, so I felt no
pressure to do so. We discussed the progress being made on the cargo
container special but agreed that it was too early to roll it out.

"Rick, it is too early to push the special, but what about letting the public know how you are employing the people who lost their jobs over the surfing movie?"

"Isn't that bragging?"

"No, it is letting people know that Jackson Enterprises is a good company to be involved with. It also will do wonders for your image. It can't hurt to have a positive image no matter your life's direction. Besides, making the special a success helps all the people who are working on it."

"Susan, you could sell ice to Eskimos. Next, you will tell me I'm selfish if I don't do it."

"See, you do understand!"

"Sigh, okay, I will do it. I have a date in Columbus, Ohio, next Friday night. I'm planning to fly over on Thursday. Try to work around that if you can."

"Could you fly to New York on Tuesday, appear on Wednesday and Thursday, and still go to Ohio?"

"That would work."

"Now, what is this about a date in Columbus? Enquiring minds will want to know."

"You know about the bachelor auction. For my date, I'm taking Judy King to her Winter Ball."

"Is that a big event?"

"I think it is a dance in their gym. I didn't ask."

"Just for fun, why don't you call Judy and get the details."

"That's a good idea. I never thought of it."

"What are you planning on wearing?"

"Well, I thought a sports coat and tie would do."

"Where are you taking her to dinner? Are you planning on ordering a corsage? Have you arranged transportation, and how about an after-party?"

"Uh, I had better call her soon."

"Have you made airline reservations yet?"

"No."

"That's good because we would have to change those. Also, now we can get your interviews to pay for most of it, first class, of course."

I replied, "Of course," in my most posh British accent.

We both gave a small laugh at that and said our goodbyes. I would call Judy after school and then get back to Susan.

Working on my multi-engine stuff until lunch made the time go fast. After eating, I drove down to the gun shop that had been set up for my shooting lessons. It had an indoor range, and I had never seen one before.

My new instructor was really big on gun safety. He had me show him my new weapon. I was careful not to point it at him or put my finger inside the trigger guard. I broke the pistol and showed him the cylinders were empty, then handed it to him.

"Good practices, Rick. I thought you hadn't had any formal lessons."

"I haven't, but they are strict on the movie sets, well, at least off-camera. On camera, they do some pretty stupid stuff."

"I've noticed," he dryly told me.

He provided me with a box of shells and asked me to shoot at a target. After loading, I aimed. He gently asked me if I thought ear protection might be a good idea.

That had never been an issue before, but it made sense to smother loud noises when you could. After all, I didn't want any hearing loss. Why, it might even affect my singing voice if I couldn't hear correctly. I donned the muffs anyway.

As requested, I fired off six shots at the target. He reeled it in.

I thought it reasonably good as all my shots were in the black, though none in the bullseye.

He then taught me the Weaver stance, named after the FBI agent who had standardized it. This time, I had a tighter pattern, with one tearing the edge of the ten-ring.

He thought I had a pretty good sense of targeting and would improve with practice—the more, the merrier.

He told me to shoot the rest of the rounds from the box of fifty. I did this with the patterns remaining tight but only an occasional hit in the middle. I did it differently when I was down to my last two rounds. I shot from the hip as I did when I was with Elvis in the desert.

This time, there were two overlapping holes in the ten rings.

That got my instructor's attention. He brought out another box of shells. This time, I overlapped six rounds in the center.

He told me he had never run into anyone with proprioception like mine. That was a new word for me, so I asked for an explanation. It was a fancy term for eye-hand coordination.

He told me to forget the Weaver stance. Just shoot at the target.

He had me assume several awkward positions, including on my back on the floor. If I could see the target, I could hit it. Not always a bullseye, but close enough.

"Rick, your lessons are done. That said, the more practice you do, the better. Lastly, most law enforcement officers go a whole career without having to shoot someone. Since you aren't going to be an active officer, odds are you will never draw this in danger."

Somehow, that didn't make me more comfortable.

He then set me up with several holsters. One was for my hip with a place for my badge, another to fit in the small of my back, and finally, a shoulder harness.

The shoulder holster was bulky enough that I would have to modify my sports coats or buy new ones. I wasn't going to fly to England for suit fittings.

The shooting lessons took most of the afternoon, so I returned home and studied schoolwork until dinner.

At dinner, I was quizzed about my day. That was when I remembered I was supposed to call Judy. I would do that immediately after getting up from the table.

While giving the details of my gun range experience, Mum nodded.

"You got that from my side of the family. That is one of the reasons you are so good at some sports."

She wanted to know what sort of shoulder rig I had been given. I had no idea, but the name was stamped inside the holster.

I was tasked with obtaining another shoulder rig and back holster to send to my tailor in England. They, in turn, were to make another suit to fit, and then I would send all my suits back for modification. I thought that would take forever, but I learned about a new service called air freight.

That got me thinking, and I made a note to investigate how air freight was loaded. Maybe there was a container solution for them.

I headed directly to my room to call Judy as soon as dinner was over. It was so important I even passed on a second helping of bread pudding.

The operator was able to connect us in short order. Judy sounded happy to hear from me.

Chapter 36

"Judy, I called about the Winter Ball next Friday. I have no idea how formal of an event it is. I imagine it is in the gym, and a sports coat will do?"

I was soon disabused of that. It was very formal in the ballroom of a major hotel in downtown Columbus. White tie and tux formal! She guided me through the events of the evening. It would start with us going to dinner. After arriving at the ball, we would pose for photographs. Next would be her introduction to society.

We had to back up at that point. I had been confused, thinking it was a high school event. No, it was the annual debutante ball of the Daughters of the American Revolution. We would be at the top of the stairs and announced.

Yikes! I had dodged a bullet with this phone call. I better do something nice for Susan Wallace.

Judy told me she would make dinner arrangements as we would be going as a small group. I was directed to reserve a limo for a party of six. I did ask for advice on where to order a corsage.

After those details were worked out, we spent some time updating each other on our week. I was torn about telling her about the child predator but knew it would come out. After giving her the basic details, I felt better. Nothing gory about brains on the sidewalk.

She accepted it very well. I was to let her know what TV shows I would be appearing on so she could plan to watch.

We ended up talking for over an hour, but it flew by.

When I hung up, I realized I had a silly grin.

I called Susan right away. She asked me what color Judy's gown would be. Lucky for me, Judy had told me because I would never have thought to ask.

"Why is it important to know?"

I must say Susan had no reason to sound so exasperated.

"Well, it might affect what flowers you order!"

"Oh."

"You said you have a tuxedo; it is not what you wear at a white tie event. By any chance, do you own a tailcoat?"

"Probably. I was outfitted in England, and there were so many outfits I have never opened some of them."

"Check it out; better yet, ask your mother for help."

Now that was a good idea. I told Susan I would do precisely that and get back to her. After hanging up, I went directly to Mum. She quizzed me until she had all the information I had. Maybe interrogated would be a better description. She treated me like I didn't pay attention to detail or was obtuse on social events. In other words, like a guy.

"Rick, I will call Susan, Judy, and her mother. As things stand, there is a disaster in the making."

"Oh?" I've been saying that a lot lately.

"Going to dinner in a white tie outfit doesn't work. One spill and it's over, plus the natives would take one look and either laugh or beat you up. In the meantime, I think you and Eddie have a Boy Scout meeting to attend."

Yikes, I had almost forgotten it.

Luckily, my uniform was all set up. I changed quickly, and we left for the meeting. Eddie was excited and thought it would be nice if they were having a camping trip this weekend. Mum had bought Eddie his first scout uniform at JC Penney, so he was ready.

Arriving at the scout building behind the school, we found the troop just starting to gather. The Scoutmaster was easy to spot as he joined us as we were getting out of the car.

I explained we were relatively new to the area and that Eddie wanted to start scouting, while I needed to be affiliated with a troop. Eddie was sent to an adult in charge of registration.

The Scoutmaster recognized me as I was pretty famous in scouting circles, with my picture appearing on the cover of *Boy's Life* several times. I thought he would ask me about my knots, but he was more interested in my Spanish translator's badge.

"Is your Spanish any good? If so, could you help us with an immediate problem?"

When there are problems, it is not the time to be humble.

"It is considered native."

"Great, come with me."

We went over to the school building into the cafeteria. There was a Cub Scout meeting in progress. Over to one side was a man in his fifties, a woman who looked about twenty, and a girl about eight years old. The young lady wore what looked like a Cub Scout uniform, but it was one I had never seen.

"Rick, this couple showed up with the girl for the meeting, but they have no English. We're totally confused."

I went over and introduced myself to the group. To say they were relieved when I introduced myself is an understatement.

The man proved to be the driver and the young lady the nanny for Silva De Bourbon-Anjou. Her father, a widower, was the Argentine Consulate-General. They had just moved to Los Angeles for his new posting. Silva was a Cub Scout in Argentina and wanted to continue here. Her father thought it would be a good way for her to learn English, so he sent them here.

I explained that American Cub Scouts did not include girls. Silva's face crumpled on hearing that. Her heart was set on being a Wolf Scout.

While we were talking, several young ladies about Silva's age joined us. Their mother stood behind them. They were there to watch their brother receive an award.

The girls said, "*Hola*" to Silva. She replied with a half-hearted smile. The mother asked me what was going on. When I explained, she nodded.

"I thought that was what they were saying, but my Spanish isn't that good. Ask the young lady if she can't be a Cub Scout if she wants to be a Brownie in the Girl Scouts."

I explained that girls had their own group, and she would be a Brownie at her age. I stumbled a little in explaining the program. The mother, who I did not know, helped; her Spanish was better than she thought.

It turns out she is a Girl Scout leader, and her two daughters are Brownies. I gave a card to the nanny and told her to have the father call me if he had any questions. I then headed back to the Scout hut.

My having to leave turned out to be a good thing, as Eddie was sitting with his new patrol and fitting right in. That means they were learning to tie knots and making jokes about farts. An assistant Scoutmaster was keeping it down to a dull roar.

If their mothers had been there, they would have died. This was in the building. If mom ever saw what could happen in the woods, she would have a heart attack while having kittens.

I could remember seeing the results of trying to pee into the wind, a prayer stick disaster, and losing my eyebrows due to a Coleman lantern mishap. Then there was the catapult that would launch large water balloons for boys to catch on a hot day, being loaded with a cow patty. Mothers and camping trips just wouldn't mix.

The Scoutmaster had just finished a Scoutmaster's conference, so I joined him and explained what was happening with the Cubs. He was relieved to hear the girl had been connected with the Girl Scouts. It would be unthinkable for girls to be in the Boy Scouts.

I was assigned to a Leadership patrol. It was for older boys who had gone through all the ranks. We were to help the adults and try to stay out of trouble. I told him I had plans to build a catapult on our next outing.

I met the other three guys in my patrol. They were a little reserved until I told them I had little interest in being the patrol leader. I was here to get my little brother going in Scouts, and I would probably miss more events than not because of my schedule.

They knew all about me because of *Boy's Life* and the fact this was Hollywood. Their parents had connections in the industry, so they weren't awed by me. At least they didn't act like it. They asked for a bit of help on our next camping trip. Could I bring fifty feet of shoreline and maybe a left-handed smoke shifter?

I told them to pull the other one. We were going to get on fine. They were all younger than me, around fourteen, so I would never be close friends with these kids.

On the way home, Eddie talked nonstop. He was going to love scouting and had made friends already. He couldn't wait for the monthly camping trip in the second week of December. It would be a winter outing!

Of course, I had to tell him about real winter outings in Ohio. I got him to shiver when I told him about the marble seat in the Yellow Springs outhouse. I will never forget the feeling.

I told Eddie I would go to the first several meetings with him, but I think I was getting past Boy Scouts. He didn't seem to have a problem with it. His main concern was getting a ride to the meetings. That wouldn't be a problem.

At home, he had to describe the whole meeting. I think Mary was the only one to appreciate the fart jokes. Well, Denny pretended that they were beneath him, but he kept snickering.

I spent the evening typing up a paper for my schoolwork. It wasn't that long until I would have to start some final exams. I was so ready to finish high school.

Thanksgiving Day had always been a quiet day in the Jackson household. We never had company. Dad would make the dressing while Mum did everything else. We kids would do the dishes.

I had been told the entire staff had been given the day off to be with their families. So, I assumed it would be just the family, including Mrs. Hernandez.

Thinking this, I threw on a house robe and searched for coffee. There must have been quite a look on my face when I saw Anna Romanov and Sharon Bronson in the kitchen with Mum.

I tried a hasty retreat, but it was too late. Mum and Dad had invited all our friends who didn't have family in the area to spend the day with us. That was great, but I wished they had told me. At least I would have worn a better house robe.

When I mentioned this, Sharon called it whinging, but it wasn't, well, maybe a little whine. Mum reminded me that she had mentioned it at dinner on Monday and Tuesday and that perhaps I should pay attention.

Knowing enough to stop digging when I found myself in a hole, I grabbed a cup of coffee and went to get cleaned up. As I left the room, Mum told me a suit and tie were not required during the day, but plan for it at dinner.

Later, I asked Mum about Sharon being here. Her parents live in the area. I was told that her parents asked her not to come home. It seems the pastor of their church had denounced her as a daughter of Satan and forbade them to have anything to do with her. I thought my head would explode.

The day turned out to be wonderful. The younger set hung out in the basement game room. The adult men watched the Packers beat the Lions 24-17. The women hung out in the kitchen and kept an endless flow of food coming. I wandered between groups.

For the record, I even helped with the dishes. How many people can say they did dishes with Anna Romanov and the wife of a state senator?

Mr. Monroe was there, and we were cordial with each other but avoided any conversation about the film or my future in them.

I snuck out back and practiced loading a muzzleloader on the run. I did it maybe twenty times, only nine hundred and eighty to go. After my first shot, I started to collect an audience. That lasted about twenty minutes, and they got bored and wandered away.

The last guest left after a late sit-down dinner. Well, most people sat down for the whole meal. I was part of a group that did the serving. It was fun; everyone was in a good mood.

I changed into casual clothes after they left and returned to schoolwork. I wanted to be done with it.

Chapter 37

I had the bright idea of playing golf on Friday. Boy, was I surprised at the number of cars in the parking lot. When I inquired about a tee time, they just laughed. How was I to know this was one of the biggest golf days of the year? The women started their Christmas shopping, and the men headed to the links.

Every tee time was taken by a foursome all day long. I asked about standing by and was told I could do it, but don't get my hopes up. They put my name down so if someone didn't show up, I could take their place. I went to the driving range. A runner would be sent for me if there was a no-show.

I went through two buckets of balls. I worked on the accuracy of my drives. I could put them in place out to two hundred and seventy yards. After that, things got a little dicey. The club pro had given me some advice about long hitters.

I would pay a price with back problems someday if I kept it up. He recommended that I find my natural, accurate distance and only try to hit beyond that rarely. It made sense to me. With the leverage obtained from my height and speed, it didn't take much imagination to see my back going out of whack. Hmm, is that a pun?

Next, I spent an hour on the putting green. So many people were warming up that I even had to wait there. I could see today was not my golf day. As the old joke went, it would be hit the ball and drag Charlie for the entire round. I let them know at the pro shop that I was giving up. I was told that Saturday and Sunday would be the same.

Since it was close to lunchtime, I stopped at an In-and-Out and had several cheeseburgers. From there, I headed to Ontario airport and rented a plane for the afternoon. I racked up another four hours in my logbook.

When I returned home, I found out that the local police were having a press conference tomorrow morning about the child molester that I had killed. They wanted me there. My first instinct was, No!

It was explained that I would meet with the little girl's parents before the conference. They wanted to thank me. This gave me no choice, but I wasn't thrilled about it. At least Susan would be there to help me through it.

Mary was quiet after dinner, uncharacteristically so. I asked her what was wrong.

"You won't let the bad men get me, will you Ricky?" She had heard us talking about the press conference. I picked her up and assured her we would never let the bad men get her. And if they did grab her, the whole family would rescue her.

Thankfully, this meant she didn't remember, at least consciously, when the Russians had kidnapped her. That, in turn, reminded me that I had better start carrying. People had gone to a lot of trouble to provide me with self-protection. I would look stupid if I didn't use it.

If I had my pistol with me the other day, could I have just drawn down on the guy?

I spent the rest of the evening playing pool with Denny and working with Eddie on his Tenderfoot requirements.

The press conference wasn't until after lunch, so I went horseback riding after my regular morning exercises. No tigers or chipmunks were in sight, so it was a peaceful ride. It was nice to slow down and enjoy the morning. It felt as though I had been going ninety miles an hour recently.

There were so many loose ends right now. Did I want a movie career? How would I make peace with Mr. Monroe? Where would I go to college? I had started businesses. Did I want to run them? Would I ever have a girlfriend that I could get close to in all senses of close?

After my ride, I got cleaned up, dressed, and headed for the press conference. Susan was waiting for me in the parking lot. There were several news people there, and they tried to ask questions, but Susan told them to wait like everyone else.

The police chief escorted me into a small office where the young lady's parents were waiting. She wasn't with them. They introduced themselves as Steve and Judy, with no last names. I respected that.

Their thanks weren't effusive but were heartfelt. I told them I felt lucky to be there to prevent that man from taking their daughter. There wasn't much to say after that. Before it got awkward, the police chief told me it was time for the press conference. Steve and Judy wouldn't be attending as they wanted to keep their daughter completely out of it.

On the way out, the chief told me those conversations were always awkward, but he'd had too many over the years where things had gone poorly. I was just lucky it had not gone the crying and hugging route. He was right about that.

Chief Wilson started the conference with a statement about the event and the follow-up about bodies being found in the basement and that they were still digging on the grounds. Inquiries were coming in from all over to see if any of their missing children were involved. At this time, they had twelve bodies and counting.

He then turned it over to me for questions.

The press conference had the usual questions until one bright young man at the back of the room asked, "Did you enjoy killing him?"

"I enjoyed rescuing that little girl. His death was an accident. I didn't even know he was dead until it was all over."

"Yeah, but didn't that give you a thrill?"

I looked at Susan. She pulled her finger across her throat.

"Since there are no more useful questions, I will turn it back over to Chief Wilson."

The chief took the center podium and spoke to an officer in the back.

"Please go out and ticket any illegally parked cars. For those members of the press, that means any car parked in a police officer reserved spot."

I was impressed with how quickly the room emptied. It ended the conference.

Susan complimented me on my handling of the conference. I thanked her for her support and direction, especially at the end. After our mutual admiration moment, we parted ways.

I went to my office. No one was in, as it was a long weekend.

I typed up a memo. In it, I outlined my thoughts on air cargo containers. I asked that a preliminary market study be performed. Aircraft manufacturers would be contacted for internal dimensions. Projected costs and if, in general, the idea was feasible.

After that, I went home for a late lunch. For fun, I checked up on the progress at my beach house. It was still a work in progress. Work was the keyword, with progress far behind.

From there, I drove down to the beach and walked. Some guys were out surfing, but it was too cold for me. I stopped in at Katin's. They updated me on Corky. He had won big down in Australia and was now attending a South African meet.

Back at home, I practiced some more loading a rifle on the run; many more runs to go.

After that, I got back into the textbooks. I had some tests soon, so I needed to start revising, a wonderful term the British used. I always called it reviewing. I wasn't going to argue the semantics. It just sounded cool.

I went flying on Sunday. I flew up to Santa Barbara. I had lunch on the pier and checked out all the shops downtown. I liked the way they had preserved the look of the town.

While at the beach, I saw a restaurant, Sambos. I didn't go in, but it was interesting. They had the story of little black Sambo shown in tiles on the wall. I thought they would do well if they ever went national.

They sold hats at one of the downtown shops, so I bought a cool-looking straw Panama. I had on my sunglasses and was wearing a sports coat to conceal my weapon. Just call me Jackson, Richard Jackson.

I spoiled the image by laughing at myself.

This attracted the attention of a foot patrolman. He had enough experience to know a shoulder holster when he saw it. He was calm as he approached me without making a scene. He asked to see my license to carry a concealed weapon. I opened my coat jacket so he could see my badge, which I had pinned inside the coat.

He asked for some identification. I shared my marshal's ID. He was skeptical, to say the least. I had to show him my driver's license as a backup. Another patrolman had driven up and stopped. They conversed for a minute and made a call on the radio.

The cop didn't seem worried about me as he hadn't cuffed me or confiscated my weapon. That seemed a little too laid back to me. That was until I realized there were two other officers behind me.

The guy on the radio came back.

"He's good."

That eased everything up. They were curious about how someone as young as me became a US Marshal. They backed off when I explained that I had some run-ins with the Russians and couldn't talk about it.

What impressed me most was they had singled me out on the street, then checked me out and never raised a commotion. The road was busy, and no one had broken stride to see what was happening.

Then the coin dropped that I was the actor Sir Richard Jackson, and I had to sign autographs all around. They also had heard about the guy I had tackled earlier in the week and told me that was righteous.

I had never heard it used like that before, but I liked the ring of it.

From there, I headed home.

I spent the evening watching *Maverick, Lawman,* Dinah Shore, and then Jack Benny with the family. I wasn't a tremendous TV fan, but this was my favorite night, well, except for Red Skelton on Tuesdays.

After my morning workout, I practiced loading and shooting on the run. I had finally got it through my head to let security know in advance what I was doing. For some reason, gunfire made them nervous.

The older black powder gave off a more resounding boom and was louder than modern powders, which gave off a high-pitched crack. Jim, the guard on detail, thanked me for the call. I had saved him some gray hairs.

I was firing into the stone fence wall at the back of the house behind the garages. Behind the wall, it was woods. The rifle was accurate to about two hundred yards or so, but the ball could go out to a mile. Even though there were no nearby trails, I didn't want to take any chances.

I had been firing on the run and had pretty poor accuracy. By stopping for a moment, turning, and firing, I hit the wall every time and the target ninety percent of the time. It took practice and trial and error with lower loads to achieve this.

As far as I knew, I had never had a flyer. I could tell from the number of flattened balls at the base of the wall. I had drawn a rough human-sized target with charcoal and was hitting it consistently.

Anyway, something odd happened when I fired the next time. The ball kicked up dust as it bounced off the ground in front of the target. My aim was not that far off. Had I used enough powder? I know that I spilled some while loading. It was just like when I first experimented with light loads.

At first, I went "doh" and thought it was funny. Then I thought about what if I put too much powder by mistake. That wasn't funny. Even I knew these things could blow up.

That gave me some food for thought!

After getting cleaned up and having breakfast, I called the director of *Over the Ohio*, this being the latest working name for the movie. It would probably change several times before a final title was settled on.

He wanted me to stop by and pick up some music. They wanted me to sing the song while the scenes were being shot. That would make doing a voice-over from someone who could sing much easier. Those were my thoughts, not his words. He just said an easier voice-over.

Chapter 38

As I was getting ready to walk out the door, there was a phone call for me. It was from the Argentine Consulate-General Juan Carlos De Bourbon-Anjou. He wanted to thank me for my assistance at Scouts the other night. He had no idea of the differences in the programs.

Our conversation was in Spanish, and he complimented me on my accent or my non-accent, as far as he could tell. I would be sure to let Mrs. Hernandez know; she would be pleased.

He asked if I was the actor Sir Richard Jackson. When I acknowledged the fact, he invited me and a guest to an event at the Consulate on Saturday. December 19. He assured me an invitation would be in today's mail. He stopped short.

"Oh, I forgot it is a white-tie event. You will have to rent a suit for it."

"Not to worry, I own a tailcoat and its accoutrements."

"Oh, that is unusual for an American, but then you are an unusual American."

I didn't know how to respond, so let it go. Besides, I had more important things on my mind, like using the word accoutrements in a conversation for the first time.

We exchanged compliments and ended the call. First, I let Mrs. Hernandez know about the compliment on my accent. She was thrilled but, as a Spanish Republican, was not impressed by a compliment from any Bourbon-Anjou. I would have to look that up.

I called the studio, and the director for *Over the Ohio* had time for me as soon as I could get there. Mum and Dad were right; the sound of that guy's head hitting the pavement was less real as I drove by the school.

The director, Ryan Bayless, saw me right away.

"Rick, it is nice to see you again. How have you been?"

"Fine, sir, and you?"

"Just great, Rick. This movie is coming together better than I thought, but I have to bring up something I'm not sure you will like."

"What is that?"

"You're singing in the movie; I'm going to ask you to work with a voice coach."

"I thought I was only singing to help the lip-syncing?"

I could feel my temper rising.

"That is true, but we have a concern: what if an unauthorized recording made it off the set? We don't want anything horrid coming to light. It would make a laughingstock of our efforts."

I could see that, but why didn't it ring true?

"Rick, I promise nothing is going on here. We just want to protect you."

Now, I was concerned. However, I didn't want to be a jackass about it. It did make some sense.

"I never did ask what song you would have me singing."

"At first, we thought "Danny Boy" but discovered it was only written fifty years ago. So, we went with a lively little tune, 'Soldier, Soldier, Will You Marry Me'. Here is a copy of the words. It's a tune with a little kick at the end. It fits the picture we want to create for your character."

I read the words and did think the ending was funny.

Soldier, soldier, will you marry me,
With your musket, fife, and drum?
Oh, how can I marry such a pretty girl as you,
When I have no hat to put on?
Off to the haberdasher, she did go,
As fast as she could run,
Bought him a hat, the best that was there,
And the soldier put it on.

Soldier, soldier, will you marry me,

With your musket, fife, and drum?
Oh, how can I marry such a pretty girl as you,
When I have no coat to put on?
Off to the tailor, she did go,
As fast as she could run,
Bought him a coat, the best that was there,
And the soldier put it on.

Soldier, soldier, will you marry me,
With your musket, fife, and drum?
Oh, how can I marry such a pretty girl as you,
When I have no boots to put on?
Off to the cobbler, she did go,
As fast as she could run,
Bought him a pair of the best that was there,
And the soldier put them on.

Soldier, soldier, will you marry me,
With your musket, fife, and drum?
Oh, how can I marry such a pretty girl as you,
When I have no pants to put on?
Off to the tailor, she did go,
As fast as she could run,
Bought him a pair, the best that was there,
And the soldier put them on.

Soldier, soldier, will you marry me,
With your musket, fife, and drum?
Well, how can I marry such a pretty girl as you,
With a wife and three kids back home?

I agreed to work with a voice coach, but the whole deal still didn't feel right.

After agreeing to something when I just knew nothing good would come of it, I headed out to the stuntmen's area. I had a question or two.

I was lucky some guys were there who fired black powder. I explained my event this morning about a weak load. They both agreed that I could overcharge while trying to load on the run, and why would I try to pull such an idiot stunt like that anyway?

I told them about the movie and what Kenton, Wetzel, and others could do. They both thought it was insane and couldn't wait to try it.

I learned that the cap on the end of the powder horn was usually a measuring cup to hold the necessary charge. That would add an extra step, so they showed me another trick.

I could kick myself. It was so simple. In those days, soldiers had learned to put powder and ball in a twist of paper. They would bite the end off to free the powder and then ram it home.

In my case, I could bite the end off, pour powder and ball down the barrel, and just stuff the paper into the barrel. This would hopefully keep the ball from rolling out if I tilted the barrel too much.

We drew several Kentucky-long rifles from the armory and tried it out. It worked like a charm. They also had a couple of trials of loading and firing on the run. I made a mental note to ask for Mike as a stand-in for me. He could run and fire!

From there, it was almost lunchtime, so I headed home. Dad was there. He was in a good mood. I asked him how things were going.

"Rick, they are going great for me, but what do I hear about you throwing the cat amongst the pigeons?"

"What do you mean?"

"Your new airfreight container idea."

"I just left a note about it the other day."

"Well, from that note, a phone call was made to Flying Tigers Airfreight. They went wild about it. Your management team is meeting with them later this week. It's not a question of doing it. The question is, how soon can containers be available."

"What about the fit of the container in the hold?"

"Lockheed and Douglas representatives will be there to provide input."

"How long will it take for our factory to tool up?"

I learned a few industrial terms along the way.

"Not long at all. The most time-consuming part of the project is making and fitting a rolling platform for each aircraft configuration."

"Rolling platform?"

"It is a floor for the aircraft, a bed of ball bearings which you can use to roll the container into lockdown position. After landing, you unlock and roll off. A forklift will lift the containers in and out of the plane. They already make lifts with extended forks to handle the load."

"Will it be profitable?"

"In the tens of millions to start, and it will grow from there."

"What about a patent?"

"Already being worked on; you will have some papers to sign next week."

It just didn't seem real to me: a casual request for information on a thought, and tens of millions are being discussed.

After lunch, I drove down to the airport for another multi-engine lesson. My instructor seemed determined to find new ways for me to fall out of the sky. Fortunately, I had learned enough to prevent that from happening. As I landed after a dozen touch-and-goes with him turning off an engine to simulate a failure on the glide path, he told me I wasn't doing too bad.

What do you say to that? He was alive. What more did he want?

After dinner, I spent time with Mum, who helped me pack for my trip. My fancy clothes for the big dance had been shipped airfreight to the Neil House in Columbus to be held for my arrival.

I asked if a room had been reserved, and she had the information written down for me. When I saw that there was a limo for six people and three bedrooms in the suite, certain ideas went through my head.

Mum must be a mind reader, as she told me with a smirk, "Judy and her friend Connie will have one room, her escort Steve and you will share one, and the girls' mothers will have the last one."

There goes that dream.

After packing was completed, I spent the rest of the evening on schoolwork.

Chapter 39

After getting up at what Dad calls zero dark hundred, I took a limo to the airport. I managed to get back to sleep, so I missed most of the long commute to LAX. For some reason, there weren't many people traveling today, so getting from the counter to the gate was easy.

Usually, I would sit in a window seat in first class, but they were all booked. The window seat next to mine was empty when I got on. Before the seat's occupant showed up, I was invited to the flight deck. This seemed to be my new normal with TWA. I stayed there until we were well in the air. I had hoped that they would let me fly the jet, but that didn't happen.

Oh well. I had hopes of a pretty young lady sitting next to me when I returned to my seat. Not to happen. It was a grumpy-looking old guy. He must have been fifty.

I nodded when I sat down but said nothing. He gave what could be described as a grunt and ignored me. I pulled out one of my ancillary readings for my class. I tried to read; however, the guy was talking to himself. It was hard to ignore, so I gave up reading.

Being forced to pay attention to him, I realized he was reading and grading papers. From the number of red marks he made, I wouldn't want to be in one of his classes.

I got engrossed in trying to read the papers as he graded them. They appeared to be MBA business plans. I must have been too obvious because he turned to me and commented.

"All these damn kids think they are going to be another Richard Jackson."

"Would that be a bad thing?"

"Not if he were real."

"You mean he doesn't exist?"

"Oh, he is a living person. He is an actor, and I think that is what he is doing for the business called Jackson Enterprises. They paid him to act as the inventor of the cargo container. Give me a break; no kid could do that."

"I read that he got the idea because he worked on an ocean freighter."

"Nonsense, no parent would let a child that young work as crew on a freighter."

Maybe I should introduce him to Mum.

"I understand that he has several patents."

"Again, nonsense. I will never believe it until I see his name on them."

"I have to disagree, but further talk makes no sense."

I then returned to my book, and he resumed grading. I also pulled out a sheet of notepaper and wrote several things. I enclosed them and one of my engraved cards, which had "Sir Richard Jackson, Queen's Messenger," in an envelope.

We landed in St. Louis for fuel. My professor friend was getting off there, so I handed him the envelope.

"Here are some items you might want to look up."

He dismissively took it from me and stuffed it in his suit coat pocket. In it, I listed the patent numbers and name for the hairdryer, flexible shower head, cargo containers, the *Pride of Liberia* sailing date, and the Union Hall address where he could find the crew listing. I also noted that his students would write about the airfreight container business next.

I would have loved to see his face when the truth dawned on him; nah, more fun thinking about what it would have been like.

The rest of the trip was not as interesting. Unfortunately, a pretty girl did sit next to me. She recognized me immediately and never shut up from Saint Louis to New York. Her first name was appropriately Cathy. I made a point of not getting Chatty Cathy's last name. I couldn't get off that plane fast enough.

In the morning, my first stop will be *The Today Show*, so they had a driver and escort waiting for me. After retrieving my luggage, I was driven to the Waldorf Astoria, where a suite had been reserved for me. I would be staying here for the whole visit.

As I was checking in, an older man came up and introduced himself. It was Mr. Conrad Hilton, owner of the hotel and founder of the chain which bore his name. He told me how much he admired my shower heads and had them installed in all his hotels.

They were a time saver for travelers who didn't want to get their hair wet. A shower also used less water than a bath, so the hotel saved on that. Plus, a shower could be cleaned quicker and easier than a bathtub, so it was a win for management and workers.

He told me when he found out I was to be a guest, he had my suite upgraded to an Astoria-level suite. I thanked him politely. I did ask if they were buying the showerheads from Detroit Faucet or another outlet. He wasn't sure but would look into it. He wanted the best.

My suite was absolutely the best suite in décor I had ever stayed in. There seemed to be a rule of thumb when traveling: the shorter the stay, the nicer the room. You could live in one of these.

The phone rang. I assumed it was the front desk asking if everything was okay. This was after the bellhop went out of its way to show me how everything worked. It was a man's voice asking if this was Sir Richard Jackson. I was immediately on guard, thinking it might be a reporter or worse, a papa rat's eye. I loved Mary's term for them.

Instead, he asked me to hold for President Hoover!

It was the ex-president. He had lived here at the Astoria in his own suite ever since leaving office. He invited me to join him for dinner at the Bull and Bear restaurant here in the hotel. He wanted to talk to me from one engineer to another.

Wow, this is from the man who was president when a dam was built that bears his name.

So, instead of dressing casually and having room service, I had dinner with a past president of the United States. It was an exciting and educational conversation. It started with general topics like the Dodgers beating the cursed White Sox in the World Series. We both agreed that it was weird calling them the Los Angeles Dodgers.

He was interested in the hairdryer and showerheads, which Mr. Hilton had told him about.

We went on to talk about the disaster last week in Malpasset, France. We both speculated on the cause of the failure. It could have been a tectonic fault due to blasting in the area weakening the dam, the face angles being off from the water pressure, and poor geological surveying. President Hoover knew the technical terms like a tectonic fault. I had read of the term, but I called it earth slippage when I mentioned the possibility.

At this point, there was no way to tell. One item that had already come out was that earlier in a day of heavy rainfall, permission was asked to open the dam to relieve pressure, which was denied.

From there, he segued to the Aswan Dam in Egypt. He felt it was a play by the Egyptians to get more aid from the US. The Soviets wanted access to a warm water port with Atlantic access and would do anything to get it. That was the basis for supporting North Korea in the Korean Police Action.

What he was most interested in was the cargo container project.

It came out that he had several talks with President Eisenhower on this subject. He was interested in the logistics of converting a port, especially foreign ports, which didn't have the same support as American ports.

I had kept up on how this was being handled. Jackson Transportation had chartered several cargo ships and made them into support vessels. Everything needed was carried on board. At first, this caused some concern because the local companies wanted the contracts. We demonstrated that costs would be held down by doing it our way.

Of course, we had to share the rice bowl, so we used the locals in every way possible. We couldn't allow shoddy materials, which would have occurred due to local corruption in some cases, not all, but enough to cause us to take steps.

There was also the hiring of local leader's relatives. While we would pay them, they were never allowed near anything critical. I had heard of one nephew hired as a librarian for the safety manuals. It would have helped if he could read English. Fortunately, we also hired a person who could. As far as I know, the nephew had never been to the library.

Hoover chuckled at that; he had several stories on the subject. It was a very enjoyable meal.

He went on to tell me if the Chinese ever approached me about a container system, the current administration wanted me to cooperate. Of course, I was to let them know I had been contacted.

I raised my eyebrows.

"Why would the Chinese approach me? And what do you have to do with any of it?"

"Well, Sir Richard, it is known that you have acted as a messenger between the United Kingdom and China, so they know of you, and you have earned some trust. Also, they are not getting along with the Russians, and it appears to be getting worse. Since you have problems with the Soviets, they see you as someone with a common goal."

"The Soviets made big promises to the Chinese about modernizing their economy. Having their own problems, they haven't been able to follow through, thus discord between the two. As to my involvement, you will find it common for offstage people like me to act as middlemen to give deniability if needed."

"Will this be soon?"

"No idea, but it will probably be in the Nixon administration."

"So, he plans to run for President when Ike's term ends?"

"Yes, we think it is an almost done deal."

In the meantime, he invited me to a theater in the hotel for a private showing of *North by Northwest*.

After a final cup of coffee, we stood to leave for the suite that had been converted into a theater.

Chapter 40

Another gentleman was seated near us. He said hello to President Hoover, who returned the greeting. The president was kind enough to introduce me to General MacArthur, another hotel resident. The general was pleasant, but it was evident that he had no idea whatsoever who I was.

Man, I was flying in high company tonight.

When we got to the theater suite, thirty people were present. One room had been set up for cocktails. I noticed Cary Grant talking to a group of people. We had met casually several times, but I didn't feel I could just walk up to him.

President Hoover asked for one quick word before the movie.

"I think dinner went very well, and the message was delivered."

I must have looked lost because he explained.

"At the next table was a man identified as an information broker. He was listening to us very carefully. If things go well, we hope he will sell this information to the Chinese. They will tend to believe it since they will be paying for it. So, we may have set you up as our first conduit to the Red Chinese."

"Oh." This was getting to be my go-to expression. "Can I tell my parents about this?"

"Yes, because odds are nothing will come of it. At the same time, if anything does start, they can give immediate advice."

After all that, the movie, which was supposed to be a thriller, wasn't that exciting. Here I am watching it, gun in my shoulder holster, badge in my pocket, next to a former president of the United States and involved in real international intrigue. My name is Jackson, Richard Jackson.

I couldn't wait to return to my room to call home and let them know who I had dinner with and met afterward. Dad didn't seem impressed. He still held Hoover accountable for the depression and called the general "Dugout Doug."

I don't think Dad liked any of the previous world leaders. Well, that's not right because he had nice things to say about Winnie. Since he had never stayed at a Hilton, he didn't bad mouth the hotelier either.

I also told them I had something to discuss when I got home. I didn't want to relay my conversation about China over the phone. They bugged phones, you know.

I had trouble going to sleep, so I read the entire novel about the guys who wore a bundle of bones as earrings.

I slept until the last minute I could and didn't have time for my morning workout. Instead, I relied on a pot of coffee. My first stop was with the *Today Show*. As expected, Mr. Garroway wanted to talk about the child molester and my taking him down.

By this time, I had repeated the story enough times that I was able to present it as pure happenstance that I was the one there and that his death was an accident. When asked if I was sorry he was dead, I replied with a simple "No."

He then proceeded to ask about my latest movie venture. I played coy, telling him that not everything would be as it seemed and that my role was minor. I was going to be listed as either a producer or director, but I did play a part.

He asked me directly if I was going to sing. It appeared that he had some inside information.

"Yes, I will be singing so they can lip-sync correctly, but my voice will not be in the movie."

These words were going to cause me all sorts of grief later on.

He went on to ask how I liked the Waldorf. I told him it was a fantastic hotel and that I planned to stay there for future visits. I hope that plug paid Mr. Hilton back for the excellent room upgrade.

After that appearance, I went to an interview at the *New York Times* office. They did discuss the molester but were more interested in the container business. When they asked me what direction I would like to take, I told them that I thought there would be a large market in Asia in the future.

They wanted to know what ports I was considering, but I told them it was a thought rather than a plan. For all I know, maybe China would be interested. That was my international mischief for the day. Let them and the Chinese sort it out.

My driver for the day told me that he had called the hotel as they instructed him. It came to light that the concierge kept track of the whereabouts and timing of certain guests. He was going to take me a different route to my room. There were some fans of mine in the lobby.

By stating on the air where I was staying, a few teenage girls had shown up. Several hundred of them! The lobby was in pandemonium.

The driver dropped me at the curb at Grand Central Station. A uniformed bellhop from the Waldorf was waiting for me. We walked smartly to a door off the main concourse. From there, it was a long hallway to a locked brass door for which he had keys. We descended a long set of stairs.

Opening another door, we stepped out on a dirty train platform that was decorated as though it came out of the 1920s. I asked about it.

"This is track 61. It is part of Grand Central. It was built in the 1920s for private railcars to connect with the hotel. Because of the depression and the war, it never got used as such. A coal-fired power plant was down here, so they hauled the ashes out from these tracks."

This was not a small siding. There were three rows of tracks. On one of them sat an old passenger car.

"I bet that car has some stories it could tell."

"Rumor has it that Franklin D. Roosevelt used it. He did come this way several times. They snuck him in through here when his polio got bad. They even brought his limo this way. It was an armored Pierce-Arrow. They took it up the freight elevator to the garage."

"Blackjack Pershing was the first famous person to come this way. Since then, Truman and Ike have used it, and I expect others will in the future. That reminds me, I need you to sign the log."

"What log?"

"Some bright person had General Pershing sign the log, and it has been used by every visitor since, or at least we think so. It is rumored that one of the Kennedy boys snuck a girl in this way. I don't know the truth of that."

From his smirk, he must have been the escort. The logbook was a book used by the engineer of the ash train to sign for the number of cars. The last real entry read: J. Nelson six cars of ash dated October 15, 1931. After that, it had a list of fifty entries, many of which were repeats.

While he was not logged in, I noticed from the wall that "Kilroy was here".

I was taking an exclusive route. I made a mental note to ask my godparents what they thought of the place. Not that it could be construed as bragging to them!

When we exited the huge freight elevator, Mr. Hilton was waiting for me.

"Sir Richard, you have us at sixes and sevens. They won't go away, and we don't want to use force."

"What if I sign a few autographs?"

"It will be more than a few."

I now understood why Susan Wallace insisted I have a package of photos to sign. They came two hundred and fifty to a package, and I hoped it would be enough.

We came up with a quick plan. While I went to my room to do a rapid coat change and lose the tie, they prepped a ballroom. It had a low stage, so they put a table and chair for me there. They were good at crowd control, so they had plenty of brass stands and red velvet rope to guide the crowd in.

When I returned by a service elevator and back hallways, I was amazed at what had been set up.

They provided several service stands and handed out free soft drinks and snacks. When I thanked Mr. Hilton for this, he raised his eyebrows and informed me that I would see this on my bill. They were a business, after all!

I couldn't complain as this was taking care of an awkward situation. Besides, how many Cokes could teenage girls drink? When I saw my bill at checkout, I found it was a lot and at New York prices. Oh well.

With things under control, it went smoothly. At one minute per girl, signing the pictures took over four hours. I only turned down about a hundred requests for dates. I told them that I already had a girlfriend.

A society reporter was there, so I knew that would make the papers. Since I named Judy King, I hoped she would forgive me.

Some of the young ladies had Eastman Kodak brownie cameras, so I posed for pictures. This could have been a bad idea as I saw many cameras coming out of purses—also, some disappointed young ladies who didn't have one.

The society reporter had a cameraman with her. I asked him if he had a bunch of films with him. He did and could send out for more. I then asked the society reporter about her favorite charity. It was the Children's Aid Society that originally ran the Orphan Trains. She agreed to be the recording secretary if all proceeds went to them in her and the cameraman's name. She was kind enough to include me.

For one dollar, each girl would have her picture taken with me. Anyone who had their camera could use it but still had to pay a dollar for the charity. Four hours is a long time. By the end of it, the Children's Aid Society had people there to help out and a booth set up.

I talked to the people manning the booth. They were Lee Nailing and Alice Ayler. They thanked me very much for doing this. The Children's Aid Society always could use the money, and besides, it was fun being around so many young people, especially young people doing well in New York City. Both of them had bad experiences in the city.

The local ABC channel was doing a remote broadcast interviewing the young ladies. They all agreed that I was fab. I thought that was a detergent. In the meantime, more people were showing up as school had let out. I ran out of pictures, and my hand was cramping badly.

I would rest it for several minutes and get back to work. It got down to having each girl write down their name and address and how they wanted it to be signed. I promised they would be mailed to them, and in the meantime, the *Times* sent out a second photographer and another lady to help the original reporter.

Where there are girls, the boys show up, hundreds of them. They, of course, had no interest in me, just the girls. Mr. Hilton, the ever-consummate host, opened another ballroom with service.

Of course, I would see it on my bill. It didn't matter; I just wanted to get out of it alive. I had been to many events, but they had been well-controlled. This one was on the border of being a riot. In Texas, it was one riot, one ranger. Here, I don't think one marshal could cut it.

Chapter 41

No sooner had I thought of that than about twenty-five of New York's finest walked in and took positions around the rooms. This was not the Waldorf's or New York's first rodeo.

The cops didn't make a big deal about it, but the noise level went down if nothing else.

In the meantime, I went from having a cramped hand to permanent blue dots from the flashbulbs going off. Since I didn't have to sign anything and could just pose with girls, I had a few conversations. Nothing memorable, but who doesn't like to be told how great and good-looking they are? I think I had better take a hint from the victorious Roman generals who had a person whispering in their ear "*memento more*." Remember, you are mortal.

When the band started playing rock and roll music in the next room, I thought things had gone overboard.

The society columnist saved me from making mistakes when she approached me and told me how impressed she was with my turning a potential disaster into a fun event. There would be publicity agents all over the city crying in their beer tonight because they would get calls from their clients demanding the same type of events.

That calmed me down. When they started playing "The Stroll" next door, I joined the line. Almost everyone there joined in so they could all say they danced with me. As soon as it ended, I went to leave. No luck there.

So, I'm on a bandstand in New York City singing "Rock and Roll Cowboy" followed by "Brothers". I was joined by the band's lead singer, a guy by the name of Lou Reed. The band had just started and wasn't that great. Reed himself had it, whatever it was. I had just met enough people who had made it in the industry to know one if I saw one. Of course, luck and timing would play a role in it.

We chatted during a break for several minutes. I told him about Track 61 and how cool it was. He thought it would be a great place for a party. I told him if it ever happened, I wanted an invite.

When the caterers set up a paid buffet in a third room, I figured out I was dealing with one of the best professional groups in the world. I wanted to know how they did it. Before I left for Columbus in the morning, I wanted to have a serious conversation with Mr. Hilton. I caught up with him as I was leaving. The band had packed up, the lights turned down, and the last of the kids herded out. I had to give a last interview to the gathered three radio stations, two TV crews, and who knows how many newspapers and magazines.

No, this was not a planned event. Many thanks to the fine people of the Waldorf Astoria, the New York City Police Department, the Children's Aid Society, which had raised over a thousand dollars, the *New York Times* for its support during the day, Lou Reed and The Velvet Rollers Band.

With that, I returned to my room with a ringing telephone. I almost didn't answer it. I'm glad I did; it was Susan Wallace. She wanted to know what I was doing, and was I crazy? I confirmed the lack of sanity and filled her in on the day. She calmed down after hearing about the professional support I received.

I asked her how she had heard about it.

"It was on the nightly news about an almost riot in New York City that you caused. Oh, can you call your mum?"

I did. She was a lot cooler about it than Susan. She just wanted to make sure I was okay. She also told me the *Today Show* had been trying to contact me. She had a number, and would I please call them at any hour?

I thought about it for a New York second and called Susan back. I told her there was no way I was going back on the program. Look at what today's appearance had caused. She came up with her usual Susan brilliance.

"So, you are going to let them control the narrative of what happened yesterday?"

"You don't fight fair, Susan."

"You don't pay me to fight fair."

"Okay, I get it. I'll call them."

"Do I have to remind you not to reveal any of your immediate future locations?"

"No, mother."

"Be nice, Rick."

"Okay, sorry, but this is all a little overwhelming."

"At your age and experience, you are doing a wonderful job. I don't know how we could have planned today to turn out any better. Your fans had a good time, you helped a charity, and most of all, you prevented a lot of bad press if things got out of hand. That's called turning lemons into lemonade."

"I just reacted to events as they occurred."

"Yes, but you reacted correctly. I have had clients who would have freaked out and made it worse. You have good instincts."

"Okay, I will call them as soon as we hang up."

As expected, they wanted me back on tomorrow morning's show. Speaking of which, I had to get to bed as it was already tomorrow.

After too short of a night's sleep, my phone rang. It was President Hoover.

"Rick, what you told the *New York Times* was brilliant."

"What do you mean?"

"By working in China into possible plans, you have given credibility to the information broker. He will be hot to sell it to the Chinese now, and they will be interested in buying it. From my point of view, that is an excellent outcome. However, the Soviets aren't going to be happy about this. They are still trying to repair their relations with China. Be careful."

"I don't see how I could get the Soviets any more upset. I have to go armed as it is."

"I find that to be deplorable. A young man in America having to go armed because of KGB agents."

"Well, I don't think it is just the KGB. By now, it's their whole alphabet soup of agencies."

"Well, again, be careful. Downplay it a little if you are asked about doing business with China again. Say it was an example. The message has been delivered. The ball is in their court. They won't respond overnight. It may be several years. They don't move quickly."

"Good advice, sir; it has been a pleasure meeting and talking to you."

"Good luck in your future endeavors. You are an interesting young man."

On the *Today Show*, of course, they introduced me as the young man to whom exciting things happened. Then Mr. Garroway wanted me to tell them about my day yesterday.

I had given in to the whole thing, so I related the day from the moment I gave out where I was staying to the band showing up.

I was asked if there were any lessons learned.

"Yeah, don't tell people on TV where you are staying until after you have left."

"What was the highlight of the day?"

"It was when we turned the event into a Children's Aid Society fundraiser. Oh, then there was an unforgettable moment when General Douglas MacArthur, a hotel resident, came out of the elevator to a crowd of two hundred teenage girls. He retreated quickly, and he was muttering something. It wasn't, 'I shall return.'"

I looked into the camera and said, "If you are watching, sir, please forgive me, but it was funny."

Mr. Garroway surprised me by holding up a copy of the *New York Times*.

"What about the story in the *Times* that you are going to open up China?"

"China was an off-the-cuff example. They would have to invite my company in, and I don't see that happening soon."

"Well, you never know; things seem to happen around you. We should call them 'Happenings.'"

"That will never catch on."

My flight to Columbus was uneventful. I did remember that I had wanted to talk to Mr. Hilton about the way they handled yesterday. I wanted an idea of what resources were needed to do that. However, I had to leave early for the *Today Show*, maybe some other time.

The cockpit crew had me up front before we took off. We exchanged pleasantries, and that was about it. The only other notable thing was that so many people were now asking for my autograph that an announcement was made.

"Please wait until we have completed service so the aisle will not be blocked. After that, we are certain Sir Richard will give you his autograph."

That worked for me; I wish they had asked me beforehand. My hand was still sore from yesterday.

Chapter 42

A limo was waiting to take me to the Neil House. It was right downtown, across from the Ohio State Capitol building. It was a short walk down to Lazarus, where I had bought my electric typewriter. It was well worn in now.

The front desk let me know that my suitcases had arrived from California. As instructed, they had opened them and ensured there were no wrinkles and that everything was as it should be. They had taken the liberty of hanging up everything in my room in my suite.

They also asked me not to let the general public know where I was staying as they didn't think they could handle a crowd like the Waldorf did.

I was glad to relax for the rest of the day in my nice suite. I was getting spoiled; it didn't compare to the Waldorf Astoria. I wouldn't tell anyone that, as it would be rude.

I didn't feel like eating a full-blown meal, so I put on jeans with a shirt and sweater and walked north on High Street to the Clock restaurant. The Clock was unique. It was a diner a block long. You walked in off High Street, and the diner extended to the next street over. It was so narrow that booths lined one wall and a diner bar along the other side of the building.

The Clock's clock was still stopped at 10:05. I saw no sign of Colonel Pritchard, and the sidewalk had been recently shoveled so that I couldn't see any footprints.

No one recognized me, so I had a quiet meal of steak and eggs. After all, it was a diner.

On the way back, I stopped at a newsstand and bought the latest edition of *Amazing Science Fiction Stories*. I don't know why they kept changing the name. At least it still only cost thirty-five cents. When I returned to the hotel, I called Judy to let her know I was in town and checked in.

She and her friend Connie would come over for lunch tomorrow and then spend the rest of the afternoon in a beauty salon. Good to know. I will make myself scarce.

I asked, "What about Connie's boyfriend? When will he get here?"

"Oh, he won't be coming that evening. She has an escort for the evening."

"Why an escort? Where is her boyfriend?"

"Stupid boy, how many teenage boys do you think own a white tie outfit? Why, you can't even rent them in Columbus. Steve Johnson, a senior at Ohio State, owns one and hires out for these events."

"It's nice knowing I can earn a living if needed."

"Are you worried?"

"No, just teasing."

"Oh good, I don't have to scale back on our wedding plans."

I think I almost dropped the phone.

"Wedding plans," I squeaked.

"Just teasing, seeing if you can take it after dishing it out."

"That took it to another whole level. I think my life flashed before my eyes."

After that, we talked for a few more minutes. I was careful not to get near the W-word again. That was plain mean! We said good night, and I read about the "Deadly Satellite". It wasn't that good of a story.

At least I had a good night's sleep.

Having a car and driver at your beck and call is handy. My driver, Tom, took me to the Park of Roses, where I had my first good run in days. It felt good. I wish I had time to run in Central Park. I liked it there. If I ever got a place in New York, it would be close to it so I could run.

I returned to the hotel, had a large breakfast in the main dining room, and got cleaned up. I put on some comfy jeans, a shirt, and a sweater. I spent until lunchtime reading a book on my suggested reading list.

It was about the War of 1812. It had one story about how the 39th Infantry, a regular army unit, was sent to Andrew Jackson as reinforcements. He only had militia with him, and they had not performed. The book told me that he made false charges against an eighteen-year-old boy and ordered the 39th to execute him as an example to his militia.

Despite many people stating his innocence, Jackson had a young man executed for running from the enemy. I would have to research more. If this were true, it tarnished Jackson's reputation in my mind. I already had doubts about him because of his role in removing the Cherokee from Georgia.

Judy and her friend Connie showed up, along with their mothers, just before lunch. Judy immediately gave me a hug and a light kiss, more of a peck than a kiss. I hoped for better, more like a bushel of kisses.

She introduced me to Connie and her mother. Mrs. King acted pleased to see me. I was told to order room service for lunch as there was much to do. Not being a dummy, I ordered food.

While waiting, I was quizzed about the events in New York. The Kings had watched both interviews and Connie and her mother the second one. Only one dangerous question came up. It was from Judy.

"Rick, were there any good-looking girls there?"

Some quicksand I had learned to recognize.

"Scads of them. It's a shame about events like that. You have no time to speak to anyone and get to know them."

"Oh, would you like to learn more about them?"

When in a hole, quit digging.

"No, I'm lucky to be getting to know you better."

I thought the two mothers were going to choke to death as they restrained their laughter. I was lucky that Judy accepted that answer and moved on. She and Connie wanted to know what the girls in New York City wore.

My first impulse was to say clothes, but I stifled the words.

"I didn't notice much difference from what you are wearing now. Well, I didn't see any of those sack dresses."

"What about the colors?"

"All the bulky sweaters were very bright, bold colors."

"And what did they wear with these bulky sweaters?"

"Either a thin-looking skirt, I mean not flared out, or jeans with a skinny-looking cut, unlike mine."

"So, the latest fashion for teenage girls in New York City is a bright, bulky sweater with jeans or a pencil skirt."

"That's it. Also, many of them had a class ring on a yarn thread around their neck. The rings were also wrapped in yarn. I'm not sure what that was all about."

"The yarn is angora, and some lucky girls get their boyfriend's class ring to show they are going steady with them."

I wondered if that was a hint.

After an inquisition like that, I was glad for lunch to show up. We had just finished lunch when Steve Johnson knocked on the door; he had a garment bag. After introductions all around, I asked him if he had eaten.

"Yeah, I grabbed a hotdog from a street cart."

The ladies all adjourned to their rooms to freshen up. I took Steve to our room to hang his outfit. He asked how long I had been in the escort business.

"I'm not. How about you?"

"A couple of years. Connie needed an escort, but I think I was the only one who owned a white tie and a tailcoat. Do you own a white tie outfit?"

"Yes."

"Wow, I inherited mine from an uncle who was an ambassador to the Court of St. James."

"That's why I ended up with one. It was thought I would be attending events at the Palace, but it hasn't happened yet."

It was about that time the coin dropped for Steve.

"You're Sir Richard Jackson, aren't you?"

"Yes, but call me Rick."

Females! It turned out that Connie hadn't told Steve who Judy was going with. They say men were dense about things. I'm not sure about women. Wait a minute. I'm very sure about women! They are different from men.

"So, does the escort business pay very well?"

"I get one hundred dollars for this. I do it about six times a year. It almost pays my complete tuition."

"If I may ask, what is your major?"

"It's Aeronautical Engineering with a minor in Electrical Engineering."

"That's a pretty heavy load to carry."

"You're still in high school, aren't you?"

"I am but pushing to graduate by summer. I will be doing eleventh and twelfth grade between New Year's and Memorial Day."

"I've read about your self-guided study with Warner Brothers."

Steve proved to be quite easy to talk to. He had questions about people I had been in movies with. His hero was John Wayne. I shared a few funny stories about John but didn't tell how he could sometimes be a mean drunk.

When the ladies returned, the younger set wearing jeans and non-bulky sweaters, we went downstairs to the ballroom for the rehearsal. From the clothes, I figured a trip to Lazarus was in their near future.

The rehearsal went quickly, at least for Steve and me. All we had to do was move to the top of the stairs with our girls on our arms. While pausing there, they were given their formal introduction, which went like: Miss Judy King, descendent of Captain Marsh Duvall of the 25th Maryland Regiment and escort.

Then, with their right arm resting on our left, we would walk them down the stairs. It was our job to make sure they got down the stairs safely. It was emphasized several times this was about the girls, not the escorts, and we weren't to attract attention. Why they looked pointedly at me, I don't know.

It went as smoothly as such an event can go. From the looks of them, ninety percent of the girls had paid escorts. I guess most teenage boys in Columbus, Ohio did not have a tailcoat hanging in their closet. It was noticeable how cliquish the girls were. If Judy and Connie weren't together, they would have had no one to talk to.

Well, they could have conversed with us guys, but we were treated like the furniture right now. You use furniture; you don't talk to it, well, unless you trip on it. Then you can accuse it of being things like a son of a beech tree.

Chapter 43

After being dismissed, Steve and I walked around Lazarus. I was trying to get some of my Christmas shopping out of the way. I bought another one of the new dolls for Mary, along with several outfits.

We got dressed for dinner. The girls' choice was just to eat at the Neil House. Steve and I wore slacks, sports coats, and ties as instructed. We met up with the girls and their mothers in the sitting room of our suite.

All the ladies were dolled up to the nines with their hair up but not a beehive, makeup, nails done, or other mysterious things they did. They all looked great.

Connie and Judy both wore slim skirts and bulky sweaters. Connie had a class ring on a long necklace. The ring had been wound with angora so that it would fit her.

Steve and I were smart enough to say admiring words like, "You all look great."

The timing looked right, so I whispered to Judy, "You don't have a class ring since you dumped that guy. Would you like mine?"

She grabbed me in a hug and shouted, "Yes!"

I took that as a positive answer and brought out my class ring from the studio, Warner Brothers's version.

Like an engagement ring, all the ladies gathered to ooh and awe. Of course, that sent Judy and Connie back to their room to break out the angora.

Steve and I had a Coke while waiting; the mother's a glass of wine. I asked where they got it. "Room Service," was the short answer.

After Connie and my new steady girlfriend returned, we went to dinner.

Dinner at the Neil House dining room was a relaxed affair. Connie asked me how often I could see Judy as I lived on the other side of the country. Depending on our social schedules, I told her I would try to fly out every other week or so. If there was a dance or event, there was no reason I had to miss it.

Connie's mom commented, "Money doesn't seem to be an object here. I gather you are well off for a sixteen-year-old. The movies must pay very well."

It wasn't a secret, so I told the table about my various business ventures without going into amounts. Steve took the opportunity to tell me he would be job hunting as he graduated early in June. I gave him a card and told him to call me.

We finished our meal and were standing up from the table. I saw what happened but could do nothing about it. A man stood up from his table and pushed his chair back without looking.

The chair bumped into a waiter carrying a tray with a glass of red wine. Following Murphy's Law, the wine spilled all over the one guy in the room who wore his tailcoat to dinner. It went all over his white shirt. I suppose the coat got wet, too, but the shirt turned red.

This prompted the young lady sitting with him to flee the table in immediate tears. Her evening was now a disaster. I assumed it was her mother who followed her.

Fortunately, I was in a position to help. I quickly went up to the soaking-wet young man who was trying to fend off a waiter from ineffectually wiping him off. I told the young man, Mike, that I had a spare shirt in my room, and we looked close to the same size. He immediately took me up on my offer.

The gentleman who caused the problem was apologetic and offered to pay any damages. He handed Mike and me a card. It stated that Woody Hayes was the head coach for the Ohio State Buckeyes football team. Like everyone from Ohio, I knew of him.

In turn, I gave him one of my cards. You never know when you might want tickets to a game.

Our entourage, including the second girl from Mike's table and her mother, returned to my room where Mike tried on one of my shirts. It fit pretty well. The other girl's mother, whose name I didn't get, called Mike's girl's room and let them know a shirt was found.

They all joined us in our suite. I ordered a display of desserts brought up by room service. I mean, it had been twenty minutes since we had eaten, so I and the other guys were ready for some more.

That, along with coffee, got us set up for the evening. The ladies were all talking away. I was one of the topics and saw my class ring displayed to the newcomers. I think Judy was marking her territory, though I wasn't dumb enough to say that.

We proceeded to our respective rooms and prepared for the big presentation and ball. I must say I looked reasonably good dressed up. It was nothing to how Judy looked. I would have been proud to present her at Queen Elizabeth's Court.

Later, when Mum asked for a description, I could tell her it was a light blue ball gown. This didn't satisfy her, as I was then grilled. Short sleeve, off the shoulder, full or tight, cut low or neckline? After ten minutes, I told her enough to end the inquisition.

She repeated back to me, a standard prom dress, a princess top with no sleeves and open neck, layers of tulle floor length.

"Yeah, that's it."

This grilling occurred on the weekend when I got home. Pictures would be sent after the film was developed from pictures of us at the top of the stairs.

We went to the staging area where the girls lined up in the presentation order. The guys were told to stand over in a line and join our dates when told, and please be quiet.

There was a stir in the line. One of the girl's escorts wore a standard suit with a white bow tie. She was moved to the back of the line. From what I could figure out, he was her brother, and they hadn't understood the dress code or couldn't obtain the tailcoat.

By placing her last, it was to be hoped that her faux pas wouldn't distract from the event, at least not much, again a young lady in tears.

I asked Steve if any of the escorts did double duty. He told me that he had never heard of it. I went over to Judy and explained my thought. She replied she knew I was a knight in shining armor. Well, I am a knight, no armor though.

I then approached the woman in charge of lining up the ladies. When I explained my thought, she hugged me.

From there, I went to the young lady named Diane and told her that since Judy was one of the first in line, I could escort Judy down, take a service elevator back up, and escort her down if she would like that. I received a very tight hug from the well-endowed young lady. This Rick to the rescue was working out well! I looked over at Judy; she held up her nose but was smiling.

I was introduced to the mother and a relieved brother. It went down quickly; I do not remember their names to this day. Then, to avoid logistics problems, I found a Neil House staff member and explained what was happening. He showed me the route I would have to take in reverse. No one was allowed now on the grand staircase.

It all went off without a hitch. Judy was introduced to society, a service elevator back up, a five-minute wait, and then escorting Diane down. I took Diane to her table, where her family was waiting.

I had introduced myself as Rick Jackson, and I don't think they realized who I was. This was fine with me.

Judy and I had a wonderful time waltzing together. She didn't hesitate to get up close and personal. We worked our way around to the other side of the room, where I got a hair-curling kiss.

This gave me hope for later, but after the dance, we and the mothers retired to the suite. Steve packed up and left because he had things to do on the weekend. This left me as an odd man out and unable to get with Judy privately.

It is nice being woken up by a kiss.

"Rick, quick, get up and brush your teeth. The moms just went to breakfast, so we have a little while. Connie is our lookout."

Now, that was a wake-up call! In a flash, I was out of bed, peed, brushing my teeth, and dreaming of the glory to come. It was not to be. As I rinsed my mouth out, I heard Connie hissing "Judy."

The mothers had forgotten something and returned to the suite to pick it up. I heard Judy's mom as I was pulling on some clothes.

"Oh, good, you girls are up. You can join us for breakfast. Is Rick awake?"

"I don't know mom."

I knew when to cut my losses, so I told them I was getting dressed and would be with them in a minute.

I wondered why the two mothers looked at each other in the elevator and laughed. I think I knew what they had done.

"Did you find what you had forgotten?" Butter wouldn't melt in my mouth.

This got the girl's attention.

"Mother, do you mean you returned to the room to check on me?"

"Should I have, dear?"

Fortunately, we arrived at the lobby, so Judy never had to answer that question, at least when I was around. We had a nice leisurely breakfast and then returned to our rooms to pack. A bellhop took the bags downstairs while mine was to be forwarded to the airlines to be shipped home.

The ladies all accompanied me to the street, where my limo waited. They had their vehicles in the hotel parking garage.

I thanked everyone for a wonderful time. I hugged Judy boldly, and she turned it into a kiss. It was the sort you would do in front of your mother. Still, it was nice. The hug also reminded me of how well nature had provided for her.

Her mother didn't take offense. I said a final goodbye until our next date. I was reminded to call Judy when I got home.

The trip to the airport and boarding the plane was uneventful.

Chapter 44

I had a window seat as usual. A nondescript man sat beside me.

He introduced himself as Fred.

He recognized me as he started quizzing me after takeoff.

He asked how I felt now that I had murdered a guy. I didn't have to punch him out as the co-pilot came back and invited me up front. I couldn't get there fast enough.

I thought it was the usual invitation I got from TWA flight crews because of my earlier adventure with them. It was different.

"Rick, do you know the guy sitting next to you?"

"No, but I don't like his attitude."

"Our head stewardess recognized his name on the passenger list. He is Fred Otash, who works with the scandal sheets. Be careful what you say to him."

"Thank you and the crew very much. You have helped me dodge a bullet. I've not been approached like this before."

I returned to my seat. Mr. Otash stood up to let me in.

"Thank you, Mr. Otash, and I have no comments."

He grinned and said, "It was worth a try. I saw you in the lounge and found out the seat next to you was empty, so I upgraded."

"Well, you paid for a first-class seat. I'm not certain about the upgrade."

Not the smartest thing to say, but I doubted he would ever be a friend. I spent the rest of the flight reading one of my schoolbooks. Let them report that. I can see the headlines now.

"Star can read."

"Sir Rick resorts to books as he can't find companionship."

Or my favorite, as the book includes the Salem witchcraft trials.

"Sir Richard Jackson is into witchcraft."

They will print what they want, and I will ignore them.

As we were getting off the plane, Otash spoke to me.

"Mr. Smartass, this trip will never see print, so you have missed some publicity."

How do you even respond to that? I just nodded and kept moving. I did thank Miss Carlson, the stewardess who had recognized Otash. I wondered what she reads that she knew of him. I owed her sincere thanks no matter what she read.

A limo was waiting, and I got home just in time for dinner. My trip was the main topic of conversation. The guys wanted to know more about Track 61. Mum and Mary about the ball.

There were so many questions that we adjourned to the sitting room and continued.

Dad was most interested in my descriptions of President Hoover and General MacArthur. Mum more so with anything connected with China. By the time it was done, I understood what a spy must feel like after being debriefed.

I did remember to call Judy. We both agreed that we had a wonderful time and that her mother was a fink. I told her that while flying home, I realized that having a car and driver on my trips wouldn't ever allow us to be alone. I was thinking about buying a car in Columbus.

She thought that was a neat idea. I could leave it at her house, and she could pick me up at the airport. And, of course, I wouldn't mind if she used it occasionally. I told her that sounded okay with me. I realized that I had just effectively offered to buy my girlfriend a car. I would have to think this through some more.

After hanging up, I read the rest of the stories in my magazine and called it a night.

I didn't know it was possible to wake up tired, but I did. I guess the last week was a tough one. By the time I did my workout, ran, and then cleaned up for breakfast, I was in better shape.

I decided to take it easy today, no studying. I certainly wasn't going flying. I don't think I was mentally sharp enough for it. I did saddle up and go riding for several hours. Again, I was lucky with no critters attacking me.

After lunch, I took a book to the tower and lay in the sun. It was protected from the wind, making it nice on this seventy-degree day. I pity my friends in Ohio.

We later had dinner and then played Monopoly. Mary cleaned the house, and she didn't have any help from Mrs. Hernandez. I wondered what she would be when she grew up. After that, we watched TV and called it a night.

I felt better today than yesterday, not one hundred percent, but much better. Last week was a tough week. After my workout and run, I was ready for the day. A hot shower had me prepared to go.

At breakfast, Mum had yesterday's *New York Times*.

"Anything you forgot to tell us, Rick?"

"I don't think so."

"The newspaper says you have a girlfriend."

"I had to say something to the reporter to help keep all the girls off me."

"Does Judy know about this?"

"Not that, but she is now my steady girlfriend. I asked her in Columbus."

"You gave her your class ring?"

"Yes."

"So, you will probably be allowed to live."

Mary had to ask, "Did you kiss her?"

"None of your business squirt." But my blush gave me away.

As I left the room, Denny, Eddie, and Mary chanted, "Rick and Judy sitting in a tree, K I S S I N G."

Now, what to do besides run away from the brats? That decision was made for me with a phone call from the studio. Their voice coach was ready for me, and the school wanted me to contact them. I told the secretary I would be there in an hour. I also asked her if she wanted donuts and coffee. Always keep the secretaries on your side.

I stopped at Randy's Donuts, which is distinctive because of the giant donut on top of the store. I started to order a dozen, then thought better and made it five dozen. It was a large office with lots of secretaries. They also had coffee in carafes to go.

Waving at the new guard who let me through based on my sticker, I got lucky and found a parking spot up front. I carried everything into Mr. Monroe's outer office and gave the coffee and donuts to his office assistant.

"These are for secretaries only today. If they want to share, they can, but don't have to."

There, that would get things stirred up. It would soon be known which bosses were liked and which weren't. As you can tell, I wasn't feeling very charitable with the studio management.

I worked my way back to the music studio area. Helen Marshal was waiting for me. She was a contract worker trying to break into the music industry. She did voice coaching to pay the rent. This was a typical story around here.

We hit it off fine. First of all, she had me read the song to her. It was an easy read. Then she told me to read it faster. I did. In doing so, I noticed that the song had a natural rhythm. It was not quite a chant. Next, it was faster. Before you knew it, I was singing the song.

The funny part is that it didn't feel forced as all my other attempts. She had me run through it several times, making sure I took breaks in between and sipped on water.

I asked why I could only sip the water; was too much bad for my voice?

"Not too much, and you will have to keep taking breaks to pee."

"Oh."

For that, in my next run-through, I used my British accent. She got a funny look on her face.

"Do it again the same."

I did. She then turned on a tape recorder. After another trial, she played it back to me.

I was stunned. It didn't sound like anything I had ever done before. It was a lively, fun tune that made you want to tap your feet. Most importantly, it sounded good!

Next, she handed me a fiddle. This is a downhome word for the violin. I asked if there were any differences between the two.

"A fiddle is used by those who want to interpret the music their way. The violin is made to play the music as directed. The arch of the bridge of a violin is higher, so it is easier to play a single note as directed. That said, they both can be used, but a fiddle would sound blurred in an orchestra.

"Rick, I won't be able to teach you how to play the fiddle, but I can teach you how to fake it."

My fake playing turned out to be large motions with my arms and shoulders. Any close-ups would be a real fiddle player's hand. She made a phone call, and we were joined by Louis Spohr, who would be my hands double. We did several run-throughs of the song for him.

He then proceeded to play the song on the fiddle. It had a bounce to it. I wanted to dance a jig or whatever was appropriate. When I asked, I was told a Virginia reel would work. When I asked what that was, I learned it was what I called square dancing.

Louis had fun with the song. When the girl would run to buy something, he would walk his fingers across the instrument in a running motion while making the sound of the steps with his other hand. The soldier got a martial beat when his turn came.

We then performed the song with me singing with my accent and Louis playing the fiddle. It was special; that is all I can say.

I wasn't the only one who thought that.

When we were finished, Helen said, "Rick, this is too good to let go. You need to sing in the movie."

Insanity took hold. "I agree."

Before I could withdraw that statement, she was on the phone again. After a five-minute break, Mr. Monroe and the movie director walked through the door. Well, I said I would do it. Not being one to back down from my word, I sang the song once more with my British accent.

No one said anything for a minute after we finished.

"Rick, do you want to release the record before the film release or after? There are arguments both ways."

"Mr. Monroe, if the song bombs, the movie might bomb. If the movie makes it, the song might. The bigger investment is in the movie. We should protect that."

"As usual, your thinking is clear. We will do it that way.

"That said, you are a bad boy; I have had complaints all over the place about why some people are getting donuts this morning and others aren't."

"You should talk to those not sharing. There is probably a pattern of several secretaries not sharing with a particular boss."

"Oh, you are a right bastard, aren't you?"

"Aside from the language, I have learned from the best of the best."

He had the grace to blush. I couldn't help but start laughing. After a moment, he joined in, and just like that, our problems were past us.

Chapter 45

He invited me to lunch. As usual, the scene was colorful, with extras walking around in their costumes. There were the normal cowboys and Hercules types, 1920s gangsters, and college preppies, but WWII Soviet soldiers were different.

What caught my eye were Mr. Sinatra, Mr. Martin, Mr. Davis Jr., and Mr. Lawford sitting two tables over. I had to say hello to the famous rat pack. Mr. Sinatra told me they were in the process of robbing Las Vegas. I wished them luck.

Mr. Sinatra went on that I still owed him another song. I stuttered and admitted that I hadn't given it much thought. My brain caught up with my mouth, and I told him about "Soldier, Soldier". The group got a laugh at it. We talked briefly, and then I rejoined Mr. Monroe, who had ordered for us.

"Rick, would you like to do a walk-on in their movie?"

"Not really. I have so much going on right now that I don't have the time. I'm still going to finish high school by next summer."

"More power to you. I feel like we are losing you from our business."

"I haven't completely decided yet, but it is possible. I will go to college somewhere full-time, and then there are my other business interests."

"Are your other businesses doing well?"

"Let's put it this way: I'm almost at the point I could buy the studio."

"My God, Rick, I had no idea."

"It seems unreal to me, but the money keeps flowing in. My financial people predict that I could become the richest person in the world. I don't see that, but money will never be an issue. If nothing else, my parents have almost as much."

"Your family is an incredible group, Rick."

"Just wait until Mary is let loose on the world."

He didn't know what to make of that, so he changed the subject. "Have you thought about financing your movies?"

"That is a no. I have seen what goes on in this world. It is too much of a gamble for me. Well, except for the documentary on the container business."

"How is that going?"

"It's going rather well from what I have been told. My only part will be as a background commentator and to be seen with the presidents and prime ministers of the countries involved."

"You say that like you are used to meeting presidents every week."

'Well, I did meet President Hoover last week."

"I read about that event at the Waldorf. How long did that take to put together?"

"About fifteen minutes."

"What!"

I then proceeded to tell him the whole story. He got a kick out of General MacArthur. People seemed to love or hate the general, with few in between.

My next stop was the school to see Miss Sperry. She wanted me here at this particular time. I wondered what was up. When I entered the one-room schoolhouse (used as a set when needed), she and a person I hadn't met were there.

"Thank you, Rick, for stopping by this is Dr. Dixon. He is with the State of California Department of Education. There are some concerns with your academic standing. I didn't realize that until this meeting. He called and requested it without expressing them, so I'm just as much in the dark as you. He has given me a complete set of new exams."

From the nasty glare he gave her, he didn't like her sharing what she had. It was apparent he was not on our side after ambushing her and now me.

"It is nice to meet you, Dr. Dixon. Do you have a card?"

Start nice, but be sure you know who the players are. I handed him one of mine to force the issue. It was an accident that he could see my shoulder holster when I pulled my card case out.

"Young man, is that a gun I see?"

"Yes, a .38 special. The load is a little light for my taste, but that is what the marshal's service issues."

"Marshal's service?"

This allowed me to show him my US Marshal's badge and ID. This was a blatant attempt to get this person off balance. I don't think he is my friend.

"Well, I will have to ask the department about this. Students are not allowed on school property armed."

He has never been to a small town on the first day of the hunting season.

"Well, this is studio property, so I'm not violating any rules. The studio has armed people all over."

I wasn't going to tell him most of them were props.

"Now, what did you want to see me about?"

"I'm new to this job and have been reviewing student records. There is no way you could be progressing this fast. I'm afraid of irregularities occurring."

"What type of irregularities?"

"That you are being credited for work that you haven't learned."

"So, you are accusing Miss Sperry and me of cheating?"

"I didn't say that."

"Then what do you mean?"

He was getting a little red in the face. I didn't help when I went to the phone and called the front office and asked to be connected to the legal department.

"This is Rick Jackson. I need some legal representation on a studio matter. Could you have someone come over to the schoolhouse?"

It took ten minutes, and I had three attorneys; it must have been a slow day in legal. The studio lead attorney asked what was going on. I explained to them that I had heard, and Miss Sperry confirmed.

"Well, Dr. Dixon, Peter Dixon, do I have that right?"

"Yes," he replied reluctantly.

"What are these irregularities you are referring to?"

Do you ever have that sinking feeling when you know you are in over your head? That was the look on Dr. Dixon's face.

"I just don't see how he could have learned this much this quickly."

Miss Sperry is sharp. I found how sharp she is.

"Rick, you have passed all the exams once. Are you ready to take two of them today?"

Talk about a quick right turn.

"Yes, I am."

"Dr. Dixon, if Rick takes the exams right now and passes them, will that satisfy you?"

"He doesn't have enough time; it is now two o'clock, and each test is three hours. That would put it until eight tonight with no breaks to take two of them. Then he would have to finish up tomorrow."

"I can do that."

"Well, I quit work at five, so it can't be done."

What a loser!

"Fine, I will do each exam in an hour and a half with little or no break in between."

"You can't do that. If you fail, trying to do them fast, you will lose the whole year."

"I thought I couldn't do it anyway?"

"Err, yes, I suppose you should have the chance if you want to risk all."

Miss Sperry made a point of handing the unopened packages with the exams back to Dr. Dixon.

"Please open them and proctor the exam. That way, we can be certain there will be no question of irregularities. Oh, can we have one of the studio attorneys stay to ensure all goes well?"

Boy, she knows how to stick a knife in. As usual, the junior attorney was tasked with watching me take a test. For me, I wasn't concerned. I could have taken these exams months ago and passed them. I have been reviewing the material ever since.

Not that I was trying to show off, but I completed both exams about four-thirty and had a fifteen-minute break in between. Dr. Dixon graded the Geometry while I was taking the English exam. It took him almost as long to grade the English exam as it did for me to take it.

It was five-thirty by the time he was finished. At least he was honest in his grading. He showed me what answers I had wrong on both tests. I agreed that I missed them. I still had an A on each of them. At that point, he said with poor grace, "I misunderstood that you were working with a genius."

Rather than point out that my IQ had been tested at 118, a far cry from genius, I let it go. Miss Sperry didn't. She let him know my IQ and my work ethic. If regular students were allowed to work this way, using my study ahead and read-everything methods, there would be no need for half the teachers in the system.

Obviously, she took that irregularity accusation personally. I think Dr. Dixon was glad to get out of there with a whole skin. Miss Sperry asked me if I wanted to come in tomorrow morning and finish my other exams so I could be done with tenth grade. That sounded like a plan to me. We agreed upon eight o'clock.

We woke the junior attorney up from his nap and headed out.

At dinner, I updated my parents on my afternoon. Dad laughed and told me that I could be in more danger from government bureaucrats than the KGB if I kept it up.

As I had thought, Mum didn't see any humor in the situation.

Eddie let us know he was ready for his first camping trip this weekend. Dad had taken him to an outdoor store and bought him a backpack, tent, and other gear he would need.

Then it was Denny's turn. He had been working at Sam Nielsen's photography studio in Dad's office building doing vanity pictures. He was making good money. It was neat that it brought in business above and beyond Sam's regular customers.

Sam was picking up all sorts of family and wedding work from contacts made through Denny's portraits. I asked him if the term "portraits" wasn't a little highbrow for his work. He didn't take it well. He fled the table.

At least, I thought he fled the table. Mum was just about to give me an earful when he returned with an album.

I had to eat crow. My little brother was taking portraits as good as any I have ever seen. He has a knack for making everyone look good by highlighting their best features. I'm not a professional at this, but this work was so good it couldn't be ignored.

Mary was quiet during all of this. She looked dejected. I asked her why she looked sad.

"Oh, I'm practicing for my next audition. It is for a little girl who didn't get the doll she hoped for on her birthday. I have to look excited when opening my gift, then sadly disappointed when it isn't the doll."

"So, you are, okay?"

"Yes, I am!"

As she said that, her face lit up, and her arms, which had been at her side, were up and waving.

"Rick, this is me being excited. Am I doing okay?"

Mum muttered, "She has been doing this all day."

"You're doing great, Mary. You should keep showing Mum so she can track your progress."

Mum slapped me up the back of the head.

"You and that Harmon boy will be the death of me!"

At a charity event, Mum had met his father, Tom Harmon, and the young Mark tagged along. He liked to joke around and caused mild grief when he appeared anywhere. I would like to play around with him if he weren't only eight years old.

When he and Eddie were together, they were always in trouble. This ranged from putting bubble bath soap in a fountain to frogs in the girls' dressing room at a charity beauty pageant.

I heard a sob, turned, and there was Mary with large tears running down her cheeks. She spoiled it by yelling, "Yes, I knew I could do it!"

I told Mum I was sorry for everything.

Chapter 46

After breakfast, I drove to the studio the next morning to take the rest of my finals. Miss Sperry had it all set up. It was much more casual than yesterday. I started my first exam and finished it in an hour, but it took another fifteen minutes to review everything.

It was my History exam, and I was pretty certain I had a one hundred percent on it. Every one of the multiple-choice answers jumped out at me. None of them were in doubt.

Next was Biology II. Again, I did well, but it wasn't a given like History.

While I was taking that exam, the phone rang, and Miss Sperry spent a long time on the call.

My last exam was in Spanish. It felt like cheating to take it, but I wasn't a glutton for actual punishment, so it was nice to have one course that would go easy.

Mandarin would have been a better choice, but it wasn't available.

When I finished my last exam, Miss Sperry informed me I had passed the first two. History was one hundred percent as I thought. Biology was a respectable ninety-six percent. She graded my Spanish exam while I waited.

It was ninety-seven percent. Considering how fast I had taken the exam, that was okay. I falsely thought I had just passed the tenth grade for a second time.

"Rick, that phone call I had earlier was from the California Department of Education. They feel that even though you passed those exams yesterday, you should demonstrate a firm understanding of the tenth grade before allowing you to take the eleventh and twelfth together.

"What are they asking for?"

"They want you to appear before a panel for oral exams."

"I thought that only happened at the graduate level in college."

"You are correct. I am going to talk to our management about this. They are trying to discredit our entire program."

"Why is that?"

"The straight answer is we are non-union. Union teachers feel threatened by the success of our programs."

"That's not right, and there is the fact that you haven't been teaching me anything. I get my required work from you, turn it in, then take the exams."

"I know Rick. I would be really upset if they asked for oral exams from one of our regular students. They are just like most other students, doing enough to get by. You, on the other hand, are going beyond all expectations.

She continued, "I would like to ask you to keep an open mind on appearing in front of them."

I responded, "Everything will be okay if they stick to the textbook and the first level of recommended reading. I have read all of it. If they go to the recommended reading in the guided reading books, I'm in trouble. I only had the time and interest for a few of them."

"That's why we would insist that I and our lawyers be present to ensure they don't go beyond the course curriculum. For the average student, they would stick to the textbooks."

"I want to talk to my parents about this. I'm not certain that a high school diploma is worth all this."

"But Rick, how will you expect to earn a living...Oh, silly me, you don't have to put up with this, do you?"

"No, I don't. I will let you know tomorrow. In the meantime, let your management know what is going on."

To say I was upset was putting it mildly. I took a long walk around the backlot to cool down. After I quit using bad language internally, which would have gotten my mouth washed out with soap, I went to the commissary for lunch.

By the way, Mum washed my mouth with soap when I was ten years old. Never again!

I had an appointment with my voice coach right after lunch. It was fun. Listening to a playback, using my British accent, it didn't sound like me. Maybe that is why I could stand it.

For fun, I did "Rock and Roll Cowboy" using it. Now that was plain weird. A British accent and Rock and Roll just didn't work. I pity any Englishmen who tried to make it in America.

Before dinner, I had a serious conversation with Mum and Dad about the requirement to face oral exams. They were not pleased. Dad would be talking to our attorneys in the morning.

After dinner, I practiced loading and shooting on the run using a paper cartridge. It worked like a charm. I could quickly load while running, then stop, shake a little powder into the priming pan, close the frizzen, and fire at the target. I had given up on loading powder in the priming pan while running. It was only seconds. If they were that close, I was done for anyway.

My accuracy improved as the stress of loading on the run was removed. My stress went right back up when security came running around the corner. I had forgotten to call them.

After going to *Mea Culpa* many times, they let me off the hook but pleaded that I remember to call them in the future. I told them I would but that I had the process under control. Heck, a stand-in might be doing it all in the movie. I was doing this for my pleasure.

When I returned to the house, I found Mum and Dad in front of the TV. I asked if we could talk. Dad got up and turned the TV off.

"What do the regular teachers have against me?"

Mum answered, "Probably nothing, Rick."

"Then is it the teachers' unions?"

"Rick, no one is out to get you as an individual. It looks like you are an individual caught in a power struggle between two systems."

"What systems?"

"It appears to be the public sector represented by the teachers, teachers' union, and school boards and the private sector represented by the private schools such as the studio schools."

"Why are they fighting about what power, and why me?"

"You are an innocent bystander caught in the middle. They are out to limit or eliminate the other group. You happen to be a battle that the public sector thinks they can win, and in doing so, limit the private sector."

"That doesn't seem fair."

"The systems don't care about fairness; they care about the process. You are not an individual to them, just a data point to be argued."

"I thought the teachers were good."

"They are. Over ninety-nine percent of them don't even know you exist, and almost none wish you ill."

"Then why are they allowing this?"

"They aren't. The union is forcing the issue."

"Then is the union out to get me?"

"Not as an individual. As an abstract group, the union wants you to fail so they can use this as proof that the private system doesn't work. At the same time, the private system wants you to succeed to prove that their system works. Neither side cares about you as an individual."

"I think I understand about the private side, wasn't it some Supreme Court justice who said, 'Corporations have no soul?' That implies the individuals within the corporation only work for the good of the corporation and their position within it."

"And what makes you think that the teachers' union is any different?"

"Well, they are working for the teachers, not themselves."

"It is correct that when a union is first formed, they work for the forming group. However, when any group gets above a certain size, the group members start working for their benefit. Larger groups work for the good of the group. They become disconnected from their original mission. Very few are like the Salvation Army, which has remained true to its mission.

"That is how a large union can sacrifice one of its member groups for the good of the whole, and more importantly, its good."

"So, unions are bad when they get too big."

"Not bad. Who are we to say their objectives are not good? They are fighting for better pay and conditions for the individuals they represent. Unions are earned by poor management. No one wants to pay dues to fend off good management.

"Remember, the union workers are like you, and the teachers, as individuals, most are good people. Their interest doesn't coincide with yours. Certainly, there is always a bad apple or two, but they are found within all parts of society. That is called the human condition."

"This is very confusing. The teachers and their union are fighting the private sector for students. Why should they care?"

"Follow the money; that is why corporations exist, to make money, so their side is easy to understand. Teachers are human, so they want good pay and benefits. They as individuals can't get it from the school boards, so they form unions."

"Though they haven't started this particular battle, the corporation will use your success to demonstrate they can teach more at a lower cost."

"But as I told Miss Sperry, she hasn't taught me anything. She has just provided the material and tracked my progress."

"That's not what the outside world will see. They see a Rick that attended the studio school and exceeded expectations at a lower cost."

"So, the private and public sectors are fighting over a slice of the pie, and if the private sector wins, the pie will be smaller. Why wouldn't the school boards be all for this?"

"Maybe because the school board as an organization has grown large, and it is looking out for its own best interests rather than the public. If the private sector wins this argument, why have a large school board with all of its employees?"

"Well, if the school board isn't looking out for the public's interests, why aren't they voted out?"

"Who says that they aren't looking out for the public who voted them in? People with children want good schools and are willing to pay for them. People without children and seniors whose children are grown and moved away ask themselves, why pay for a system that doesn't benefit them?

"Then there is the majority who don't pay attention and don't even bother to vote."

"So, if I understand it correctly, no one is out to get me as an individual. The teachers, unions, and the school board struggle with the private sector for the good of each group. The group's members will benefit if their group wins.

"From this, I shouldn't be angry at individuals but decide what my best interests are as a group of one, and my power is very limited as a group of one."

"Welcome to the real world, Rick. However, you have money, and money can buy some power, which in this case is a strong representation in the legal system. Without money, you would have no hope. With money, you hire lawyers to fight for the best outcome."

"But if I understand what I have just learned, I have to be careful about what group of lawyers I hire because if they are too large, they will be working for their firm's best interest, and it may not coincide with mine, and as a corollary, I have to watch out for bad apples as they can appear in any group."

Dad laughed, "People often confuse lawyers and bad apples."

"Is that because half of all lawyers are working against you?"

"Well, that and some lawyers are bad apples, while others become politicians, which is another conversation."

"So, what should I do?"

"First, let's see what our lawyers tell us. They will probably refer us to a group specializing in this sort of case. They will appeal to a judge for an injunction. The judge will either allow the oral exams or not. If he or she allows them, there will be conditions set. I predict the exams will be allowed as it is within the school board's prerogative to set the conditions of success for its students. Your lawyers will try to ensure the conditions are fair within the bounds of what you should have learned."

"When will I be old enough to drink?"

"Not tonight. Go to bed."

Instead, I went to the library and started the process of reviewing every textbook and recommended book in my tenth-grade curriculum. I couldn't take the time to read any of it in depth. I would have to skim through it all, hoping to remember enough.

Just as I was falling asleep, I remembered I hadn't called Judy about the reception at the Argentine Consulate. I doubted her parents would let her fly out, but I had to give her the opportunity.

Chapter 47

After my morning rituals, I drove to the country club on Tuesday. John Jacobs didn't have anyone yet, so he caddied for me. The rest of the world would go away when I was on the golf course. Today, I wanted it to go away.

After some warm-up time on the driving range and then on the practice putting greens, I went to the first tee. There weren't many people playing golf today, so I was allowed to tee off by myself.

John and I spent our time walking down the fairways catching up. He was glad to see me back out here as the New Year and the US Open qualifications were coming up. I asked about his family, and all was well. With my paying him and the extra he had been picking up by caddying here, they were in the best shape they had ever been.

I told John that I wasn't planning on a career in golf, so he should keep it in mind as he went forward. He told me not to worry as he could make a good living caddying right here. He had caddied enough to qualify as a fully registered caddy at this course and several corresponding clubs.

After talking about it, we decided after the first of the year I should play a round at Pebble Beach and maybe Torrey Pines. He would go along and start to learn those courses. It sounded like fun.

By the time we got to this point in our conversation, we were ready to turn onto the back nine. A hot dog at the refreshment stand was served as lunch. The back nine went smoother than the front nine. I couldn't seem to miss the greens, and the golf balls had eyes in them as they rolled into the hole.

Enjoying the day, I hadn't kept track of the score. In the end, it seemed as though I had tied my course record. More importantly, I had spent the morning without stressing out over school.

After thanking John and probably over-tipping him, I headed home. I was hoping that Dad had talked to his attorneys, and they had told him there was no way they could force me to take oral exams.

Well, he had talked to them, and it wasn't good news. It appeared the school district had the right to do whatever it wanted in testing. After discussions with my parents, the lawyers went to a judge to see if an injunction could be granted. Since the school board had called Miss Sperry and told her I was to appear at Hollywood High at eight o'clock on Friday for my exams, the injunction hearing was to be on Thursday at ten o'clock at the courthouse.

So, the rest of the day was spent reviewing everything I had done since September. In the next two days, I had to review every textbook, additional recommended reading, and paper I wrote. The books and papers were all in the library, so I planned to live there for the next two days.

The one thing I didn't do was try to think of ways to get out of it. I just had to face the fact I was taking oral exams. I hadn't any concerns as I had been going to the dentist for years. That poor joke showed how nervous I was about the whole affair.

In the middle of the afternoon, while I was studying, Mrs. Hernandez brought me coffee and a light snack. Her definition of a light snack was even better than mine, so it was welcome. My brothers and sister checked in with me as I took my break. They seemed to think I was going to face a firing squad.

When Mary tried to talk to me, her voice was so scratchy that it was hard to understand her. I told her not to try to talk if it hurt as much as it sounded. She pealed laughter and, in a clear voice, told me she could teach me how to talk like that so they wouldn't test me. I hope she doesn't turn to a life of crime.

I spent the rest of the afternoon going through my stack of books. I wasn't trying to learn anything new, just refreshing what I had already studied. There was so much I didn't think I had a prayer, but I wasn't going down without trying.

After dinner, I called Judy. She thought it would be neat to fly out for the reception, but she didn't believe her parents would agree, and she had already accepted an invitation to an all-girls sleepover. I did ask her why she had to specify all-girl. Did they have boy-girl sleepovers in Columbus? She told me I was dreaming.

She did ask her parents, and I heard the resounding "No" that was given in reply. I didn't understand why her parents wouldn't let her skip a day of school and fly halfway across the country to go to a formal dance for the fun of it. I would have fallen over if they had said yes, but I got boyfriend points by asking. I'm not completely dense.

I then went back to my books. This was the longest I had ever crammed for anything. Mum came into the library at midnight and sent me to bed.

The following day, I took a long workout. I didn't go to exhaustion, but I was wide awake. It was then back to the books. Mrs. Hernandez served me lunch in the library. I worked for another two hours and then ran two miles to stretch my body and refresh my mind. It did help my body; I don't know about my mind. At least I was wide awake.

It seemed like I had just returned to the books, and it was dinner time. Dinner was quiet at the Jackson house. Well, that was until Mary started giggling, and giggling, and then giggling some more. I thought she had lost it and said so.

"Silly Rick, a little girl has to be cute in the ads. To be cute, you have to giggle. I'm practicing."

"It is a little annoying, but please don't practice bawling your eyes out."

Mum said dryly, "That was earlier while you were studying."

"Hmm, has she tried to look demure yet?"

"Rick, what's demure?"

"To be demure, you look shy, bashful, and innocent at the same time."

"Oh, that is my normal look."

That set the table laughing. Of course, that upset Mary, and she started to tear up. I reached out and said I was sorry. Then she giggled and said, "Gotcha."

Sororicide came to mind again. Maybe I will tickle her to death.

"When are you auditioning for a part in a movie?"

Mum kicked me under the table, but it was too late.

"Maybe I could audition for yours?"

"I don't think any cute little girls are in it."

"Then you will have to write me a scene. I can be at the dance where you sing your song. I will tell you I love you and will marry you when I grow up. You will be nice about it, no promises, but to check back in twenty years. That will make your character even more likable, so it is even more shocking when the audience finds out you are the killer."

I didn't know what to say to that. First of all, she was right. Second of all, who was this girl? Where did she get this idea? I don't see how she would have even known enough about it to be able to come up with this. I saw Denny smirking across from me. I glared at him.

"You shouldn't leave scripts lying around. I was reading it. Mary asked what it was. She wanted to know if there was a scene for her. There wasn't, so Eddie, Mary, and Mrs. Hernandez made one up. Well, I helped, too."

"Mum and Dad, what is your opinion of Mary being in the movie? The scene actually could be made to work."

Dad was very proactive. "Peg, what do you think?"

Way to go, Dad! Mum surprised us all.

"Talk to your producer and director. If they agree, it is okay with me."

"I will. You seem more agreeable to this than I thought you would."

"Mary and I have an agreement; she is allowed to be in one movie or one advertisement this year, and that is it."

I thought for a moment.

"Mary, you would make more money from an advertisement."

"Yes, but I would get more exposure by doing a movie."

"Where did you learn that?"

Mum answered, "Spend enough time waiting for your turn to audition, and you learn a lot about the business."

Mary added, "Mum, you still haven't explained what a 'casting couch' is."

"I will when you are my age, dear."

Dad turned red in the face and left the table. I don't know if he was going out to laugh or get his rifle.

I retreated to the library, even giving the dessert a pass. There are some conversations to be avoided at all costs. I think Mary's acting career may be on hold.

As can be guessed, I spent the rest of the evening studying.

Chapter 48

I expended all sorts of energy during my workout but still felt like I had a live electric wire inside me. Talk about nervousness! Not too nervous to skimp on breakfast, but nervous.

For the event, I wore a suit and tie. Neither of my parents had to tell me to. It just seemed like a good idea to look serious. We took the limo. I think it was more for all the boxes of books rather than us. We placed a small handcart in the trunk to unload them on the other end.

Dad and I unloaded everything at the courthouse and took them up to the third-floor courtroom using the elevator. Our corporate attorney was there to introduce us to another lawyer who worked on cases involving the school district. I found that interesting. The school district merited an attorney who specialized in challenging them.

Next came in attorneys representing Warner Brothers, and then another group from the school company along with Miss Sperry. Talk about interested groups, and they all represented their employer's interests. Of course, they may be from a large firm only interested in itself.

I wished I still lived in my little world where things were black or white.

They huddled together, and I was glad to see Dad's attorney, Mr. Hopkins, take the lead.

Mr. Hopkins gave me the expected talk: look at him before answering any questions. If he nodded yes, then answer that question only and do it truthfully and as briefly as possible.

I noticed one of Dad's newspaper reporters sitting in the back of the open courtroom. I wonder who tipped him off.

We had timed it closely, as we were no sooner settled, we were told, "All rise for the presiding judge, the Honorable Thomas Thornton."

We all stood. The judge was no-nonsense, getting right down to business. The court clerk read off the reason for the hearing.

The attorney for the school board was asked why they were there.

"Your Honor, the School Board of Los Angeles County is here to ensure that it is allowed to proceed as its right, to have Richard Jackson take oral examinations to demonstrate that he has the knowledge to graduate from the tenth grade."

"Oral examinations. I thought high school only did written exams."

"That is the normal practice, Your Honor. However, questions have been raised about if the young man has gained the required knowledge."

"Has he taken the written exams?"

"He has Your Honor. We are not convinced there weren't irregularities in the exam process."

I started to stand, but the lawyer on my left touched my shoulder to indicate I should sit still. He had assistance from the large guy on my right, who held me down with a grip of iron. I wondered why he had joined us; I think I understand now.

"Your Honor, we have provided you a copy of the school board regulations, and it is very clear on page sixty-one, paragraph three, sub-section four that the board has the right to use various means of examination."

"I have read that. What does Mr. Jackson's counselor have to say?"

"Several things, Your Honor. As almost a side note, I will start with the quoted regulation. Within the text of the regulation, it is apparent that this section is meant for subjective items like grading a piece of art or gymnastics. We have been able to find no cases of the school board ever requiring oral exams previously for academic subjects.

"The second and most important item is the accusation of impropriety on the examinations Mr. Jackson has taken and passed. The examinations were unopened when handed to district employee Dr. Dixon, who administered the examinations. They were then graded in his presence."

Turning to the district's attorney, the judge asked, "Is this true?"

"Yes, Your Honor, it is, but there is no way that this kid could have learned a year's schooling in less than four months."

"Objection on characterizing my client as a kid!"

"Objection upheld. Please be professional in your references."

I noticed two things: the judge didn't seem to be a fan of the School Board's attorney, and there would be no Sir Richard in this American courtroom.

"I apologize for not following the forms of the court; my contention still stands that Mr. Jackson couldn't have acquired a year of studies in less than four months."

He didn't apologize for calling me a kid; he apologized for not following the court conventions. I don't think I'm a fan either.

"How would these oral examinations work?"

"A committee would put together a list of questions on his textbooks and its required and suggested readings. Each examination would be allowed the standard three hours of questions."

"So, fifteen hours of grilling on all materials covered?"

"Yes, Your Honor."

"Mr. Hopkins, your comments."

"The opposition has just asked for a very open-ended set of conditions."

"In what way?"

"They have asked for an examination on all textbooks, required and suggested reading. May I show the court what this entails?"

"You may."

"After reviewing the tenth-grade curriculum, here are the textbooks." He pulled my five textbooks from the top of one of the eight boxes we had lugged in.

"After reviewing the course requirements, we found that reading five English literature books was required."

He pulled out the five required books from English Lit.

After those ten books, there are the suggested readings found at the end of most chapters. At that, he and the assistant who had held me down unpacked 153 books and stacked them on the table.

"Your Honor, all of us went to high school. I suspect we all had suggested reading at the end of each chapter. I read none of them and still passed my tests well enough to graduate."

The judge was frowning as the books were being unloaded. His frown got deeper and deeper.

"I will now retire to my chambers to consider what has been presented. The court is adjourned for one hour."

I felt elated. From what I had seen, we had won the case. I expressed that thought to our group. Mr. Hopkins shook his head. "I've known Tom Thornton for a long time. He usually gives the benefit to those with written rules on their side."

We went downstairs to get some air. A Coke machine was there, so I put in my dime and got a bottle. That is when I noticed the entire bottle opener and the cap catcher had been removed. There I stood with a bottle I couldn't open.

I got lucky. A policeman stopped and bought a bottle. He smiled at me and said, "The opener has been gone for a month. Come with me."

We went outside, where his squad car was parked in front. We both placed our bottles with the caps on the lip of the bumper. Next, we smacked down on the lid sharply with the palms of our hands. It worked like a charm.

"Thanks, officer."

"Anytime, kid."

From him, I would take being called a kid.

At the appointed time, we all were back in our seats in time to rise once more.

"After reviewing what I have been presented, here is my judgment. The School Board has the right to give oral exams. Even though the regulations had examples that weren't all academic, they do not preclude them."

I felt like a hammer had hit me. There was a stirring on the School Board side as though they felt victory.

"However, I have concerns. It hasn't been demonstrated that there is any reason to think that irregularities occurred during the School Board exam. The Board appears to believe that learning faster than their lesson plan allows is impossible.

"On top of that, I do not appreciate the fact that a far beyond a fair set of conditions were attempted. I also attended high school and never read any of the suggested books. Does the School Board of Los Angeles want to imply that I shouldn't have graduated?"

The other attorney was up like a shot.

"Not at all, Your Honor."

"Glad to hear it.

"Because of the above, I'm setting the conditions of the oral examination to be given. First, it will be in this courtroom starting at 9 a.m. tomorrow morning. It will last for three hours. The stated case for this examination is for the young man to demonstrate he has acquired the knowledge necessary. A sample of it rather than in-depth testing should suffice."

"Additionally, all questions asked will have citations for the questions read out so that Mr. Jackson's attorneys may look them up. He will sit in front of them and will not be able to see the books. I don't have a number to judge by, but a large portion of the questions must be directly from the textbooks."

The attorney for the school board objected, "Your Honor, we will not have time to prepare!"

"Strange, you were trying to have young Mr. Jackson appear before you tomorrow. What has changed?"

At that, the School District attorney looked frustrated.

"I'm not certain. Your Honor, that was my instruction."

"Will the gentleman from the school board enlighten us?"

The man who stood up looked like someone you wouldn't want to buy a used car from. Of course, I may be biased.

"Your Honor, we had a panel of five professionals ready with their questions. With your conditions, some of the questions will be disallowed. We need time to come up with new ones."

"Would that be because most of the questions would be from suggested books rather than the formal textbooks?"

You could see the guy stop and think about lying in court. Well, that is how it looked to me. He caved.

"Yes, Your Honor."

"The exams will be given here as stated tomorrow morning starting at 9 a.m."

"Your Honor, that is unfair. Our people will have to work late!"

"If they are college graduates, they have pulled all-nighters before. Court dismissed."

And with a bang of the gavel, the hearing was over.

Chapter 49

The judge called out my name.

"Mr. Jackson, you may want to check your shirt pocket."

My effort to look good had failed. My fountain pen in my shirt pocket had leaked badly. The shirt was ruined. Heck, even I was probably dyed Esterbrook blue.

"Thanks, Your Honor. This just hasn't been my day."

"I think you will do very well tomorrow."

Outside the courtroom, Mr. Hopkins explained to me that the judge had done everything in what he interpreted as his power to give me a fair shot.

I'm not sure the outcome was fair, but I saw I wouldn't gain anything by arguing. We left the books in the courtroom cloakroom. We were assured they would be okay.

When I got home, I changed, tossed the shirt, and showered to wash the ink off. As I suspected, the stain would take a while to disappear from my skin. It looked like a Rorschach tattoo.

I then went for a run. I had to work off the stress. After three or so miles, I started to let it go. By the time I returned to the house, I was a lot calmer. Instead of whining about my fate or whinging, as Mum called it, I went to study. Oh yeah, we had left the books at the courthouse.

After a late lunch, I had a package waiting for me. It was a group of quotes for my workshop. One of them stood out from both price and quality standpoints. The quality was the fact they made several suggestions to improve the space. The others were going to build it as I had requested. All the prices were within ten percent of each other, so I signed the Yankee Home Improvement contract.

Wonder how the Yankees ended up in California? Hmm, I guess I'm a Yankee by strict definition, as I grew up in Ohio, but I was a

Limey by birth. However, I was born in southern England, so what was I?

The construction time was estimated to be twelve weeks and wouldn't start until after the first of the year.

Next, I started to go to the beach to go surfing. I did stop at the Beach House to see how things were proceeding. They were making progress, but at this rate, it would be next summer before it was done. I was hoping for early spring. The construction foreman I had met before told me the problem was getting inspectors out to sign off each step.

I was beginning to not like the government I saw in action. I bet if I checked into it, there would be a particular interest group pushing the inspection department to make things harder so the special interest would profit.

Was every government like this, or were we just bad?

Instead of surfing, I drove to Dad's office and found he had time for me. I asked him about the opinion I was forming.

"Rick, that is the beauty of the United States. Each state can make its own regulations. Special interest groups, whether trade groups or voter groups push the laws. But if you don't like the laws in one state, you can move to a state where you like the laws. It's like the United States is made up of fifty laboratories to try ideas out."

"What about the Federal Government?"

"Our Constitution specifically spells out the Federal powers. The states reserve all other powers."

"What about commerce?"

"That is a concern. I'm hoping that the Supreme Court someday will reverse itself."

"From what I've learned the last few days, the Federal Government as an organization will try to expand its powers as all organizations do."

"Unfortunately, you have paid attention, and I'm afraid that is the eventual outcome. But that will take many years to occur. In the meantime, all we can do is vote against it."

"Well, we are becoming a large, vested interest; maybe we can influence events."

Dad looked horrified.

"Rick, you aren't thinking of going into politics, are you?"

"No, I'd rather work behind the scenes."

"You scared me for a moment. I saw your soul going straight to Hell."

"Dad, it can't be that bad."

"If you heard what I hear in business daily, you would believe it."

Note to self: don't go into politics if I want to go to Heaven.

"Well, on that cheerful note, I'm going to buy a milkshake. Want to come along?"

"Sorry, I can't, Rick. Too much to do. There is one other thing I want you to start thinking about. I wanted to wait until after your exam so it wouldn't create extra pressure. However, I know you face things better if you have a Plan B. Pass or fail: where will you finish school?"

That never occurred to me. Fail, and I would have at least to spend the rest of the year in tenth grade and a full year every grade after that. Pass, and they would make my life difficult as I tried to continue.

"Thanks a lot, Dad. I never thought of that. Want to sit with me as I'm awake worrying all night?"

"It's not that bad. I made a couple of phone calls. The studio schools are spread out over several counties so that you could transfer to one of those schools."

"Don't you have to live there?"

"Live or work there. I bet you could develop a project in the county of choice."

That got me thinking.

"If I needed to attend a class, I could fly to school."

I didn't share the next thought that skipping a class and then buzzing the school might be fun.

"Or if you wanted to push it, you could go to school in another state."

"Wouldn't that be the same, but just further?"

"Just like when you moved to California, you could request to take placement tests to see what courses you needed to graduate."

"Oh, wow. That would reduce the number of classes I would need to take."

"Or you could go to England and take your O-levels. You can do that at sixteen. Many US universities will accept you if you have passed five O-level exams and have good ACT or SAT scores."

"You mean I could fly to England, take the exams as a citizen, come back here, take the SAT, and get into college?"

"That's what it sounds like. Of course, I would check with the school you intend to go to first."

"Can I skip tomorrow and fly to London instead?"

"No, you would be viewed as cowardly and running away if you didn't face the exams. By doing it afterward, you are working around an unjust system."

I felt as if the weight of the world had come off me.

"I can't lose now, no matter what. If I fail, and that will only happen if they are unfair in their questions, I can show they are wrong by passing the O-levels and getting into a university. If I pass, the same outcome, other than I don't have to fight them to graduate. Thanks, Dad!"

"Rick, your Mum and I are always on your side, even those times I had to spank you."

Even today, I remember those spankings. Never again will I hide under a table with two canes from the fairground and pull Denny's feet from under him. It wouldn't have been so bad, but he had a glass of milk. The glass broke. He didn't get cut. Mum did as she was cleaning it up. Thinking back, I deserved it.

"I know, Dad. At times, I wonder how you put up with me."

"I wonder how my mother put up with me. I guess children are our punishment for how we treated our parents."

"And on that note, I'm out of here."

"See you at dinner and relax for the rest of the afternoon."

I did that. Well, I went home after getting my milkshake and broke out my books on flight. It was a nice change of pace. I finally understood how that pesky Newton came into play on the subject of lift.

This was after asking Mr. McGarry to explain it several weeks ago. He had me work out the math involved with the lift from the Bernoulli Principle and Newton's Laws on a Cessna 172 wing. The numbers were amazing. Way to go Sir Isaac!

After dinner, I played Mr. Potato Head with Mary and Eddie. Denny spent most of his evenings in his darkroom. His work was getting better and better. He told us at dinner several days ago that he wanted to enter them in a professional contest. I think that he would do well.

My Potato Head was the goofiest looking, but the others thought theirs were. Mary won, which was no surprise. I think she had loaded dice. All cute five-year-old girls do.

Before going to bed, my parents and I discussed tomorrow. We all agreed that all I could do was show up and answer the questions as best as I could and let the chips fall.

Chapter 50

I had a light workout in the morning, cleaned up, and went to breakfast. I even went light there as I didn't want to feel sleepy during the exam. Luckily, I even went to the bathroom, so I was good to go.

I rode with my parents in the limo. We seemed to be using it more and more. I had to restrain myself from bouncing out like I usually did. Our guard, riding up front with the driver, would get out first and check the surroundings before opening our door.

There were no difficulties, so we went directly to the courtroom. Others were there ahead of us. The setup was different. In front of the judge's bench was a table with five chairs. Facing the table was a single chair. A portable blackboard was on one side of the room where a jury would normally sit. Another table held copies of every book that my lawyers were now just bringing in from the cloakroom.

Miss Sperry sat with Mum and Dad. All the other lawyers were at a table behind me.

We were no sooner in the room, and it was, "All rise."

Judge Hopkins got right down to it.

"Is the school district ready to ask its questions of Mr. Jackson?"

"Yes, Your Honor."

At that point, four men and one woman walked over and sat down. They had an individual for each subject. I walked up to the chair, preparing to sit down. The judge raised a question,

"Do you plan to have Mr. Jackson sit in that chair for the next three hours?"

"Yes, Your Honor."

"Bailiff, bring in a small table, a glass, and a pitcher of water for Mr. Jackson. Also, I see the questions are written down. Do they have the correct answers with them?"

"They do, your Honor."

"Good. Please provide me a copy."

"Your Honor, we didn't mimeograph extra copies."

"That is alright. We have one of those new Xerox machines. Give my secretary the answer sheets, and she will take care of it."

It took about twenty minutes, and we were settled in. The first question was a math problem, and I walked over to the chalkboard and solved it. It would be a breeze if the rest of the day went like this. I stayed at the board waiting for the next math problem.

Instead, the next person at the table asked me a question in Spanish. I responded in my very fluent Spanish. It must have been good enough because the man said, "Bueno," and I never heard another question in Spanish. Of course, that meant I would have more questions in other subjects.

And so it went, the remaining four asking questions in random order. If they were trying to get me off balance, it wasn't working because the judge appeared to be on my side. He required them to give the citation for each question. My attorneys would look up the question and then nod to the judge that it was in the book.

At first, they stayed in my textbooks, but as time passed, they went deeper into suggested reading. Since I was given time before answering, I didn't feel stressed and could think clearly. It was amazing that I could almost see the page before me when they gave the citation. Not word for word at all, but the general thrust of the topic.

When that tactic didn't seem to be working, they switched.

I was asked, "Young man, you have taken Physics. Please explain the principles of flight simply."

"There is thrust, drag, Bernoulli's Principle and Newton's Laws to take into account."

For the first time, I heard, "Incorrect."

Did that mean I had all the others correct?

"Newton's Laws play no part in the physics of flight, not if you keep power to the plane."

"Sir, I beg to differ if you would let me explain."

"You are wrong, next question."

Bang went the gavel.

"I would love to hear Mr. Jackson's explanation."

Taking him at his literal word, I explained directly to the judge, ignoring my questioner.

"Your Honor, Bernoulli's Principal only plays a small part in the lift provided to the aircraft. It depends on the principle of equal transit time.

I drew the standard wing profile on the blackboard, as shown in most of my flight manuals, with arrows denoting airflow.

"The common thought is that the air when it hits the leading edge splits, some over and some under the wing. In both cases, the air hits the trailing edge at the same time. That is equal transit time. Since air on top has further to flow, there is less air pressure, so the air flowing under the wing provides lift."

"Now, we calculate the speed and distance from Bernoulli's Principle. From there, we can calculate the amount of lift required. Simple mathematics tells us that to generate the lift for a small plane, for example, a Cessna 172, the distance over the top of the wing would have to be fifty percent more than under the wing."

I then drew a picture of a wing segment resembling an offset mountain or a right-skewed bell curve.

"Just imagine what the wing of a 707 would look like. That Cessna 172 would have to fly at over 400 miles an hour to obtain enough lift."

Having previously worked out the very arithmetic for this problem for Mr. McGarry and his flight instructions, I could jot it down quickly. The judge had me pause and asked if my math was correct.

He received a pained-sounding "Yes" in reply.

"Proceed."

"If this were the only reason an aircraft could remain in the air, an inverted flight wouldn't be possible. The plane would lose lift and dive."

"Now, to Newton: the wing must change something of the air to get the lift. Changes in the air's movement will result in forces on the wing. To generate lift, a wing must divert air down, lots of air.

"The lift of a wing is equal to the lift generated by Bernoulli's Principle plus the equal and opposite reaction to the mass and speed of the air that it diverts down. Momentum is the product of mass and velocity. The lift of a wing is proportional to the amount of air diverted down times the downward velocity of that air. So, F=ma. The wing can either divert more air or mass or increase its downward velocity for more lift.

"Now, when the air goes down, it does not create a void above the wing. The air above the wing fills the almost void in, creating lower air pressure above the wing." According to Bernoulli, the air below the wing will now provide lift until the air pressure on both sides of the wing is equal, while Newton tells us that the mass of the air will provide additional lift accelerated downward. Since we are moving forward until we provide less velocity by reducing speed or changing the configuration of the wing, we will have the needed lift.

"The viscosity of the air creates the downwash of air off the back of the wing. When a moving fluid, such as water or air, comes into contact with a curved surface, it will try to follow that surface. Picture water running over a water glass. It will follow the curve of the glass rather than falling straight down at its first opportunity. I think the fountain in front of this building demonstrates this principle.

"So, the air follows the wing to its end, then tries to follow the curve. It cannot reverse its course and flow back towards the front of the plane because of the velocity of the wind flowing under the wing. Thus, it is forced straight down. This is referred to as the bound vortex or circulation model."

"Thank you, Mr. Jackson. May I ask where you learned this?"

"Your Honor, it was mentioned in passing in one of my flight manuals. I couldn't figure it out, so I asked my original instructor Mr. McGarry, and he explained it."

"I thought so. He beat it into me. Your explanation is correct, and the school board's instruction incorrect."

"They didn't instruct me in this. They just came up with the question. If you noticed, they didn't give a citation for this, just a general question as to the principal of flight. While the Bernoulli Principle and Newton's Laws were covered in Physics, they were not in the context of flight. That wasn't covered in the textbooks nor the suggested reading."

"I find that interesting. Will the attorneys approach the bench?"

There followed a whispered conversation that quickly got down to being accompanied by sharp gestures by the judge and the school's attorneys. A soon disgruntled-looking group returned to the school's table. Mine had a barely suppressed grin.

"Questions have been asked of Mr. Jackson for over two hours now. He has had the correct answer to all of them and proved the questioners to be wrong in one instance. I think we have had a fair sample of this young man's learning. He has demonstrated the knowledge I would expect of a graduate student. I also noticed that only ten percent of the questions came from his textbooks, the rest of which no normal student would have been able to answer.'

"Mr. Jackson, by order of this court, is graduated from the tenth grade and promoted to the eleventh. This court is dismissed."

And bang went the gavel.

As the judge stood, he waved me over.

He quietly said, "Well done, United States Marshal and Queen's Messenger, Sir Richard Jackson," and left the courtroom before I could respond.

I heaved a sigh of relief. That lasted for two minutes. One of the school's attorneys approached me.

"Just so you know, the rules are being changed so that nine consecutive months must be spent in a grade before you can move on."

"Thank you, that makes my next decision easier."

He looked at me funny and walked away.

Dad shook my hand, and Mum hugged me. All the kids were there. Denny and Eddie congratulated me and wanted to know if they would have the same exams. If so, they had both decided to flunk out. Mum didn't look so happy at that. As usual, she wore her I want to break something face.

One of the opposing attorneys saw her look and couldn't leave the room fast enough.

Mary had the best thought.

"You should bring whoopee cushions the next time."

We headed home. I spent the rest of the afternoon helping Eddie get ready for his first camping trip. I had planned to go with him but had accepted the invitation to the event at the Argentine Consulate.

It was fun showing him how to set up his tent. I swear by the time he put on his backpack, with his sleeping bag and tent attached, the rig was bigger than him. I did give him a present for his first scouting trip: my official BSA folding pocketknife.

Dad drove him to the Scout building. I tried to help with dinner in the kitchen, but Mrs. Hernandez threw me out. She was muttering about not having enough room to move with a big lummox present.

I called John Jacobs to have him set up a tee time for me on Sunday. All in all, I was like a wet dishrag, a very mellow wet dishrag.

After sleeping late on Saturday, I spent the morning and afternoon in a rental plane, racking up some hours. Just huge lazy circles and a few touch-and-goes at small airfields.

I dressed once more in my coat and tails with a white tie for the event at the Argentine Consulate. I didn't know what to expect. I was glad Judy hadn't flown out for it, as it was mostly boring. There was one small encounter that got my blood racing.

My host introduced me to Colonel Frade. As we shook hands, he said we had just missed meeting each other when I was last in Argentina. Before letting my hand go, he asked if I was planning to visit shortly. I told him I wasn't, and he let my hand go after that. I think he broke one of my bones.

It just became more urgent to have to get all my suits and tuxes modified so I could carry my .38 Special. Between the KGB and irate fathers, I needed it.

After that, I fled to the bar for a Coke. They were serving a beer I had never seen before, Quilmes. Apparently, it was brewed in Argentina. As the waiter used a church key to open the can, I thought of my bottle of Coke at the courthouse.

There was no can opener, but I was able to open the bottle using a car bumper. What would you do with a can without an opener? I would have to think about that.

After being thanked profusely by my host for helping his daughter with Scouts, I left the event early, pleading tiredness. He must have thought I was a wimp. In a way, I was. I didn't want to be in the same room as that colonel any longer than I had to; besides, his daughter wasn't there.

Ouch, there would be a scene, Judy and Dorotea. I was glad my driver was waiting here instead of having to come from Jackson House. As I got into the limo, I noticed an old man in a long trench coat. He had one hand under the coat as though he was holding something. I gave a brief wave that was returned. I was so glad to be out of there.

Sunday was a nice day for golf. John and I hit the links around ten o'clock. At the first tee, I thought I would get him. I held out my hand and asked for a long nose. He handed me the driver. He probably figured that was the club needed, no matter what I called it.

Later on, I asked for a bulger at a par five fairway. He handed me a fairway wood. He was on to me. I hit close to the green, so he recommended I use a niblick. He confirmed it when he handed me a spoon later on. To rub it in, he complimented me on using my cleek.

It was a wonderful golf outing with no course records, just a relaxing day to end the week.

Eddie had just returned from his first camping trip when I got home. He was a dirty, stinky, happy mess. He jabbered all through dinner, telling us about it. The best part was that he had qualified for his Tenderfoot badge.

Chapter 51

After my morning workout, I felt like staying outside, so I saddled George and took a long ride. I did come across the young lady who had sprained her ankle a while ago. She thanked me once more. We apparently had little in common, so each went our separate ways.

While riding, I kept thinking about the beer cans and how to open them without an opener. The can would have to have some sort of opener attached. I wondered if you could do it as the corned beef people did; they had a key soldered to the bottom of the can.

I had a bright idea after getting cleaned up. I called the Mexicali Delight Brewery and asked if I could have a tour. I was told they had scheduled tours that I could sign up for. This was one of the few times I used my name and fame. When I explained who I was and that it might get disruptive if I showed up in a crowd, they invited me to come in whenever I wanted.

I told them to expect me after lunch.

Another thing that had been on my mind was Christmas. This was Christmas week, and I had no idea what to get Mum and Dad. The kids were easy.

I had picked up a couple of camera filters that Denny could use. I had previously called his studio and asked Sam Nielsen what Denny needed. After snooping through his gear, Sam gave me recommendations. He was even kind enough to order those I had chosen.

For Mary, I got a Pony Liner blanket for Misty when it got cold, which was seldom. Also, a fleece-lined exercise sheet and saddle pads for English and Western saddles. They were all deep green, like British racing green, and I had Misty's and Mary's names and the Jackson coat of arms embroidered on each piece.

For Eddie, it was an all-BSA Christmas. It included the Boy Scout Field Book; he had the Handbook, a compass, a mess kit, a flint fire starter kit, a first aid kit, ground cloth, and a canteen. The canteen was the only piece that wasn't official Boy Scout gear. I picked up a World War II surplus army canteen. I know the boys thought these were cool.

On the way to the brewery, I stopped at Nielsen's because I knew Denny was home. I settled up for the lenses and filters. Next was the tack shop. I put everything in the trunk, which already held Eddie's gifts.

On the one hand, it seemed like I was cheap because I had spent less than one hundred dollars on each of my brothers and sister. At the same time, we hadn't been in the money that long and were used to much less for Christmas. Just because we had it was no reason to throw it around.

What to get Mum and Dad had deviled me for a while. Then I realized we had a family membership at the Rivera Country Club, and they didn't play golf. Dad had messed around a little in Bellefontaine but never followed up when we moved to California.

I bought them matching golf bags, white with British racing green trim; I was now thinking of it as Jackson green. The golf pro attached Riviera Club tags with their names on them. I also bought each of them a gift certificate for a set of clubs designed for them, plus ten lessons. This would give them something they could do together. It was way over my budget, but I didn't care.

I had no idea what to get Judy. I called her mother when I knew Judy would be in school. We discussed what would be appropriate at our age and stage in our relationship. I bought her a Cashmere sweater and mailed it to her Mom, who would gift wrap it for me.

An old brick church across from my office was doing gift wrapping for donations. I dropped everything off there to be wrapped and was to pick it all up on my way home.

When I arrived at the brewery, I was introduced to the general manager. He inquired about what I was interested in. I explained how I had noticed that while there were ways to open glass bottles without an opener, that was not the case with a can.

He disabused me of that notion quickly. He took me to their maintenance shop, which had the most jumbled group of equipment I had ever seen and picked up a greasy screwdriver. At least he wiped it off with an orange shop rag. We then went to the filling line. He grabbed a can of beer off the rapidly moving conveyor belt and drove the screwdriver into the top. With beer foaming everywhere, he took a large drink.

"Ah, that hits the spot. As you can see, you can open them without an opener."

"I see."

What I saw was half a can of beer wasted on the floor.

"How does it fill them and put the tops on?"

He proceeded to show me a filling line that could make you dizzy. They filled over 100 cans a minute with what he called a carousel filler. The filler had 60 filling heads. A can without a top would be fed onto a platform under the filling head.

As the can rode around the carousel, it would be filled by a tube. The tube went to the bottom of the can and would rise as the can filled, always remaining just below the surface of the beer. This was called a subsurface fill and prevented the beer from foaming over.

The newly filled can would then pass onto a conveyor belt, which moved the can under a device that dropped the lid on top of the can. The next station would crimp the lid into place. After that, they would flow onto an accumulator table, lining them up to six rows across. A device would push an empty beer case into position. The full cans would be lifted six at a time by a set of vacuum fingers and put into the case. Another machine to the side was taking flat pieces of cardboard and assembling and gluing them together to make the cases.

The line operators would keep materials fed into the line and clear it if it jammed up.

I asked if I could have some of the can shells and lids. He gave me a tube of lids and several cases of can shells. The tube was how they were received from the can manufacturer. They would tear the top off the tube, turn it upside down, and pour it into the lid-dropping device. I supposed all this equipment had special names, but I just thought of them by their function.

I thanked the general manager for his time. I had the forethought to bring publicity photos, so I spent time in the office signing enough for everyone, including the floor workers.

On my way home, I even remembered to pick up my Christmas gifts, all brightly wrapped. My donation must have exceeded expectations from how they received it. From the careworn look of the place, they spent more time on the people they served rather than the building. I made a mental note to have a donation made to them, maybe in Eunice Carpenters' name.

I had the gift cards for Mum and Dad; their golf bags were in my room and would be brought out at the last minute. I had even thought to buy a large bow to put on each of them.

Upon arriving, I placed the gifts under the tree in the family living room. This was the tree we had put up as a family. A professional team had decorated the central part of the house. Tomorrow night was our open house, and Mum wanted the place to look good. Our tree was about seven feet tall. The one in the main ballroom was every bit of 15 feet tall.

Mum and Dad's gift cards were in an envelope, which I placed prominently on the front center of the tree. I loved the fresh-cut smell of pine trees. However, this was overpowered by the delicious odors from the kitchen, so I had to check them out.

Mary and Mrs. Hernandez were baking gingerbread men. There was a sheet of them sitting on the counter. A cookie-cutter had been used on them, but the excess hadn't been removed yet. I grabbed one. I got most of the sheet. The cookie-cutter hadn't been pushed all the way through. Of course, this set off cries of outrage from both ladies.

I fled the scene with the incriminating evidence as fast as I could. The evidence tasted pretty darn good. I may have to commit some more criminal acts in the kitchen.

An odd thought occurred to me. What if you scored the top of a beer can with a cookie cutter but didn't go all the way through? In theory, you should be able to remove the cut out without tearing the whole can. Of course, you would have to have some sort of lever to pull on.

Then there was the question of how deep the score would be; too deep, and the pressure of the beer would open the can if shaken or got hot sitting in a delivery truck; too shallow, and it wouldn't open at all or not without a jagged tear.

I wished my workshop were up and running.

I wondered if attaching an aluminum pull-ring lever with a rivet to a pre-scored wedge-shaped tab section of the can top would work. The ring would be riveted to the center of the tab. When pulled off, the tab would leave an elongated opening large enough that one opening would simultaneously serve to let the drink flow out while air flowed in.

The only real question would be, could I cut the tab thin enough to resist the pressure of the beer under the worst conditions, shaken while warm? While simultaneously being easy enough to open by pulling on the tab.

One thing I had learned from missing out on the electric curling iron was that time was of the essence. I called Mr. Goodson in Transportation. He was surprised to hear from me, to say the least, as I never was involved with the day-to-day business.

I explained that I had another thought I had to pass by a patent attorney as soon as possible. He must know who to call since he had handled the airfreight container idea.

He did. Rather than getting into a series of callbacks, he set up what he called a conference call. This was my first experience with one of these. I knew I would be doing more of them in the future. I had read that AT&T was going to make it possible to have a television screen attached to the phone so the people talking to each other could see each other. That would be cool. It was supposed to be available in the next year or two, 1963 at the latest.

Anyway, he asked many questions when I explained what I was thinking. I was glad I had thought to take measurements before calling. While the final dimensions and depth of the cut were not absolute requirements, they helped. I gave depths of 25, 50, and 75 percent of the lids .011-inch thickness. The tab shape was rounded at each end, the drinking end twice as wide as the other end, the air end. The total hole would be 75 percent of the top of the lid in its longest dimension.

An engineer joined the conversation, and I talked him through what I had in mind. Once he could give me feedback on what I was thinking, they promised to start the application. In the meantime, I was to start prototyping and testing to see if the idea would work. Hopefully, I would know before the application was filed.

I told them this would be a high priority after Christmas.

I had no sooner hung up the phone than it rang. Answering it, "Jackson House," it was for me. It was Hank Smith, my multi-engine flight instructor. They had scheduled a flight examiner for tomorrow morning.

The person to be examined had an unexplained family emergency and had to cancel. Hank thought I was ready. Was I interested in taking my check ride at ten o'clock tomorrow morning? I told him yes.

Immediately after hanging up, I said out loud, "What was I thinking?"

It was close enough to lunchtime that I braved returning to the kitchen to see what was being served today. Keeping a close eye on Mrs. Hernandez and her large wooden spoon, I found out it was to be cheeseburgers, one of my favorites.

I then made a tactical error. I turned to leave without backing up from a striking distance. It was a quick rap, but it stung. That propelled me out of the room to the sound of laughter and giggles. I tell you, kitchens are dangerous places. They should be labeled as hazardous to your health. The state required warning signs on everything else.

After lunch, I drove to the studio to spend time with Helen Marshall, my voice coach. Before that, I checked in with the pretty Miss Sperry. She was cleaning a chalkboard in a cloud of dust. She immediately handed me two erasers and told me to bang them together outside.

After that chore was done with me almost choking, I had to load fresh chalk into the music staff device. Now that I had been reminded who the teacher and student were, I was allowed to talk. I thanked her profusely for her help in the oral exam and her whole efforts in helping me pass the tenth grade. The third time was the charm.

She told me it was the most interesting school year she had gone through. No teaching, just providing materials, proctoring, and grading tests, then going through court fights. Not your typical year. But then, I was not her typical student. She didn't know if that was a good thing or not.

If it became the norm, teaching schools would have to add a law degree to their requirements. We both agreed that would never happen as there would probably not be another lawsuit involving a student in our lifetimes.

She wanted to know my plans. I informed her that I would be flying to England the second week in January to take O-Level exams, which would finish me out in high school. I would also check out the A-Levels as they were the same as graduating with distinction, which would help with better universities.

"Rick, I wouldn't recommend it for anyone else. However, you have the knowledge and maturity to pull it off. There is probably room for more mathematics, but you can pick that up as needed.

As far as the social aspects are concerned, I can't see you fitting in with any of your age groups. That is meant in the best manner possible. Most of them should be put in a barrel and fed through the bunghole until they are twenty-one."

Now that was visual.

The afternoon had fled, so I headed home for dinner. I barely had time to clean up and change into a sports coat and tie for our meal. Of course, as I was going down the steps two at a time, I noticed a mustard stain on my blue tie, so it was a quick trip to change to a regimental stripe. Which regiment, I had no idea.

At dinner, we caught each other up on our days. It was a happy conversation all around, with some silliness mixed in. My biggest news was taking my multi-engine flight exam tomorrow. Oh yeah, I had a patent filed on a beer can with the opener built in. This led to further conversations about where I could get someone to build a prototype.

Dad thought he knew of a machine shop that might be able to do it. We made plans to check them out next week.

After dinner, Mum, Dad, and I adjourned to a small sitting room. We didn't use it very often. I don't know why. It was done up as a man's room, all in leather and wood paneling, with pictures of English hunting scenes. Tea was served for Mum, while Dad and I had coffee.

We seriously discussed flying to England and taking the O-Level and possibly A-Level examinations. They were supportive. It would take a while to arrange as we had no idea how to go about it. Mum thought I should call Mr. John Norman, head of the Queen's Messengers, who probably could find out what needed to be done.

This made sense to me as I hadn't had any contact with him since I was last in England. This would renew the relationship. We all agreed that I probably should wait until the end of the first week of the New Year. This would let him settle back in after the end-of-the-year festivities.

About this time, the phone rang. It was for me; it was a very distraught Judy King. It seems the paparazzi had been making her life miserable. I hadn't taken this into account. I lived behind a wall and had security, so I never had many concerns. It was only when I was in a large public event that they found me.

They had gone to Judy's house and had taken pictures through her bedroom window. One of the national rags had printed them. They weren't that salacious, but the idea of the whole world seeing her in baby doll pajamas freaked her out.

I thought privately that I had to buy a copy. I was not dumb enough to say that to anyone.

I tried to reassure her, but it didn't seem to help. After a while, her father got on the line. He wasn't upset with me, but you could tell he didn't care for the situation. He was having a fence erected around their property and no trespassing signs put up.

The bottom line was that it affected the whole King family, and they didn't know what to do. They didn't want to overreact, but at the same time, this was a shock to them.

The call ended on an inconclusive note. It knocked my good mood in the head. I explained it all to my parents. They had no idea what to do. We, as a family, had the same issues. The only difference was we had walls, guards, and limousines.

On that note, I retired to my room for the evening. I tried to read some fiction, but it held no interest. Instead, I reviewed my multi-engine textbooks.

Chapter 52

I was awake early for my big day. Unlike my first training flight, I felt confident and looked forward to it. My morning workout and run flew by. After cleaning up and dressing in my tan chinos and a yellow polo shirt, I went down for breakfast. I kept it to a moderate breakfast of French toast. I went light on the coffee as I didn't want to be jittery or have to pee badly during the check flight.

Now, this is usually where the wheels flew off my plans. Something would come up to turn an ordinary event into something that would make the news. Today, it didn't. I arrived on time and got the written portion out of the way. As we walked out to the aircraft, I noticed butterflies in my stomach.

My check ride examiner didn't know me from Adam or didn't care, which was fine by me. I performed the aircraft walk round completely and carefully. There were no surprises. Everything was in order. My examiner asked casual questions about the aircraft as we walked around. This was the beginning of the oral questions.

I taxied out and performed a compass check. I made no smart remarks to the tower as I followed the radio procedure to the letter. The butterflies disappeared as I fell into the routine I had been taught.

When I filed my flight plan earlier, my examiner had provided a course he wanted me to fly, so I followed the plan without any further instruction from him. When we arrived at the designated area and had clear turns and were 3000AGL, my examiner asked me to perform some maneuvers.

It started easily with steep turns. Power was 20% at 2400 RPM, followed by a 50-degree bank. I managed it at 53 degrees, which was within the plus or minus five degrees allowed. Next, he had me perform a right turn of 360 degrees and then a left turn of 360.

Next was a slow flight. Power was set back to 15. I put the gear down as requested at 150 mph. When down to 130 mph, flaps were lowered. I put the mixture/prop forward. Power was brought up to 19 to maintain altitude. My airspeed was reduced to 90 mph. During all this, I had to pay attention to pitch controls, airspeed, power controls, and altitude.

This sounds like a lot, but I had over fifty hours practicing all this when only three hours were required.

Then there was slow flight recovery using full power, pitch up, climbing the blue line. I also remembered to clean up the aircraft configuration by raising the flaps and landing gear.

After that, it got more interesting as I had to perform a power-off stall. I set the power at 15, put the gear down as the aircraft slowed to 150 mph, then flaps at 130 mph. At 110 mph, I set the mixture/prop forward. Next was setting power to idle at 90 mph while maintaining altitude into the stall.

I internally chanted Pitch-Power-Drag-Climb. While chanting this, I pitched the nose just below the horizon, then went to full power. As the engines revved, I reduced drag by raising the flaps and the landing gear. I heaved a sigh of relief as I climbed the blue line.

The examiner snorted as I sighed.

He told me, "I always tighten up a bit when this starts. At least until I see I won't have to take control. You are doing fine."

Hearing this took the pressure off my chest. I didn't realize how stressed out I was getting. It was nice to know the examiner wasn't out to get me. He had a job to do and was doing it. It was also in his best interest not to have me crash the plane.

"Okay, now it will be power on, stall and recovery."

I set the power at 15 and 75% power. This is what we had been taught, and without any further instructions, I was going with what I knew.

At 110 mph, I set mixture/prop forward while keeping the nose just above the horizon. As soon as the stall started, I repeated my mantra of Pitch-Power-Drag-Climb. All went smoothly.

I then went through the Vmc demonstration showing that I could power up smoothly (I thought I had been doing that all along). I had to set the prop throttle to full, doing it smoothly. I had to guard the rudder until there was an imminent loss of directional control. Power was idled on the good. I set pitch to the blue line, next adding power smoothly at the blue line. I also had to maintain airspeed and directional control on a single engine.

I didn't have to do a drag demo as that was for a Multi-engine Instructor only. I had been shown what to do, but since I wasn't asked, I wouldn't volunteer.

The last air maneuver I had was an emergency descent. I was told the port engine was on fire. Now I thought Chop-Drop-Prop, as I set the power to idle, dropped landing gear down, and put the prop to full forward. I set the pitch for 150 mph and banked away from the burning engine at 30 degrees.

I was directed to return to the airport. I was prepared for the last instruction as we turned onto the taxiway. I heard, "Abort, Abort, Abort." That startled me even though I was expecting it. I immediately set the power to idle. I then glanced at the examiner. He rotated his finger to indicate that I fire it back up.

As I returned the aircraft to the hangar apron, my examiner commented that I had good directional control on the runway. I brought the aircraft to a complete, smooth stop. After powering down and making certain that no bits had fallen off in flight, I made an entry in my logbook.

With a pleasant smile, my examiner countersigned my book, shook my hand, and congratulated me on a fine check ride.

"I see that Bill McGarry was your initial flight instructor. I'm glad you didn't try to strafe the runway."

"Well, it seemed a waste of time since the aircraft isn't armed."
He chuckled and walked away.

What's with Mr. McGarry and strafing runways?

Just like that, I had completed a major goal without any drama.

Hank Smith was waiting for me. They had prepared a nice, framed certificate from their school. I was then escorted to the office of their owner. The office had all the decorations you would expect in such an office: his I love me wall, a wooden propeller, and in pride of place, centered on the largest wall, there was a framed piece of old canvas from an early aircraft. The canvas had a hand-painted picture of an opened mouth Chief Sitting Bull.

The owner, Mr. Larson, a tall, lanky guy, made a request that surprised me, though it shouldn't have. He wanted to use me in their advertising.

In return, he offered a refund of all my fees plus the instrument rating on multi-engines. All I would have to do was pose for some pictures. I would be allowed to approve the wording in the ad. I didn't see anything wrong with this, so I told him yes, I would love to do it for him. I was rich, but this was easy money.

That reminded me. With Mr. Baxter retiring, I needed a new agent. Mr. Larsen told me they would draw up a contract for my review. It would be ready the day after Christmas. He was in a hurry as he wanted to put out the ads as early as possible in January, as many pilots made New Year resolutions to obtain or upgrade their certifications.

I told him that if that was the case, we should try to get the photo shoot in the last week of the year as I was heading to England for a while. I then asked him who his photographer was. He didn't have one. I suggested Sam Nielsen's studio. I pointed it out to him in the *Yellow Pages*. He told me he would call them.

In fairness, I told him my brother was employed at the studio and might catch the assignment. After that, I flew home. Well, it seemed like I was flying. I was so high from passing my check ride.

Mum and Dad were at the table when I went down for lunch. I stopped at the doorway in mild surprise at this unusual occurrence. With their busy schedules, someone was always out and about.

I was bursting to share my good news, so I blurted it out.

"I passed my check ride!"

"That's great, Rick."

Mum stood up and hugged me. I almost shied away from this unusual display of affection from my English mother. Almost was the keyword. This was praise as high as it could get for me.

Dad shook my hand while giving me a half hug. My smile must have been a mile wide. Well, at least as much as my mouth could open, like the Chuckle Lion in Dad's story.

With my hands swooping up, down, and around, I gave a play-by-play of the examination. I must have babbled a little as Dad told me to slow down. This did bring me down to earth. Well, at least to ten thousand feet where I could breathe again.

Mum enthusiastically asked if I could now fly them around. Sadly, the answer was, "No, I can't do that until I'm seventeen."

That didn't change my mood. I could fly my new airplane as soon as it was delivered. That thought reminded me that I should call and see if the delivery date could be moved up by any chance.

We chatted as we ate our mac and cheese about how things were working out. That, in turn, generated another subject. I had left early enough this morning that I hadn't seen the papers.

The headlines on the local page of the *LA Times* read, "Jackson talks his way out of tenth grade."

That didn't sound friendly to me, but it was well done as you got into the story's text. They gave both sides of the issue from the organizations' point of view. I was depicted as being caught in the middle.

I had another big grin on my face as I read about the oral examinations and how I handled them. They skimped a little about how the school board had tried to stack the questions from the standard textbooks to the suggested reading.

The story did spell out my answer to the physics of flight in more detail than usual. They used that to illustrate how Judge Thornton, being a pilot, brought that knowledge to bear when the school board had misinformation.

I didn't know ignorance was misinformation, but I wouldn't quibble.

His comment about Mr. McGarry and strafing the runway led to a sidebar story about Bill McGarry being one of the Flying Tigers. He had been interviewed about why he taught his students to shoot up the aircraft on the ground.

"Well, it is more interesting than doing another touch-and-go. Those things can get boring, especially if you don't have holes in the rudder, your landing gear is locked down, and no smoke is coming out of the engine. I try to liven it up for them. Besides, you never know when you will have to go to war again."

The article's tone made me think of dinosaurs. The reporter didn't think we would ever have to fight an air war again. I hope he was right.

Mum had already informed Susan Wallace that I would be doing no interviews on the tenth-grade issue. My back went up a little when she told me that. It was my life and career. Luckily, I came to my senses before I opened my mouth.

First, I didn't want another round of interviews; second, the issue was so complicated I would probably put my foot in my mouth and then shoot myself in the foot. Best left alone.

"Thank you, Mum."

"You're welcome, Rick. Now you had better change. The first guests will be arriving at any time."

From my blank look, she stood up, walked behind me at the table, and slapped me on the back of the head.

"Christmas Reception, lots of company coming. Many of whom you had put on the guest list? Ring any silver bells?"

Yikes, I had forgotten about the Christmas Reception! I hurriedly went to my room rather than trying to fake my way around it. It was not deserting the battlefield; it was a strategic retreat.

A quick hot shower, followed by blowing my hair dry with the latest version of my hairdryer had me decent-looking, clean-looking. Putting on my blue pinstriped suit made me neat and trim. I liked my Christmas tie with the little Santa in his sleigh pulled by eight tiny reindeer. Must have not been any fog as Rudolph wasn't there.

The reception had two parts: a drop-in from 2 to 4 p.m., then an evening dinner starting at 5. Mum had fretted about what would happen at 4. Some of the dinner guests would be there and would expect to stay.

Some who hadn't been invited to the dinner would hang around. She didn't want to tell them to leave, but had no way of seating everyone for dinner, and didn't want to upset people who left on time and heard about it later.

Dad suggested that we tell the dinner invitees to discretely adjourn to the tower, where cocktails would be provided. I was one of those detailed to pass the word at the reception.

The hope was that at 4 p.m., the only people left in the ballroom would be those invited for the afternoon. One could hope they would have the common sense to leave. This was to be encouraged by the staff starting to clean up.

The last choice was for Mum to announce another event she had to prepare for. She would not say it was dinner here and that they weren't invited.

Man, these things can get complicated, and if not handled right, feelings could be hurt. Since some reporters would be invited as guests, it was Dad's job to let them know this was a private event and there would be no stories.

Chapter 53

I was on hand to greet guests, especially those I had invited. The lobby was festive with a large Christmas tree, blue spruce I had been told. It had white flocking to simulate snow. The white lights were like candles, and they twinkled. The color on the tree was provided by many silver, gold, blue, green, and red ornaments. A shining star topped the tree.

Garlands ran up the grand staircase. On the ground floor opposite the elevator were several tables loaded with fruit baskets. These were to be handed out by the elves as people left.

Yeah, we had elves named Denny, Eddie, and Mary. You can guess which one loved her role, the others not so much. They had professional green elf costumes rented for the occasion. There were even extensions for their ears. I thought the curly-toe shoes with bells on the end were a bit much.

Their duty would be to help with hats and coats and then hand out the baskets. Since several hundred people were expected, many more baskets were in a room just off the hallway.

Dad had spent most of the afternoon yesterday delivering baskets to the local police and sheriff's offices, plus our fire station and sanitation department. When I asked Dad about it, he told me he thought Mum had read one too many books on how the rich did it in the nineteenth century.

It seemed like a nice thing to do. It's not as though we couldn't afford it.

The first two people on my list to arrive were the tall, straight arrow-looking Mr. Bell, my archery instructor. Yes, the pun was intended. It was especially neat that he was accompanied by the built-like-a-tank Mr. Pearson, retired Marine and unarmed combat instructor.

I led them into the ballroom, which again was a winter wonderland. This time, the Christmas tree had an old English theme. The ornaments were decorated with fox hunting scenes, the Union Jack, and red telephone boxes with the royal crown on their top.

There must have been a hundred poinsettias sitting around, well maybe not a hundred, but a whole lot. The men headed directly to the bar before I even had a chance to point it out, with the Marine leading the way.

After we had refreshments in hand, their whiskey and my ginger ale, we chatted about the latest events at the studio. It seems Basil Rathbone still could take on anyone at swords. No one had fallen in a horse trough recently. I was invited to visit. I wondered if there was a connection. I don't think I will chance being near a water trough for a while.

The subject of my skills came up. Mr. Pearson was concerned that I hadn't progressed any further and was in danger of backsliding. I tried to argue that since I was now an armed US Marshal, I didn't have to rely on unarmed defense. I only needed the skills for any movies I might be in, and none were on the horizon.

He had a slight twist of his mouth as I told him this.

"So, you are just going to shoot everyone?"

"Well, no."

"Then how will you defend yourself?"

I remembered several things. When in a hole, stop digging, and if you can put a decision off for mature thought, do so.

"You make a good point. Now I have to figure out how to make the time."

"You know where I am."

Mr. Bell was more laid back.

"Rick, your archery is good enough for any movie scene. At most, some practice would bring you back to your peak. Have you thought about entering any other archery contests like last summer?"

"I hadn't thought about it, but I might enter again if I'm in England next summer. I wouldn't make a special trip for it, but if I'm in the neighborhood."

I had a fleeting thought that things had changed since Bellefontaine last year, "in the neighborhood," what sort of world was I living in?

I excused myself when I saw other arrivals that I had invited. An unlikely couple was drinking wine and having a lively talk. I wondered what the short red-headed surfer Nancy Katin and tall blonde Miss Sperry, my studio teacher, had in common.

When I joined them, I received an enthusiastic hug from Nancy and a handshake from my teacher. Nancy was wearing a Santa hat that clashed terribly with her hair, and whoever let her out of the house with that floral dress should be arrested. Miss Sperry, with her dark-rim glasses, wore a severe dark suit. They both looked like they had dressed for a casting call, but in different movies.

Nancy was on top and bubbling over with news about Corky Carroll. He had taken first place in the South African Open surfing tournament. This ensured him sponsors in the future. Of course, she encouraged me to keep helping him. I told her I would for another year, and then we would revisit the need. Corky would be back in the States in February. Maybe we could get together then.

Not wanting to leave Miss Sperry out of the conversation, I once again thanked her for all her help this year and support through the oral exams. She graciously let Nancy and several other people who had joined our group to listen know that it was my hard work that had made it all possible.

Before she was done, my ears must have been red.

"Rick, have you looked into what you must do to prep for the O- and A-Levels?"

"I didn't know you could prep for them."

Without coming across as superior, she told me in a matter-of-fact voice that it was like taking the SAT. You could take prep classes. Some pre-examinations could be taken to see what you need in the way of tutoring to prepare you for the examination.

This was all news to me and told me I would probably be in England for longer than I had thought.

"And that, ladies and gentlemen, is how Miss Sperry has helped me. Yes, I did the work, but she made certain I was doing the right work."

Then, with a dramatic bow, I took her right hand and brushed my lips close to the back of her hand without actually touching.

"Oh my, Rick, you have been in too many movies."

That may be, but I saw several women close by start to fan themselves.

"Probably so, but you are one teacher I will always remember."

With that, I withdrew. Know when to hold 'em, know when to fold'em was a saying Dad learned from a young country singer while playing poker. I quit while I was ahead.

I spotted Mr. McGarry in the growing crowd and drifted towards him. On the way, I saw a lady with the biggest hair curled up I have ever seen. She hadn't used orange juice cans to curl her hair, more like Quaker Oats boxes.

Mr. McGarry had been joined by Hank Smith, my multi-engine instructor. As could be expected, they were talking flying with their hands. Everyone in their vicinity kept their drinks held close.

Once more, there was an exchange of handshakes and congratulations on my recent check ride. I related to Mr. McGarry how everyone who knew of him mentioned strafing the runway.

"As I said to that newspaper reporter, I do it to keep my students interested, plus I destroyed more planes on the ground than in the air. Our bonus was based on planes destroyed; they didn't care where. I think I will add shooting up trains next."

That gave us a laugh as I edged away. More people were showing up all the time, and I had to do my rounds. I was starting to regret my wool suit; the room was heating up.

John Baxter and Susan Wallace were standing to the side, so I joined them. It was near an open window with a slight breeze.

"Mr. Baxter, how are you enjoying retirement?"

"It didn't last very long."

"Why, what are you doing now?"

"Well, I told you I was retiring. Then you sprang that documentary about your company on me. I no sooner got that settled than I got a call from a young actress that I couldn't say no to, so I am representing her now."

I started to ask him why he couldn't say "No" when a cute little elf showed up.

"Mr. Baxter, I'm so glad you could make it. Did you get a chance to review the contract that Mr. Monroe sent over?"

I fled the scene to the sound of laughter.

I joined Roberta Grimes, Sam Nielsen, Mark Downing, and Sharon Bronson at a table with a poinsettia centerpiece. After ten minutes of listening to the merits of various honeymoon sites and other wedding subjects, I stood and told them I would see them all at dinner. I knew they were invited to the later event.

Passing by an open French door, I saw Popeye standing on the veranda. He was smoking a cigar, so I joined him for the fresh air and to escape from the crowd. He looked comfortable with his tie askew.

"Popeye, I think I enjoyed chipping paint better than this. I like everyone in there but in small doses."

"Same here, Rick, except I don't know most of them. How much longer does this have to go?"

Glancing at my Bulova watch, I told him at least another couple of hours.

Waving his large stogie around, he told me he might make it last that long so he could stay out here. It seems Aunt Sybil only lets him bring one cigar, hoping to keep him in with the crowd.

John Jacobs joined us, tugging at his collar.

"Man, it is getting hot in there."

"Mum and Dad have been talking about getting one of those machines that will cool all the air in the house. I guess it works like a refrigerator. In the meantime, I think I will hang out here."

It was around sixty-five degrees and a beautiful sunny day, at least at our place on top of the hills.

Mr. Dawson, my sword instructor, was the next to join us. Mr. Danson from the school came out with a six-pack of Mexicali Delight beers.

"Anyone want one?"

Ben Carpenter was the first to take him up on the offer.

They didn't last a minute. This started a trend of men coming in and out to get drinks. Soon, many of them were having a smoke. Popeye appeared to be the only one with matches. He was striking them off the sole of his shoe constantly.

All good things have to end. Mum appeared in the doorway and summoned me with a twist of her hand.

"Rick, we need you in here to keep conversations going like a good host."

I opened my mouth to reply but then shut it. When in a hole, stop digging. I thought my being out here was entertaining many of our guests.

Dennis Lawson was by himself near the bar, so I joined him. I asked him how his on-air reports were going. That was the right question. I could drink my Coke while he related what had been occurring. There was a market niche, and he was the first one there.

His program started with twelve radio stations and was now up to 415. The show was syndicated and projected to be in every major market next year. He thanked me several times for the opportunity.

I didn't see any reason to share that a comedy of errors made it happen.

Thankfully, it was nearing 4 p.m., and the crowd was thinning out. Dennis made his goodbyes, and I looked around to see if I could help people out the door.

I needn't have bothered. The elves had it well in hand. Mary would march up to a group, followed by the two boys, each carrying several baskets. Mary would thank them for coming. The boys would present them with a basket.

In the meantime, the bar had been closed, and the staff was clearing tables.

Everyone took the hint.

The guests staying for dinner had discretely taken the elevator to the top of the tower, where hors d'oeuvres were being served. Also, two guest rooms had been set aside for the ladies to freshen up.

I took the opportunity to retire to my room, shower, and put on fresh clothes. I kept the same suit and tie but changed everything else. That kept my look but made me look and feel fresh and clean-cut. I had learned to do this between scenes in my movies.

John Wayne had told me to do this. It made me look cool, calm, and collected. What I thought of as the James Bond look. The image John Wayne practiced was the just came in from the range look.

I checked the map that had been set on an easel outside of the dining room. Mum told me I would be seated next to an unescorted lady and that I was to be certain to introduce myself and seat her at the table.

As a dutiful son, silently repeating "Why me, Lord, why me?" I went up the tower and introduced myself to Miss Doris Tucker, former owner of Tucker Academy.

She was not what I expected at all. This was not a frumpy lady in a lavender ball gown. This was a woman who had aged gracefully dressed in the proverbial black dress with a strand of pearls. Her hair was done in a style of long ago, but on her, it looked natural.

She was in a group with Anna Romanov and Mum.

Using my best manners, I waited for a break in the conversation and introduced myself.

She looked me over and commented, "A little young, but he will do."

The ladies thought this was funny. I wasn't sure what to think.

If nothing else, this taught me that not all was as expected. She turned out to be a witty conversationalist and a pleasure to have dinner with. While not dominating the conversation, she steered it so that all seated near us were included in the discussions. There was no backbiting.

I was amazed at the life this person had led. I began to think the movie *Auntie Mame* had been modeled on her life. The only difference was the movie was more restrained.

Dad gave the welcome speech to thank everyone for sharing their holidays with us. There was the traditional champagne toast to all. The meal was a mere seven courses.

There were enough wait staff. Each waiter served four guests which kept things moving nicely. The caterer had a field kitchen set up in tents behind the house, so all the food was done at the same time.

The touch I liked most of all was the Christmas poppers. Mum had ordered them specially made in England. The gift for the ladies was a diamond tennis bracelet. Men had onyx tie tacks and cuff links, also with diamonds.

I thought it would be too expensive when I first learned of this. I quickly learned that this sort of gift was de rigueur in our new level of society, and besides, the diamonds weren't of the first water. I had to look up de rigueur in the dictionary.

We all popped our poppers and wore our silly paper crowns, except Mary, who was no longer a little elf. Somehow, she had transformed into a little princess, tiara and all.

I didn't think the diamonds in her tiara were real, but I no longer was going to guess at any of it. I had a real disconnect moment. Was I on the set of *The Great Gatsby*?

Bellefontaine, this wasn't.

The moment lasted exactly that—a moment. Looking around, I saw many people I knew having a relaxed good time. There were none of the frantic, forced looks I envisioned from the large parties on the verge of the Great Depression.

Dick and Janice Wyman, who looked like she would deliver before the night was over, sat next to Mr. Monroe and his secretary Donna. Across from them were Mr. and Mrs. Baxter.

Don Pearson and his spouse sat across from Todd Goodson and his wife. They appeared to be having a good time, but you could see Mrs. Pearson was mentally taking notes of what the other women were wearing.

Mark Downing and Sharon Bronson seemed to have become attached to Roberta Grimes and Sam Neilsen. This was to be expected as they were the same age and both couples were engaged. Joining them were Ben Carpenter and his blacksmith girlfriend, his plus one. I couldn't think of her name. I'm not even sure I had ever heard it.

Popeye and Sybil were at the center table with Mum and Dad. I would have bet Popeye, as an old ship's bosun, would be the most ill-at-ease person there. Instead, he looked and acted as though he were born to it.

Anna Romanov sat with Sam Wingate, and you would have thought they were an old married couple, they were so comfortable with each other. Mrs. Hernandez was accompanied by a very distinguished gentleman of Spanish descent. With his silver-gray hair, it looked like he should be in the movies.

Looking at the people sitting at our table, I realized it was our real new life. For the first time, I think it sank into me the changes that had occurred and the high bar set for me and my family.

Mary was the well-adjusted one as she cheerfully flitted around the room to say hello to everyone. She was young enough that this life must seem normal to her.

The dinner was not the opulence of the Gilded Age, but it was fancy. At least I didn't have to wear a tux or, worse yet, a tailcoat and tie, although it would have been fun to see all the ladies in hats with large feathers.

Some of the ladies had small pillbox hats that were coming into fashion. None wore white gloves, so I guess their time was done.

After dessert, which was a baked Alaska, the men adjourned to the veranda for a cigar and whiskey, the ladies back to the reception for tea. Well, it said tea on the card, but I noticed the sideboard had a large variety of liquor. To fortify the tea, I imagine.

I took the opportunity, along with my siblings, to return to our rooms. The vibrant Mary had run out of energy, and I ended up carrying her to her room. I helped remove her shoes and tiara. She made me turn around as she put on her pajamas, but I was allowed to tuck her in. As she snuggled down, she smiled at me.

"Sweet dreams, Princess."

And with that, the day caught up with me. I read for a while, then went to bed early.

Chapter 54

Christmas Eve was a quiet day at the Jackson House. We all seemed to be recovering from yesterday's parties. All the shopping had been done and presents wrapped. We hadn't put the cat out as Mittens had decided she was a house cat.

The kids spent time shaking packages from each other that were under the tree. I was above such childish endeavors; besides, I had my turn early before I went out to run.

Mary was the worst. She kept asking me what I got her. I broke down and told her I had given her a new blanket. What I didn't add was that it was a horse blanket. For some reason, she didn't believe me when I told her that, so she just kept on for most of the morning.

After lunch, I went surfing in the afternoon. I wondered what they were doing in Ohio besides shoveling snow.

After dinner, we retired to the family sitting room with Mum's British Christmas tree. There was a small fire in the fireplace. The veranda doors were opened to let in the cool evening air. Candles were lit around the room.

Mum, Dad, Mrs. Hernandez, and Ben Carpenter were waiting.

Our family tradition was to allow us to open one present from each other. Mary chose to open one of those that I had bought her. She was excited to get a blanket in the Jackson colors with "Misty" embroidered on one side and "Mary Jackson" along with the Jackson coat of arms on the other.

I opened my present from Eddie. It was a BSA logo knife to replace the one I had given him, a cool Swiss Army knife that I could put on my key chain.

Ben was pleased with a new veterinarian bag, which looked like a doctor's black house call bag to me. This was from Dad.

Mrs. Hernandez opened a gift certificate for a day at a beauty spa. She blushed as she told Mum her timing was good. I would have to look into this. I think our housekeeper was dating!

Christmas morning wasn't the pandemonium that we normally had in Bellefontaine. I think it was because we had a larger room to spread out. Also, someone had thoughtfully placed a plastic trash bin in the corner for all the wrapping paper.

We all sat in a large circle of chairs and couches. Everyone had housecoats and slippers on. The kids wore their elf hats.

The first present I opened from Mum and Dad was a new Jepsen case for my flight log and maps. It had my initials embossed in gold. We went around the room, each opening our gifts one at a time. It took longer, but we saw what each had received.

In one corner, next to the golf club bags for Mum and Dad, were three new Schwinn bicycles. I doubted any of them were for me. Maybe a new car in the driveway? A Ferrari would be good.

A kid can dream, can't he?

Instead, my gift from "Santa" was in an envelope. I had trouble figuring out what it was. I finally sorted it out that it was a new airplane hangar.

Dad explained what it entailed.

"Rick, the only place with hangar space available for your new plane is out in Ontario, which is a long drive. On the other side of the park, there is a World War II airfield that was used for training purposes. The whole facility is just sitting there."

"I made some inquiries, and it seems the US Forest Service would love to have it as a general maintenance area and as a base for water-tanker planes and their crews during fire season. It would also be a designated rest area for the ground fire crews. The only problem is they don't have the money in their budget."

"We struck a deal. Jackson Enterprises would pay to refurbish the runway and barracks. They would take care of the rest of the infrastructure. In return, we get to place your hangar there and fly in and out."

"Wow, that's neat. By road, it is what? About fifteen minutes?"

"About that, but the good part is that it is only two miles from here as the crow flies."

"I know that area from my runs. There is a deep ravine that runs between us."

"That's why part of the deal is that they build at our expense a roadway that connects us and a trestle bridge over the ravine."

"That means I could be in the air quickly."

"It also means that you can fly the family out of here in need, without anyone knowing, and that the next stop could be in Ontario, where we will hangar the family jet."

"That will confuse the papa-rats-eyes."

As I said that, I thought about Judy and how they had upset her. I had better call her today and wish her a Merry Christmas. It would have to be later, as I knew with the time difference, they would be in church.

The staff had the day off, so we made do with a cold smorgasbord brunch.

After that, I called Judy. Her mother answered the phone. When I asked for Judy, her mother told me she wasn't available.

"Could you have her call me when she is?"

"Rick, I hate to tell you, but she probably won't be calling you."

With a sinking feeling, I asked, "Why not?"

"We had a bad experience in church today. We sat in our normal pew. A stranger, a boy about Judy's age, was sitting there. We didn't think anything of it. Judy went in first, as usual, and sat next to him. He grabbed her quickly and forced a kiss. As this was happening, a man in front of us turned and started snapping pictures."

They both then ran out of the church. We know these pictures will end up in the scandal sheets.

"Tell Judy that I'm not upset with her."

"We didn't think you would be after you heard the truth. However, her father, Judy, and I don't want this life living in fear wherever she goes. She is mailing your ring back. Would you please let your publicity people know she is no longer dating you?"

I was in the middle of an emotional storm of anger and grief at the unfairness of it all. I still managed to remain polite and told her Merry Christmas as I hung up. That was the most unfelt Merry Christmas I have ever given.

I had made the call from my room, so no one was present to see me pound on the arm of my chair. Of course, they did hear my scream of anguish.

I had a roomful of family within a minute.

I explained what happened.

Mum told me she would call Susan Wallace and make certain that the full story got out.

That ruined the Christmas spirit for me. I spent the rest of the day escaping in a story about flat cats.

Boxing Day, the day after Christmas, we had the house open for our local employees and their families. It was a casual dress day to make everyone comfortable.

There were refreshments set up in reception. We gave guided tours of the house. The nosiest group was Eddie's. He had all the boys about his age. They ran everywhere they went, sounding like a thundering herd. They ended up in the basement game room, which was the last we heard from them for a while.

Denny's group appeared to be all the girls that should have been in Eddie's. I noticed he was giving one blonde a special guided tour. By that, I meant he was squiring her around with her arm over his.

My group consisted of all older kids plus the girls that were Denny's age. Several of them were flirting outrageously, but I ignored them. The older girls were much more reserved. When they looked at me, I felt like a bug under a microscope. As a group, we settled in what I thought of as the Olde English sitting room.

We had grabbed soft drinks from the kitchen. I started the conversation by making certain I caught each name of the nine of us. That was the last thing I had to do. The grilling, uh, the questions started.

"What is it like being in the movies?"

"Who have you met?"

"What is Judy King like, and do you get to see her very often?"

That one stopped me.

"Not at the moment."

I went on to explain what had happened yesterday. They all agreed that it was unfair.

"So, are you looking for a new girlfriend?

This was asked by a girl who looked like she was twelve.

"I haven't had time to think about it, but not for a while."

"Okay, I will leave my phone number for when you start dating again."

Talk about shutting a conversation down. The older girls looked like they wanted to sink into the floor. Several of the boys asked for her number. I guess straight questions can open doors.

There were small gifts for all and an unannounced Christmas bonus for their parents.

I think the highlight of the day was Jim and Connie describing the great water fight. The way they told it; it was the funniest thing they ever had been involved in. Jim also let everyone know they had been lucky to keep their jobs and that it wouldn't happen again.

The whole thing must have been set up because Mary had a special gift for each of them. The squirt guns from the fight had been mounted on a plaque with the date and participants of the great water fight.

These were going to be mounted on the wall of the guard hut. All in all, it was a good day for us.

Sunday was spent riding, horseback in the morning, and cruising in the afternoon just to do something.

I had a serious talk with Mum and Dad about my immediate future. I didn't plan to try to date anyone. I wanted to get high school out of my way. I needed to finish up my current movie and singing projects. After taking and passing the O-Levels and maybe some A-Levels I would have to decide where I would go to school.

We all agreed that more information was needed before that decision was made.

Christmas week had been fun, but at the same time tiring and stressful. I was looking forward to next week when I could just bum around.

Chapter 55

I was up and at it on Monday, I wanted to get my exercise in and then check out the airbase on the other side of the park. After my physical workout, instead of running my usual trail, I drove the T-Bird up the hill on the winding road to the airbase.

My estimate of fifteen minutes was off by ten minutes. Using the road, it took twenty-five, and I didn't drive slowly. The suspension on the T-Bird was not the best for this sort of twisty road. Mum's Morgan would be better. Luckily, there were no police on the way.

The turnoff to the airbase was marked by a wooden sign which must have been impressive many years ago. Today it was a half-fallen over rotten wreck. If you didn't know what it was supposed to identify, you couldn't tell.

The only reason I knew it was the correct turnoff is that I had looked it up on a map of the area. The road back to the base was broken asphalt with plants growing in the cracks and in one case a good-size tree growing in the road. I was able to drive around the tree.

About a mile off the road was a parking lot for visitors who weren't allowed to take their vehicles on base. I parked there as the main gate to the base was padlocked shut. This wasn't an impediment to entering the base.

The main gate was in fairly good shape. However, the fencing next to it was down so I was able to walk around the gate onto the base. I jogged the internal perimeter of the whole base. The runway was over a mile long. You could tell it was the runway because the concrete was in rather good shape.

The winters weren't harsh like in the Midwest so there wasn't the freezing, thawing effect. There was no apparent earthquake damage, so it didn't look like a major rebuild would be needed.

I wondered why it hadn't been used as a drag strip. It would have been ideal. I bet a few illegal drag races had been held here. My theory was supported by a fire pit and thousands of beer cans at the end of the runway next to the hangars. From the way it was all grown over it had been many years ago.

The buildings were another story altogether. To me, it looked like it would be better to level the existing structures and start over. They had been thrown together quickly during the war and had had little maintenance since.

The barracks may have been painted at one time but were bare wood now. The roofs were collapsing. Not much to recommend them.

I was able to look inside one of the barracks. It had a sizable bat colony attached to the ceiling. From the amount of white guano on the floor, it had been there for a long time. I decided not to try to go inside.

The only buildings that looked like they were worth saving were the large metal hangars at the near end of the runway. Aside from needing rust removal and repainting, they were still sturdy-looking.

A man-sized door was open on one of the huge doors used for aircraft. A look inside revealed a big open space and nothing else. I guess I had been hoping for an abandoned aircraft from World War II, maybe a hangar queen that wasn't worth moving.

There was a headquarters building that had been maintained. The door was locked and had a large sign stating it was the property of the US Forest Service, Keep Out.

Peeping through a window, I saw it looked like it was used for equipment storage. Whatever utilities for power there were long gone. There was a huge metal water tower that looked intact, but it gave no clue as to the water supply of the base.

I ran closer to the water tower and almost stumbled into a sunken trench. It was most likely the remains of a collapsed septic system. This was going to cost a small fortune to rebuild. Since it would be through my company it would be my small fortune.

Having learned enough about how things were expensed in the business world, I suspected Uncle Sam would pay. That seemed reasonable to me as the US Forest Service would be getting the most benefit.

After an hour of nosing around, I headed back to the house to get cleaned up. I had an appointment with my singing coach. Today we were going to record the song.

When I got home, Denny was there and all excited with his latest news. He had a call from Sam Neilsen. The studio had been hired by Mr. Larson to take the photographs for the flight school ad campaign and Denny was to take the pictures.

He was being driven to Sam's studio. Sam would accompany him to LAX to the flight school to get things ironed out. How many kids his age are chauffeured to work? I was thrilled for him and what it might do for his budding career. It was beginning to look like Mum and Dad wouldn't have to worry about their retirement.

Helen Marshall and Louis Spohr were waiting for me at the studio. We had a small recording studio reserved for the day. It was nothing fancy. It was a room lined with dark grey acoustical tiles with no frills.

There were two inner windows, one for the sound engineers to see us from their recording room and another for any audience we might have.

The engineers were surrounded by banks of equipment. It was a wonder they could turn around. The heat from all the tubes in the equipment must have made it extremely hot in there.

The room for the spectators wasn't much better. No chairs, just a place to view the singer. This facility was made for work and not show.

We spent the first hour doing sound checks. They needed to know where to place the microphones for me and Louis.

They fiddled around, the sound engineers, not Louis, for over an hour before they were happy. At the engineer's signal, we started to play and sing. I didn't get through the first verse before it was shut down.

Another half hour or more was spent on additional sound checks.

And so, it went one false start after another.

Finally, the engineers were happy, and now it was our turn for false starts. I would start to sing the song and lose the thread. Louis would be playing fine and hit a false note or lose the beat when he played the part of the soldier march or the young lady running.

We took a late break for lunch. I moaned about how bad it was going. Mrs. Marshall was quick to correct me.

"Rick, this is going smoothly compared to many a session I have been in. Everyone was on time and sober. The sound checks went faster than normal. What did you expect?"

"I thought we would walk in, sing the song once or twice, and be done."

"You have done other songs. Did it go like that for them?"

"Pretty much. The Beach Boys like to party, and it showed that day."

"What about Frank Sinatra?"

"He wasn't there. I did a couple of run-throughs, sang the song, and they blended us later."

"None of those were normal. This is easy compared to most sessions."

The lunch was pleasant. We ate at the commissary with the usual mélange of actors in costumes. I think I saw every superhero but Batman stroll down the street. It would be neat if they made a movie about him someday.

I turned when I heard my name. It was Mary and Mum. They joined us for lunch. Mary was here to rehearse for her role in our movie. We will do some filming tomorrow. They had started several weeks ago, but they hadn't needed me for anything. Most of the scenes for Lew Wetzel would be performed by an unidentified stunt double.

I was glad to see that Mary was wide-eyed at the people and bustle around us. I would hate to think that she was blasé at her age.

I may have had that thought too soon.

"Mum, my tiara is better than hers."

The young lady referred to was dressed as a princess. Were they doing the Cinderella story?

"Now Mary, it isn't nice to compare dress in public."

"Okay, I will say bad things about her when we get home."

"Why would you say bad things about her?"

"Look who she is walking with. That must be the Evil Prince, and she isn't even talking to Prince Charming."

"How do you know he is the Evil Prince?"

"Well, he is shorter than her. His hair looks greasy, and he has one of the eye-glass thingies that only have one glass. Only bad guys wear those, and he is dressed in a black uniform. Prince Charming has a blue coat with white pants plus he is a tall blonde."

You couldn't fight that five-year-old logic. After all, that is how all the stories went.

"Do you want me to report them to Mr. Monroe?"

"No Rick, maybe she loves him. You never know what goes on behind the scenes."

Louis looked a little shell-shocked. I know I was. Mum and Mrs. Marshall were trying not to laugh.

After that pleasant interlude, it was back to the salt mines. Well, the recording studio.

Someone had left the sound studio door ajar on the way out, and apparently, it destroyed the acoustics in the room. We spent another hour doing sound checks to get it back correctly. Since no one accused me, I didn't volunteer that I was the last one out at lunch.

Finally, we were back to singing. After several successful run-throughs, I thought we had it. Not. We did several more. It was like we had peaked and were going downhill. Each repetition was rougher.

Finally, I had it.

"Stop. We are getting nowhere!"

"Say that again, Rick."

"Huh?"

"Shout like that again."

"Stop. This is stupid."

"Shout once more, please."

I did and my voice was getting tired and cracked. My shout came out hoarse.

"Now please sing the song again."

I thought she was crazy, but I did it. All along I had been doing it with my British accent, the high-tone version, not the born within hearing distance of Mary-le-Bow.

She had them play it back. I couldn't believe what I heard; it certainly wasn't Rick Jackson. Since it wasn't me, it was good. I mean good. It was a different sound than I had ever done before.

I thought using the accent made it acceptable. My voice, being hoarse put it over the top.

Suddenly, I felt alive and was enthusiastic about this project again. Louis was smiling. One of the sound engineers gave me a thumbs up.

We performed the song once more, and of course, I screwed it up. Altogether we had to run through it another nine times before I was told, that's a wrap.

It was a good thing; my voice was about gone.

By the time I got home, it was time for dinner. I barely had time to change shirts and put on a jacket and tie. Murphy was alive and well as I grabbed the mustard-stained tie. I had to see if a dry cleaner could get the stain out.

Dinner was a round of roast beef along with mashed potatoes and gravy. The nice clear gravy, not the flour-thickened stuff I hated. Dessert was a dish of butterscotch pudding. I would have to check out the kitchen later to see if any was leftover.

Denny and I talked about the photo shoot for the flight school ad. He wanted to do it on Wednesday or Thursday. I told him we could try for Wednesday but with the film schedule, it would probably be Thursday.

Mum and Dad talked about a New Year's Eve party they were attending. I had no plans for the night. That left me and my brothers and sister home alone. It would be a quiet evening for us. Nothing would go wrong.

I was at a loss for what to do after dinner. I had no schoolwork nor flight manuals to read. It seemed odd after the last few months.

I sat down to watch TV but couldn't get interested in anything. I went to the basement and demonstrated once more how futile it was for me to play pool against Denny. After that, I went to my room and thought about something I had to arrange. I owed some revenge to a paparazzo for costing me my girlfriend.

I had an idea, but I would have to make a phone call to set it in motion. My first instinct was to shoot the guy, but that seemed a little extreme. He seemed to like to take chances in his work. Maybe I could help him push the edge enough he would fall off.

After that, I fell asleep quickly. You would think I had a busy day.

Chapter 56

Tuesday started as a grey day, but the newspaper said it would clear up later. It was not quite the rainy season yet, but it was coming. I wore a light jacket over my chinos and polo shirt—no sense in getting dressed up when my first stop would be costume and then makeup.

Before I left home, I called Susan Wallace. In my revenge plan, she was to leak to the specific paparazzo who had taken the pictures of Judy that I would be doing a photo shoot with some hot models out at a private flight school near LAX on Thursday.

She told me she knew just who to call. She didn't ask why I wanted this leaked, and I didn't tell her. What she didn't know couldn't get her in trouble if this went south.

I let Denny know that the photo shoot had to be on Thursday. He was okay with it. I didn't share my plans with him either.

I went past the grade school and got caught at the traffic light. Looking over and thinking about what happened there seemed unreal. The kids were running, shouting, and playing. It was as though nothing had ever happened here. I guess life goes on. At least this time, it was the good lives going on.

I was flagged down at the gate by a new guard. He acted like I was trying to sneak in. Even when I pointed out the permit on the windscreen, he made me show my ID. From there, he made a telephone call to see if I was on the current admittance list. He was either extremely new or there had been a problem.

I had the time, so I stopped by the main office and asked Donna, Mr. Monroe's secretary if anything was going on.

"No, that new guard, Tony Lip, is trying to be noticed and get into the movies. He will be gone by the end of the week. I suspect he will go back to Manhattan and never be heard of again."

"He is a bit of a pain, but he was doing the job the way it is written up."

"He is? How do you know?"

"Remember when I worked with all the departments? I read their manuals."

"Maybe I should bring this up to Mr. Monroe as he is ready to drop the hammer."

"Good idea. Now I need to get to costuming."

"Well, you better hurry. There is a young actress that has a scene with you. She is fretting that you won't show up."

I wondered where Mum and Mary had gone when they left the house early. Duh!

Costuming was a breeze. They had my size down pat. All I had to do was change into a rough, homespun cotton shirt and pants. I was even allowed to keep my shoes and socks as they wouldn't be shown.

Makeup was a different story. I spent two hours there as they kept me the same but simultaneously made me different. That sounds weird, but they made me look dark, not as in skin tone, but as someone you would not want to meet in an alley. They highlighted my features so that I looked a lot harsher. Oh, they did put a two-inch long scar on my right cheek, ending at my eye.

All in all, I liked the look, dangerous.

When I walked on set, the crew was ready for me. The set itself was done up as the interior of a barn. The extras were dressed for a frontier barn dance. That meant there were no fancy square-dancing costumes. All were in clean, rough, and ready clothing.

One little girl was in a gingham dress and a white cap. She was as cute as a button. Well, at least until she stamped her foot while looking at her wristwatch and told me it was about time. All these people had been standing around waiting for at least an hour.

"Well, onto the movie, Mary. Isn't it a fine day?"

"It is, Rick, I'm so excited."

About that time, we heard, "Places everyone."

I moved to the slightly raised stage in the center of the set. My place was marked by an X taped to the floor. We then did a walk-through of the scene. Everyone hit their marks, so we went for the first live take, with me pretending to play the fiddle and sing.

I made the broad hand gestures I had been taught. At the same time, I sang the song quietly. We were halfway through the song before the first of many cuts were called. It seems the way the dancers were moving, they were blocking the camera.

This resulted in the changing of the starting point of the dance. It was moved four times before the cameramen were satisfied. Next, I was the problem. I was singing softly so my mouth wasn't showing up on the screen as it should.

So, we went on and on. Typical for a movie set. I could see Mary getting restless on the sideline. Everyone looked frazzled, so the next time the director yelled, "Cut," I walked over to him.

"I think we are ready for a change of pace. It is getting worse as we go."

"That's for damn sure. What do you have in mind?"

"Let's do the scene where Mary tells me she wants to marry me, and will I wait until she grows up."

"Can't hurt, and it will be a step forward."

Of course, this led to a change in lighting and camera angles. Once the set was ready, Mary did a walkthrough of her lines. She had them down cold, so we went for it. She delivered them letter-perfect and with a sincere look. I wasn't certain she was acting.

The director had us run through the scene twice more, but it was a formality. She had nailed it the first time. I didn't do too badly myself. I promised her I would wait until she grew up. To do a scene like that, you must have something real in your mind as you pretend.

For me, it was easy. I just pretended that I was at one of Mary's tea parties. We had done enough of them over the years. I could say absolute rubbish with a straight face, "Why yes, Mrs. Bear, I would love to have sugar with my tea; two lumps, please."

The director made a big deal out of it, "That, ladies and gentlemen, is how a professional does it. On-time, dressed correctly, knows her lines, and does the job."

I had been about to open my mouth but decided not to say anything. Mary had left on her wristwatch. I wondered if they would catch it somewhere along the line. They didn't, and it made it into the final cut.

It made the trade rag as an error when they reviewed the movie. Just as I was ready, the director sent us all to lunch. The movie business is a lot like the military; hurry up and wait.

Mary and Mum had left the studio as her part was done. I doubted if she would be called back for a retake. Like everyone else, I ate at the cookout setup immediately outside our studio. I had never seen fifty-five-gallon drums cut in half to make a grill, so that was neat.

I spent my lunch with the set crew rather than the other actors. Not that I was a snob, but the actors were all temporary people who worked as extras trying to get a break. Trying to get the break also entailed bringing themselves to the star's attention, hoping to have a good word put in.

I didn't know any of these people and was tired of them thinking I owed them something. By hanging with the working crew, I avoided the extras and spent time with people I knew. Not all of them, of course, but I had worked on different movies with several of them.

I asked how everyone was doing and how the parts of the movie that I hadn't been there for were going. I found out the crew was in a good mood and that this movie was going fine.

They were more interested in the documentary about Jackson Enterprises. The whole industry knew how it came about. They concluded that I'm a good person. I felt good about it but tried to downplay it. The more I tried, the more they told me I was the greatest.

I finally bowed to the pressure, stood up, and took a real bow.

"You all may kiss my ring to pay me proper homage."

That took care of that. I had offers to kiss other parts of them in turn. I ignored the peasants. It was a good lunch with a lot of laughter.

After lunch, we went back to me playing the fiddle. The change of pace had helped drop the frustration level of all present. We had five more takes, and the director was satisfied.

I had to appear in three different barn dance sets to build up my character as a likable guy. I had to change clothes twice more and have my makeup refreshed each time. I didn't have to sing in the last two, so it was easier for me.

All I had to do was make the broad hand motions and smile. They would cut in Louis's hands for the close-in work. The two scenes took only seven takes, which must have been a record.

From there, it was back to costuming for me. Now, I had to do several talking scenes with me being a nice guy and admired for my feats without describing what those feats were. This required three costume changes as the writers wanted to build a solid image of me. By the time these scenes were shown on the screen, people would wonder what I added to the movie.

Several women in the scenes showed interest in me, but I did not return the favor. By the time this was all displayed, I would have a firm image as a good guy in the movie, at least with the white settlers. While all the other named actors in the movie had an interaction on-screen with the Indians, I didn't.

It went past dinner time and late into the evening. They brought us cold cuts from the commissary. We ate standing, just wanting to get it done. I was yawning as I played the fiddle and joked with people. I wonder how they would keep that out of the picture.

The director called it a night sometime after midnight. I think he would have kept going, but the square dancers were all danced or squared out. They looked like they were staggering around the stage. I had "forgotten" to sign the log with my hours. I hope the state didn't check.

I drank black hot coffee from a paper cup before getting in my car to head home. It was bitter, but it did the job. I managed to keep between the Botts Dots. Well, I did run over a couple of dots.

Mum and Dad were waiting up. This was the latest I had been out for a long time. I didn't have a curfew, and they knew where I was. They just wanted to know I was safe. I felt good about that as I said good night.

We were back on the set by nine o'clock the following day. I spent the first two hours in costume and makeup. Yesterday, I had been a good guy; today, I was a bad guy.

They would shoot the scene where I would be revealed as the crazy killer Lew Wetzel. My clothes were changed to outdoors frontiersman, and there was a freshening of my makeup. Well, it was more than freshening up. They made me even harsher looking.

When I saw the daily rushes later, I did look like a murdering psychopath.

I would be chasing a young girl through the woods, intending to kill her.

In a previous scene that used a double, I had shot her father and killed her mother and brother with the tomahawk. I was now going to do the same with her. It was not a Blood and Gore movie, so my killing of them would be a gunshot, then an arm raising the steel-headed tomahawk for a killing blow. Contact wouldn't be shown.

The family had been built up as "good Indians" during the movie. They were relatives of the chief of the Wyandot tribe. They were shown trying to convince the chief to sign a peace treaty with the settlers. In real life, this attempted peace treaty was as close to a peaceful settlement of the Ohio country as it ever came. The family's murder by Wetzel led to wars that finalized the demise of the Indians in the Northwest Territory.

Granted, Indians had killed Wetzel's family, but he took his hate and revenge beyond any civilized bounds. His killing of Indians, in turn, caused the death of many a white settler.

This set up what we hoped would be a shocking ending. The young man we built up as being admired turns out to be the villain they learned to hate during the movie. For those who gave it any thought, it would highlight the difference between then and now.

All I had to do for the shot was run down a trail with the camera mounted on a trolley following me on a track. I would be chasing a six-year-old Indian girl with my rifle in my left hand and a trade tomahawk in my right.

Simple sounding, but I stumbled the first time and fell on my face. Not only did this ruin the shot, but I wiped my face as I got up, resulting in a redo of my makeup. Fortunately, they were used to such things happening and had the makeup artist on set with their gear.

My job was to run down the path, and then, when I crossed a line drawn across the path, I would look up. They had a white spot painted on one of the fake trees. When I looked directly at it, my face was full on to the camera.

The trees weren't fake. They were sections of real tree trunks turned vertical and mounted on a trolley to be stationed wherever needed, a forest that could move. I asked one of the stagehands if they were Tree Ents, but he didn't get it.

The tomahawk I was using had a very dull, rounded edge. It was good because I tripped on another retake and would have done myself serious harm. The safest person in the area was that young girl I was chasing.

The last time I fell, she came back and asked if I was okay. Not what I would do if someone were trying to scalp me with a hatchet, even pretend.

We finally got the scene in the can. There would be an epilogue rollover that would tell that Lew Wetzel was eventually arrested for the murder of the peaceful Indians but was freed by his friends. He went to New Orleans, where he spent time in prison for being caught counterfeiting and eventually died of old age. To this day, the Shawnee put charms on his grave to keep him there.

The day went long again, but we finished in time for me to return home for dinner. Mary was still up from her appearance in the movie. She hardly shut up the entire meal. She asked me about my next project and if she could be in it.

Mum interrupted her to remind her of the deal, one movie or ad appearance this year. Mary got a stricken look and burst into tears. Not crying, just tears running down her cheeks. I wanted to hug her, but Mum just glared.

"Mary Elizabeth Jackson, I can make your scene go to the cutting room floor."

Just like that, the flow stopped. What an actress.

"Yes, Mum, I will behave, but it was so much fun."

"I know, dear. There will be other chances."

In a spritely, happy voice, she said, "I know. I wanted to see how serious you are."

"Very."

The kid was frightening.

Chapter 57

After dinner, I called Mr. Larson and explained that there might be an unwelcome guest tomorrow and that I would love to see him arrested for trespassing on federal property. Mr. Larsen just rented his space from LAX; it was controlled by the US Government, even though Los Angeles County owned it.

He thought it would be a good idea to invite the LAX police over for coffee in case they were needed.

Today was New Year's Eve. It was a normal workday for most people, but they would probably get off work early to get ready for the night's festivities. I skipped my morning workout so Denny and I could head out to LAX early. Mr. Larsen didn't have any flight training scheduled for today and wanted us in and out as soon as possible.

On the way, I explained to Denny my plan for the paparazzo, and would he get as many pictures as he could.

Denny had taken care of the wardrobe for the photographs with input from Sam Neilsen. Sam met us in the lobby of the flight school. Even though Denny was taking the pictures, this was a new opportunity for his studio, and he wanted to make sure it went well.

He had a van with a ton or so of lights and reflectors in it. At Mr. Larsen's direction, we took it around to a hangar with several planes that would be used in the ads. All had Larsen's Flight School painted neatly on the fuselage. Denny was to make sure that all pictures included these.

To my surprise, another van and a car drove up. The van contained the wardrobe that would be used today. I hadn't given it any thought as to what I would be wearing. Now that I thought about it, my chinos, a light blue polo shirt, and a dark blue sports coat would be a bit much for every picture.

Denny had raided my closet, and Sam had borrowed some outfits from Warner Brothers, using my name.

The car had two models sitting in the back, a blonde and a brunette. This worked out well. It turns out that the papa-rats-eye had not been lied to. I knew that two LAX policemen were watching us from the window in the hangar office. Since the blinds were pulled, you couldn't see them.

About that time, the door opened, and the two cops came strolling out. They headed towards the hangar man-door, but at the last moment, they turned to the side and ran behind a plane parked there. The next thing I heard was a couple of thuds like a scuffle going on.

The police emerged from behind the plane with a man who looked slightly worse for the wear in handcuffs. As they brought him towards us, Denny and Sam were clicking away. At least I would have something to send to Judy; it wouldn't change how she felt, but it would show that I did care.

The paparazzo swearing up a blue streak was still struggling with the police. Not the smartest thing to do.

The lead policeman told Mr. Larsen, "As you suspected, there was a trespasser on your grounds and that of the LAX airport. He also resisted arrest, so that will be added to the charges."

From the cop's smirk, I wouldn't bet who started that little fracas out of our sight.

I asked, "What will the penalty be?"

"Not that much. He is probably a first-time offender. The judge will probably issue a fine for a couple of hundred and time served."

"How much time will he have to serve?"

"It will be at least until next Monday when court resumes."

Mr. Larsen thanked them for their efforts as they hauled the guy away. The guy had never stopped swearing. I thought he would bust a gut when they exposed the film from his camera and all that he had on him.

I thanked Mr. Larsen for his help.

"No problem, Rick, but he seemed to get off lightly."

"I'm not certain about that. He had the cost of a flight from the East Coast; the fine, whatever it will be; a long weekend in jail with a bunch of drunks; and worst of all, pictures of him will appear in the papers he normally sells to.

"He will be a laughingstock in the industry. I hope that will make the paparazzi think twice about messing with people. Most of all, it will show my former girlfriend that I don't take messing with me and mine lightly."

It made me feel weird when I said former girlfriend, but I might as well face reality.

The rest of the morning was spent taking glamour shots of me in various poses with a pretty girl on my arm and many a change of costume for me and the girls.

The girls were professional models hired for the occasion, and they knew what they were doing. The hangar office was used as an impromptu changing room. Sam Nielsen had hedged all his bets. He had hired one of the studio makeup ladies for the morning. I had worked with her several times in the past.

It wasn't like movie makeup; this was lightly done to emphasize cheek lines and shadows. It went like clockwork. I could see that Sam could have a future in this. He might even end up with his modeling agency. I thought this because of the questions the two models had about what other work he might have.

They were very favorably impressed with how this had come together on such short notice. Other people they had worked with would have made this a painful day for all involved.

I was proud of Denny. He worked with us on every shot, clearly having a vision of what he wanted, and was very patient in explaining it to us. Sometimes, he would set his camera down and pose us or even show us the pose. The young ladies, Cindy and Patty, weren't divas about it. They worked with him. When he had them in an awkward position, they suggested changes, which he usually went along with. It was a team effort.

A catering truck showed up at about ten o'clock, and we took a break. Sam had arranged this. The more I saw of him, the more impressed I was. As we ate donuts and sipped coffee, I asked him if he was considering expanding.

"Roberta and I have been discussing this since we received Mr. Larsen's call. It would be natural for us, but we don't have enough money to bankroll the startup. We're not certain the banks would loan us the money for this sort of venture. Even if I pledged the studio as collateral, we wouldn't have enough."

This was one of the few times my having money hit me as a good thing.

"Would you consider a silent partner?"

He raised an eyebrow at that. "Yes, if it was the right one."

"Come up with a business plan, and I will buy in."

A very excited-looking Sam nodded his head. "I will do that this weekend."

We hadn't been sitting alone during this conversation. We were at a picnic table just outside the hangar. The others present, the models, makeup artist, and even my brother, let it be known they were available at need for any projects. Mr. Larsen said he would let us use his hangars and planes as a set if needed, at a fee, of course, or paid in kind.

"Rick, you may have to be one of our models until we are more established."

I thought, *Oh, Lord, you stupid boy. What have you gotten yourself into*?

We went back to work after the break. The setup I liked most was me in a World War I flying outfit. It had been borrowed from the studio. I had a flight jacket, a leather helmet, and a long white scarf. I thought I looked very dashing. The way Denny draped the models over me cemented the thought, at least to me.

As a bonus to the models, Denny took extra shots of them alone for their portfolios. They loved how they were being treated.

Mr. Larsen also interviewed me for a few quotes he could include in the ad's script. I wouldn't want to be a model full-time as I didn't have the patience for photograph after photograph of the same basic pose. I was too used to moving around. I was ready to change my mind after changing clothes in the same room as the two girls.

They weren't modest at all. It also meant that I had to act the same. That was a little weird being in my underwear with two attractive ladies in the room. It didn't help that they openly admired the merchandise. I didn't realize how shy I was until that day. I would get over it.

We wrapped up on time. Denny and I helped Sam tear everything down. Mr. Larsen was anxious to see the pictures so he could deliver them to the magazine. Denny and Sam were going to their studio to develop them and return them to Mr. Larsen later this afternoon.

The topping on the cake for the models and makeup lady was the check that Sam had prepared for them. Work was lean for them this time of year, so this was a nice extra. I could see Sam being an attractive employer in a market where models could make or break you.

I headed home to clean up for our very modest New Year's Eve. By modest, I meant the kids and me. Mum and Dad were going to the mayor's party. We kids were staying home. I could have gone to one of several parties but had sent my regrets after Judy's breaking up with me. I didn't feel very sociable.

If I went to any parties, there would be girls like that twelve-year-old earlier who had given me her phone number, which I had promptly thrown away. I didn't feel up to that sort of attention. It would be like being a piece of meat at a steak house.

When would I ever meet a nice girl who would like me for me, not for what I did or was worth? Maybe I should start hanging around wealthy young heiresses. I wondered if Mr. Hilton had a granddaughter if I went to school in England, or maybe I could find a duchess or two.

At home, I went down to the basement playroom where Eddie and Mary were goofing off. I was no sooner within range of Mary, I heard a "ring ring." I picked up a tin can sitting on an end table.

"Eddie, it's for you."

He glared at me as he took it. I love my little sister, but there was no way I would spend half an hour listening to her troubles with her dolls on two tin cans joined by a string.

In the past, things the dolls got up to were interesting. I just hoped Mary didn't try any of those stunts when she was older. A lot of them she had heard about from Dad. What was funny to him wasn't funny to Mum. I had never heard of setting a paper bag filled with fecal matter on fire on someone's front porch, ringing the doorbell, and hiding to watch them stomp the fire out.

Dad's childhood in the depression was a little more than we could handle these days. However, I remembered fondly the noisemaker he had shown me how to make.

We took an empty wooden spool used for sewing thread and cut notches around the edges on both ends. Then we passed a long, thin string through the center of the spool, tied the ends together, and wrapped the string around the barrel of the spool.

Then, using a nail as an axle, I was supposed to hold it against a window and pull the string as fast as I could. The notches cut into the end of the spool made an unholy racket as they hit the window glass when I tried it at home.

I was in the fourth grade then because I took it to school. I had it out to use on a window in the classroom when our teacher Mrs. Jernigan saw it and took it away. She told me she hadn't seen one in school since the 1930s. I was to tell my dad he was a bad boy. She kept the spool. Dad had a big laugh when I told him at dinner, Mum, not so much.

That got me thinking about the changes in my life since then. I had hitchhiked across the country, flown coast to coast many times, and sailed to South America, Africa, and Europe. There was still plenty more of the world that I wanted to see.

I had been seen as a hero several times, most importantly preventing a gunman from shooting Queen Elizabeth. I had also caught bank robbers and cattle rustlers. Besides that, I had pulled people out of wrecked cars and burning buildings. To top it off, I had landed a jet plane to save us all.

There was fun to be had and adventure in making movies and singing professionally. That singing still left me wondering what was wrong with people's ears. I made a lot of money and gained satisfaction from inventing the hairdryer, and cargo containers for land, sea, and air.

With those inventions came production facilities and the people to run them. The last I had heard, Jackson Enterprises employed over ten thousand people. That made me one of the largest employers in the country. Not GM or US Steel but growing.

Then there were the darker moments. I had shot bank robbers in Colorado and accidentally killed a pervert in California. I tried to forget those Russians and what we did to them when they kidnapped Mary. I could try, but I never would.

Then there were the people I had met, from presidents to the queen to CIA and KGB agents. Well, I hadn't been introduced to the KGB, but they certainly knew of me.

Then, there was the little matter of World War III being averted. Every teenage boy wanted a love life, but mine had a dismal record. I forget how many girls I had dated, only to be dumped. Hope springs eternal. I guess that is how the human race continues.

Probably finishing high school at sixteen, two years early, and obtaining my multi-engine pilot's license paled compared to the other events.

I wondered what the coming year would be like.

I wasn't normally this introspective, but with the end of the year and new chapters opening in my life, it was a good time to review what had happened.

All this serious thinking had me sitting in the basement, ignoring the world around me. Big mistake! I went to stand up and fell backward onto the sofa. Thank goodness for a soft landing. I knew who the culprits were from the giggling.

Mary and Eddie had wrapped the string from the tin can telephone around and around my legs. By the time I was unwrapped, they were long gone.

I went searching for them with tickling till they peed in my mind. Lucky for them, an upside-down pineapple cake was left unattended in the kitchen. A huge slice and a large glass of milk kept my strength up for the revenge I would take.

Someone had left the TV on, and the New Year's shows were starting, so I sat down to watch Guy Lombardo welcome in the New Year. I must have fallen asleep somewhere along the way before the magic moment. I woke up to a test pattern of an Indian chief and two kids leaning on me, both sound asleep.

We had been covered with a blanket, so I knew our parents were home. I didn't hear Denny come in from his late day at the photography studio, but if he weren't home, the parents would have woken me. Rather than disturb my sibs, I went back to sleep.

Chapter 58

I was a little stiff and sore when I woke up. My workout later would take care of that. There were no kids next to me. They were getting cleaned up. The family was going to Pasadena to watch the Rose Parade. I was going to be in the parade.

This was a promotion for my upcoming movie. I would march in buckskins with a group of mountain men. No one would listen to me when I tried to tell them it was the wrong period.

During the parade, they had wanted me to run down the street and load and then fire my rifle. The publicity people thought it was a shame that I couldn't use a ball, which would be too dangerous.

I pointed out that many horses would be in the parade, which might cause a problem if I fired the rifle. They didn't like it but had to back down. Lord, help us from those in the backroom who don't have to face the consequences of their actions.

Thankfully, the parade went well. When we marched in front of the cameras and stopped in the box chalked on the ground, a reporter, a pretty young lady, came out and asked about the movie. I replied that it was a good, entertaining show for the whole family.

"Rick, I understand your role is a little darker than you normally do."

"You will have to buy a ticket to find out."

I said this with a grin and waved my tomahawk in the air. She backed up at that. Hmm, she does have a nice head of hair.

The people at home saw the wonderful floats in all their gorgeous colors if they had color TVs; the audience along the way not only saw but smelled the many flowers. Those walking the parade route had sore feet from the cement pavement and felt lucky if they didn't step in any manure.

I was asked again if I wanted to ride a float or even be the grand marshal like Vice President Nixon. When we were lining up for the parade, being a good politician, Mr. Nixon shook as many of our hands as he could. I just happened to be walking away when he came close to me. I had met him several times and didn't care for him.

There was a bus to take us from the end of the parade back to our starting point. From there, I headed home, raccoon hat and all. The convertible top was down, so I got my share of stares and laughter.

At one traffic light, I was asked by a pimple-faced college kid if I wanted to race for pinks. I raised my tomahawk and said, "Race for hair."

He didn't take me up on it.

Returning home, we guys watched the Washington Huskies defeat the Wisconsin Badgers, 44-8. Neither team meant much to us, but we had to root for the Big 10.

After that, we goofed off for the rest of the day. We all saddled up and took a ride. We ended up at the old airbase and took a tour. It still looked dilapidated and run down. It would cost a ton of money, but it would be worth it.

A quiet evening in front of the TV ended the day.

Denny and Sam had the ad photos done up in several layouts. They met Mr. Larsen and me at the airport. They all looked good and bad. Good pictures, but they had me in them.

Mr. Larsen was thrilled with them. He had the written copy ready to go. We all reviewed it and agreed it was good stuff. He only talked about the school in the copy, mentioning me as a student once. The pictures would sell themselves. Attend Larsen's school, and the pretty girls would hang all over you.

What they didn't say was the pretty girls had been paid to hang all over me.

We had the T-Bird with the top down. It was cool but sunny. We were enjoying the ride with "Cathy's Clown" on the radio. I was first in line at a traffic light. It turned green, and I started. We were almost out of the intersection when a car ran the light from the passenger side of the car.

It hit us in the rear end, spinning us around in the road; the car was still in the same lane but facing the way we had come. Both Denny and I were jerked from side to side. Luckily, the windows were down, or we would have both cracked our heads.

I was stunned for a moment. As I turned to see what had hit us, two guys were getting out of the other car. They both started to run from the scene in opposite directions. One of them was running directly at our car, intending to run past us.

I opened my car door just in time for him to run full tilt into it. That knocked him down. He was a small, skinny guy with a greased-down DA in jeans and a white tee shirt. He started to get up, so I helped him by taking hold of his arm.

I noticed he had tattoos on his knuckles. They were homemade and spelled out Love on his right hand and Hate on the left. The package of Lucky Strikes rolled up in the sleeve of his tee shirt completed the picture. He belonged on a movie set.

This went down in seconds. At the same time I was "helping" him up by holding onto him, the police showed up. I mean, they showed up. The four-way intersection had two police cars come from each direction.

The one runner who had gone in the other direction had gotten away unless his buddy gave him up. The police didn't take long to sort it out. They had the guy up against a squad car and in handcuffs quickly. It turns out the black Lincoln Continental that had T-boned us was stolen.

They had jumped a parking valet for the car. Fortunately, a police car was passing by, and the valet flagged it down. From there, it went as the old saying goes, "You can outrun the police; you can't outrun Motorola."

The T-Bird was wrecked up badly. The rear axle, among other things, was broken, so another one bites the dust. We were able to pry the trunk open to get Denny's gear out. After assuring the police we were okay, Denny and I used the payphone on the corner to call a taxi. It would cost a small fortune but would get us home quicker.

The police told me they would have the T-Bird hauled to an impound lot to get it off the road. So now I had no car and was leaving the country for an unknown period. Should I buy a new one? Hmm, maybe I would end up with a Ferrari.

When the cab dropped us off at the guardhouse, there were plenty of questions. Mum and Dad were waiting for us to see how we were. It was a puzzle of how they knew already. It appeared that a reporter listened to the police radio and called Jackson House.

One of them called the house to see how my parents felt about the whole thing. I didn't predict a bright future for the person asking such a boneheaded question.

When convinced that we were okay, Denny and I went our ways, his to work on his pictures, mine to read the afternoon away.

Sunday was spent reviewing my wardrobe for England. I would call Mr. Norman for advice tomorrow but wanted to be ready. I would ship most of my clothes by airfreight. I don't know where things had changed.

It had started that I would fly to England for several days and sit for examinations. Then, it expanded to time to take prep classes for the exam. Now, it seemed to be an indefinite trip.

I was staying at the Plaza on The Strand for the first week, but if it were going to be a while, I would hunt for a flat. I looked forward to the coming year.

Finished, for now.

Back Matter

Continued in Book 8: Oxford University[1]

https://www.enelsonauthor.com/

If you would like to be on the mailing list for new releases and a free story go to my website and contact me with Free Story as the subject.

For information on hiring Janet E. Rupert to edit your fiction project, email:

janeteditorrupert@gmail.com

1. https://www.amazon.com/gp/product/B082VGMNNX

Other books by Ed Nelson

The Richard Jackson Saga
Book 1 The Beginning
Book 2 Schooldays
Book 3 Hollywood
Book 4 In the Movies
Book 5 Star to Deckhand
Book 6 Surfing Dude
Book 7 Third Time is a Charm
Book 8 Oxford University
Book 9 Cold War
Book 10 Taking Care of Business
Book 11 Interesting Times
Book 12 Escape from Siberia
Book 13 Regicide
Book 14 What's Under, Down Under?
Book 15 The Lunar Kingdom
Book 16 First Steps
In the Richard Jackson World
Mary, Mary
Stand-Alone Story
Ever and Always
Cast in Time Series
Book 1: Baron
Book 2: Baron of the Middle Counties
Book 3: Count
Book 4: Earl
Book 5: Earl of the Marches

Did you love *Third Time is a Charm*? Then you should read *Oxford University* by Ed Nelson!

Oxford University has Rick transitioning from being a tenth-grade high school student to entering Oxford University as an underclassman. Fame, adventure and even some danger keep coming his way as he moves to Oxford, England to enter Trinity College at Oxford University. He is back and forth across the Atlantic as he takes his exams and prepares for the US Open. Somehow his courtesy job as a Queens Messenger lands him in the Royal Air Force as a flight officer. How this ends up involving a French actress and the Mona Lisa remains to be seen. For the young, this is a coming-of-age adventure; for those who lived it, a trip down memory lane, and for those with a search engine, Easters Eggs galore. This tongue-in-cheek saga is all true, give or take a lie or two.